The
# DISGRUNTLED
Wives
Club

## ALSO BY PORTIA A. COSBY

*Too Little, Too Late*

*Lesson Learned: It Is What It Is*

# The
# DISGRUNTLED
# Wives
# Club

## PORTIA A. COSBY

DISTINCT | Publishing

DISTINCT|Publishing

DISTINCT Publishing
PO Box 1034
Beaver Falls, PA 15010

PUBLISHER'S NOTE
This book is a work of fiction. Names, characters, places, and incidents are either the product of the author's vivid imagination or are used fictitiously, and any resemblance to actual persons, living or deceased, business establishments, events, or locales is entirely coincidental.

ISBN-13: 978-0-9823013-2-6
ISBN-10: 0-9823013-2-4

Cover designed by Marion Designs
Printed in the United States of America

For information regarding special discounts for bulk purchases, please contact DISTINCT Publishing at the above address or ordernow@portiacosby.com.

**Dedicated to** all members of the club;
past, present, and future

# The Disgruntled Wives Pledge

I pledge allegiance
to the club
of the Disgruntled Wives of America
And to the husbands who we love,
but can't stand
One situation
after another
until we're fed up…
Pursuing happiness and clarity
for all

# DANA

He's a thirty-five-year-old fuckup. He's my husband. And I love him. If there was a more eloquent way to put it, believe me, I would. But, there isn't. He's not just a member of the Fuckup Club; he's the president. Still, he's mine, and I'll never deny that.

I used to find it laughable whenever I heard people say you can't help who you love, but I'm a living witness to that well-known statement. Ric's been in my life for fifteen years, with fourteen of them having been peppered with questionable behavior, half-truths, and flat-out lies. To be fair, he's not a total disaster. An equal amount of our years have been filled with laughter, good times, and great sex. Toward the beginning of our relationship, he was my ideal man: thoughtful, hardworking, unselfish, confident, and good-looking. However, as the years roll by, he's becoming more and more of a train wreck.

When I met him, he was in the Air Force, had a car, understood the importance of saving money, and most importantly, he had goals. I was seventeen, and he was twenty-one. Now plagued with the complacency of struggling, he's content with purchasing a monthly bus pass instead of a car, having a mediocre job instead of a career, and living paycheck to paycheck instead of having a savings account.

Everything seemed to change after he left the military and we moved in together. No, I take that back. I'm now convinced nothing ever changed. I just wasn't aware of how he really was because we had a long-distance relationship for the first five years. On the telephone and in letters, you can make yourself into someone you aren't. You can hide more secrets, cover up lies, and make things seem so flowery that your significant other will only smell roses and not the horse shit you're placing under their nose.

That's what happened to me. Unfortunately, I didn't find out Ric's dirt until after we stood before the Justice of the Peace and said "I do." And so I did. I stood by my husband, feeling like I was simply being tested with a "for better or for worse" moment. Using the rationale that it happened before the marriage, I figured I shouldn't dwell on it. I had done my dirt while in college, so who was I to judge?

Maybe that was the problem. By the time he popped the question, I trusted him enough to believe he'd been the honest man he appeared to be. In my case, love wasn't blind. It was young, believing, and, dare I say it, naïve.

I met Ric at the Burger King across the street from my school during my senior year of high school. I'll never forget the day. It was November 22nd. My teammate, Tara, and I ran over to grab a Whopper meal before practice. It didn't take long to get our food, so we sat down for a few minutes to eat as much as possible. There was nothing worse than eating and walking simultaneously.

We panicked after Tara looked at her watch. It was 2:37 p.m., and we only had eight minutes to return to school, change into our practice uniforms, and shoot ten foul shots. We stuffed our bags into our backpacks and headed out the back door. Tara led the way with her Coke in one hand and backpack in the other.

We were barely out the door, when Tara busted her ass on the ice and snow. Weak from laughter, I could barely

2

help her up. That's when a white Chevy Caprice parked in the space closest to us, and two guys who looked to be in their twenties stepped out.

"You alright, lil' mama?" one asked.

That "one" was Ric. After helping Tara to her feet, he introduced himself as Cedric. His charm was even cuter than his smile. He wore a gray skull cap and black leather jacket. After shaking my hand, he placed both of his inside his pockets and leaned against the building. His smooth talk was slightly interrupted by the chatter of his teeth when the wind blew, drawing attention to his lips that were pleasantly juicy for a man.

As he kicked his game, I had to cut him short. It was 2:49, and at that point, Tara and I were guaranteed to run four suicides. She exchanged numbers with his friend Troy, while Ric and I did the same. In that short time, I was clear on a few things. He hailed from Pittsburgh, Pennsylvania, but was on leave from the Air Force for Thanksgiving, accompanying Troy as he visited family in Indianapolis; he was based in Tennessee; he was single; he didn't have any children; and he was interested in *me*, even though I was four years younger than he. When Tara and I walked away, you couldn't tell us nothing. We'd snagged two out-of-towner cuties in a matter of twelve minutes. So what if we were late for practice.

I still can't decide whether the day is more memorable because it's when I met my husband, or because I almost threw up after running ten suicides with Tara. Shit. Today, both memories yield the same feeling. I digress...

A week later, we were official. When I walked the halls of Ben Davis High School wearing my man's Air Force t-shirt, I used to think I was the shit. Not only was Cedric Hall a sexy chocolate drop, he was old enough to buy something for us to sip on, he had a car, *and* he was paid. Ideally, we would've been in the same city or at least the same state, but something that good had to have a catch. We dealt with it, though. Whether it was through a letter, email, instant messenger, or use of a pager, landline, or cellular phone, our love lasted at a distance for five years, evolving with technology through every turn. We took the good with the bad. Now here we are fifteen years later, having been married for seven of them.

When I say he's a fuckup, I mean everything bad that can happen in any given scenario will happen to him. Murphy's Law should be renamed in his honor. Many times, the circumstances aren't even his fault. I tell him all the time that he must've pissed off God in a major way—in this life and a past life—to have the luck he has. Then there's the shit that *is* his fault.

I knew when my phone rang that something was wrong. I almost didn't answer it, for fear our conversation would ruin my day. Just the tone of his "Baby, what you doin'?" greeting made me sick to my stomach.

"I'm out shopping with Crystal," I replied.

"Aw, that's what's up."

Red flag! He doesn't like me spending money "that we don't have". So, normally, he would've bombarded me with questions about what store we were in, what I bought, etcetera.

"Hey, do you have your AAA card on you?"

I felt my blood pressure rise. With his license currently suspended, he was not to drive my vehicle. Therefore, he had no use for my card. Yes, I said *my*. I'm all for sharing and the "we-are-one" mentality, but when ultimate liability falls on me, the property is considered mine. All I could picture was my Camry, which is barely a year old, wrapped around a tree or telephone pole.

"Are you in my car?"

"I don't have time to talk about all that. I need to handle this first. Then I'll hit you right back. What's the number?"

I heard men laughing in the background. "Who the hell is that? Where do you have my car? And why would you drive when you know you're riding dirty?"

"Man, I just came to Lenox to get somethin' real quick."

"And what happened?"

By now, Crystal was shaking her head, knowing I would be yelling profanities in the middle of the store in just a few seconds.

"The keys are locked inside."

I took in a slow, deep breath and exhaled even more slowly. "That's where they'll stay then," I replied. "That's what the hell you get for trying to be sneaky. Do your friends have a bus pass like you? If not, y'all better split a cab."

"I'll break this fuckin' window," Ric threatened.

"I dare you." I hung up and looked at Crystal. "Is Martha at your house?"

Martha is Crystal's maid and/or assistant when necessary.

"You need her to go get the car, huh?" she asked as she dialed her home. "Where is it?"

I powered off my phone when Ric tried to call back. "Lenox. I feel like I have three sons. He found the other key and took my shit. And why the hell would he go to Lenox Mall? We can barely afford to eat in the damn food court there!"

Crystal and I had this emergency procedure in place after the first time Ric took the car. I gave her the spare key along with the other keyless entry remote for situations like this. Then, if needed, she or poor Martha could ride around a given location pushing my Lock/Unlock button until the beep became audible and the flashing lights became visible. What a shame to have to babysit a grown-ass man.

I knew things were too perfect before I left home almost a week ago. He was home on time every night; he helped the

5

boys with their homework a couple times; and one night, he even ran my bath water and got in the tub with me. He made it a point to reassure me that he wouldn't use the car. He also expressed how juvenile it was of me to hide the spare key, and now look.

The only other key at the house was the valet key, which I taped to the bottom of one of my dresser drawers. That meant the fool did a thorough search of the place until he found what he wanted. So, who's the juvenile here?

I smiled while listening to Crystal relay the information to Martha. "Ask Hans to take you to Lenox Square to get Dana's car. We have no clue where it is, so you'll have to search the whole parking lot. If you see a bunch of men standing around the car, have him park somewhere until they leave…"

Who would've known my girl would be the shot caller she is? When I met her in college, she was a simple girl from Indianapolis. Now, she's the wife of a superstar—Mr. Dante Moss. Her lifestyle is nothing short of luxurious, but despite the glitz and glamour, she's still Crystal Thornton, my former roommate and forever best friend.

An hour and a half later, Martha called back to say she was driving my car to Crystal's house. I still felt a little uneasy because most likely, Ric had his younger and equally immature associates with him, and they were probably heading to our house to play the f'n Playstation. Oh well. The one thing I could control was taken care of, and I refused to worry about it.

*There's nothing I can do about Atlanta happenings while I'm in Indianapolis*, I thought while Crystal and I were purchasing a couple pieces of art from one of the vendors at the convention center.

I was back home in Naptown, celebrating the Indiana Black Expo. For the first time, I attended the professional luncheons and networking sessions. I even attended the health fair while Crystal handled business with Dante this past Thursday. This time, I actually bought items at the booths instead of collecting bags full of free pens, nail files, and church fans that I'd never use.

As teenagers, our expo experience included many nights of watching StarQuest performances and Friday and Saturday visits to the convention center to walk aimlessly around the exhibit halls for hours. The only shopping we did involved buying perch from the fish spot in the Hoosier Dome, and the only networking we did was with the fellas, exchanging numbers like they were handshakes.

I was twenty-three when I last attended the expo festivities, and after I moved to Atlanta, I never made time to return. But, what better time to return? Dante would be the headliner for the Summer Celebration Concert that evening, and I wouldn't miss it for the world. Not only is he talented, he is a great friend to me and an even better husband to Crystal. Every once in a while, I would ask him to give Ric some pointers, but it's probably a man-rule violation to point out each other's relationship flaws.

"I wanted to run to White Castle, but we better head back to the hotel," Crystal said after checking her cell phone. "I still have to pick my outfit for tonight."

"I thought you bought that dress for tonight?" I pointed to the bag in the backseat of the car.

"Oh, shit! I forgot!"

"What would you do without me?"

She reached back, grabbed the bag, and threw it onto my lap. "I don't know," she replied with a wink.

"You got this for me?" I asked.

I'm not big on charity, but the dress was baaad.

"You can't be walking around with me in that pants suit Ric told you was cute. You're not chaperoning a school dance, sweet pea. You're hitting the town, and you're gonna look sexy doing it. I feel like a prophet. That's a fuck-'em-girl

7

dress if I've ever seen one, and he didn't even piss you off until after I bought the thing."

We both howled with laughter. We used to love that 'fuck-'em-girl' saying in college. Whenever our boyfriends would piss us off, we'd hit the club hard just to remind ourselves of our capabilities. She was right. As soon as night falls, I will slide into that dress, forget about my husband's poor judgment, and remember who I am.

Fuck 'em, girl!

# WILLOW (MILKY)

"Your usual?" Gretchen asked as I approached the MAC counter with my darkest shades on.

I nodded while she reached for the Studio Finish Concealer in my color and placed two of them on the counter.

"It's been a while since you've been in," she said, trying her best to sound uplifting.

I handed my credit card to her. "Not really. Natalie waited on me the last two times."

With no words to utter, she rested her hand on mine and smiled softly. Finally, while pointing to the display of lipglass, she said, "Would you like to try our Lustreglass? I think Love Nectar would look sexy on you."

Careful not to aggravate my bruised cheek, I attempted to smile slightly and motioned for Gretchen to add the tube to my order. After I signed the receipt, she handed me the bag and covered her thin lips with the index finger of her other hand.

"I hope you feel better," she said sweetly before approaching another woman at the opposite end of the counter.

I peeked inside the bag and found a tube of Lovechild lipglass—my favorite. Before I left, I blew Gretchen an appreciative kiss. Not for the complimentary lip gloss she'd slipped in the bag, but for the thought behind it. On a day when nothing about me seemed beautiful, a subtle, nonverbal statement like the one she made lifted my spirits. God bless her.

It's a shame most of the girls at the makeup counter know me. Not because I'm so vain, but because I am constantly using their product to cover the bruises on my face—the ones my husband gives me. Wait. There I go being unappreciative. Vaughn also gives me the money to purchase the cover-up. (Insert sarcastic smile here.)

He gives me money for everything because he's the breadwinner. He's the spoiled rich kid who has been accustomed to getting any and everything he wants ever since he was old enough to grunt and point. I don't resent that at all. I just don't understand why my face always seems to take the brunt of his temper tantrums when he's having a bad day.

Complaining is not my thing, though. I could play the victim, but I'm stronger than that. I've lived through the hurt and confusion of being abandoned by my biological mother and father, eventually overcoming those ill feelings and trying my hand at motherhood. And God is good. Venus has been my saving grace and the center of my world since she was born, and in her three years of life so far, I have been my happiest.

Vaughn is a great father. Every free moment he has is reserved for Venus. He's usually the one scheduling her kiddie activities and picking up outfits for her when he's away on business trips—things mothers normally do. She's his reason for living and mine, too.

At times, I wonder if she's the only thing that connects us. We are night and day personified, as different as oil and water. Yet, we still try to mix, try to make it work. I wouldn't say I stay with Vaughn because of Venus, though. I stay with him because I love him. I stay because I took vows and am woman enough to keep them. No one ever said the road would be easy, and whenever we reach a bump on our road, I remind myself, *For better or for worse.*

It's not fair for me to say Venus is our saving grace, though. All in all, Vaughn is a fantastic man. Three hundred and fifty-five days out of the year, he's a beauty, and the other ten, he's a beast. I'm not a gambling woman and have never liked math, but that ratio doesn't seem too horrible. The only trouble with it is some nights I'm not sure whether to put on my sexiest lingerie or boxing gloves.

Our tale began with him being the perfect gentleman. I met him at a job fair after I moved down here to Atlanta. My sister, Crystal, said she'd cover my rent for three months after I relocated, and I had a little money in my savings. But, when I heard of the job fair on V103, I figured I'd see if I could snag a j-o-b after only being in town for two weeks.

Vaughn was at the J.T. Development booth talking with an older gentleman, when I approached and picked up a poorly-designed brochure. He turned to greet me, did a double-take, and the rest, as they say, is history. When I told him I could redesign their marketing materials, he confidently stated he could redesign my life.

According to most standards, we had a whirlwind romance. It was truly love at first sight. His skin resembled a Hershey's Special Dark candy bar—smooth, starting with his clean-shaven head and ending at his pedicured feet. If he knew my nickname, he would've pictured the same thing I envisioned: a swirl of two chocolates coming together as one. I remember wanting to kiss his full lips as we conversed at the job fair. I remember wanting to act like no one was around, wanting to clear the table of all its literature with one swipe and instead display our bodies for all to see. I remember thinking he felt the same as his eyes periodically bypassed my face and focused on my all-natural D cups. I listened to his every word, watching the movement of his tongue, imagining it was flicking my nipples, imagining he was imagining the same.

He spoke with intelligence, and his stature exuded self-assurance. I admired how handsome he looked in his crisp white shirt and how his tie ended with the arrow pointing to the spot that first caught my attention. When we said goodbye, his handshake was firm, but gentle, and the light touch to my back with his other hand just about sent me through the roof.

"I look forward to doing business with you, Ms. Thornton," he had said, while his fingertips lingered in the small of my back.

Four days later, I was working my magic in Photoshop, and two days after that, Vaughn and I went on our first date to the Sun Dial Restaurant downtown, celebrating his 22nd birthday. I didn't know he was younger than me until he chatted at dinner about that birthday celebration being much more reserved than his last. He then went on to give me details of his previous festivities, highlighting the fact that he was finally able to buy his own alcohol.

I tried not to let our age difference bother me. If he hadn't said anything, I would've been convinced that he was at least my age, maybe a year or two older. Really, three years isn't that much of a gap. He proved then to be wise beyond his years—wise enough to recognize a good woman like myself and put a ring on my finger. We were engaged after six months and married in less than two years. I remember…

I rushed into the house and threw the MAC bag onto the kitchen counter. Since my plane wasn't scheduled to take off until three, I used the extra time to change into the knit Capri outfit I'd bought a few days prior. As I slid my feet into my flip flops, I inhaled a figurative breath of fresh air. This weekend getaway couldn't have come at a better time.

I was looking forward to meeting up with Crystal and Dana. They'd been in Indianapolis since Tuesday, attending luncheons and other events that I would've loved to if Vaughn wasn't so jealous and suspicious. His insecurities are the reason I'm taking his father's private jet. It's all about his convenience. Since he wants me to leave when he thinks it's appropriate, he's sending me on the jet. If he wants me back home sooner, he'll send the jet to Indianapolis early and arrange for a car to drive me to the airport. I didn't anticipate a premature departure for my return flight, though. Vaughn knows he is not on my good side after last night's events.

To be truthful, I don't recall the initial reason for our argument. What I do remember is Vaughn accusing me of lying about my whereabouts, insinuating that I am cheating on him. I didn't want our dispute to turn ugly, so I tried to assure him the best way I knew how. As he looked through my phone for suspicious activity, I placed my hand on his thigh, rubbing up and down, then up some more, and up a little bit more. At first, he acted as if he didn't feel it, but as his manhood grew, so did his rage.

"Don't touch me! Get your fuckin' hands off of me. You think you can distract me with one of your slut moves?"

I could've punched him in the balls. I've only been with three men, including him, and he knows that. He also knows the pain I associate with the word "slut" after a year of being taunted by my snobby sophomore classmates who learned some of my family background and used it to hurt me because their boyfriends liked me. "Your mom was a

13

teenage slut," they'd say, "and you're gonna be just like her. I don't care who adopted you. The apple doesn't fall far from the tree."

As the words echoed in my head, I made a fist. I wanted to punch him. I was going to punch him. But then, he punched me.

The blue ice pack still lay on the bathroom counter, its gel now warm. Vaughn had handed it to me after a five-minute apology. I didn't dare tell him that his sympathetic kisses to my eye were only making the throbbing worse.

He promises he doesn't mean to harm me, and I believe him. When I look into his eyes while he's enraged, there's no one there. It's like he leaves his body momentarily, then returns once my tears fall. He says he wants to change and has even attended anger management classes, which clearly changed nothing except that he may substitute a backhand for a punch on occasion. I beg him to join me at church, but he won't do it. Whenever I speak of God's grace and His ability as a waymaker, Vaughn shuts me out. One day, I hope he'll realize God can do more for him than any anger management class could ever do. Until then, last night's incident marks our fourth this year. Not bad for July, I guess. That's less than one per month.

I looked up and faced myself in the mirror. The swelling had gone down significantly, but I would definitely have to put more ice on it once I boarded the plane. The more I can decrease the chances of Crystal seeing the damage, the better. She hates Vaughn, and if I place myself on the outside and look in, I can't blame her. All she sees are the black eyes, bruises, and bite marks; not the kisses, hugs, and subtleties that I receive far more often. As far as she's concerned, there is no excuse for his violent behavior, and I agree. It's just that I'm his wife. I know him, and I know this isn't him. It's a demon that needs to be cast out in the name of Jesus.

14

That being said, I pulled two more pairs of sunglasses from my closet and placed them in my duffle bag. When I returned downstairs, I added the MAC bag. As I zipped closed the duffle, Vaughn blew the horn. I extended the handle of my carry-on suitcase and carefully placed my shades on my face again. *Operation Cover-Up is in effect.*

# CRYSTAL

I stood at the side of the stage with Milky and Dana, waiting for the smoke to clear. Dante had completed his third wardrobe change and now wore charcoal-gray silk pajama pants, baby oil, and a look in his eyes that would send every female into panty-dropping mode.

The women in the crowd went wild as my husband gyrated onstage and crooned to the crying fan in the front row. The excitement I felt reminded me of the first three years of our marriage when I proudly hung on his arm as the woman who snagged the hottest R&B sensation of the era. Now that we've reached year eight of matrimony, I see him for what he really is: an actor. If those women only knew he has acne that flares up once a month like a woman on her period, won't shave his hairy balls, and can't live up to his lyrics about lovemaking, they wouldn't be standing with wet panties wishing he was theirs.

When he first wrote "Mr. All Night Long" and let me hear it one night before we went to bed, I loved it. It's one of those songs you can put on your "get some" CD twice. The problem is, I can only get some from him once, and

16

nowadays, I have to cheat and apply my clit stimulating cream before we make love if I want to guarantee an orgasm.

Let him tell it, his lackluster bedroom performances are a side effect of his larger-than-life stage performances. He's either too tired to even try and I end up on top doing all the work, or he flops on top of me repeatedly and pauses for extended breaks, or he gives his last ten-minute burst of energy that ends with him shriveling up inside of me when I'm just warming up.

Let me tell it, he's been doing more than he's previously admitted to with his little groupies. His mannerisms are more informal; he's not as explosive when he cums; and his stamina has decreased far more than he can blame on fatigue. If it's that serious, drink a Red Bull and let's get it poppin'.

I watched Dante pull the little hot girl on stage and sit her in the chair. 'Privileged' was written all over her face as she winked at her girlfriends in the crowd and puckered her lips at my husband. Her miniskirt barely met her mid-thigh, and when she crossed her right leg over her left, it crept up two more inches. Dante complimented her on her choice of wardrobe, then asked the men in the audience if they agreed.

*Game on.* Just as he did to the blonde in Phoenix, the plus-size beauty in New Orleans, and the ebony woman in Houston, he stood in front of the P.Y.T. and sang to her. Starting with a stroke of her hair, he made that stranger feel special. His hand never left her body as he lowered himself to his knees.

I miss the exciting Dante. Before we ever met, I would see him around town—sometimes at Lafayette Square Mall, other times at the skating rink on the Westside, but mostly at the StarQuest competitions where he'd perform with three of his high school friends. From Jodeci to Boyz II Men to

Shai, their renditions of the time's hottest music had us teenage girls open.

Dante always stood out. He was the best looking, the best vocalist, and the best dancer. So, imagine how many females became instant Crystal haters when Dante and I crossed paths again during my freshman year of college. Just add jealousy and stir.

It was homecoming, and he came to IU to perform. His visit was a big deal because he's an Indiana native who had just signed his first record contract. I was working at the sports complex at the time, and Saturday morning, I had to open the place. When I arrived at 5:40 a.m., ten minutes late as usual, Dante and his manager, Tre, were waiting by the main doors.

"Do you work here, sweetie?" Tre asked.

I didn't answer because there's no way he could've missed me placing my key in the door and opening it.

"You look familiar," Dante said, squinting as if it would somehow help his memory. "Are you from Nap?"

Being too tired to care that he recognized me, I nodded and held the door open. "Are y'all coming in?"

As they followed me to the main office, I asked if they were coming to work out.

Tre cleared his throat and activated his let's-make-a-deal voice. "That's what we're hoping to do. See, I don't know if you know who this young man is, but he's one of the hottest new—"

"His name is Dante, and he's performing tonight at Assembly Hall." I turned to Dante. "Are you trying to work out for free? Is that what he's trying to get at?"

After a nervous laugh, he nodded. "Can you get me in? I'm not feeling the fitness center at the hotel, and I don't like missing my workouts."

I glanced to see if my boss was looking, then activated the turnstile so they could go through.

18

"I appreciate it," Dante said.

I didn't appreciate the smile he had given me until an hour later when I woke up completely. Once he was done working out, he stopped by my turnstile and waited for me to finish my conversation with my coworker.

"Thanks again," he said.

"You should thank me publicly tonight at your concert," I joked.

"Are you coming?"

"I've had my ticket since the first day they went on sale."

I swear I saw him blush. "Well, hopefully, I'll see you later..." He paused to read my nametag. "...Miss Crystal." He pulled a piece of paper from the pocket of his hoodie and handed it to me.

*A V.I.P. pass?* I thought, while accepting the paper that was too flimsy to be anything important. After staring at the receipt that listed his purchases from T.I.S. Bookstore, I looked blankly at him.

"You want me to be your trash girl, too?" I asked.

"What?"

I shook my head and threw the receipt in the can near my foot. "Anything else you need before you go, Your Majesty?" I'd heard he was a little cocky, but if I was expected to perform one more favor, I was going to remind him that I wasn't on the payroll to be his little bitch.

"How are you gonna call me when my number's in the trash?" he asked before licking his lips and walking away.

That was fourteen years ago, and to this day, Dante still denies licking his lips like a lame. I tell him he ought to try licking 'em nowadays so I can feel what I felt that day. Realistically, though, the newness of love or lust can't be reenacted or rekindled. It can only be remembered.

Dana's elbow dug into the side of my arm as the girl Dante was serenading planted a kiss on his forehead. She still doesn't understand how I deal with that type of activity. I don't understand either, but as one of the other industry wives told me, it's not to be understood. It's just the way it is. We can either get mad about a chick who fantasizes about having him as her man or smile because we are living out her fantasy.

I can use the line "I know who he's coming home to", but that doesn't mean he's being faithful before he comes home. If our marriage had a theme song, it'd be a cross between MoKenStef's "He's Mine" and Monica's "Sideline Ho". Unlike the songs, though, he keeps his little floozies in check. I told him that he doesn't have to fess up to his extramarital activities, but it'll be on if I see some shit in the tabloids, hear it amongst his band members, or smell it when he comes home. Yes, I said smell it. According to our agreement, he shouldn't even be close enough to *it* to pick up its scent.

While we dated in college, he was very upfront with me. He wanted me to be his girl, but he warned me of his groupies, saying they were a part of the after-party experience just like bottle-popping and dancing. In other words, in his mind, his flings with them didn't count as cheating. I rolled with that for a while, because when it came down to it, I was damn near running a mini soup kitchen during the times I needed to get one off, and I had a list of customers who wanted to feast on a little Cream of Crystal. If men can say "sucking ain't fucking", then women can surely say "eating ain't cheating". I barely saw him anyway because he was living in L.A. and constantly doing promotional shows all over the country. With both of us having needs, we fulfilled them until we could be together again.

Once we became an official couple, we modified our agreement. His after-party experience could no longer involve penetration. Something had to be mine. Something

20

had to be sacred. And I chose Junior, the nickname I had given his eight-incher.

"You don't have a thing to prove," I told him. "If you can't say no to those thirsty hoes, you let 'em drink and that's where it ends. Be about self." He knew exactly what I meant.

Sounds stupid, right? Sure, it was a tough pill to swallow, but when I started going on tour with him and meeting the wives of the other singers, they gave me the water to help get it down. Farah gave me the clearest perspective. In a nutshell, she said a man is only going to say no so many times to half-naked or completely naked girls who meet him at his hotel. Some hoes, like puppies, wait anxiously for their chance to do a trick so they can get a treat. Others, like vultures, are bold enough to attack until they get what they want—a celebrity name to add to their list. Whatever the approach, they usually attain their goal.

"Don't take it personal unless he gets personal," Farah advised. "The problems arise when those tramps feel like they're significant."

Before we tied the knot, Dante and I sat down again for some real talk. I told him I'm no one's fool. Even though his intentions may not be to cheat, shit happens, and I wanted him to be clear on what type of shit was permitted and what wasn't. I laid out the rules under a "deal or no deal" contract. No kissing. No holding. No real conversation. No number exchanging. No sexing. No repeats. When getting head, he is to wear a condom. No one gets all of him except me. He pleases no one but me.

Of course, he said he was done with that stuff—that he would only be hooking his boys up with a little trim from then on. I can't say if he has or hasn't, but I *can* say I'm smart enough to know better. He's smart enough not to track his dirt through our house, though, and if I don't see it, it isn't happening.

21

One may ask how a college-educated woman can involve herself in such a situation. Quite frankly, millions of other college-educated women who are married to average, everyday men are in the same predicament. They just choose to turn a blind eye to their man's actions—their damn near poor-ass man's actions. Let me clarify. I'm not even close to being a gold digger. But if I'm going to spend some nights alone while my man is out doing whatever, you better believe I'll be doing so from the comfort of my eight-bedroom mansion, while watching *Cheaters* on the flat-screen TV and soaking in my Jacuzzi tub.

"You have to be one of the strongest women I know," Dana said as the song ended and the girl exited the stage. "The way she looked at him…"

"They all look, sweetie. That's all they can do. It's like shopping at Saks with an EBT card. What the hell you gon' get?"

"You and your analogies," Milky said, smiling and shaking her head.

Once the show was over, me and the girls hit the club to attend my baby's after-party. Dana was killing 'em in her dress, looking like neither a mother nor a teacher. Ironically, she ran into a guy she went to high school with who was fine as early morning snow, could dance his ass off, and spent almost the entire night dancing with her. While Milky and I lounged in V.I.P., she stayed downstairs with him until almost closing time.

Around three a.m., my stomach started feeling queasy, so I made my way over to Dante.

"I'm about to go back to the hotel, baby. What you wanna do?" I said in his ear, while caressing his neck on the opposite side.

"I got you, baby," he replied before giving me a kiss goodbye. He knew then he only had about an hour and a

22

half window to make it to the room and get some before I passed out.

I gathered the girls and we headed to the valet station.

"You look like you're gonna throw up," Milky said as we waited near the curb.

"I feel like it, too." I looked at Dana, who was fiddling with her phone. "What you doin' over there? Texting Mr. High School?"

"Girl, please. Not at all."

I twisted my lips in disbelief.

"I don't even have his number," she added.

"You're on punishment. How you gon' wear the fuck-'em-girl dress and not do your thing?"

"Probably because she's wearing that ring," Milky said, pointing to Dana's left finger.

"Right!" Dana agreed. "I did exactly what I wanted to do. I had a ball celebrating my renewed sexiness. You know I wasn't trying to walk away with anybody tonight. I wanted to forget about Ric being an inconsiderate idiot, not forget that he's my husband."

All I could do was shrug as the valet parked the car in front of us. "Let's roll, ladies."

When we got back to the room, I flipped the light switch, and Dana instantly gasped.

"Flowers!" Dana's high came down just as quickly as it went up. She walked past the table where they set and plopped onto the bed. "I know they aren't for me. Ric and I were dating the last time I got flowers."

"Shut up, fool," I said with a chuckle. "Bet Mr. High School would give you flowers."

She threw one of her heels in my direction. I dodged it and pulled the card from the plastic holder to read it. "To Willow…From Vaughn…Just Because."

"Awww!" Dana sang as she lay with the pillow covering her head. "Forget y'all and your cutesy marriages."

23

Milky admired the flowers as I let Vaughn's words sink in. "Ain't that special. The card should've read, 'Just because I went upside your head again'." I flicked a petal before going into the bathroom. "Please."

I didn't have to pee, but I found it best to retreat to avoid embarrassing my sister any further. Dana is like a sister to us, as well, so she knows the situation. Still, I like to save my verbal thrashings for when Milky and I are in private.

She didn't think I knew this time. She was flitting around backstage and at the after-party like she was all good, but I saw the hint of bruising just above her cheekbone. I told her the last time it happened that if he even thought about laying his hands on her again in any way other than seductively, I was saying something. She begs me to stay out of it, but I'm not sure how long I can keep my mouth shut.

I exited the bathroom, only to find Dana knocked out and Milky texting on her phone. There was no question of who was on the other end of that chat.

"Alright, I'm gone. I'll see y'all in the morning."

Since she was pissed, Milky didn't acknowledge me, and I didn't make time to call her out. I would have plenty of time to do that the next day. My priority was getting to my room and taking some Pepto Bismol before Dante came back and rocked my body into a seasick frenzy...hopefully.

# DANA

It was the Friday before my first in-service day at school, and I needed to get a few last-minute supplies for my personal collection. Our neighbor, Ms. Gladys, said she would keep Chase and Dalvin while I went to Staples to rack up on extra Post-It notes, pens, and Lord knows what else. My palms moistened with excitement as I approached the door. The huge red and white banner in the window indicated that everything in the store was fifteen to thirty percent off, which is definitely a teacher's dream.

Although I was done with my shopping, I couldn't resist the urge to browse the remainder of the aisles. I ended up in the furniture section near a beautiful mahogany desk. I ran my hand across its smooth finish as I glanced at the price tag.

"You like stroking wood?" a male voice asked.

With my neck cocked to the right, I turned to my left and saw Lorenzo's huge smile. Instantly, I relaxed.

"Boy, I was about to cuss you out," I said, playfully backhanding his chest. If I wasn't married, I would've definitely hit him with a comment like, "Yeah, I like stroking and polishing it, and my polish has all natural ingredients."

25

Lorenzo and I started teaching at Lithonia Grove High School the same year, and we have been close ever since our second day of in-service after he almost ran me over in the parking lot. He has joked with me for five years about how we should've met sooner so he could've been my husband. Our running joke now is that he's my seven o'clock to three o'clock husband, Monday through Friday and during the sporting events we attend together.

We checked out at the same time, and he walked me to my car.

When I caught him staring, I giggled a little. "What are you looking at?"

"So is this the year you're gonna get divorced and marry me?" he asked.

He knows nothing about my problems with Ric, but he uses every opportunity to reiterate that he's mine for the taking if I'm ever interested. I won't lie. Some days I *am* interested. I'm married, not blind. And because of the fact that I'm human and currently unhappily married, if given the right place, time, and mindset, Lorenzo could get it. Knowing this, I avoid placing myself in predicaments that may yield to such an encounter.

He's a shade away from being considered a yellow boy, and he would probably be labeled as a pretty boy if his swagger didn't have so much of an edge. He's slim in stature, but his body screams former wide receiver, and his dress shirts and slacks look heavenly draped over his perfectly defined body. Though I love a man with waves, his bald head suits him just fine, leaving nothing to distract me from his handsome face. If I had to be picky, I'd complain about his gap. I'm very particular about teeth, but outside of that discrepancy, his are flawless. Actually, as the years have gone by, his gap has become part of his appeal.

"Is this the year our football team will finally make it to the playoffs, Coach?" I fired back.

26

"If we do, will you leave your husband?"

I fell out laughing, but secretly thanked God that we were in a public place. His bedroom eyes were fixed on me, and if we were near a bedroom, there would've been trouble.

I quickly regained my focus as I drove home. It was date night for me and the hubby, and I couldn't wait. Our scheduled alone time has become predictable, but we've been consistent, which is a plus. Ric's a dinner and movie kind of guy. He doesn't think outside of the box, and when I do, he's sure to pull me back inside the box and close the lid. I'm at the point now where I take what I can get. Since he's willing to devote two nights a month to us, I make the best of it by preparing my taste buds for meat and potatoes and perusing the paper for the newest movie releases.

Ric greeted me with a kiss and pat on my backside when he came in from work. "Did you decide where you want to eat?" he asked, placing two Best Buy bags near the couch.

"I have a taste for Olive Garden, but..."

"Man, you know I can't stand that place."

"Yeah, I know. You can't stand most of the places I love," I mumbled. "Well, I guess it's Chilli's again," I said in a more audible volume.

"I told you we can check out that new spot on Peachtree," he replied.

I silently applauded his initiative, but was hesitant in agreeing. I heard the place was very classy, and Ric was not about to put on anything more than a pair of jeans and a button-down shirt. After telling him Chilli's would suffice, I went to the closet to decide which jeans I would wear. *Just once, I'd like to dress up*, I thought as the cocktail dress I'd had for two years caught my eye, tags still attached.

When I reentered the living room, Ric was sitting at the computer desk fumbling with a box.

"Are you gonna change clothes?" I asked.

"Yeah. Yeah, baby. Give me one sec. I'm checking out this editing software."

I internalized my grumble but still rolled my eyes. Ric already knew what I was thinking, though.

"It was on clearance, so I picked it up. I can use this until I get that Mac and buy Avid. We'll be straight. The major bills are paid, right?"

"I can't even go there with you right now. Can we just go?"

Dalvin and Chase surrounded Ric as he told them about the different effects he could add to the home videos we've filmed through the years. He went on and on about eventually being able to film their ball games and creating a highlight film.

Moviemaking is his dream. After he left the Air Force, he attended film school in Orlando in pursuit of making the dream come true. Sadly, he couldn't stay focused and dropped out six months into the program. His passion for the profession has stayed the same, though. He's always pitching movie ideas to me and talking about lights and cameras as if I know what he means. I smile and nod like a good wife should do. I'd love for him to get where he wants to be, but his half-stepping is holding him back. In his mind, everything and everyone else is holding him back. God forbid he ever takes responsibility for something.

We finally left the house at seven o'clock. Ms. Gladys stood on the porch as the boys skipped over to her house. After a quick wave goodbye, we were on our way.

It was 8:30 p.m. when we were seated at the restaurant. By that time, I was already annoyed, but I was taken to another level when Ric put on his phony southern drawl while speaking with the waitress.

"Naw, shawty, I said I want my steak *well* done. I don't want it breathin', mooin' at me, or bleedin'. *Well* done."

I gazed out the window to avoid total embarrassment. All of a sudden, he'd turned into T.I., King of the South, in a matter of seconds.

Once she left, I looked at him. "Since when do you speak like that?"

"Like what? Man, go 'head with that. This is how I talk."

"It's not. Stop perpetrating like you're from here. You're from Pittsburgh. You grew up eating pepperoni rolls and cod fish sandwiches, not neck bones and oxtails. Half the natives don't even speak like that. You've been hanging around those teenagers too much."

"How are you gon' tell me how I talk and how I grew up?"

*Because if you talked with such ignorance when I met you, we wouldn't have gotten past 'Let me holla at you, shawty',* I thought. Instead, I replied, "Never mind. It's not worth the argument. Let's just change the subject."

After a few awkward minutes, the mood lightened, and we engaged in more lighthearted conversation. He even complimented me on the new lip gloss I had bought earlier in the day, which I didn't think he would notice.

I became increasingly turned on as I periodically caught him staring at my lips. They're what most men usually compliment me on, but having my husband looking like he wanted to suck them off my face made me want to say, "Check, please!"

We made it through dinner without ripping each other's clothes off, thanks to his cell phone. He spent twelve minutes on the damn thing while scarfing down his steak and corn on the cob. With each passing second and each chuckle he let out, it was clear he wasn't on a date with me. He ditched me to have a date with his partner on the other end of the line. I wasn't supposed to be upset because he was talking to another male and they were talking "business", but I don't think a discussion about the best

29

Ghetto Boys song fits under that category. Five minutes into their conversation, the area on my body that was once flooding was now dry enough to accommodate a few cactuses and a camel. As my kids at school would say, I was having a WTF moment.

*****

I called Crystal the next day to see if she had talked to Willow. We were supposed to take the kids to the aquarium, and I couldn't get in touch with her.

"Milky's probably still on punishment from the expo for exceeding her fun limitations," Crystal joked.

"You are too much. Well, hopefully she'll call back before three. I don't wanna wait around too long. Oh, by the way, I looked over the proposal the other day. There are a few things I'm gonna reword, but other than that, it looks good."

Crystal started some programs for teenage girls under a foundation she named Something to Do. She's been changing their lives for five years, and I've been enthusiastically helping in any way I can for just as long. She had given me a proposal to look at that would get her more funding for mentors. So far, Crystal, Milky, LaToya, who is Crystal's business partner, and I are the only ones giving our time to the girls, and we're spreading ourselves thin.

"Cool. Thank you." Before we hung up, she asked, "How did date night go? What did y'all do?"

"You know what we did. You should've just asked which restaurant we went to and what movie we saw," I replied.

"Well?"

"Chilli's and that X-Files movie."

"And how did it go?"

30

"It went. That's all I can say. You know Ric is only gonna do the bare minimum. He was texting during the majority of the movie."

"Maybe *you* should've texted him so you could've had some attention."

We laughed.

"The best part of the night took place in bed."

"So you temporarily became un-pissed so y'all could get it in?" She howled with laughter.

"Temporarily! I can't say no to the meat. It's a special thing."

"I ain't mad at you!"

"His birthday is Thursday, so I guess I'll get ready for more of the same. Do you know of any movies coming out next week?"

Crystal doesn't know the details about my problems with Ric. Sometimes I want to vent to her, let out all my frustrations, tell her all the stories. However, I've always heard it isn't healthy to share marital business with anyone—not even your best friend. None of us share that part of our lives with each other now that I think about it. The only reason I know about Vaughn abusing Willow is attributed to the obvious. She could only fool us with the kickboxing injury story or the falling-down-the-steps-in-the-middle-of-the-night fib a couple times before we demanded the truth. Crystal? Well, she probably has nothing to complain about besides Dante not spoiling her with the damn towel warmer she's been wanting for over a year now. Everyone has their "big deals", though. Mine just so happens to be a cluster of deal breakers that I wish I would've known about before making the deal.

Before I got married, my dad said something that stuck with me. *There's nothing two people can't work out. The problems arise when you bring the third person into it.* Back then, it made sense. I remember hearing my mother on the phone giving

31

her friends a play-by-play account of her and my dad's arguments, and since she's so easily influenced, they could have easily talked her into doing and saying things that drove my dad away. Then again, he may have known she was spreading their business and acted accordingly.

Now that I'm older, more analytical, and married, I'm beginning to feel like he could've been misinterpreting his own words. Sure, two people can work anything out, but each party must be willing to bend and sacrifice a little to do so. As for the third person messing up the flow, I'm convinced that person is the other woman or the other man. Problems arise when a spouse feels like they can cheat with a third party and still participate in married life.

Maybe my mom needed an ear. Sometimes it's healthy to talk about your problems…therapeutic. Instead of seeing a psychologist, she went to her friends. Maybe I need an ear, but I'm almost ashamed to share this part of my life. Damn that. I *am* ashamed! I don't want to be looked at as the dummy I said I'd never be…the dummy I feel I am sometimes.

Even though Willow has a major problem with Vaughn, he treats her like gold—no, platinum—on most days. He has a bank account that can probably feed the state of California if there were ever a crisis, and he would give her the world if it were for sale. That doesn't make it right, but I could see small incentives there that would make me think twice about leaving. Then, there's my Ric, the cell phone store manager with a gold bus pass…and I'm with him, waiting for him to mature and catch a clue. Let me share that with my close friends and see how therapeutic that is.

I often wonder if there's a positive correlation between the type of wedding you have and the type of marriage you have. Fabulous wedding, fabulous marriage; obligatory wedding, obligatory marriage. If Ric could've gotten away with just signing the marriage certificate and not saying a vowel of a vow, he would have. We argued for five months about what state the wedding would be in, how many bridesmaids I wanted versus how many groomsmen he wanted, reception or no reception, not having enough money for the honeymoon, where to go for the honeymoon, and the list goes on.

Then when he was arrested for disorderly conduct at Dugan's Sports Bar a year into our engagement and I used the little bit of money we'd saved for the wedding to bail him out, I gave up. Financially, neither of us had the money it would take to pull off the ceremony I envisioned, and our parents had even less.

After another six months went by with no change in funds, Ric and I sat down to decide what was really important. Were we going to wait indefinitely to come up with the money? Or could we make our commitment official at the Justice of the Peace and have the full-blown ceremony for our five-year anniversary?

I threw a private pity party for a day, eventually concluding that the J.O.P. was the logical choice. We broke the news to our family and friends and wed on July 21, 2001, eight years after we met. I had myself and others convinced that I was okay with my drab exchange of nuptials, but I can't help but feel now that I settled.

These are the moments when I begin to harbor a tad of resentment toward my mother for not emphasizing the things I should consider before entering into a marriage— the things she learned from experience rather than from common sense, the things a mother should discuss with her daughter. When we got married, Ric had the essentials: a job, love for me, and ambition. It seemed like enough. What more did I need? My answer now is time. We needed more time sharing the same space to determine whether we could make it together and for me to see he probably wasn't ready to become a husband, though in his mind he was ready to get married. There's a difference.

# WILLOW (MILKY)

August seems to be the busiest month for us every year. My father-in-law Joseph and Vaughn are usually swamped with paperwork from the new developments that were built months prior, while I'm preparing new advertising materials for the job fairs and expos we have coming up. Not only do I work for J.T. Development, I also do volunteer graphic design work for the March of Dimes. I promised the director of our chapter that I would design posters for their next event, and I had to drop off the flash drive with the file by four o'clock.

*Vaughn's gonna have a conniption*, I thought, as I shut down my laptop and calling Carrie to let her know I was on my way with the file. Sure enough, Vaughn walked into my office shortly before I hung up the phone.

"You heading out?" he asked.

I explained where I was going, avoiding all eye contact. He stood in the doorway, purposely preventing my departure.

"Did you need something before I go?"

35

When I peeked at his eyes, I wished I hadn't. *Here we go,* I thought. As he wrapped his hand around my wrist and squeezed, every muscle in my body tensed.

"Don't you still have work to do here?" he asked as he pushed me further into the office and closed the door. "You get paid to be here. You volunteer there."

I could hear Joseph's voice down the hall, so I wasn't too terrified. Vaughn wouldn't harm me in the presence of others—certainly not his father. I knew he would be annoyed when I said I was leaving, but I didn't understand why he was making it into a bigger issue. Really, all of my work is done on my laptop, so I can work from home if I feel like it. I only come to the office because Vaughn likes to spend more time with me.

He pinned me against the wall and smiled. "I was coming in here to get a little personal business taken care of. Do you have to leave?"

I almost slid to the floor as he planted kiss after kiss on my neck and shoulders. "Baby, yes. I have to get this stuff…" I paused to savor the sensation his touch was giving me. "…to Carrie."

"I want to give this stuff to you, though," he said, pressing his hardness against my pelvis. "Hold on." He walked to my desk and used my phone to page Joseph. "Hey, is Mario still here? I need him to deliver something for me."

I remained against the wall, anticipating the feel of my man. These spontaneous moments are rare, but every time they arise, I'm game.

Vaughn tucked his piece under the elastic of his underwear to conceal its growth and then removed the flash drive from my hand. "I'll be right back."

In three minutes, he was back in my office, and Mario was on his way to Peachtree Street to the March of Dimes office. That's what I mean. He handles business. True to our company's motto "Everyone is a winner", Carrie, Vaughn, and I got what we needed, right on time. Yes, indeed.

*****

"How long do we have to stay?" Vaughn asked when we pulled into my parents' driveway.

In many ways, Vaughn is reserved and a little stuck-up, so he has a hard time socializing with my outgoing and down-to-earth family.

"I don't know, babe. It's not like I have an itinerary for the visit. I definitely want to be home before it gets too late, but I don't get to see Todd often. Plus, it's his birthday. I want to spend time with him. Besides, you've never met him. I think you'll like him."

*Do I ask how long we have to stay at your parents' house when your mother clearly doesn't like me?* I thought.

Todd is my adoptive brother. I rarely get to see him because he plays for the Arizona Cardinals. Because of his schedule, he was unable to attend our wedding, and every time he's been in town, Vaughn has been away on business.

He's the ultimate big brother, figuratively and literally. Standing six-foot-five and weighing three hundred and thirty-eight pounds, he's a gentle giant. That is, until he's provoked. If someone gives him a reason, he won't hesitate to put them on their back, and he's not stopping until his opponent is in a body cast. I say that because it has happened before.

For that reason, I have never told Todd about Vaughn hitting me. As my brother, he only knows how to do one thing: protect—not understand. His ears would deafen to any explanation I'd share regarding why, when, and how. If I ever call on him, hell will have broken loose, and it'll be well worth it. In the meantime, I choose not to jeopardize my brother's career with a high-profile murder case.

37

Mom greeted us at the door with warm hugs. Hezekiah Walker was playing in the background, but I also heard the TV blaring in the den. I could smell Mom's sweet potatoes from the doorway, and I couldn't wait to see what else she cooked.

"Did y'all go to church today?" Mom asked.

"Venus and I did," I replied, trying to sound unaffected.

Vaughn cut his eyes at me. He was raised in church, but I can't pay him to join me for service now. When we were dating, we went together a few times, but I was under the impression that he was attending his home church when he wasn't at New Life with me.

As we followed her into the kitchen, she went on to tell us about the sermon her pastor gave. After a few minutes, she stopped her story. "Oh! Your brother's in the den with Dante and your dad. Y'all don't have to stay in here with me."

"Where's Crystal?"

"Upstairs somewhere. Who knows what she's doing."

Before I headed for the den, I peeked at the pots and pans on the stove. "Yes!" I exclaimed, just as I did in my younger years. Her signature fried corn was simmering in a cast iron skillet, teasing me with its aroma. Mom winked at me as I took Venus by the hand and led her and Vaughn to the man cave.

Todd jumped up as soon as he saw us. "Milky!" I ran to him and jumped into his arms. He returned the love with a bear hug and kiss on my cheek. "Look at you, girl. You look good."

Venus clung to Vaughn's leg and looked up at her uncle with wide eyes. They stayed glued to his face as Todd squatted down and held out his hand.

"Do you remember Uncle T?" he asked sweetly. "Remember our Build-A-Bear trip?"

She nodded and muttered, "Bill Bear." A couple seconds later, she touched his hand lightly, but then she quickly wrapped her arm around Vaughn's leg again.

"You gettin' big, little mama," Todd told her before turning to me. "She's talking a lot better," he said with a proud smile. He then stood and extended his hand to Vaughn. "Good to see you, man. All this time you've just been the dude in the pictures."

Vaughn shook his hand and they did the universal hand-grip-chest-bump-back-pat thing that most men do when greeting each other. "Nice to meet you."

"So you married our little M.C."

He looked at me. "M.C.?"

When we were little, Todd and Crystal used to say I was a black girl trapped in a white girl's body and that I had natural soul. By the time I was eleven, they wanted to give me a nickname. Crystal was the most adamant because that was the thing to do in middle school: have a cool nickname. She went through an entire spectrum of names, ranging from White Chocolate to Cocoa. Finally, she had a teenage epiphany and came up with Milky Way, a play on milk being white and a Milky Way being chocolate. Over the course of a few months, it evolved into M.C. (milk chocolate), M.W. and M. Dub, and then finally settled at Milky. As time went on, it stuck.

Now that we're older, we understand people are people. There's no such thing as acting black or white or red or blue. However, I'll always be Milky, and the name's origin will always remind me of how my family embraced me as their own.

"Milk chocolate," Todd responded. "You probably just call her Milky, though, huh?"

Vaughn's nose turned up as if someone had passed gas in the room and he was trying his best to pretend he didn't smell it. "I call her Willow."

He hates to hear anyone call me Milky. Says it takes away from my identity. He can be so smug when it comes to certain things. It'd be different if I introduced myself to everyone as Milky, but only those people who are close to me call me that.

Todd glanced at me, and I rolled my eyes to confirm what he was thinking. He nodded repeatedly while glaring at Vaughn. "Alright then," he said before returning to the recliner.

"How are you, Mr. Thornton?" Vaughn asked before waving in Dante's direction.

My dad kept his eyes on the television. "Hello, Vaughn."

It's not that he doesn't like Vaughn, but they have nothing in common. Even when they try to discuss sports, they end up arguing because their views are so extreme on opposite sides of the fence. Dad says Vaughn is uppity, and I suppose he would think that way. He's finishing up his last two years at General Motors before retirement. Ever since I can remember, he would come in the house covered with dirt and grease after having worked a ten- or twelve-hour shift—a true blue-collar worker. Vaughn, on the other hand, wears a shirt and tie daily, and he won't even change a flat tire if he doesn't have to.

I felt a bump from behind. "When did you get here?" Crystal asked as she took Venus' hand and joined Dad and Dante on the couch.

"Just a few minutes ago."

Mom came to the doorway. "Y'all come on. Dinner is ready."

Conversation is always great at our family dinners. We make a point to share any news from our personal and professional lives. Dante usually has the most exciting information to report, but since Todd was home, he also had excerpts from the good life to share and was hopeful for the upcoming season. Crystal talked about her new ideas for

40

Something to Do; I bragged about Venus' progress in speech therapy; and Mom and Dad discussed their plans to travel the country once Dad retires.

"I know you're the prince of real estate around here, Vaughn. Can you hook me up when I'm ready to get a place?" Todd asked.

"Yeah. If you're talking condo, I'm your man. If you want a house, I have a friend I can hook you up with."

"So that means you plan on visiting more often?" I asked.

He nodded, and then turned to Vaughn again. "So what else are you into?"

"Hitting women," Crystal said under her breath.

I stared at my plate, praying I was the only one who heard her, but the grinding of Vaughn's teeth gave me a chilling feeling that he heard her, as well.

"I'm a gambling man. I'm thinking about having a house built in Vegas because I'm there so much."

"Oh yeah? Next time you're out that way, give me a call. I go there all the time. We'll hang out. You've been married to my baby sister three years, and I barely know you."

"Don't be trying to intimidate my husband while you hang out," I said.

"He shouldn't feel intimidated if he's treating you right. Right?" Todd directed the comment at Vaughn, who was losing a staring match with Crystal.

"I think that'll be great!" Crystal said with phony enthusiasm. "You guys can bond. Hey, here's an idea. Vaughn, you can recap your entire marriage from the wedding on the beach until now. He'd love to know how well you treat Milky."

"Is there something I'm missing?" Todd asked.

"Nope," Crystal responded. "Vaughn can be shy sometimes, so I want to make sure he tells you how he loves our sister with *all* of his might."

41

# CRYSTAL

"I don't know why she won't use this dishwasher," I said, squeezing the water out of the dishrag.

"You know Mama ain't into all that technology," Milky replied, while handing me the pan that was caked with the remnants of macaroni and cheese.

"Oh, hell no! The devil is a lie if she thinks I'm scraping this shit out." I filled it with soapy water and placed it to the side.

Milky laughed. "You know she's gonna say something."

"And I'll point to that dishwasher. She bugged me for years about gettin' it, and now she won't use it."

Before I placed the butcher knife in the dish rack, I offered it to Milky. "You need this tonight?" She looked confused, so I elaborated. "He's your husband, so you know him best, but he looks like he can't wait to get home and dig into your ass. He wants to dig into mine, but he values his life too much."

"It doesn't help when you instigate, Crys. Now I have to answer all his questions about why you were mumbling at the table and whatever else he comes up with."

"You don't have to answer a thing. Tell him to talk to me about it. Vaughn's known me from day one and I haven't changed. I'm not gonna put on airs like I like his ass when I know just the other day he choked you out. That makes me wrong? That makes me an instigator?"

"He didn't choke me."

"You know what I mean. Don't get technical."

"All I ask is that you respect my wishes. At the end of the day, he's my husband and Venus' daddy."

"If you ask me, he's obsessed with that baby. I don't know what it is, but something ain't natural about his love for her. Why was he feeding her like she's four months old?"

"Okay, Crystal, you're going too far now."

"You don't think he's a little over the top when it comes to her? The play dates, the shopping sprees, the playhouse in your backyard that's damn near as big as Dana's townhouse, the tattoo?"

"Venus has special needs. You know that. Maybe that's why he's so involved with her, but don't act like it's strange. He's not a new boyfriend of mine; he's her daddy." She placed a plate in the dish rack, purposely letting it clang loudly. "And I can name ten men we know off the top of my head that have tattoos of their children's names."

"But his tattoo is a picture of the world revolving around the planet Venus."

"I know what he has," she said, growing more and more defensive.

"He could've put your name *somewhere* on his body. You're sure as hell walking around with the words *Vaughn's House* tattooed on your inner thighs. Do you get it? You're not a part of his big picture."

Milky pressed her fists down on the counter until her knuckles were white.

"I know about Venus' needs," I continued, "but don't you have some, too? He should treat you with the same care.

He's destroying you mentally, emotionally, *and* physically. Do you need a specific condition to demand that he not call you bitches and sluts or hit you? Is there such a thing as Shaken Adult Syndrome? That has to be what you suffer from. Mama didn't raise you to deal with his shit."

Just then, Mama walked into the kitchen. "What are y'all in here fussing about?"

"Take a wild guess," Milky replied.

"Vaughn?" Mama asked, almost whispering.

"Ding, ding, ding!" I answered, while staring at the side of Milky's face since she wouldn't face me.

"I told you to stay out of her marriage. That's how problems occur and relationships get broken. It's either gonna be yours and hers or hers and his."

"I'm okay with it being the latter," I replied as she gave Milky's back a consolation rub.

"After all these years, you still haven't learned how to ignore her?" Mama asked with a smile.

She doesn't know why I don't like Vaughn. Much like she's done with Todd, Milky has kept Mama and Daddy in the dark about Vaughn's abusive ways. As a result, I get pegged as the overprotective sister who always has something negative to say. I'll take the title. I've had it with that punk of a man, and I don't regret giving my little sister the real. I only dish out tough love when absolutely necessary, and I'm thinking black eye number thirty-one makes her a perfect candidate for a strong dose. I couldn't help but feel bad, though, when I looked into her eyes and saw a gloss of tears covering them.

Mama took an extra dishrag and wiped the counter near the dish rack. "Willow, I need to talk to you later," she said. "Remind me when we have some privacy."

Milky looked at me for answers. When I shrugged, her eyes pierced me. *Did you tell her?* she mouthed, referring to her Black Expo black eye. Even though I'd told her I'd had enough of Vaughn's punk ass and was thinking of taking action, telling our mother was never in my plan.

*Hell no!* I mouthed back.

I felt like we were kids again. Whenever Mama wanted to chat with us in private, the conversations were far from lighthearted. We were either in trouble or something bad had happened.

Todd rounded the corner, coming from the living room. "Since I have all my favorite girls in the same room, I need your opinion." He pulled a piece of paper from his pocket and unfolded it. "What do you think?" He set the paper on the island as me, Mama, and Milky huddled to see. It was a printout of the engagement ring he bought for his girlfriend.

"Does it have to be so extravagant?" Mama asked.

"He makes over a million dollars a year, Ma. This is the equivalent of you going to Kay's and picking out something. That's not extravagant. It's what he can afford," I responded for Todd.

"You have such a way with words," Milky said.

"I think it's gorgeous," I continued. "Did you pick it out yourself?"

Todd nodded as Milky also gave her approval. While he brainstormed about memorable proposals, my mind drifted to my graduation day when Dante surprised me at the ceremony by meeting me at the end of my row with a ring. I swear I walked on air that day. Mr. Rico Suave himself had come through and swept me off my feet, and true to style, he did the same on our wedding day. Actually, we had two weddings: one in Aruba with just us, our parents, and our siblings, and another here in Atlanta at the mansion where he lived before we got married.

I tuned back in as Milky asked Todd where his ceremony would be.

"I don't know. She'll probably want to have it in L.A. since that's her hometown."

"Why don't you do a location wedding?" I asked.

"Because my little sisters already wed in Hawaii and Aruba, my top two choices!"

Milky and I laughed.

"You need a top five then," she said. "What about Jamaica or Puerto Rico?"

"Ooh. Puerto Rico sounds sexy," I added.

"What about a church?" Mama asked. "What's wrong with a good ol' fashioned church wedding? If you want to 'do it big' as y'all say, go to a mega church."

We cracked up. Though our mother is old-fashioned, she knows good and well that she enjoys using our weddings as all-expense-paid vacations.

"Whatever I do, it won't live up to yours unless I hire Oprah to do our vows or something. I won't even ask you for suggestions about the ceremony logistics," Todd joked.

"Boy, stop! It wasn't that serious." *Okay, maybe it was*, I thought as they shot me *bitch, please* looks.

Yes, we had five hundred guests, but in my defense, most of them were Dante's invitees. He wanted to include his industry peers and some members of the press for P.R. purposes. And yes, Spinderella was our deejay. It was only fitting, and she had us grooving all night.

Thinking back, our "second" big day *was* a big deal. Why couldn't it be, though? It was the one day that set the standard for the rest of our lives together. Dante treated me like his queen on April 1, 2000, and that hasn't changed in eight years.

We wed purposely on April Fool's Day to further confuse the media and paparazzi. From the moment we were engaged, rumors circulated about the four W's concerning our matrimony: who, what, when, and where. Depending on which magazine you read, we were married the same day he proposed in Vegas, had a private ceremony in Indianapolis on his birthday, had an untraditional

46

wedding while on an African safari in January, or we simply had a minister come to our house and marry us in the great room.

"I may have to bite off the horse-drawn carriage idea, though," Todd admitted. "That was hot."

"You don't wanna sing Sydney a song?" Milky joked in reference to Dante singing a song he wrote for me called "Crystal Clear".

"I'll run everybody away if I start singing," Todd replied.

Mama stood with her elbows resting on the counter and her fingers intertwined. "That song Dante sang to you was the most beautiful thing I've ever heard. I pray you don't take that lightly. Those words…" She couldn't finish her thought. "Beautiful."

"So stop hating," I said to my siblings. "You can't sing, so do what you do," I added, nudging Todd. "Tackle her as she walks down the aisle or impress the crowd by bench pressing a thousand pounds. Find what works for you."

We all rolled with laughter as Dante approached me from behind and slid his hands around my waist. "Why didn't y'all tell me the party was in here?" he asked.

"You would've known if you would've come in here to help with the dishes," I quipped before kissing him. "They were in here hating on our wedding, baby."

"Oh yeah?"

Todd explained how he wanted to do something to wow his bride and their guests.

"The glitz and glamour details aren't up to you anyway, sweet pea," I said. "That'll be for Sydney and her family to decide. If she wants a horse and carriage, she'll get it. If she wants to do a naked handstand and walk down the aisle, she'll do it. Think with your heart, and whatever you come up with for your contribution will be special. If all else fails, make Dante sing for you."

47

Mama shook her head, signifying that my words never cease to amaze her.

"I don't know, baby. You said he had jokes about our song, right?" Dante asked, while smiling and stroking his goatee.

Vaughn appeared in the doorway with Venus in his arms. "She's getting sleepy." His commanding tone was sent Milky's way.

"You can lay her in the guestroom, Vaughn," Mama said. "Do you want me to take her up there?"

"No, thanks. She needs to be in her own bed."

*Ike has spoken*, I thought.

Milky gave Todd a quick hug and kiss. "What time do you leave tomorrow?"

"Ten-thirty."

"I'll try my best to get over here early so I can see you off," she said desperately.

She followed suit with the rest of us, limiting each kiss and hug combination to three seconds. Vaughn said his unavoidable goodbyes as well before they headed out.

"What's up with him?" Todd asked Dante as soon as they were out of sight.

"He's a little weird, different. He's a young cat, too. What is he, twenty-seven, baby?"

*And crazy*, I thought, while nodding.

As the front door closed, I prayed for my sister's safety. There's no rhyme or reason to what sets Vaughn off, and I hoped she wouldn't be punished for the shots I'd taken at him.

# DANA

I logged into Ric's email account from my desk since I had a few minutes to spare before my homeroom students arrived. He had given me the password about two years ago, but I hadn't checked it in about a year. Since his internet activity has increased, though, I can't think of a more appropriate time to perform an inquiry.

Technology is a curse from the devil, and I mean that with every fiber of my being. With its social networking sites, chat rooms, and widespread porn, the worldwide web is the lead demon. I think all men are obsessed with the anonymity of the internet. They create profiles that display only half the man they are and, like fishing lines, throw them out to see what woman will bite. Throw in a webcam and, Lord, help us all. I find the whole concept to be comical. The most hardcore man will pose in front of the bathroom mirror, cell phone in-hand, with his shirt off and sunglasses on, just to post a picture that will draw a comment from a lady other than his own.

Ric has an obsession with porn, so I wasn't surprised to see all the messages from those types of sites in his spam box. They offered him white girls, Asian girls, animals, she-males, and everything in between. I prayed some of the categories were in his spam box because they were just that—spam. If he gets turned on by watching a man screw a monkey or by watching a "girl" named Lucy jack off, I have some blood that needs to be screened, and we've got some papers to sign.

What *did* surprise me was the email from his coworker, LaShay. She's a little nineteen-year-old hot ass who works at his store after she gets out of classes at Georgia State. I can call her a hot ass because most of us know we were a little hot in the tail at that age, if we're honest with ourselves.

In her message, she thanked Ric for taking her to lunch the previous day, and instantaneously, the red siren in my brain was activated. Am I the jealous type? No, but I believe in boundaries and the respect thereof. I've been a little leery of their relationship since she first called his phone after midnight seven months ago (yes, it's on my calendar).

I asked Ric to make her aware of proper etiquette to practice when communicating with a married man. He relayed the message, but that's the problem. Instead of speaking for himself and breaking down the rules, he told her what *I* said and expressed how much *I* was bothered by her phone call and their relationship that straddled the line between coworkers and friends. If LaShay was thirty-something grown and knew how to conduct herself as a respectable woman, I would have no problem with her and Ric being friends and catching a quick lunch together. Lorenzo and I do it quite often. However, a nineteen-year-old child employee and a thirty-six–year-old manager have nothing to discuss outside of "Stay in school", "Let me hook you up with my younger sibling", or "Your new schedule is posted on the back wall".

The trouble is that Ric is thirty-six with a twenty-one-year-old mind. LaShay can only do what he allows her to do, and if he keeps opening doors, she's going to skip her happy ass in. My hostility toward her stems from a real place. I've talked to her twice, the first time being when she called Ric's phone again after midnight. That's how I learned he had made me the bad guy, saying I was possessive and insecure. After a brief, but informative rundown of my stance on the matter, it seemed LaShay and I were on the same page. She apologized for inadvertently disrespecting my marriage, and that was that...

Until two weeks later when she texted him at 10:30 p.m. to ask what he was doing. He was in the other room, so I texted back, *Chillin' with wifey*. When she texted, *LOL. Sorry to hear that*, I lost it. Unlike her claim from the first time I talked to her, she was purposely disrespecting my marriage. I marched into the living room and presented the messages to Ric, who could only ask me why I took the liberty to text her. He eventually said her "Sorry to hear that" response was an inside joke. I then made it clear that if he thought it was cute to mock his marriage, he could go play high school games with her *outside* of our house, and I'd call that my *outside* joke. That was the last I'd heard of her until today.

I looked at my watch. It was 7:20 already, and in ten minutes, the bell would ring and my classroom would be packed with rowdy eleventh graders. Ten minutes was just enough time for me to see Ric had been corresponding with LaShay via email all this time. He had a whole folder devoted to their emails—most of which were full of frivolous nonsense, and others which contained too much personal information for my taste and sexual innuendos that were surrounded by "LOL's" and "j/k's" as if they weren't meant to be taken seriously.

Just as I logged out, my phone vibrated in my purse. I retrieved it and read the text from Ric. *Hope you have a great first day, baby. Tell them lil' young bucks to back up off of you. You married. I don't wanna have to hurt a kid. LOL. Muah.*

*My sentiments exactly*, I thought, as I texted a smiley face in return.

*****

During my free period, I completed my seating charts and finalized a few lesson plans before getting back on my computer. I saw a few notifications from Connect.com in Ric's inbox, and I wouldn't be the thorough woman I am if I didn't log in to that site to see what I could see.

Connect.com is a website that was created for networking and finding friends. You create a profile where you can post your picture and general information about yourself. You can also upload other photos you'd like to share with your friends or the entire Connect.com community. It's a great concept. I've found friends from many stages of my life, dating back to elementary school. I make a point to mainly add people I know, though there are maybe twenty people I accepted friend requests from because they, too, are teachers and we can use that commonality to network.

Ric and I are friends on the site, so I can access his page to see some of what his friends are saying to him. He's not that foolish, though. If he wanted to keep anything from me, he'd simply tell his friends to send a message to his email account on there, an account I could only access if I had his password.

I signed in under his name and typed in the same password he uses for his regular email account. Two seconds later, the invalid password message appeared on my screen in red. I tapped my fingers on the desk. *Think. Think. Think.* A quick change to the last two numbers of the password, and I was in.

As I figured, LaShay was his friend, and they'd been communicating on there. Again, there was nothing blatant that proved they had more going on than inappropriate conversation, but that didn't make their communication acceptable. His inbox only had messages to and from his Connect.com friends who were a part of the independent film industry, so I was pleasantly surprised.

I sighed, thinking maybe I was overreacting and that his interactions with LaShay could be as innocent as mine and Lorenzo's. Still, a nagging feeling kept telling me to keep my antenna up and my radio tuned in.

I moved the mouse pointer to the top in preparation to sign out, when a chat box appeared at the bottom of the screen. Some girl named Vita Applebottom Milner typed, *Hey, boo! How've u been?*

I logged out, vowing to nip this mess in the bud when I got home.

*****

Chase and Dalvin played on the living room floor, while I poured gravy over the cubed steaks and finished perfecting the cheese sauce for my macaroni and cheese—Ric's favorite. The green beans simmered on the back burner, and the house smelled so good when he came home, he probably tried to taste the air.

He was in a great mood. He ran over to the boys and hit them with some playful punches, then entered the kitchen and kissed me on the cheek. "Ooh, baby, I didn't know you were making mac and cheese. Damn. I must be doing something right for once," he said jokingly.

"I wouldn't go that far," I replied, minus a smile.

"You straight? What's wrong with you?" he asked.

I shook my head.

"It has to be something. Spit it out. Did something happen at work?"

I nodded.

"Talk to me. What happened?"

"It has nothing to do with work. I just saw some things while I was *at* work." Careful to withhold some of my

53

information, I asked him his purpose for being on Connect.com.

"Aw, shit. Here we go. Get to the point. Did you see something on my page or something?"

"I just see that you have over seven hundred friends, and I bet five hundred and sixty of them are female. And why do you get little messages on your wall with these chicks calling you 'boo'? Am I missing something?"

"And? Do you know how many women call me 'boo' in the course of a day? If that's gonna be a problem and have you so insecure, you might as well divorce me now. And as far as the ratio between males and females, I can be friends with whoever I want."

"You don't even have friends in real life! You've said it yourself. You consider Omar to be your best and only friend, and y'all talk what...quarterly?"

He shook his head. "That's your problem. You take things too literally. I'm not friends with all those people on my list. They're my acquaintances. And you don't know how often I talk to Omar. I don't report to you about shit like that."

My eyes shot daggers into him as I failed to believe he had more than seven hundred acquaintances.

He looked away from me. "Man, you trippin'. I'm a businessman. Networking is what I do. I'm tryin' to handle business."

"What kind of business? Prostitution? What do these random girls have to do with your *business*? You sell cellular phones. I'm pretty sure you're not getting a bonus from work for getting five hundred bitches to change their provider."

"You got jokes?" he asked, looking at me again.

"Take it how you want. I'm sick of this shit." I pressed the cheesy spoon against his chest. "Get one of your

Connect.com hoes to cook your dinner," I said before I stormed off.

Destination: the bathroom. Mission: to cry.

*I am so weak*, I thought as I struck my forehead rhythmically with the heel of my hand.

I'm not the wicked wife who is determined to drain all the excitement and normality from my husband's life. I just ask for discretion. I'm registered on Connect.com, as well. However, my two hundred and thirty-six friends are mostly people I went to school with or my coworkers, and none of the men are writing sweet nothings on my wall. He thinks being called "boo" is nothing, but I bet if Lorenzo or any other random man put that on my profile, he'd be ready to fight.

I wonder if my mother went through this with my dad. I'm sure she did, because she eventually found out he was cheating, but technology takes cheating and opportunities to cheat to another level. Back then, women only found out their husbands were cheating if a girlfriend saw them out on the town or if some evidence was left behind. There was no way to research his infidelity outside of a good ol' fashioned slipup like finding a hotel receipt he left in his pants pocket before doing laundry.

In an age where technology makes everything faster, easier, and more convenient, here I am. I'm making the history button my friend, logging into my husband's accounts as if they're my own, and preparing to look through my file cabinet for old cell phone bills to see who he's been sharing sentences with.

What's better? Staying in the dark for years like my mother, or finding evidence in an easier fashion from the convenience of my computer and possibly ending my marriage in a faster manner? I'll say it one more time. Technology is a curse from the devil.

55

# WILLOW (MILKY)

"If she can't use your comb, don't bring her home."

That's Mrs. Ella's, Vaughn's mother, philosophy. So imagine her surprise when Vaughn first introduced me to her. She knew I worked with Vaughn, and she knew he was seeing someone from work; but she never thought we'd be one and the same. Joseph was aware of the romance brewing between his son and me, but he kept one detail from the Mrs.: I'm white.

She threw a fit for about a month. Vaughn would try to downplay her attitude and attribute it to her going through menopause, but I knew better. I saw the way she scowled at me. I heard the questions behind the questions when she'd ask about my family. She was floored that I was raised by a black family and that I refuse to refer to them as my "adoptive" anything in conversation.

I waved to her and Venus before getting into my car. She smiled like it didn't hurt her to do so this time, and then she knelt down to Venus' level to return the wave.

To her, I'm false advertisement in the flesh. I love fried corn, can make collard greens that'll make you want to smack somebody, and attend a predominantly black church.

That translated to me being black when Vaughn initially spoke of me. Tell me that's not inflicting stereotypes on her own race. Trust me, I get it. I see how she could've thought that. It's her reaction when she learned the truth that makes our relationship shy of friendly. I'm being nice when I say we're cordial, and I only give that much of myself because she's my mother-in-law.

One time, early in our relationship, I dressed like a Stepford wife and attended dinner at their house. Vaughn looked like he'd seen his grandmother naked when he opened the door to greet me. He knew me well enough by then to decode the message I was sending. If my skin color was such a problem for Mrs. Ella and since she was so into stereotypes, I decided to give her the ultimate white woman look. I even baked an apple pie and brought it to add an extra touch of smart-assness. Ever since that evening, I haven't had a problem out of her. She saves her adverse talk about me for her husband and has learned not to tell Vaughn a thing if she doesn't want me to hear it. Venus' entrance into the world has softened her a bit, too. She now has a biracial grandchild who brings a smile to her face every time she sees her. I imagine it's tough to hate the woman who used half of her genes to create her.

I am who I am, and that's Willow Thornton Townsend—daughter of Raymond and Janice Thornton, and sibling of Todd and Crystal. I am the light-skinned one of the family, taken into their household at one week of age, loved unconditionally from the moment my mother walked in the house and said to my father, "Look what I found on the post office steps."

I was someone else's trash, but became the Thornton's treasure. I didn't even know I was adopted until fourth grade when Randy Connolly argued me up and down that Crystal wasn't my sister. Then he bet me three dollars that black people and white people couldn't be related. When I

57

told my mother, she asked me to name any differences in how she treated me, Todd, and Crystal. When I couldn't name one, she said, "Okay, then. You're mine. Do you understand? Another woman gave birth to you, but you are *my* daughter. If that boy wants three dollars tomorrow, you tell him to come out to the car and ask me for it."

Her words pacified me then, but as the years went by, I struggled a lot with my identity. Even now, I struggle to an extent because I don't know my roots. Who was the woman who left me outside for anyone to take? What kind of monster is capable of such a heinous act? All that aside, I'd just like to know my medical history, where I get certain personality traits, and what my last name was originally. Mom said my biological mother was nice enough to safety pin a note to my blanket with my first name on it, but there were no other identifiers—nothing else to say who I am.

My existence humbles me. Unlike many people, I don't take my life for granted. I thank God that my mother found me instead of a pedophile. I'm grateful I didn't become a ward of the state, and that I don't have horror stories of how I bounced from one foster home to another, waiting for someone to fill out an order form saying they wanted me as their child. I almost feel spoiled. I've been loved beyond measure—first by my family and now by Vaughn. The simple ways he expresses his love make my heart smile. The way he holds my hand, the strong embrace that makes me feel safe when he holds me, the gentle strokes of my hair when we lie in bed at night, even the way he says my name...I feel wanted when I'm with him. I feel needed. And because I know there's something in his actions that makes him feel the same, I endure the wrath when he lashes out. I understand his inner war, though I can't name his specific battles. Trouble don't last always, and with more prayer, we'll both become comfortable enough with ourselves to truly live out our fairytale.

*****

Mom rang the doorbell at two o'clock. I was expecting her at one, but she said her doctor appointment took longer than she'd planned. I led her into the sitting room, where she eased into the chaise. "I'm exhausted," she said after releasing a long sigh.

"Do you want anything to drink? Eat?"

She shook her head with refusal. "What in the world have you bought now?" she asked as she took a mental count of the shopping bags in the room.

"We're going to Aspen, so Vaughn had me buy clothes and a few other things." I placed my new turquoise coat at the end of the couch and sat in its place. My nerves shot anxious impulses through my system as I patiently waited for my mom to stop analyzing my finances and tell me what she'd come to talk about.

"What's that you were looking at?" she asked, referring to the packet of paper resting on the arm of the couch.

"A copy of Venus' new IEP. They're changing her goals for this year at preschool. I told you that I met her new speech therapist last week, right?"

She nodded. "Now what's an IEP?"

For the hundredth time, I said, "Individualized Education Program, Mom."

"She's gonna be just fine. As long as there's a God, my baby will be alright. She'll be talking your ears off before you know it."

*Lord knows I can't wait for the day*, I thought. Venus was diagnosed with a speech disorder called developmental verbal dyspraxia a year ago, which affects her ability to communicate effectively with us. Though she tries hard, many of her words are unintelligible, and the words she does use are often missing sounds. Mom tells me to stay in prayer because she knows deep down I wonder if I did something wrong while I was pregnant with her. The doctors say that's not the case, but I'm her mom, so I feel responsible. That's another reason I'd like to know my biological family medical history.

"Well," she finally said, "I guess you want me to stop the small talk and tell you why I'm here."

I nodded.

"I've been in touch with someone for a couple months now. She contacted me because she found out we're related, and she wants me to relay some things to you."

I scanned my brain for any recollection of someone who would be looking for me or something I could've done that would prompt someone to look for me. "I'm lost," I said after a few moments.

"Honey, her name is Rebecca Sinclair. She lives in New York City, works on Wall Street, and has a husband and two dogs. After throwing her money around to the right people, she found me and gave me a call one Sunday afternoon." A long pause separated her sentences. "She's your biological mother."

My body temperature rose, and my heart rate doubled. "What?" I asked, though I'd heard her loud and clear. "What does she want? What are you supposed to relay to me?"

"I told her I'm not relaying a thing. She needs to be woman enough to speak with you."

"So you gave her my number?"

Mom joined me on the couch and placed her arm around my shoulders. "Never. I gave her my word that I would talk to you about it. She wants to meet you, baby."

"What do you think I should do?"

"That's not for me to answer, baby girl. If you're worried about my feelings, don't be. I know I'm Mama. She don't have nothin' on me," she said with a nudge and a smile. "Think about it. Pray about it. If you need me, talk about it. I know you've had to wonder about this woman over the years. *I've* wondered about her. *I* want to meet her to get some answers."

My emotions combined to form a cluster of confusion. I wasn't sure if Rebecca reaching out to me was good news or bad news, a gift from God or a curse from Satan. I've been praying for clarity, praying for confirmation of who I am, praying for answers to Venus' developmental issues. *Are those prayers being answered? Is this going to be a classic case of "be careful what you pray for"?* Unsure of what to say or do, I placed my face in my hands and cried.

# CRYSTAL

*TING...TING...TING...TING!* Dante's drummer, Nigel, stood on the stage in our basement with his champagne flute held high, banging a spoon against it.

"I need everyone's attention, please. I want to make a toast to the birthday girl. Here's to the band's favorite brownie maker. May you never lose your touch as the years go by."

"Here, here," almost everyone said in unison.

"Whoa!" Nigel exclaimed as he avoided leaning into my stripper pole.

The whole room burst into laughter.

"Don't be afraid of the pole, Nigel," I said. "Just in case you're worried, I wipe it down after every use."

"Do you have the wipes ready for tonight?" Dante whispered in my ear from behind, while pulling me into him.

"They're always ready."

Ever since I mastered a few moves from my pole dancing exercise class and tried them out at home, Dante has been hooked. Just from pleasing him, my abs are more defined than ever and my core has never been stronger.

62

Those are just added perks to the rain showers of hundred dollar bills that he likes to throw at me. After four years, my acts still haven't gotten old to him. A sistah knows how to keep it sexy and fresh at the same time.

The basement looked like a miniature club. It seemed like all seventy-five invitees showed up to my birthday bash. They were ready to let the good times roll, and mine had been rolling three hours before the party when I started with my first bottle of Moscato.

*I'm amazing*, I thought, as I walked gracefully in my five-inch heels. Just from watching my stride, no one would believe I'd already had a whole bottle of wine to myself. I joined Vaughn and Ric, who seemed to be engaged in an intense conversation with two women from the P.R. firm that represents Dante.

"Boys," I said, smacking them on their backs, "thanks for coming! Where are your better halves?" I stretched my neck in every direction trying to locate Milky and Dana. Before they answered, my girls appeared with plates of hors d'oeuvres.

"What y'all over here talkin' about?" I asked.

"Ric was talking to us about his movie production company," Kandi said.

"Don't forget about me," he said. "Since you don't have your business cards on you, I can't flood your inbox."

"I won't forget," she replied.

Dana rolled her eyes.

"So how many movies do you have in production now?" I asked Ric.

"Well, one was in production, but we had to stop indefinitely because one of our actors had a family emergency." He turned to Kandi and Rhonda. "Y'all know how it is." They nodded, and he addressed all of us. "I have about five other movies in pre-production, though."

"Aw, shoot! Don't hurt nobody! You think you can give Tyler Perry some competition?" My balance was challenged when Dana elbowed me.

"Man, he's not even on my level. My films will blow his out the water. Next year is my year. Mark my words."

"I believe it. You just make sure you have my premiere tickets ready when you hit Hollywood. Ladies, you better get on board and represent him. You'll be sorry if you don't!" I said before turning my head to laugh.

Dana's face was priceless. She hates when I pump Ric up like he's the next big thing because we both know he's all talk. I just do it to entertain myself when I need a good laugh.

She stepped back to speak in my ear. "I'm gonna kill you," she said through clenched teeth.

Rhonda extended her hand to Dana. "Hi, I'm Rhonda."

"I'm Dana, Ric's wife."

"You rude bastards!" I said. "I thought you all had already been introduced."

"My bad," Ric said. "Yeah, Rhonda, that's my wife. Baby, that's Kandi."

We waited for Vaughn to speak.

"Oh! This is Willow," he said.

"She's my sister," I added.

"Okay. Do you work at J.T. Development, too?" Rhonda asked.

"As a matter of fact, I do, but I'm also his wife," Milky said.

Vaughn smiled uncomfortably as Kandi and Rhonda raised their eyebrows and Milky shook her head with disgust.

Dante approached us with another bottle of wine. "What do you say, baby?"

I held my glass in front of him. "The birthday girl is always thirsty."

64

"I need your next glass to be filled with water," Milky said. "You're gonna be sick in the morning."

"I don't get sick, sweet pea. My body knows how to handle this," I replied before taking my husband by the hand and dragging him to our dance floor.

I sang along with Lil' Wayne, telling Dante that I was gonna li-li-li-li-lick him like lollipop, and although he laughed at me, his Blow Pop was digging into me every time I moved in close. He knew he was in for a treat when the party was over. That deal was sealed as soon as he handed me the box containing my new diamond earrings and showed me the customized pink interior he had installed that matches the exterior of my pink Hummer.

As the night progressed, the wine caught up with me. My sexy two-step turned into a stationary bop with an occasional finger snap. Thirty-three felt great, though. I celebrated with my baby, my best friends, and my fun-loving associates.

I woke up at six a.m. and scared myself when I rolled onto my back and saw my reflection in the mirror on the ceiling. I giggled on my way into the bathroom, thinking of how clueless I was. I had no recollection of how my night ended. The last thing I remembered was doing a slow motion version of Da Butt with Dana, then falling on my favorite loveseat with cushions that are reminiscent of a water bed. I didn't even recall making love to Dante, but the dried whipped cream in my hair and the tenderness of my young lady suggested it went down.

Dante wasn't in the room and his cell phone wasn't on his nightstand, so I knew he wasn't home. I called him twice without getting an answer, and my return phone call didn't come until almost four hours later.

"What were you doing up so early, baby? I thought for sure you'd sleep 'til noon."

"Maybe I would have if I didn't have so much wine stretching out my bladder," I replied. "Where are you?"

"At the studio."

"How long have you been there? Did you just bone me and leave? At least tell me my young lady was so good to you that you had to go write a song about her...something."

He laughed.

"I'm pretty sure 99.9 percent of that wasn't a joke. What the hell, babe? You said this whole weekend was mine. Your last full weekend here before the remainder of the tour is supposed to be mine."

"I'm on my way home right now, babe. It's just that Nigel started tapping this beat on the bar last night. So, me and the boys had to go to the studio and put a little something down to it. You'll love it when you hear it. And like I said, baby, I didn't even think you'd be awake right now."

"I would've *loved* to wake up in my husband's arms on my birthday weekend. I don't give a damn if I didn't wake up until two in the afternoon, you should've been laying here with me."

He groaned. "Does this mean you're gonna have an attitude the rest of the weekend?"

I stretched and returned to the bathroom to run my bath water. "Nope. This means I'll stop getting my hopes up. I'll see you when you get here."

*****

Before I settled into my chair under the dryer, I grabbed the magazines that the mailman had just delivered. Arraya, the shampoo girl, was standing there sorting through them and kept her hand on the *Dirty Dish* magazine I was trying to slide toward me. When I pulled at it again, she resisted again.

"Is there a problem?" I asked.

66

"Uh, no, Mrs. Moss. I just needed to look at something in here real quick…if you don't mind."

"Honey, you have all day to look at this thing. I have a half hour. If it'll make you feel better, I'll read it first and give it to you as soon as I'm done."

She reluctantly released the magazine, and I stared her down during my walk to the dryer. She lowered the hood over my head and then rushed to Haven, my stylist.

After sending a few quick texts and emails from my BlackBerry, I crossed my legs and prepared to read my favorite literature: entertainment mags. I love them all, from the tabloids to the more reputable and reliable ones, but I must admit I get more of a kick out of reading some of the tabloids. They're like my comic books because eighty-five percent of the information is outrageously fabricated nonsense and the other fifteen percent seems unbelievable, but it's surprisingly true.

As I had promised Arraya, I started with *Dirty Dish*. Its pages are devoted solely to the exposure of the music industry's finest. People read it to find out where the stars vacation and with who, who's beefing with who, who's knocked up, who's knocked somebody up, who's had plastic surgery, and any other private matter that the public would love to know.

According to the cover, this was a special issue exposing twenty "dirty dogs", male and female. The carefully chosen images were intriguing. Twenty bodies dressed in indistinguishable clothing graced the glossy cover with all of their faces blacked-out and replaced with white question marks. Immediately, I turned to the index to see which page would reveal who was behind the Photoshop disguises. I was wondering if any of the paparazzi caught of glimpse of what I'd seen about a month ago: a certain married R&B diva stealing kisses from a very famous young rapper during an ASCAP event. I know if that leaked, her career and her marriage would be in danger since her husband is also the producer who made her hot in the first place.

Sure enough, they busted her on page sixteen. There was a full-size image of the two initially making lip contact, eyes closed and all, next to the title *BUSTED: What They DO Know WILL Hurt Them*. I shook my head. Since I know her personally, my heart ached for her and her husband. How embarrassing it must be to see your business in a nationally distributed magazine. How troubling it will be when her husband sees. I glanced at my BlackBerry, but ignored the itch to text her.

What would I say to her? The only thing they had ever reported on Dante and I was a vacation we'd taken in the Caribbean, and I was mad because the camera angle they used made me look twenty pounds heavier. I could empathize with her situation, but why make contact?

I glanced at the smaller pictures on the next page, then flipped the page to see who else made the cut. Immediately, the caption *Mr. All Night Long Doesn't Necessarily Mean He Spends the Entire Night with His Wife* caught my eye before the picture came into view. Above it was a picture of Dante looking at his phone, while the girl in front of him puckered up for a kiss.

The report said he met with the mystery woman at his studio the day after my birthday, then took her to the airport after their rendezvous was over. I stared at the photo of him wearing the same Sean John jeans and charcoal gray sweater that he donned when he returned home from the studio weeks ago—the day after my birthday. I noted the rose-colored bricks that his favorite studio was constructed of. I noted that as much as I wanted the story to be in the eighty-five percent category, it had fifteen percent written all over it.

Just like that, I knew exactly how it felt to know the whole world is aware of your spouse's infidelity. I tried to

68

hide my shock, tried to close my mouth, because something told me Arraya and Haven were watching me like a hawk. Poor Arraya didn't want me to see the article. *That's why she was trying to keep the damn magazine*, I thought.

I removed my phone from my lap and saw a missed text from Dana. *I see y'all finally made the tabloids for something juicy. I took a magazine away from one of my fourth period students, and it has some nonsense about Dante having an affair. LMAO. If they only knew. I'll call you when I get off.*

*No, D, if you only knew*, I thought, while sending her an *LOL. I saw it* text in return. She seems to think Dante is a golden boy incapable of engaging in the extramarital activities his peers partake in. Who am I to ruin her belief in fidelity?

Neither Haven nor Arraya said a word about the article. They followed my lead, laughing at my stories about the teenage girls I work with, but I could tell their hearts were shedding tears for me. I wanted to tell them not to cry for me, but somebody has to cry. It'll never be me, though.

When I returned to the house, I was surprised to see Dante's Hummer parked in the driveway. According to his itinerary, he should've been on the way to Tampa. I entered slowly, anticipating a bullshit explanation for the story I'd just read an hour before.

He met me in the foyer. "Baby, I thought something was wrong. I've been calling and texting you. Is your battery dead?"

"Nope."

He studied my face. "You okay?"

"Stop the games. You know this is my day at the salon, and you know damn well I read magazines while I'm under the dryer."

"Don't tell me you believe that shit. She was a fan, Crystal. She asked if she could have a kiss and puckered up. I kissed her on the cheek. Look at the picture, babe. I was texting you while she stood there. I wasn't even paying her any attention."

"Stop trying to explain yourself. I told you to keep your shit out of the tabloids. Was that asking too much?"

"Think about it. Nothing has come up in the eight years we've been married. These rumors are only starting now because this is my biggest album ever and people want to find something to knock me off of cloud nine."

"You don't need them to knock you off cloud nine. I can handle that."

My blood boiled from the hot air he was emitting. I hated to think he'd leave our bed to go get it in with a groupie, but the article sure sounded believable. *Dirty Dish* knew small details, too, which suggests an inside source was behind the exposé.

Was the picture alone enough to anger me? No. It was the mention that the girl was from Indianapolis and that they'd hooked up previously. It was the realization that she was the same girl he pulled onstage during Black Expo weekend after I studied her picture for the fourth time. He had broken our agreement—an agreement that gave him too much freedom to begin with. Who does that? A cocky superstar who thinks he's on cloud nine...that's who.

"So what all did you do with her, Dante?"

"Nothing."

"Oh, okay. We're playing that game." I stepped out of my heels and kicked them to the side. "Be careful," I said with a smile. "That 'It wasn't me' shit will get you shot. Shaggy lied to y'all."

He followed me as I started up the stairs. I stopped on the sixth one and turned to him. "Don't you have a show tonight?"

"Yeah, but I wanted to come here and make sure we were okay. My family comes first."

"Go do your show. It'll be more beneficial to you. Break a leg."

# DANA

Ric came home from work on time for a change. The past few weeks, he'd been running about an hour late, which did nothing but add more stress to our household. Not only was I left to cook dinner, help Dalvin with his homework, give both boys their baths, and fight them to go to sleep, I also had to wonder if my husband was working late with LaShay. He wasn't lying about being at the store because I made sure I called. I just couldn't help but picture them exploring the things they pretended to joke about in their emails. I thought about asking him if she was there, but it would've been like asking to be lied to.

Without being prompted, he sat with Dalvin and they started his homework. Chase was glued to the floor watching *Sesame Street* in the bedroom, so I retreated to my room to enjoy the rare "me time". As usual, Ric's jacket hung on the closet doorknob, and as I had done for the past four days, I checked his pockets.

*You never fail to let me down*, I thought, as I felt the metal piece between my fingers. His ring was in his pocket again. I believe it's safe to assume he's been placing it there for quite some time, but I'm just now finding out. And it's his fault that I know. He's the dummy who asked me to get a receipt from his pocket four days ago. When I found the ring and asked why it wasn't on his finger, he had an elaborate excuse about not wanting to get it caught on something while rearranging the cases and shelves in the store. I bought that. Now that it's three days later and he's been putting in extra hours, I know good and well that everything has been rearranged. As small as his store is, it probably took all of two hours to do. What's the excuse now?

As much as I hate to admit this, I'm the passive-aggressive type. I don't like confrontation, so I make my bold statements in other ways. I removed the wedding band from his pocket and placed it between the mattress and box spring on my side of the bed. It would do just as much good there as it did in his jacket.

The next morning, he never even missed the ring. When he came home that evening, though, he searched the computer desk, the kitchen counter, the couch cushions, and the dresser. I acted like I didn't notice a thing as Chase and I built a castle with his blocks.

Eventually, Ric reentered the living room. "Baby, have you seen my ring?"

"Umm hmm," I replied casually, never looking up from the castle.

"Where is it?"

"It was in your jacket pocket."

"I just looked in there." He fidgeted. "Shit! I hope it didn't fall out."

"You seem so concerned."

"Why wouldn't I be?"

"Because it was in your jacket to begin with. I'd say it deserved to fall out."

I felt him staring a hole into the back of my head. "Where's my ring, Dana?"

*Oh, look out. He's calling me by my real name. That means he's mad*, I thought, stifling my smile. "Why are you asking me?"

"Because you have it. I know you. You saw the ring and took it. Where is it?"

"Don't worry about it. It's in a safe place."

"Stop playing fucking games and tell me where it is!"

"You watch your mouth in front of our child."

"You stop actin' like an ass in front of our child."

"Oh, I'm the ass, but I know where my ring is."

"What you want? Two points? I knew where my ring was, too. You didn't have any business taking it."

"If it's not on your finger, it's fair game. Evidently, you don't want to wear it. Why even front like you do? I'm making it easier for you. Now you don't have to put it on before you leave the house and pretend you wear it all day. I'm pretty sure you haven't been moving display cases all this time."

"Here we go again. You and this assuming shit. I take my ring off for a lot of things. You know I take it off when I wash my hands. Sometimes I forget to put it back on."

"Well, forget no more. This will be one less thing you have to remember in your day. No ring, no worries. You think I'm really supposed to believe that hand-washing shit? It's real gold, so there's no need to remove it."

"That's not why I do it! I don't like how it feels when I wash my hands."

I nodded. "Okay. Apparently, you don't like how it feels at all. Stop with this act, Ric. You don't care about that ring. At this point, you're just arguing for the sake of arguing. This isn't about the ring. It's about me taking the ring. I'm not going to continue this conversation in front of him."

"I am until you tell me where my ring is."

"Then you're ignorant."

"You're ignorant! You're playing childish games and trying to act like you're such an adult."

I chuckled and shook my head. "It's under the mattress on my side, Ric. Feel better?"

He stood there for a few moments, then grabbed his keys. "I'm out. I don't have time for this bullshit."

"Tell LaShay I said hi."

After he slammed the door behind him, Chase looked at me with widened eyes.

I scrunched my face and mocked Ric. "Daddy's being a big ol' grouch." I threw two blocks in the air and caught them. "Back to the fun stuff!" I yelled, eliciting a joyous response from Chase. We played for a while longer, and then Chase, Dalvin, and I watched *Spiderman* before I put them to bed.

I was awakened by a tap on my shoulder. When my eyes finally focused, I saw a bouquet of roses. Ric knelt beside the bed with his jacket still on.

"I'm sorry, baby. I'm sorry I snapped at you. You're right. I should just keep the ring on all the time so we won't have this problem. I never want you to think I'm not wearing it because I'm ashamed of you. How could I be ashamed of you?" He kissed me on the forehead.

I've often wondered the same thing. Early in our marriage, he would "forget" his ring at home six and a half days out of the week, would only carry pictures of the boys in his wallet, and only gave our house number to family members. Of course, there was always a lame excuse for all those things. When he grew accustomed (if that makes it excusable) to being married and after a tumultuous argument, the ring was on every day, the family picture found its way into his wallet, and our home phone became more than a family hotline.

"Do you forgive me? Huh, baby?" he asked as I fought hard to hold back my tears. Ric sees crying as a sign of weakness, though my tears are usually a sign of frustration.

I shrugged my shoulders, fearing that if I spoke, my voice would quiver to the point of unintelligibility.

"I know you're still upset. I guess I can't blame you, but I love you, Dana. I don't want to lose you, especially over no bullshit like this. If I have to, I'll superglue the ring to my finger."

I couldn't help but smile in response to his silly statement, but I didn't want him to see it.

"You know I'll do it, baby," he said, smiling, too. "I'ma go put these in some water for you. I'll be right back." Before he left the room, he planted a few more kisses on my dry lips.

Upon his return, I could expect him to pull me close so we can spoon. Then after a few minutes, I would feel something hard pressing against my butt. After that, there would be kisses and light stroking followed by the removal of my underwear that isn't as sly as he thinks it is. Twenty-five minutes later, we would have finished making love, and all would be forgotten...in his mind. He subconsciously believes his dick is the cure-all for any problem we face. Making love is his way of showing me how much he cares. The deeper the stroke, the deeper his feelings, the more he wants me to believe him. He's done the freakiest things after our falling outs just to prove how much he loves me.

I know I don't help his thought process by giving in to his sexual advances, but he's my husband and he turns me on—even when I'm mad at him. If he touches me and I'm horny, I'm going to make love to him, and I'm going to climax without faking it. When we're done, I can go back to being pissed.

76

\*\*\*\*\*

I arrived at Crystal's just as Dante was leaving. His driver, Elgin, stood with the door of his Bentley open, waiting patiently as he and I chatted. He was on his way to the airport, heading to St. Louis for another show.

"What's Ric up to?" he asked.

"Same ol', same ol'."

"Yeah? He hit me up the other day, but I was in a meeting."

I rolled my eyes. "Is he harassing you?"

He laughed. "Nah. He said he wanted to run a video idea by me. I didn't know he was really serious about filmmaking."

*It'd be nice if he was serious about something that was making him some money right now,* I thought. "I don't think he did either," I replied with a smirk.

He chuckled. "Support the man. That's your husband."

"And that's the only reason I haven't told him how ridiculous he sounds at times. I don't want him to think I'm trying to crush his dream. Anyway, have a good show. I'll see you later," I said.

He thanked me and told me to let myself in the house because Crystal was already getting the flowers together in the kitchen. I was there to help her prepare vases of pink roses that would be delivered to breast cancer survivors and sufferers. It would be her second year heading the campaign, and I volunteered to help after hearing her horror stories from last year.

Crystal's inspiration for the project came from her mother's diagnosis of breast cancer in 2004 and her subsequent remission in 2005. Mrs. Thornton proudly testifies about being cancer-free for three years now—something many other women can't brag about.

After meeting other women at her mother's chemo and radiation appointments, Crystal gained more respect for cancer and its dangers. More importantly, she gained respect for the strength the women displayed as they fought off the disease. Though she does things for them throughout the year, she's goes all out in October since it's National Breast Cancer Awareness Month.

"Hey, you," I said, nudging her as I walked in. She'd already completed eight arrangements. "I told you not to start without me."

"There are plenty more to go around, sweet pea. We have a hundred to do."

My mouth dropped as she smirked and nodded. "I didn't realize you did so many."

"I do a total of two hundred, but I put the girls to work today. They need more community service hours anyway, need to do something more productive than listening to their iPods during our downtime."

Crystal has enough money to pay a florist to supply and arrange all two hundred, but she feels being hands-on makes the deed more meaningful. I stood at the station she set up for me and started on my first vase.

"This has been one of the longest days of my life," she said.

"Why? What happened?"

She proceeded to tell me about the sixteen-year-old who tried to clown her during her presentation about the new mentors they'd meet next week. "That little thing raised her hand and said, 'Are they gonna give us something to do, because it sounds like the program should be called 'Nothing to Do'?"

"No, she didn't!"

"Ask LaToya. Honey, those little heffas are a mess. I almost snatched that little girl's glue-in weave off her scalp for disrespecting me. I told her if she opened her mouth again, that little scrap of hair would meet her in Decatur, because that's how far I was gonna throw it. If she wants

78

something to do, she can go get a damn sew-in," Crystal replied. "You know she's new to the program, but after today, I believe she's clear on how I roll."

My phone vibrated on the counter. It was Ric calling again. We had been arguing all day about him overdrawing the account, and I wasn't going to get into it with him in front of Crystal. I pressed Ignore and grabbed some baby breath to add to my arrangement.

Still, I was agitated. Not only were our finances becoming more of an issue, Ric's involvement with his female "friends" was taking more a toll on me, especially that damn LaShay. I had checked his email and read that she'd dropped him off at the MARTA station a few times after work and was questioning why he wouldn't let her drive him home.

"Hello?" Crystal said, waving her hand in front of my face. "Where did you go?"

"What?" I asked.

"I've been talking to you for like three minutes, and you're over there zoning out."

"I'm sorry, girl."

"Don't apologize. Spill it. What's up?"

Against everything I was taught, I did just that. I couldn't keep my problems with Ric bottled up anymore. I started with his denial of our marriage years ago and ended with the emails I'd first discovered in August—the ones he was still receiving.

"You mean that negro made the time to click 'New Folder', name it, and then transfer all of their emails to it? Like, it's in a special place? Oh hell no. Out of order. He is totally out of order."

"I don't know if that was his way of trying to hide them or not. Maybe he did that thinking if I was still checking his email I'd only check his inbox or something. Does he think I'm stupid or just slow?"

79

"I'm not even on that right now. Here's what the problem is: he's made that girl significant. She has a special place in his email account. I don't want to scare you or put anything in your head, so don't take this the wrong way. But, if he's set aside a special place in his email account, nine times out of ten, he's set a special place aside somewhere else. It's up to you if you want to find out whether it's on his dick or in his heart."

Her words made my stomach turn.

"I had a feeling something wasn't right. I hadn't checked his account in almost a year, and the day I decided to take a gander, look what the hell I found."

"Women's intuition is a bitch, ain't it? What does your gut tell you?" Crystal asked.

"I feel like he's cheating, but I can't prove it. If he was just my boyfriend, I would've been gone, but I can't go off of pure instinct when I have a marriage and two children involved."

"Welcome to the club," she replied.

I cocked my head to the side.

"Dante's *been* cheating on me. Correction. At this point, I don't even call it cheating. I don't even consider what we have a marriage. It's more like we're each other's comfort blanket. We have an arrangement. He's not going anywhere, and neither am I." She was so casual, yet so serious.

"Are you talking about the girl in the tabloids?"

"Her and whoever else. Naptown New Booty isn't the first chick he's messed with. She's just the first one to blow up his spot."

"So you two have an open marriage?"

"We had a marriage with allowances. I say 'had' because I believe he is in breach of our agreement."

"You're okay with that?"

Crystal stopped arranging the flowers and looked into my eyes. "You think Ric is cheating, but you're still with him. Are you okay with that?" she asked.

"No!"

"Right. So like I said, welcome to the club."

"I hate when people say that. What club?"

"The disgruntled wives club. You don't like the situation you're in, but as soon as you're done bitching about it, you go right back to the same shit."

"Sounds like the stupid wives club."

"We're not stupid; we're married. We're where most of the single idiots wanna be." She stood back and admired the arrangement. "If they only knew…"

I handed her another vase and thought about her statement. Thought about how I was going to return home, cook dinner, put the kids to bed, and have sex with the husband I think is cheating on me. Indeed, I had just been inducted into a society that blurred the lines between love and self-respect, lies and truths, "I do" and "I don't".

There went my theory that one of my friends had a happy marriage. Crystal's news about Dante crushed that. Between her, Willow, my coworkers, and me, love and marriage is turning out to be a farce. It felt great to share the things that were weighing on me with my best friend. And though it sounds insensitive, it was relieving to hear that she and Dante have problems, too. I don't feel like I'm such a failure at keeping my husband happy now.

# WILLOW (MILKY)

"Okay, babe. I spoke with the travel agent earlier, and she said we're all set for Aspen. We'll be back three days before Thanksgiving, so thank God we're going to your parents' house for dinner." Really, I wasn't happy that we were going to his parents' house. I was happy because I wouldn't have to spend hours in the kitchen cooking and cleaning for a one-day affair.

"Good. And she got the cabin we wanted, right?"

"Of course," I replied, while passing him the dinner rolls.

He handed one to Venus and took one for himself. "It'll be nice to get out of here. We both need the escape."

"You can say that again. Too bad we still have to wait a few weeks."

"It'll be right on time, babe," Vaughn said.

We took a moment to laugh at Venus, who was entertaining herself with her fork and two strands of spaghetti. Then Vaughn addressed me.

"Have you given any more thought about meeting your mother?"

I shrugged. "I guess I've been putting it off. When I think about it, though, I'm like, what's the rush? She's taken thirty years to contact me."

Vaughn smiled softly. "So are you going to wait thirty years, too?"

I shrugged again, but this time with a smile that mirrored his. "What does she want?"

"Maybe she just wants to meet you, babe. People start reflecting on things they've done as they get older. She probably feels bad for giving you up. You know she doesn't want money. She works on Wall Street."

"With the economy the way it is, you never know. And how do we know she really works on Wall Street? How do we know she's even my mother?"

Vaughn swirled the spaghetti around on his plate, much to Venus' delight. "I have a confession," he said after taking a deep breath. "I called Rebecca today."

"You *what*?"

"Babe, you've had her number two months now. I know you. You've been wanting to call, but you don't know what to say. You don't know how you feel about her, so you'd rather avoid contact with her. As far as her being who she says she is, it's true. I looked her up, and she's a bigwig in Manhattan."

In a sense, I felt relieved. He had grabbed the reigns and taken control of a situation that was secretly taking control of me. "So what did she say? What did you say?" I asked.

"I just introduced myself, and the conversation took off from there. She seems nice enough. She asked a lot of questions about you, but I told her to save them for when you see each other...which will be in February."

"It's October."

"That's the only time she—"

"Could pencil me in?" I finished. "This is looking real promising."

"You know I'm not defending her, babe, but she's a very busy woman. From what I learned during our conversation, she's always traveling."

"And I guess she was busy when she left me outside for anyone to take, too."

It was exactly what I was afraid of. How could someone be so anxious to meet the daughter they literally left out in the cold, yet schedule the big day months down the road? An unexplainable sense of disappointment wrapped around my spirit, and suddenly, I was nine years old again, wondering why I'm not good enough to capture my mother's attention.

As my tears welled up, I refused to cry. Even when Vaughn came over to hold me, I didn't let them fall. Rebecca Sinclair doesn't deserve my tears, and I'm beginning to think she doesn't deserve to meet me.

*****

Sunday didn't come fast enough. I couldn't wait to get in the sanctuary so I could hear some of that good word. Ever since Vaughn told me about Rebecca, I felt a disturbance within, and my soul had been thirsty for a calm that only God could provide.

I puckered my lips and admired the Love Nectar shade Gretchen recommended to me months ago. It was the first time I tried it, and it instantly looked like a hit. After a slight adjustment to my suit jacket, I was ready to go. I exited the bathroom and slipped into my heels. I glanced at Vaughn, who was sprawled in our bed still engaged in a deep sleep. *Not today. I will not be annoyed*, I thought. It'd be nice if we could go to church as a family at least once a month, though.

"Let's go, princess," I said, helping Venus down from the bed.

"Daddy not coming?" she asked.

"No, pooh, he's not coming. It's a girls' day."

When we returned around 1:30 p.m., Vaughn walked two steaming hot plates of food to the dining room table. Venus' plate was already in place with her food waiting at the perfect temperature.

The smell of his rosemary chicken with a Cajun twist overpowered the hint of attitude in me that remained from his absence from church—just what he wanted. Vaughn is a great cook, and the way he arranged the chicken, roasted potatoes, and roasted asparagus on the plate would fool someone into thinking he went to culinary school.

Venus and I removed our coats and took our seats. "Looks good," I said with toned down excitement.

He leaned over and kissed me on the cheek. "Next Sunday, babe. I promise."

# CRYSTAL

Nigel climaxed and quivered beneath me. I kissed his sweaty forehead. "Thank you," I said, before dismounting him. I sat on the edge of the bed and waited for my legs to stop shaking.

"Damn. He must've really pissed you off this time."

I smiled. "And you like when I take it out on you."

Sexy Nigel has been Dante's drummer for five years, and I've been screwing him for three of them. It took nearly a year for me to convince him that Dante wasn't setting him up with some weird test of loyalty. We're a perfect fit, only we can't be together—at least not out in the open.

I never intended to cheat on Dante, but after too many nights alone, I had to do what I had to do. Dante was always busy entertaining his groupies when he should've been home giving me something I could feel. Enter Nigel.

As with most of the guys in the band, I'd seen him around and we'd hung out in groups. But, after a night at the hottest club in Miami and a walk on the beach, my young lady was screaming for attention, and my husband wasn't around to hear her. Nigel, on the other hand, was.

Nigel's a talented lover, full of variety. He can tap me like a snare, intensify his thrust like a bass, or speed up his pace like a high hat. Much like his line of work, he'll throw me a beat, and I'll ride his rhythm to the very end.

That one night was supposed to be just that—one night. The problem was we would see each other too frequently on tour and couldn't control our hormones. While all his band mates were freshening up at the hotel after the show in preparation to hit the town and find new booty, Nigel was greasing up his legs and trimming his pubs for me. I'd kiss Dante goodbye after he promised to come back early "for real this time". He'd say, "I'm just going to show my face, take a few pictures, and sign a few autographs. After that, I'm out. Keep it hot for me."

And I would. I'd relax in bed for a while, sip champagne, and then take a nice long bubble bath. I'd close my eyes and think about my baby's two-toned gentleman holding strong in mid-air, waiting for my attention. About halfway through my X-rated thoughts, my fingers would wander, stopping at my entry for a little playtime. Deliberately, I'd heat myself until I simmered, and tease myself thereafter until my baby came back to send me beyond my boiling point.

When he keeps his word, we're the talk of the tour bus the next morning. Onyx, Dante's musical director, always rooms next to us when we don't get the penthouse, so he complains of being awakened either by my screams or Dante's throughout the night. After years of being on the road with them, I don't even get embarrassed anymore when he mocks me.

Shit, Onyx wishes he could make me scream and wants to know what I'm doing to make Dante scream. All of the guys do, and probably some of the females. A couple of his dancers have given me way too many compliments on my body for me not to consider that they are checking me out.

87

Hey, I'm no Halle Berry, but I hold my own and work what I have. You may mess around and mistake me for her cousin, though. One word to any of my husband's faithful few, and I promise their loyalties would no longer lie with him, but rather in the bed beside me. The proof was lying right behind me as I looked over my shoulder and winked at Nigel's sexy self.

He shook his limp penis and asked, "What time will he be back?"

"Seven at the earliest. His in-store appearance isn't over until five, and you know traffic will be hellacious."

"He doesn't have a jump-off to go visit?"

"We don't visit jump-offs," I replied, watching as he stroked himself. "They come when they're called." Seeing him grow made both sets of my lips salivate. I glanced at the clock that displayed 4:50 p.m., then back at him. "Why do you do this to me?"

After retrieving another condom from my secret stash spot, I placed it on him and asked, "You ready?"

It was encore time, and Nigel had the best drum solo of our sexual career. I thought my booty was two bongos for those ten minutes, and though I know it's virtually impossible, I quietly wondered if Martha heard us downstairs. Not that I'm worried. Martha wouldn't dare tell Dante a thing.

Some days, I just want to tell him what I do to pass time during my otherwise lonely nights, but he could never handle it. All the men I know can fuck the daylights out of every woman who speaks to them, but let them find out you held a simple conversation with a man, and they feel some kind of way. That in itself is a testament to the strength of a woman. We can learn of our man's adulterous ways and somehow find it in our hearts to forgive him.

In my case, I found an unorthodox way of dealing with Dante's escapades after my heart had no more room for understanding and forgiveness…and after talking with other industry wives. I love that man more than a wedding vow could express, and I believe he loves me just as much. The problem is his music was and still is his first love, and I agreed to accept that and the lifestyle that comes with it when "I do" left my lips. Only now, I also say "I do" when Nigel calls and asks if I need company.

Nigel got dressed while I took my shower. As he usually does, he stayed to admire my naked body and watched me until I dried off and put my robe on. I paged Martha on the intercom to let her know Nigel was ready to go and then walked him downstairs. Since he can't park in our driveway, Martha picks him up from my friend Kristen's house down the street and transports him back and forth.

"Are you coming with us to London?" he asked.

"I haven't decided yet. I may come for a couple of the dates and then come back. Don't worry. You'll be the second to know."

As we said goodbye, Dana rang the doorbell. Nigel and Martha continued out of the side entrance while I went to the front to greet my girl.

"Go get some clothes on!" she said. "I thought you were gonna be ready."

"How many years have you known me? Did you really think I would be ready on time?"

"No. That's why I came twenty minutes late."

I laughed. "It won't take me long. I'll be right back."

Before I turned to go up the stairs, she pointed to my robe. "What's that? An earring?"

I felt near my breast, and sure enough, a diamond stud was embedded in the terrycloth.

"Shit." I pulled the cordless phone from my pocket and waited for Nigel to answer. "Hey," I said once he picked up, "you left your earring here. Do you want to come back and get it or wait?"

"I'll wait," he replied. "I'm sure I'll see you sooner than later."

"Bye, Nigel," I said before hanging up. Dana stared at me with narrowed eyelids. "What?" I asked.

"Nigel was here? The sexy drummer?"

I nodded.

"You aren't..."

"What makes you say that?"

"You don't have any clothes on, and you have his earring attached to your robe. If it looks like a duck and walks like a duck..."

"Quack, quack!" I said. "You need to save your detective abilities for Ric's ass and let me get dressed," I joked.

She gave me the finger, and I blew her a kiss.

"Be right back, sweet pea!"

*****

A monumental day had arrived, and I wanted to host an intimate event to honor it. It was November 4th—Election Day. I took my eighteen-year-olds to the polls to cast their votes, beaming with pride. Not only was I proud to be the one to help them with their first voting experience, I was proud they had the option to vote for a black presidential candidate. Fittingly, I made "Yes We Can" the theme for November, focusing on goal-setting and overcoming rejection.

LaToya and I decorated the rec room with the colors red, white, and blue, hired a caterer, and turned on the flat screens to set the mood for the Something to Do Election Day party. All of my girls and their parents were invited, as well as the program mentors, and Milky and Dana.

We all mingled and entertained each other as the map of electoral votes was continuously updated on the screens. Ric kept me entertained with his intellectual take on the entire campaign. I would've been able to take him more seriously if

90

he didn't distract me with his hand gestures and d-boy swag that was immature to say the least. When my fifteen- and sixteen-year-old girls say he reminds them of a guy at their school, there's a problem.

As the end of the night drew near, the adults all gathered at a separate table and discussed current events. Dana was visibly annoyed with Ric, who was too preoccupied with his phone to weigh in on our hot topics.

"Care to share with the class?" I asked, as he received a new text message.

He laughed slyly. "Naw, I'm good."

"Why don't you give that thing a break and enjoy the company around you? We can't be that boring."

He didn't look up from his keypad and only responded with more laughter, so I did what Dana probably wanted to do. I snatched the phone from him and read what I could. *I might come check u out after everybody's sleep. I'll hit u up later tho. Watching the—*

"Stop playin'!" he said, almost tackling me to get his phone back.

Vaughn caught me after I tripped on Ric's foot. Ric and I stared at each other. His eyes begged me to keep my mouth shut about his text to LaShay, while my eyes threatened to tell Dana what I saw.

By the grace of God or just plain ol' dumb luck, one of my girls interrupted the visual showdown that was quickly heating up by yelling, "He won! He won!"

All of our attention turned to the televisions, as we watched the United States of America's first black president give his speech in Chicago's Grant Park. I glanced at Dana, who was totally mesmerized by Barack Obama, and read her thoughts. A man with his intelligence and of his caliber is who she deserves and who she imagined herself with from the time she was a nerdy little girl. Pan left to view the man she calls her husband. *Whomp, whomp, whomp, whooooomp.*

If she ever opens up about Ric again and thinks she should leave him because of his shady ways, I'll take that opportunity to say, "Yes, you can, and yes, you should!" To deliberately disrespect my girl as if she's nothing is a no-no.

# DANA

"You have got to get over here now. We've got a Code Red in this bitch," I said as soon as Crystal answered the phone. Code Red is a phrase we made up in college when major trouble arose and we needed backup.

"Are you gonna give me a synopsis before I get there? Do I need my black on? What's up?" she asked.

"I can't even sum this up. You just have to get here...please."

"I'm in Stone Mountain, so I'll be there in fifteen, tops. Milky's with me."

"Thank you so, so much. I'm losing it over here."

"Are you shaking?"

"Like an addict in withdrawal. I don't think I've ever been this pissed."

We hung up, and twelve minutes later, they were knocking on my door. I opened it quickly, praying the thuds didn't wake Chase and Dalvin. Crystal breezed by me and walked into the living room.

"Spill it," she said, as she paced near the computer desk in her studded Louboutins.

"Look at the computer screen," I said, unsure whether I should be showing them pictures of my husband's penis. Then I remembered he was showing them to the world.

"You did not call me over here to look at a damn porn site. I know you wouldn't do something that simple," she said, phrasing it as a question-like statement.

"Scroll up," I said.

Willow joined her at the desk and squinted. "Is that Ric?" she shrieked.

"Oh, hell no! I wasn't even trying to know him like that!" Crystal added before scrolling to the very top to view the website's name.

I sat on the arm of the couch, wringing my hands and nervously shaking my left leg. It was four in the morning, and I hadn't seen Ric since he left the house after *The First 48* went off. He was supposedly riding to the store with one of the village idiots who lived four houses down, but I knew damn well it didn't take six hours to drive 2.5 miles down the street to Wal-Mart, pick up a few things, and come back. They could've power shopped and still been back in an hour and a half. To make matters worse, he wasn't answering his phone.

I was antsy between eleven and twelve, and livid by one-thirty. At a quarter to two, my fury turned to worry as I thought of other circumstances that would have him out of the house for so long, unable to answer his phone. I proceeded to call all the major hospitals and county jails to see if they had Cedric Hall in their facility, only to hear "No, ma'am" each time.

Exhausted mentally and physically, I laid down in an effort to get a little rest, but I couldn't stop tossing and turning. Every twenty minutes, I'd roll over and check my phone, thinking I'd missed his call. Finally, I sat straight up in bed. I swear I heard, "Check the history in the computer," clear as day, but when I looked around, no one was in the room. I hesitated for a while, then rushed into the living room and sat at the computer desk.

After a quick scan, my eyes zeroed in on EZBooty.com. I hadn't seen it before, but it was obviously a new porn site Ric had discovered. When I clicked to expand the selection, I found out it was much more.

When the site loaded, a naked woman appeared with her index finger pressed against her lips. Above her head was the site name in huge font, and across her titties were the words, "It's not that hard to get some." Just below that was a prompt to log in again because the previous session had expired.

Much like the time I had a CT scan and they injected me with contrast, a warm sensation came over my whole body, starting at my throat and ending at my feet. For a few seconds, I felt like my air was being cut off after I realized my husband actually had a profile on the convenient cheating website. He was smart enough to use a password I couldn't figure out, so at three a.m., I was creating a fictitious profile that would enable me to search all profiles on the site. First stop: BigDicRic.

His main picture was one I'd taken of him while we were in Florida on vacation five years prior. He was standing on the beach with shorts on and no shirt. I clicked on his photo album, and to my dismay, there were three other pictures, all of his dick.

I have tolerated Ric's affinity for pornography. I used to be offended that he would want to look at other naked women and pleasure himself, but I learned not to take it personal. After surveying many of my friends and associates years ago, I found out that most men are into looking at it, and I adopted a new perspective of it. When I'm feeling frisky, I'll even stop by the adult toy store and bring home a DVD with an accompanying accessory that we can play with while we watch.

95

I've long been aware of him indulging in his guilty pleasure on the internet, and that's okay. All he can do is look at the girls showing their surgically-enhanced body parts and doing the sick XXX things that fall way outside of my boundaries. No harm, no foul. The only real problem I've had with his pornography obsession was when he borrowed movies from a female associate a while back. I made it clear that that was a no-no, and we moved on.

I know he's a fuckup. He's been one for a while, so I expect some of this behavior. Something is wrong with the universe if he doesn't do something stupid or inconsiderate once every two or three months. It's an idiosyncrasy I expect no one to fathom. Some things, though, aren't excusable— things like having a profile on a porn site where he's showcasing skin that only I should see and posting a sexual résumé as if he's seeking somewhere or someone else to work. I didn't know what else to do, so I called Crystal. Fast forward to her and Willow viewing the profile in my living room, still in their party dresses.

As Crystal stood in disbelief with her hand on her hip, she finally exclaimed, "Easy booty? Does that fool put effort into anything he does? Only his ass would find a website with that name."

I remained silent while Willow looked at me with worry.

Crystal read the information he posted in the profile. "Man of steel? Who told him that? Did you tell him that shit, D? One hundred percent chocolate, five-foot-eight-inches tall, nine-and-a-half-inches long, all night long, down for whatever as long as it's discreet." She stopped abruptly. "I can't read this shit. So where is his down-for-whatever ass? With some bitch he met on here?" She scrolled down to read the messages posted on his profile wall.

"That's what I wanna know," I replied. I felt lightheaded after seeing the pictures, so I never got to Ric's bio. Those details Crystal read aloud only twisted the knife. I explained his disappearing act, then told her and Willow about all the phone calls I made.

"He couldn't have ridden with his friend because he has your car," Crystal said.

"He doesn't have my car. I saw him and his friend pull off."

"Did you get the garage door fixed and park inside? There ain't no white Camry in the driveway."

"Could it be stolen?" Willow asked.

I closed my eyes for a few seconds and tried my best to breathe through my tightened diaphragm. Then I approached the kitchen counter and grabbed my keys. Without looking out of the window, I pressed the Lock button on my keyless entry remote. I didn't hear a thing. I tried again. Still nothing. A confirmation peek through the blinds confirmed what Crystal had already told me. Ric took my spare set of keys, pretended to leave with his buddy, and then came back to get the car when he figured I was fast asleep.

"I'm sick right now. I'ma kill him."

"You don't have an idea where he could be? Milky can stay here with the boys while we ride out," Crystal suggested.

I shook my head. Ninety-five percent of Ric's conversations take place via text messaging, so any locales he may frequent are unbeknownst to me. We'd reached a roadblock.

"Sorry if I ruined your night, ladies. I just had to call somebody, and I figured you'd just be leaving Shandra's release party."

"You didn't ruin a thing, so shut up."

"I wish there was something we could do to help," Willow added.

"If you know of any hit men, that will help."

97

Crystal burst into laughter. "That's one way to eliminate the problem." She went into the kitchen and searched my pantry. "You need a drink. That'll help."

"Do you guys ever sit down and talk about your marriage—like what's working and what's not? Maybe that could help," Willow offered.

"A conversation like that with him would be the equivalent of talking to this couch I'm sitting on."

"Were you two ever on the same page?" she asked.

"Oh yeah. It's just that now I'm finding out we've been on the same page, but in different books."

"Men are from Mars, and women are from Venus. You've heard the statement."

"And read the book," I added. "That's not even it. Nobody holds anything sacred these days. I really don't know what has happened with Ric. I have plenty theories, but nothing real."

Crystal weighed in. "You've got the real. He's giving it to you. I'll tell you what happened. You signed up for holy matrimony, and he signed up for holey matrimony. He just won't say it. At least Dante and I signed up for the same thing. We're married with single benefits."

"That's not how we were raised, though," Willow said.

"So? When I chose Dante, I chose this life. I knew what I was getting into. Don't even start with me, Milky. We weren't raised to take an uppercut, either."

I quickly returned to the original topic. "I don't get it. If you feel so apathetic about marriage, why did you get so mad about Ric?"

"I'm apathetic about my marriage because I already knew what to expect. I was in training all those years I dated Dante in college. Ric is a coward. You didn't get into your marriage knowing what his real intentions were. I'm not affected by Dante. Ric's shenanigans affect you. Don't think I haven't noticed you've lost more weight since we got back from the expo. That's why I'm mad. I'd never judge you for staying with him, though, because you love him, and I know how that feels. But, on the flipside, I wouldn't stop you from handing his ass some walking papers."

Most college students have horror stories about their roommates, but I found a gem in Crystal. When I was eighteen and shaking her hand on move-in day, I never thought we'd be best friends fourteen years later. When she says she won't judge me, she means it, and I know she just wants me to be happy...whatever that entails.

"Do you want us to stay until he comes back?"

"What are we gonna do? Jump him?" Willow asked with a hint of laughter.

"Y'all go home. It's six in the morning. Hold up. Milky, what are you doing out this late? Vaughn must be out of town."

"Vegas," she replied.

"I told her to take Venus to our parents and put on her sexy gear so she could roll out with me. You would've been summoned, too, if you had a babysitter," Crystal said. "No more sitting in the house while our *husbands* are out doing their thing."

*Says the woman with no children*, I thought.

"Well, I'm glad you ladies came to my rescue. I was on the verge of a nervous breakdown. Thank you for the emotional release."

"We need to do this more often. I like that...emotional release," Willow said.

We were subconsciously planning ahead for future pain, bracing for the inevitable. Nevertheless, I was game.

"I'll host it!" Crystal said.

Shortly after our goodbye hugs, Chase woke up complaining of a stomachache. By seven-thirty, he'd thrown up three times and ruined a pair of underwear, and I'd washed a load of towels that were soiled from his accidents.

Dalvin trudged into the living room at a quarter after eight and found me and his brother on the couch. After waving hello and rubbing his eyes, he asked, "Where's Daddy?"

*****

I heard the jingle of keys and saw the doorknob turn just after Dalvin finished his Frosted Flakes. Ric entered slowly, nervously making eye contact with me for all of two seconds. Dalvin spoke to him, while Chase lay with his head in my lap, still drained from the hours before. I never parted my lips as I turned my attention back to *Handy Manny* on the TV screen.

Ric approached the couch from behind and placed his hand on my shoulder. "Hey. I know you're mad. I have a reason for not being here, though." His tone was as gentle as his touch, but the heat from his breath made my skin crawl. "Sam's car broke down after we left Wal-Mart, and—"

"And you couldn't walk home?"

"If you'd let me finish…We left Wal-Mart and went to this spot in Lawrenceville because he had to pick his partner up. That's where we got stuck."

"So you were there all night?"

He snickered. "Hell yeah. Three grown men scrunched up in a damn Hyundai, cold as hell, tryna get some sleep. You should've seen us, baby. I told Sam he needs to invest in AAA. We could've been home. Then my fuckin' phone died, so I couldn't even call you. Man, it was crazy. I know you were blowin' me up." He pointed at Chase. "Is he sick?"

I nodded, then held out my hand. "Give me my keys, please."

"What keys?"

"The keys you used to take my car last night. Where did you go, to see AppleBottom770? Did she call you?" Before he spoke, I held up my index finger. "And don't ask me who, because you know who the hell I'm talking about."

100

He reached in his back pocket and placed the keys in my hand. "You can have your damn keys. It's stupid that I can't even drive the car I help pay for anyway. Don't worry about me. I'll get where I need to be."

"Oh, I don't doubt that. Hope your night out was worth it."

"Man, I don't even know what you're talkin' about. I don't know no AppleBottom770. I went to get some drinks at Dugan's, and then I chilled with Sam and Dougie. I drank too much, so I passed out. I came home as soon as I woke up."

"So that's your story now? It seems to be getting better, so let's try one more time and shoot for the truth."

"I told you the truth. You're the one thinking you have me figured out. You must want me to cheat. You keep coming up with these outlandish scenarios and shit."

I laid Chase's head on a pillow and walked over to the computer. A quick nudge of the mouse woke it from its sleep, and the screen showed the login screen for EZBooty. I logged in and pulled up his profile.

"Outlandish like this?"

He clenched his teeth.

"Dalvin, go get washed up and get your clothes on, babe." I waited for him to leave the room before addressing Ric again. "How desperate are you? What the hell? You act like you don't get ass-on-demand at home! That's not enough? You need easy booty, too?"

"There you go making assumptions again."

"I believe it's safe to assume you have been or are planning to fuck around when you create a profile on a porn-slash-matchmaking site stating you want a no-strings-attached fling and posting pictures of your smiling face and hard dick."

He hung his head.

101

Leaning toward him, I asked, "What you say? I can't hear you. Then, I read shit that these sluts post and see that you've exchanged numbers with Miss AppleBottom770."

"It's not what you think."

"Oh, it's not? Why does she need your number? You gon' give her a job? Does she need to change her cell phone plan?"

Frustrated, he looked at the ceiling and took a deep breath.

"Why don't I grab the digital camera and spread 'em for the world to see and tell you it's not what you think?"

"That would be childish."

"Did you just call me childish? You with the oiled-up dick and multiple camera angles?"

"Well, I made a mistake," he replied as if it was no big deal.

"It's looking like I'm the one who made the mistake."

"What's that supposed to mean?"

"It means I'm the only one who is married here. We both showed up for the ceremony, but it's obvious I'm the one who didn't consider it a dress rehearsal."

"If that's how you feel…"

"That's how it is."

"So why are you with me?"

"I don't know, but I'm about to seek professional help because something has to be wrong with me."

"Why seek help? It sounds like you already know what you want to do."

*Yeah, I know what I want to do—not what I'm going to do,* I thought as I watched him grab a beer from the refrigerator and pat his pockets to check for his bus pass.

"Let me guess," I said. "You're out."

"You damn right. You just told me you're the only one married, so why should you give a fuck that I'm leaving?" he said before pulling out his phone and walking out.

*Maybe he'll stay gone this time,* I thought. Ric deciding to leave would be much easier than me deciding I can no longer stay.

# WILLOW (MILKY)

The wind blew so briskly across my face that I thought my nose and lips were going to whisk away with it. Vaughn and I stood in the breezeway of Atlanta Hartsfield Jackson Airport. Rebecca had contacted Vaughn to tell him she had a two-hour layover before she boarded her connecting flight to Miami, and asked if I was available to meet her. As we stood near one of the entrances, I had a sixth thought. On the drive there, I'd already gone through my second, third, fourth, and fifth ones.

Vaughn read my mind. "We're here, babe. Let's just go say hello. If you want it to stop there, so be it."

I turned abruptly and snatched the door open, leading the way into the atrium. With the bravery of a one-woman army and the heart of a mouse, I marched toward the gift shop where Rebecca said she would be. Vaughn nearly ran into the back of me as I stopped suddenly.

The woman fiddling with her BlackBerry had to be her. She looked nervous, like if we were cartoons, she'd be vigorously biting her nails and the shavings would be flying everywhere. She wore her hair curly, yet it still fell past her shoulders. The square BCBG sunglasses resting on her

104

crown indicated she was Miami-bound, because there was certainly no use for them in Atlanta on a cloudy December day. The sight of her full lips crushed the ridiculous story Crystal fabricated when we were in high school about Mom getting me Botox injections when I was younger to help me blend in with them. I stared at them, convinced she used to be a habitual teenage lip-curler, a sure sign of a stuck-up chick from the good part of town. You know, the kind of girl who would drag out the end of almost any word, especially "Whateverrrrrrr."

"Willow?" she asked, interrupting my vision. After I nodded, she said, "I'm your—I'm Rebecca." She instinctively extended her hand as if I was a business associate.

I couldn't help but chuckle just a bit as I kept my arm wrapped around Vaughn's and addressed her simply with, "Hello."

Her eyes took in my appearance like a scanner, adding every detail to her memory. She glowed as if she were proud, as if she had anything to do with who I am outside of donating her chromosomes and passing on her full lips and curly hair.

"Vaughn, we finally meet. I feel like I already know you," she said. He was much more cordial, extending his free hand to shake her once rejected one.

"Are you guys hungry? We could sit over there in Houlihan's."

"I don't have an appetite," I replied.

"Okay…we can just have a seat near that window."

We settled in a semi-private area, and she sat about a foot away from me on the bench.

"I don't know where to start. Wow. I knew this would be awkward, but…Wow. You look so much like me."

"That tends to happen when you have a child. Listen, Rebecca, I don't want to be a total bitch, but let's get to the heart of this. Why?"

"Why did I want to meet you?"

"Why did you want to meet me? Why did you abandon me? Why are you selfishly interrupting my life right now?"

"I was under the impression that you wanted to meet me, too, Willow. If I'm wrong, I'm sorry, and I'll leave now and never bother you again."

"How could I not want to meet you? Wouldn't you want to know if you laugh like your mother or if you're tall like your father or if glaucoma runs in your family? Do you know how it feels to stare at a new patient form at the doctor's office and not know what boxes to check or leave blank?"

She lowered her head.

"Are you in touch with my father? Do you even know who he is?"

She jerked her neck back, offended that I would say such a thing. "Uh, yes, I know who he is. Scott was my boyfriend of two years, for Christ's sake."

"So his name is Scott. Scott what?"

"Knight. Scott Knight." She hung her head. "He's gonna kill me," she said under her breath.

"Don't worry. I won't bother him. You see I didn't bother you. You searched for me."

"I don't mean it like that. It's just that he thought I went through a real adoption agency, and…"

"You don't want him to know the truth."

"This isn't going well at all," she said with an uncomfortable laugh. Deep breath. "I'm not a bad person, Willow. I've made bad decisions. Leaving you there that day was probably the worst one. You want to know why I gave you up? Because I was a spoiled sixteen-year-old whose parents didn't know she was sexually active, and I was afraid that having a baby would ruin everything I had going for me."

106

Though her words stung, I appreciated her honesty. She went into detail about how she hid her pregnancy from her family. In their affluent Geist neighborhood, such a thing was frowned upon, and she didn't dare bring shame to the Sinclair name. She and Scott reviewed their options, and in a half hour, my fate was decided. They didn't want to abort me, but they didn't want to keep me. Adoption was the solution.

There was a problem with the legitimate adoption process, though. Her parents had to be involved. In her mind, there was only one other thing to do: leave me in a high-traffic area in a "decent" neighborhood—nowhere near Geist, though. She couldn't run the risk of someone mysteriously putting zero and two together.

She admitted I wasn't a big deal at the time; I was just a baby. She'd seen *Lifetime* movies where babies were taken in off the street and figured that was the norm. No one would pass up a cute, crying baby. Lucky for her, the angel watching over me was much more powerful than the devil that was influencing her. I've always known kids who live in Geist are rich, but I didn't think they were clueless...until that moment.

"So let's try this again," she started. "I'm Rebecca Sinclair. Outside of being the deadbeat bitch who gave birth to you, I'm the VP of Capital Formation at my firm; I'm the mother of two adorable Shitzus; and I'm sorry for any pain my actions have caused you." She kept her hands in her lap this time instead of attempting the informal handshake again.

I nodded. "Well, you know my name because you gave it to me. Vaughn and I have a beautiful little girl, and I'm a graphic designer." She was lucky to get that out of me. I felt like I was either introducing myself at a pageant or involved in a bad episode of *Love Connection*. "You just have dogs? No children?" I asked. My words smiled, anticipating an answer like, *I wouldn't have been able to live with myself if I had more children—not after the way I handled matters with you.*

Instead, she said, "No. After years of trying, I found out I couldn't have any more children." She shrugged as if she didn't care, but her eyes told a different story.

The Christian in me muted the "Good!" outburst that was ready to jump off my tongue.

Her phone beeped twice. "Do you mind if we go back toward the food court? I have to take medicine, and I need to eat something with it."

I looked at my watch. "Oh, that's fine. We have to go anyway."

Before we left, I asked if she was still in touch with Scott Knight. She said she hadn't spoken with him in twenty-five years, and the last she knew, he was in California. Since he graduated a year ahead of her, she hadn't run into him at a class reunion. I wasn't sure if I wanted to meet him anyway, so that was fine.

"If it helps, you should know he was 6'2" his senior year of high school. He played a sport every season. He had amazing legs, and it's pretty obvious you inherited those from him. His hair was black, he had blue eyes, and he was good at science. He was also a great artist, but he only drew occasionally for fun." She tapped her heel on the floor as if she was trying to strum up more memories. "Um…he's a Virgo. His middle name is Russell, which he hated back then. I don't know about glaucoma, but cancer runs in his family. His paternal grandfather and one of his aunts died from it while we were still in school. As for my family, we're fortunate to have not battled with any major illnesses."

"Thank you," I replied with a warm smile. In less than an hour, I had obtained many missing pieces of my puzzle. Rebecca's extra effort to paint a picture of Scott in my mind in substitute of placing his business card in my hand meant a lot. She gave me what she could, and once the residue of resentment leaves my heart, I'm sure I'll believe she gave me what she could on October 2, 1978—the opportunity to be raised in a genuinely loving family.

"Are we still on for February? If you don't mind, I'd like to meet Janice and Ray then and thank them for what they did. I can bring pictures of Scott, too, if you'd like to see what he looks like."

Vaughn squeezed my hand gently after I took a while to answer. "Sure," I said.

"Great! Well, I'll be in touch before then. I'm so glad I was able to meet you."

We had a weird what-do-we-do-now moment that ended with a quick wave goodbye and closed-lipped smiles. It had finally happened. I had met my biological mother. During a time I should've felt something—joy, anger, sadness, relief, closure—I felt nothing significant, only gratitude for the information she'd shared.

As if my day wasn't trying enough, I had to lie down that evening and make love to Vaughn. For the first time, I felt nothing. I thought he was selfish for doing anything more than cuddling with me, but I choose my battles. Having sex would be much less grueling than arguing with him about why I wasn't in the mood. Besides, it had been two weeks since we'd been intimate due to technical difficulties.

When we were done, he rolled over and was fast asleep within ten minutes. I, on the other hand, stared at the ceiling, frightened that my empty feeling would spill into the days that followed, but relieved that Vaughn didn't sense it that night.

# CRYSTAL

I haven't worked since my senior year of college, but my days are still jam packed with things to do. My occupation is keeping myself up, keeping my friends company, and keeping my husband happy. It was Thursday, so that meant it was Crystal Day.

As a ritual, I go to my favorite spa to get a facial, full body massage, manicure, and pedicure. When I looked down in the shower earlier, I also saw it was time to add Brazilian wax to the list. Instead of my usual landing strip, I figured I'd surprise Dante with the martini glass, his favorite. Once he got a glimpse of the triangular patch of hair, he'd lick me until my "glass" overflowed. And so it was done. I spent four and a half hours of my day being pampered by the best beauty technicians in Atlanta.

When my toenails dried, I slipped back into my pink Ugg boots and made a mad dash to my car. I was supposed to be in Buckhead for my teeth whitening appointment in ten minutes, and I was easily twenty-five minutes away. I called Malory, the receptionist, to let her know I'd be a few minutes late, but arrived a half hour late thanks to a fender bender on 400.

Once Dr. Knight was finished with me, my teeth were three shades whiter. I practiced my smile for the big night in the mirror and then replaced it with one of satisfaction.

"Thank you, dear. They look fabulous, as usual," I said.

"It doesn't take much to make you look fabulous," he replied.

"Don't you start," I said, getting up from the chair. He and I always flirt during my visits.

As I was paying Malory, my phone rang. It was Dante.

"Hey, baby, I've got bad news."

"How bad?"

"We can't leave for L.A. tonight."

I waved goodbye to Malory and headed to the car. "Why not?"

"I just broke this dude's camera, and I have to make sure everything is everything before we go."

"What dude? What do you mean?"

He explained his encounter with an overaggressive paparazzo who was snapping pictures of him and his sister, Traci, looking to break the next story about his cheating spree.

They were leaving AquaKnox, a restaurant Traci always visits when she's in town, when Dante said a group of six men surrounded them with video and still cameras. According to him, all backed off when asked except the guy whose camera he smacked to the ground.

Paparazzi have always been his biggest pet peeve, but in the past, he's gotten mostly positive attention from them. Now my golden boy of R&B is losing his luster in his personal life, and everybody is watching. Another shot of him with another woman could easily result in his Big Brother/Big Sister commercials being pulled. Distribution of his underwear print ads, on the other hand, would probably spread to every magazine worldwide...even *Highlights*. A man stretched out on a couch in his Perry Ellis boxer briefs is great publicity if he's a cheater.

"Dante, you can't do that. They're just doing their job. Maybe if you hadn't given them any material in the first place, you wouldn't be so mad. What are you gonna do when there are twice as many in your face before the nominations?"

"We're going in the back way, so that won't be an issue."

"Whatever. Just remember there's never a need for damage control if you don't do any damage."

"And what's that supposed to mean?"

"Hay nunca una necesidad para el control de daño si usted no hace ningún daño," I said, surprised at how well the sentence rolled off my tongue. I haven't used much Spanish since I spent a semester abroad in Spain my junior year of college. "You got it in Spanish and English, and it means the same damn thing. There are no lines to read between. You want it in Chinese, too?"

"I didn't call to hear this bullshit."

"Good. We can solve that," I said before hanging up.

Things haven't been the same between us since that photo surfaced. He still doesn't know that I remember the girl as the one from the concert. I've decided to sit on that information until I know exactly how I want to use it.

My sealed lips have given him a false sense of security, but I notice everything. I've noticed how he makes an extra effort to make love to me after shows or long nights in the studio. He used to be too tired to give me that kind of attention, and I'm sure he still is. He just doesn't want me to think he's letting Junior out to play in someone else's yard. I've noticed that he has a third cell phone that's contracted through a different carrier than his business and personal ones. I first saw it in June when I searched his Bentley for an earring I'd lost. It was placed under the passenger floor mat where it wouldn't be noticed unless one was feeling under the seat like me. It was strategically placed there so he could lie and say someone must have dropped it and not realized—as if I wouldn't turn the thing on to see whose it was if I found it. What a silly rabbit.

*****

The nomination ceremony was buzzing with nervous energy, industry gossip, and great performances. Dante sat with his fingers intertwined and his teeth clenched as his first potential category was announced. I rubbed his thigh as I stared at Justin Timberlake, wishing he'd hurry up and say the names of the nominees. Tre mouthed *You got this* to Dante, but something told me he didn't. Six of the twelve songs on his album were hits, but the others were just okay. As we listened to the names, it was painfully clear that the committee agreed with me.

He controlled his facial expression, but I could tell he was disappointed. Even when they announced that he was a nominee for Best Male R&B Vocal Performance, he didn't give a genuine smile. Traci was hands-down the happiest person at the table. As soon as she heard her brother's name, her fingers went to work. Since it was entirely too loud in the room and inappropriate to make a phone call at the moment, she texted everyone in her contacts to share the good news.

Tre flinched in his seat as if he was startled. He pulled a phone from his pocket and read the screen. I cut my eyes in his direction and snickered at what I saw. It was the same model as Dante's secret phone, but I know they didn't stop making that model after Dante bought it. It could've been Tre's new phone.

"That boy's wild," Tre said as he laughed and showed Dante the message.

113

Much like I'd done with Ric at the election party, I contemplated snatching the phone from Tre. I'm too classy to cause a scene, though, and too calculating to show my hand prematurely. I knew what was up, though. Tre was not only managing Dante's career; he was also managing his groupies.

Dante laughed half-heartedly after a quick glance. Then he poured himself some champagne. "You want some more, baby?" he asked, while hovering the bottle over my empty glass.

I stared at him long enough to make him uncomfortable. My number one pet peeve is disrespect, and with Tre's help, he had just disrespected me from six inches away. I wasn't supposed to know that was his phone. So, I definitely wasn't supposed to know some bitch was texting him to congratulate him on the nomination and tell him something cheesy like she has another kind of award waiting for him.

I wondered if she was in town, wondered if she was staying at our hotel, wondered how long it would take Dante to decide he wanted to go "to the studio" when we got back to the room, wondered if he'd make her feel significant or if he had already done that. I wondered why after all these years I had to wonder. I've always been secure, and though I'm not willing to categorize myself as being insecure, I feel like I ran across a Sherlock Holmes hat on a bad hair day and decided to keep wearing it because I keep getting compliments.

"Baby!" Dante said again.

"Go ahead," I said as he tipped the bottle to fill my glass. I was clearly feeling too much, and one or two more glasses would numb my heart.

Milky is concerned about my drinking habit. I can admit it's a habit because it has become therapeutic for me, but it isn't a problem. I'm sure that's what alcoholics say, but if someone dare throw a stone, I have always kept a few with me to throw back. I'm not an alcoholic; I'm a product of my environment. I'm a social drinker who drinks more often than most social drinkers because I attend more social events. Drinking and shopping help me maintain a smile and stay at a neutral five when my temperament would normally be on ten. Needless to say, the other wives and I have bars that look like we moved the V.I.P. room to our houses.

I'm quick to call Dante an actor, but I guess I'm one, too. I've been trained to adapt to an unconventional set of relationship rules from the moment I agreed to go on our first date. What can I say? I fell in love. If I keep getting disrespected, though, Dante's going to be the one falling — the kind of fall that results in a major injury. I'm a team player until the game becomes unfair.

# DANA

My fever had gone down to 101.4, which was much better than the previous reading of 102.8. Ric and I had been in the E.R. for two hours, and after reading my chest x-rays, the doctor confirmed that I was suffering from walking pneumonia. I had been coughing for almost a month, but my primary care physician was convinced it was bronchitis. Really, I didn't feel like I was sick until I woke up with a low-grade fever yesterday. As it progressively became worse, I gave in to Ric's demand to take me to the emergency room.

Once they released me, Ric became my doctor. He placed me on bed rest from the moment we got in the house and ordered the boys not to disturb me. He cooked—if chicken nuggets and Velveeta shells and cheese count as cooking. He cleaned, did homework with Dalvin, screened my phone calls, ran my bath water, delivered soup to my bedside, and massaged my aching muscles. After the first two days, he realized I wasn't eating while he was gone, so he'd come home on his lunch break and make me eat, even if it was just a cup of Chase's applesauce. To accomplish this, of course, he needed to drive my car. I was seven pounds lighter, ridiculously weak, and mentally exhausted, which meant I didn't fuss one bit when Ric asked where my keys were Wednesday morning. Thank God I didn't even have the mental capacity to worry about whether he'd get pulled over while he was gone.

During the week I was out of commission, I never let a day pass without thanking him. He was going above and beyond, and I fell back in love with him a little more as each day went by. He was Cedric again—the guy who swept me off my feet when I was seventeen. He was charming and attentive, concerned and compassionate—qualities that only make guest appearances in our marriage, but were staples during our courtship. Every time I get a taste of how it used to be, I hold on to the hope that it may transform back to how it always was then. Permanently.

I'd learn quickly enough. The record for chivalry's longevity within our marriage is two months and three days, set during our second year. If Ric could keep up his good behavior beyond three weeks, I would be pleasantly surprised. I see a month's worth of stripteases and whatever-you-like nights of passion in his future if he breaks the record.

I certainly haven't forgotten about EZBooty.com, just as I haven't forgotten about the girl who called me during my freshman year of college saying she was pregnant with his baby, or the picture of him and a girl who I later learned was his girlfriend, too, posing near the Grand Canyon with the date stamp proving it was taken a month after our two-year dating anniversary. The list goes on.

He hasn't forgotten either. The first day he came home to feed me lunch, I thanked him for being so sweet, and he replied, "I try to do my best, even though this is just dress rehearsal for me."

For 3.3 seconds, I felt like eating my words from weeks prior, but the visual of him holding his hardness in front of

117

the webcam put me back in check. I want him to remember what I said because when I express myself, it's what I mean. I didn't say it just to hurt him. I said it because he needs to know how his actions are perceived. Communication is the corridor to understanding, and understanding is the stairway to longevity. Unfortunately, Ric sees my attempts to communicate as an excuse to argue. So, he hears me without listening and doesn't understand where I'm coming from. Often, "I'm sorry" is his response because he just wants me to shut up or because he would rather make love at the end of the night than lie next to my coldness.

His practice of saying all the right things after doing all the wrong things is such a gamble; and gambling is an eluding game. It's designed to let you think you're in control, think you've got everything figured out, and have you believing you can't lose once you're on a roll. Much to the contrary, you have no control, and by thinking you can't lose, you reach the point of no return. That's when you increase your bet and lose it all.

Ric has been one lucky bastard, caught up in the illusion that he is playing his cards right because I've stayed with him through all the bullshit, unanswered questions, and lies. I pray he gets it together before I do.

*****

Ric surprised me with an impromptu date night. We usually forgo it in December because we are low on time and money after shopping for Christmas gifts, but he received a bonus check and wanted to do something special.

He actually put on some black slacks and a button-down shirt I'd bought him for his 32nd birthday and had been begging him to wear ever since. We went to Atlantic Station and ate at Strip, which is outside of his comfort zone. He considers restaurants of its caliber to be glorified versions of Applebee's or Outback Steakhouse. He's such a weirdo.

118

"See? I'm trying," he said as we dined. "Are you enjoying yourself?"

I smiled and nodded.

"You know this isn't my thing. This is all for you." He pulled the collar of his shirt. "I got dressed up like you always want me to do."

*Don't ruin the moment,* I thought. "So is this just for tonight, or will I get this more often?"

He shrugged. "I mean, it won't be every time we go out, but I'll put in a little extra effort sometimes." He leaned closer and smirked. "If I do, will you do that little trick?"

My eyes flirted back with his words as I bit my lower lip and laughed. "You're so nasty."

"Is that a yes?"

"I guess you'll have to find out when we get home."

He cut through his steak as if he was suddenly in a hurry to leave. I genuinely laughed out loud at his silliness.

We didn't go straight home after leaving Strip. Ric asked if I wanted to have a couple drinks, and I happily agreed. We ended up at Luckie Lounge. It was my first time being there, but apparently not his. I learned this when he told me a story of how the two gay bartenders, who are supposedly in a relationship, started throwing drinks at each other one night because one thought the other was flirting with a woman.

I tried to stay focused on his story, but I couldn't stop wondering who was with him, when, and why. So I asked, "When was this?"

"I don't remember. It was in September some time, I think." He bobbed his head to the music, oblivious to the fact that I may have had follow-up questions.

As my heart rate sped up, I took some deep breaths and chased the air with a gulp of the sweet tea concoction the bartender created for me. *Don't trip, Dana. The night is going well. Keep...your...mouth...closed.*

119

"I wanna dance," I said. "Watch my drink."

"Damn! I can't come with you?"

Ric is not a dancer. It's not that he doesn't have rhythm. He can bob his head on beat. However, when it comes to coordinating his hips and feet to create fluid movement, it doesn't always work out. He often just resorts to standing there, bobbing his head, and holding my hips while I do all the sweating. Don't get me wrong, I don't want him to break out with the Soulja Boy. It would just be nice to be able to get it with my husband the way I do with other guys when I'm at the club with my girls. They know how to move when I move, and as a result of spending my teenage years at the skating rink, I love a man who can move.

"That's fine. Any other time I ask you to dance with me, you don't, so that's why I—"

"You assumed."

I rolled my eyes and finished my drink. After setting the glass down, I reached out for Ric's hand. "Let's go, baby. Don't let me find out you've been practicing," I said with a smile.

We danced through a few songs before his phone vibrated. He pulled it out, answered it, and then gave me the index finger as he rushed toward the door. I was confident the boys were okay because the babysitter usually called my cell phone if there was a problem. So, I was hoping nothing was wrong with any of my in-laws. Whoever was on the other end of the line had something important to say for Ric to dash out like he did.

I danced nervously with a guy who seemed to keep missing my give-me-eight-inches cues. If Ric returned and saw us dancing so closely, there would be a problem. After missed cue number four, I excused myself from the dance floor. I needed to find Ric anyway to make sure everything was okay. When I stepped outside, I found him leaning against the building with the phone still pressed to his ear.

"Is something wrong?" I asked quietly.

He frowned and waved me off as if I was a panhandler asking him for a dollar. "Wait. Repeat that. Somebody was talking to me. My bad," he said, before tuning back in to the conversation.

After a half neck-roll and placement of my right hand on my hip, he placed the caller on hold.

"Yes? What do you need?"

"I *need* my husband to get off the phone and return to his date, unless he's making funeral arrangements for someone."

"This is important. I'll be off in a minute."

"It's always important. When will I ever be important?" I said under my breath.

"What?"

"Nothing. Let's go."

"I told you it would only be a min—. Nevermind. Cool. Let's roll." He walked off as if he had the right to be pissed. As if it was a good look to walk six feet in front of your date on the way to the car.

Forty-five minutes passed before he hung up. I knew he was speaking with a female just by listening to his tone. I could also hear her voice, though he tried numerous times to lower the volume of his phone. He spoke with her while he pumped gas, while we sat in the drive-thru at Krystal's, and the whole way home.

He finally hung up when we pulled into the driveway. I kept my cool long enough to pay the sitter and walk her to the door. Once I saw that she was safely in her car, I closed the door and glared at Ric.

"Who was that?" I asked.

He sighed loudly.

"Oh, are you disgusted? Good. Me, too. Who was it? I know it was a female. I could hear her voice."

"LaShay," he mumbled.

121

"You spent forty-five minutes on the phone with that girl during our date." I shook my head in disbelief.

"She had somethin' goin' on and needed to talk."

"And you're the only person she knows?"

"She can't trust her friends with something like this."

"What makes her feel she can trust you so much?"

"I don't know. I guess 'cause I'm older."

I nodded, never taking my eyes off of him. "So what was the crisis?"

"That's not your business. If she wanted you to know, she would've told you."

"*You're* my business! And maybe she would feel comfortable talking to me if she were a family friend. Opposite sex friends should be friends of mine and yours."

"You're crazy. Your little male teacher friends ain't friends with me."

"That's because you don't want them to be. And guess what? They don't call me to share their personal problems and ask me my favorite sexual positions and shit."

He shrugged. "I don't know that for sure."

My eyes bucked. "Excuse me? You can go through my phone right now, sweetie. There's nothing to see."

"I don't need to do that," he said, while heading to our bedroom.

I followed. "Because you know that will entitle me to look through yours."

"There isn't anything going on. Me and that girl don't do nothin' but talk on the phone."

"You don't need to talk to another female on the phone."

"You don't dictate who I can and can't talk to. We have work stuff we talk about, too."

"And what the hell do y'all need to discuss about cell phones at one in the morning? How many night and weekend minutes you use on each other?" I sat on the edge of the bed and changed into my pajamas.

"As a matter of fact, tonight, I had a question about something the district manager said in the meeting Wednesday."

"Here's a thought. Pay attention while he's talking. You're the manager! Try setting an example. And y'all sure as hell weren't talking about the meeting when you were in the car."

He changed out of his dress pants and put on some jeans. "You weren't even around for the first part of the conversation. I'm not about to listen to this."

"I'm sure you're not. You'll go listen to her, right? You gon' call her while you go for your angry walk? You gon' catch the bus to her house? Oh, wait. It's too late for that. Is she gon' pick you up?"

"If she calls me and needs to talk, yeah, I'll listen. That's what friends do. She's goin' through some stuff right now."

"But I tell you what I'm going through, and you ignore me."

"You're strong. She isn't."

I fell back onto the pillow and covered my face with my hands. "Are you kidding me?!"

"I can't believe you're intimidated by that girl."

"Intimidated? Please."

"I can't tell."

"Forgive me if I want to know who you're wasting all your consonants and vowels on and why. You'll talk to her for an hour at a time, sharing the details of your day, but you're on vocal rest when you're with me."

"We just talk. You act like I'm fuckin' her."

"*You* act like you're fuckin' her. And if you're not, you're emotionally bangin' her brains out. Your time is more valuable than your dick. She has a piece of your heart, doesn't she?" I asked.

He substituted answering me with rolling his eyes.

123

"You don't have to answer that. The mere fact that you're arguing with me about this girl, defending your communication with her, says enough."

He shook his head and shook me off. In a turn of events, I put on some sneakers, got my keys and purse, and left. Destination: unknown.

*****

December 19th didn't arrive fast enough. It was the night of the school district's Christmas party, and I was more than ready to let my hair down. The festivities were at the Hyatt downtown and set to begin at seven. I stood in front of the bathroom mirror to check my ensemble one last time.

"Why are y'all having such a fancy party this year?" Ric asked as he watched me put the finishing touches on my eye makeup.

"It's no fancier than last year," I replied.

I knew what was really bothering him. I was looking good in my red dress, and he knew it.

"You didn't wear nothin' like that last year."

"Okay, and?" I brushed past him and checked my purse to see if I had everything.

I had achieved my goal. I wanted Ric to have questions about my actions so he could see how it felt. I'm tired of being the model wife of a defective husband. I felt liberated last month when I lied and told him the party was for employees only, no spouses allowed. After the stunt he pulled on date night, I didn't regret it one bit.

"You know how to get there?" he asked since he knows I'm not a fan of driving downtown.

"Nope, but I'm meeting up with some coworkers and we're riding together."

I kissed the boys and continued my trek to the door with Ric on my heels.

"What kind of coworkers? Male or female?"

"What difference does it make? Business is business, right?"

I left him speechless and even more curious as I strutted to the car and pulled off without a second look.

As planned, I met Lily and Michelle in the school parking lot and rode with them downtown. Michelle's husband accompanied her, but Lily was rolling solo like me.

It seemed like everyone arrived at the ballroom at about the same time. It was beautifully decorated, and the holiday tunes provided a warm ambiance that provoked happiness as soon as we stepped inside. The tables were draped with red cloths and accented with fake snow. Four beautifully adorned artificial trees placed in the corners served not only as admirable décor, but great scenery for the pictures we'd be snapping throughout the night.

I spotted Lorenzo standing next to the coat rack, which was very convenient for me. I just so happened to have a coat that needed to be hung.

"Hey, you," I said, removing the wool trench to reveal the red number that turned Ric's head. "Who told you to come out the house looking like that?" Lorenzo asked with widened eyes while looking around. "Where's Ric?"

"I told you he wasn't coming."

"I know, but if he knew better, he would've accompanied you anyway. You couldn't be my wife walking around like that without an escort." He hung my coat, but his eyes never left my hips.

"You better cut it out before your date thinks something is up. Which one did you decide on? Andrea? Lauren? Brandy?"

He chuckled. "Don't even play me like that. I'm solo." His eyes invited me to change that status.

"Seriously? Why didn't you bring a date?"

"Because someone had to be your date."

125

I'm learning more about myself as I continue to deal with Ric's nonsense. I have lightened some of my inhibitions, believing what's good for the gander is good for the goose. The difference is I don't act out; I just act up. Right or wrong, it is what it is, and with Lorenzo's fine ass offering himself as my escort for the evening, it was what it was.

He sat with me, Lily, Michelle, Matthew, and two teachers from the art department. Our personal interaction felt natural—maybe a little too natural—as we tried our best to act like we simply had a professional relationship and not the teeny physical attraction that was probably looking more like the neon green elephant in the room. I found myself engaging more with everyone else to avoid looking into Lorenzo's eyes.

Though the free alcohol had a little to do with my feelings, my attraction to Lorenzo was way past the developmental stage. To me, foreplay starts at 'hello', and he has been stimulating me for six years.

What a great night. We all had a ball doing the Electric Slide, Cha-Cha Slide, and even the Cupid Shuffle. The highlight of the evening was seeing one of the football coaches teach our oldest teacher, Mrs. Crawford, how to "walk it by yourself" during the Cupid Shuffle. At sixty-four, she still had some moves. The most memorable moment of my evening, though, came when Lorenzo and I two-stepped to Donnie Hathaway's rendition of "This Christmas". Twenty years from now when I hear that song, I will still remember his smooth glide, the way he gently held my hand as he spun me around, the way he slightly bit his lower lip when he knew he was jamming, how hard his chest was when he pulled me close…everything.

During last call, we stood at the bar, pretending not to notice the mistletoe hanging above our heads. Well, maybe I noticed it. Maybe I was hoping he'd come and stand beside me. Maybe I knew he'd go in for a gentlemanly kiss on my cheek when someone called the greenery to our attention. Maybe *I* knew I would let him. What I didn't know is that our faces would remain just an inch apart as we stared at each other's lips, soon remembering we were in the company of others and backing away.

# WILLOW (MILKY)

I called the girls early in the week and scheduled an emotional release session for Friday night. I had pretty much kept to myself for a week because I was terribly emotional and confused, but I wanted to catch up with their lives and fill them in on mine. Dana and I left our little ones with their daddies and joined Crystal in her "chill room", a cozy space on the second floor that overlooks the indoor pool. The three of us sat in the plush chairs near the fireplace with our feet resting comfortably on the matching ottomans. Crystal, of course, had a glass of tequila in-hand.

"So what's up, stranger?" Dana asked me. "I thought I'd be the only one calling these meetings."

I smiled and ran my fingers through my hair. "Oh, I think I just need to vent. I guess it's my turn."

"Honey, please. I'm sure we all have something to contribute," Dana said.

Crystal nodded and raised her glass before taking a sip.

"Well, it's not what you're probably expecting," I started.

I knew Crystal was checking my face for bruises from the second she saw me. Neither of the girls knew I'd met Rebecca, so I shared that story.

"When did you say she's coming back?" Crystal asked in her protective big sister tone.

"February. She wants to meet the whole family."

"No, she doesn't! Since she likes to play seek and find, let me take her down to West End and leave her on the post office steps. Let's see who finds *her*. I bet she won't find justification for that. Naw, she don't wanna meet *me*."

"It's in the past now. What can I do? If I keep holding on to that anger, I'm still gonna be the only one affected. She has clearly moved on. She even tried to have more kids. There's no need for you to get all upset about it."

Crystal went on and on as only she can do. There was no interrupting her rant, until Dana answered her vibrating phone and got our attention with the outburst that followed.

"No, I don't know when I'll be home," she said loudly. "Did you tell me when you'd be home when you snuck off with my car? Or do you need to know how much time you have with LaShay? Is that little bitch over there with my babies?"

Crystal and I looked at each other with raised eyebrows.

"Yeah, whatever. Goodbye, Ric," she said. Her trembling voice was in rhythm with the quiver of her hand. She placed the phone on the ottoman and poured a glass of tequila and Minute Maid Limeade.

We looked her way, awaiting an explanation.

"I'm sorry. Go ahead. What did I miss?"

"Un unh," Crystal said. "What did *we* miss?" she asked, pointing to the phone.

Dana told us how Ric ruined their date by taking a phone call from that LaShay girl. "He only called to piss me off. I haven't said more than twenty words a day to him for the past week and a half, but he knew I would answer

129

because he has the boys and I'd want to make sure they were alright."

"Please tell me you were lying when you said he told you he'd answer her call whenever she needed him," Crystal said.

"I wish I could," Dana replied. "I'm at my wit's end. If you ask me today, I'll say hell yes, I'm getting a divorce."

"He is really feeling himself," I said.

"Tell Ric he can bypass your ass and kiss mine. I mean that. I'm starting to believe he really thinks you're stupid," Crystal said.

"Yeah, that's bad," I cosigned. "What if you did that to him?"

Crystal wasn't finished. "Better yet, offer him a straw. His lips aren't even good enough to touch your ass or mine."

"They say love can stand the test of time, right? Maybe it's just a phase he's going through. This could be his midlife crisis," Dana offered.

"Who are 'they'? And have 'they' traveled down the same path you're on? If you think about it, marriage is more about tolerance than love."

I had to interject. "I disagree."

"So you *love* how Vaughn treats you on a bad day, or do you *tolerate* how he treats you on a bad day?"

"I tolerate his actions because I love him."

She waved me off.

"This is hilarious," Dana said. "We should be telling the nativity story and talking about Jesus right now, but we're sharing horror stories about our husbands."

"That reminds me," Crystal said, while reaching into her purse and pulling out two jewelry boxes from Tiffany's. "Merry Christmas, you miserable bitches."

Dana and I laughed as we accepted our respective boxes.

"From the secretly miserable one herself," I replied.

I flipped the top open and was almost blinded by the flash from the ceiling light reflecting off of the diamonds. Crystal bought us 14-karat gold, diamond encrusted dog tags that looked like membership cards. "DWC" was engraved in fancy letters on the front, and my signature was on the back with the words "Member since 2005" engraved below it.

"That's your proof of membership," Crystal said.

Our running joke about being the Disgruntled Wives Club had been taken to another level.

"How did you get my signature?" Dana asked.

"Remember the papers you two signed for the mentoring program?" she answered with a smile.

I handled the piece carefully between my fingers and examined my reflection. "This will be interesting to explain when Vaughn asks what DWC stands for."

"I already have that covered. It's our initials. I didn't realize that until I had the man design them."

"That *is* right! Dana, Willow, Crystal. What a damn coincidence," Dana said.

"And what about the year on the back?" I asked. Vaughn and I were married in 2005, and I could see him figuring that out.

"I don't know. Make something up! If you don't want it, give it back. Shit, I didn't buy an explanation *and* a warranty."

I apologized and thanked her. I was confident I could think of an explanation for the date—even if it was something corny like it being the year we all became close.

"Now back to you, Dana. You need to fall back from this love talk for a second and use that super nerd brain of yours. He messed around when y'all were dating, correct?" Crystal asked as Dana nodded. "Remember what I told you after you said he made a folder for her in his email account. She's significant. He confirmed that when he left you on the dance floor. I know you two overcame a lot, and I won't discredit that, but why would the game playing stop simply because you stood in front of a stranger, repeated what he said, and signed a piece of paper?"

"That sounds like what those women say who live with their men for over ten years and never get married. 'Marriage is a state of mind,'" I added, laughing slightly.

"Is it not?" Crystal asked.

"She's right," Dana said. "I never thought of it like that."

"You know I'm not that friend who is on that he-ain't-no-good stuff, but as your girl, as your sister from another mister, watch yourself," Crystal added. "Ric is a careless little somethin', and if he's sliding in somebody else, I doubt he's wrapping that shit up."

Dana nodded and looked as if she had already thought the same thing. "How do I go about it, though? Do I bust out a condom all of a sudden? Withhold sex?"

"If that's what it takes. Maybe he'll get the message if you pull out a Trojan like he's a fuckin' stranger."

"I say withhold sex. Why would you want to have sex with him anyway if you think something's up with him and that girl?" I asked.

"The same reason you spread 'em for Vaughn after he choke slams you," Crystal said after swallowing the last of her drink.

"Touché, jerk," I replied.

"You know what? I should just divorce his ass and become celibate," Dana said.

"Now I know you're on some drunk shit. Did you have a drink before you got here?" Crystal responded. "Stop while you're ahead."

"Listen. I'm beginning to think I only keep him around for sex. I can please myself with my toys or my fingers and eliminate the drama that comes with having a husband I can't trust."

"Bullshit. Being celibate and using toys is like being on a diet and not eating cake, but eating cake batter. It doesn't add up. We both know you're with Ric because you love his trifling ass. Vibrations and spirit fingers get old after three times a week, sweet pea. Stop playing yourself. Matter of fact, maybe you need a stronger drink to pull you out of this nonsense you're talking." She topped off Dana's glass with more Patrón. "And stop mixing this with juice. You're ruining the experience!"

"It doesn't sound like an issue of whether to have sex or not, Dana. You're substituting that decision for the decision of whether you're going to work on your marriage or not."

Dana shrugged. "Damn psychology majors. Y'all heifers make me sick."

"We'll send you an invoice," Crystal said.

I shook my head and looked at my sister. "What about you? You are so anti-marriage now. You're like the marriage Nazi."

"I am not. I'm anti-ignorance. I'm anti-obliviousness. I'm anti-LaLa Land. Marriage is what it is. It's your job to figure out what IT is, because you agreed to deal with IT forever."

"You haven't been the same since the article came out about Dante and that girl. I think that has a lot to do with your attitude," I said.

"I've been like this. It's the only way I've survived being married to a man that millions of women want."

Ever since we were little, my sister has never settled for less than the best of anything. I studied her eyes. "I'm not buying it, Crys."

"Good, 'cause I'm not selling anything. Dante is used to getting booty without putting in a bit of effort. He can get those girls to do the nastiest shit to him without asking. He lived that way for years. Just like I asked Dana, am I supposed to believe he stopped when we said 'I do'?"

"Yes!"

"Milky, please. Come out of the clouds. When we woke up the other night after the Grammy Nomination Party, there was lipstick smudged on his pillowcase. He was kissing on somebody, and it wasn't me. I don't wear that cheap shit."

"Oh my God," Dana said empathetically. "What did you say?"

"I didn't say a word."

"What?!" Dana and I said in unison.

"I just packed the pillowcase in my bag when he wasn't looking and tucked it in a special place when we got home."

"Ah," Dana said, "evidence."

"Not really. I kept it so I can smother his ass with it when the time is right," Crystal replied with a chilling calmness.

"Why don't you just leave?" I asked. "I don't care what you say. A part of you is not okay with that."

"Because I took vows," she said, unable to hold a straight face longer than ten seconds. After she finished laughing, she added, "It's not necessarily right, but it's okay."

Dana frowned. "Isn't that a Whitney Houston song?"

"Really, though, let's say I leave Dante. Then what?"

"I'm sure you'd meet a better man later," I told her.

"Define better."

"One who won't cheat on you."

"But who is otherwise subpar? I'll pass. I'm gonna say something that will probably make y'all think I'm shallow, but y'all know me well enough to know better. Dante's been a part of my life for fourteen years. In that time, I've become accustomed to a certain lifestyle. I'm spoiled. Y'all know that. I'm not settling for less than my norm, and no one can touch my norm except another celebrity. I'd be leaving one cheater to be with another."

I shook my head. "I don't believe that."

"Milky, if I say the grass is green, you'll say it's magenta just to disagree with me. If you don't believe it, go marry a professional athlete—one of the best in his league—and let me know how that works out for you."

"I'm just saying infidelity isn't always the problem in a marriage."

"Duh!"

"You've never suspected anything with Vaughn?" Dana asked.

"Early on, I wondered if he cheated on me with black women because of how he plays me in front of y'all. Now? No. I just think Vaughn's idea of marriage is screwed up. He wants to be my provider, my lover, my friend, my protector, my everything, and that's sweet if he's those things in moderation. He's extreme, though. It's like he signed the papers and said, 'Okay. I own her. I can do and say what I want to her now.'"

"Thank you, Jesus!" Crystal said with her arms outstretched. "She has finally seen the light."

"Well, your theories don't apply to me and Vaughn. He didn't hit me before we got married, so I didn't know to expect these tantrums of his. I didn't walk into this as an informed party like you two."

"You're informed now," Crystal shot back.

"But I don't think Vaughn can control his behavior," I said. "His possessiveness comes with insecurity, which he'll never admit to having, but his insecurity comes from something else."

Crystal simulated the sound of an airplane crash. "And the shade is back down, folks. She is back in the dark!" she said, using her closed fist as a microphone. "You should really be concerned if you feel he can't control his behavior!"

Dana turned to me. "Most cocky men are insecure," she said, while I nodded.

"Bullshit. Don't try to give him a pass for abusing you," Crystal said.

"I'm not. I'm just saying he doesn't hit me because he's a possessive, angry monster. It stems from other things." I paused before continuing, careful about what I would reveal. I believe Vaughn's struggle factors in to his anger, but I wasn't sure if it was appropriate to share with anyone else. "Okay. I'm gonna tell you guys something, but you have to promise you won't say anything." I took extra time to direct my words at Crystal.

After they agreed, I continued. "Vaughn has erectile dysfunction." I closed my eyes in preparation for Crystal's response.

It was quiet for a moment. Dana kept her hand over her mouth, so I couldn't tell whether she was in shock or applying tension to her quivering cheeks to prevent herself from laughing out loud.

Crystal stared out the glass wall that overlooked the pool. "And that's his excuse for whoopin' on you?" she eventually asked.

Dana tried to help. "It must be all that pent-up aggression and energy."

"Damn that. You should be whoopin' *his* ass for walkin' around with a limp piece of meat. I'm not buyin' that misplaced anger bullshit. He better get his ass some Levitra and a cock ring, and sit his ass down somewhere—keep his hands to himself."

"Or on his nightstick!" Dana added before they busted into laughter. "That's what he should be beating!"

Unable to withhold my laughter, I joined the two in their mockery of Vaughn's problem. "He's resorted to a pump."

"Hell naw! I wouldn't be in the mood after waiting for his ass to pump up his pitiful Johnson. He'd be hard, and I'd be sleep." Crystal gestured as if she were using an air pump between her legs. "Y'all can't even be spontaneous!"

"He's not like that all the time."

"If he'd stop getting his blood pressure up from hollering at you, maybe he'd have some flow down there. It's going to all the wrong places. That's priceless advice right there. Your invoice will be in the mail, too.

"Man, if I would've known you were dealing with that, I would've gotten you a platinum dog tag," Crystal continued. "You deserve that and a gift certificate to Inserection so you can get a premium toy."

It felt great to finally tell someone about my dwindling sex life. Even better, I was able to laugh about it for the first time after all the nights I have retreated to the bathroom and cried because my husband couldn't make love to me before we went to sleep.

"There are so many questions floating in my head," Dana said.

"Every time we're intimate, I just pray all goes well. It really affects him. He flies off the handle and blames the impotence on me. It's hard."

"No, it's not hard!" Crystal said. After gaining control of her laughter, she apologized. "Seriously, little sis, can you deal with that and his violence until death?"

"No, but I believe God will deliver him so I won't have to make that kind of decision."

"Well, I believe God will deliver one of y'all so the mailman doesn't end up delivering my mail to the prison."

# CRYSTAL

I logged on to Connect.com after I ate breakfast and saw I had six friend requests and two messages. One of the messages was from Cheyenne, a college friend I haven't heard from since shortly after graduation. In her message, she expressed wanting to confirm my identity and asked me to reply with the ending to a story she recounted therein. It was one that only she and I knew, and I cracked up as I recalled the two of us using a sheet to rappel down the wall of the neighboring dorm after almost getting caught in two football players' room after hours.

I responded right away, and within ten minutes, we were on the phone.

"It's so good to hear from you, Big Time!" she said. "I was hoping that was you on Connect, but I had to quiz you in case you were an imposter."

"Riiight. You know these folks are crazy. There are a bunch of profiles named 'Mrs. All Night Long' or 'Mrs. Moss'. That's why I use my maiden name and don't have a profile picture. If someone really knows me, they'll send a message like you did."

We caught up on the basics. She and I used to sing together in the IU Soul Revue, and I was glad to hear she used her musical capabilities to land a teaching gig at a college in Florida. Though she can sing her ass off, she decided to focus on the technical aspect of music production.

"Dante records there sometimes," I told her. "It's a beautiful school."

"Yeah..." she said slowly. "I've seen him here a few times."

"Did you say something to him?"

"No..."

"Well, you two only met a couple times at school. I forgot."

"How are y'all doin'?"

"We're good, girl. I'm pretty sure you've seen the picture, though. If you're doing music, you probably read *Dirty Dish*."

"I won't lie. I saw it months ago when it came out. I stopped procrastinating and decided to reach out to you, though, after what I saw last night."

*****

Dana came over at noon. Ric was off work for the day, and she was still home for Christmas break. Her goal was to stay away from the house as long as possible. She was still avoiding their issues, still avoiding him.

We hung out in the theater room for a couple hours, then went downstairs to the bowling alley.

"So guess who I talked to today," I said after contemplating whether or not I would share what Cheyenne revealed to me just a few hours prior.

"Who?"

"Cheyenne."

"Cheyenne who lived on our floor at Briscoe?"

139

I nodded. "She found me on Connect.com. Guess who she knows."

She picked out a ball and joined me at the lane. "Dang, I came over here to relax, not play the guessing game, chick," she said before snickering.

I pushed the side of her head. "I'm serious. Guess!"

"Nigel."

"What the hell? No. Naptown New Booty."

"So I assume she saw the pic? How else would she even come up in the conversation?" she asked.

I told her how Cheyenne said she'd seen the article in the October issue of *Dirty Dish* when it first came out, but felt obligated to contact me after confirming their involvement wasn't just a tabloid rumor.

"It turns out that Cheyenne is an instructor for recording arts at Full Sail in Florida. Dante uses their studios from time to time. Naptown New Booty started school down there in January, and all she does is brag about her experiences with Dante."

"What kind of experiences? As his technician at the studio or his technician below his waist?" Dana asked.

I held up my index finger. "It gets better. Last weekend, Dante booked studio time there, and guess who was with him both days?"

"So she knows they've been intimate?"

"Something's up! Dante rushed home from his tour just to lie to me about not knowing that girl. Now I find out they kick it on the regular. That's all I need to know."

Dana studied my face. "Talk to me. Are you mad? Upset? Feeling victorious because you found out more information?"

I wasn't expecting that reaction from her. "Maybe I'm all of those," I answered. "All in all, I'm amused that he can't man-up and tell me that he's been booed up with this heffa."

"Does he know about you and Nigel?"

"Hell no!" I replied as Dana raised her eyebrows. "Don't look at me like that. I'm not a hypocrite. I haven't told him about Nigel for his own good. That man would have a shit fit if he knew I've been giving his drummer some all this time. He'd go insane, and his career would be shot. We have too lavish of a lifestyle to maintain for him to end up on *Behind the Music...Return of the Has-beens*."

"What do you mean lavish? Everybody has a four-lane bowling alley in their house, don't they?" Dana joked. "Okay. Give it to me straight. You're not sickened by the thoughts of him laying up with her? I know he's a celebrity, Crys, but that doesn't make it acceptable."

"I don't think about it. Why would I want to? And the concept of cheating husbands didn't just come into play this year with our men. A man can be homeless, filthy rich, a nobody, a celebrity, skinny, fat, insecure or secure. As long as he has a dick—big or small—he'll use it on whoever will let him. I'm just picking my poison. Do I stay with my first love and continue to live this life I've grown accustomed to, or do I move on to a second love who has less to offer *and* will still play Show and Tell with any woman who's interested?

"In my opinion, if I want to find the perfect guy who is sure to stay faithful, I'll have to pay some whiz kid at Georgia Tech to create a mechanical man with faux flesh and a nine-inch super penis that knows how to give it to me without asking."

"Well, what about Nigel? You don't have feelings for him?"

"Yeah, lust! My young lady has feelings for him. We wreck shop in the bed, yes, but outside of that...no, honey."

"I thought you said he's a nice guy."

"He's a nice guy who's screwing a married woman. He's giving it to his boss' wife. Is that really nice? There are a lot of nice guys, but that's relatively speaking."

Nigel is a good man on most levels, and he's great when it comes to me. That would look perfect to an outsider like Dana. When it's all said and done, though, Nigel is the other man, and it's his job to do whatever he can to make me happy. It's his job to show my husband up whenever he can. When I explained this to Dana, I put it in terms she could directly relate to. I'm the teacher, and Nigel is the teacher's pet.

She laughed, then asked if he brings me polished apples.

"No. He just comes to polish my apples."

"I truly believe there has to be a better man for me," she said.

"I'm sure there is, but he'll be better where Ric is lacking and then come up short in the areas where Ric is a champ."

"He's a champ at sex," Dana said, laughing. "The list was longer a few years ago. He used to be such a good guy."

"You've got two children, Dana. At this age, what man are you gonna find that's ready to deal with them and a loco ex-husband who ain't fifty-five with a receding hairline and saggy, wrinkled balls? All the rest of the fools our age still don't have their shit together."

Dana toppled over on the couch with laughter. Once she could breathe again, she said, "Well, I bet the old man would have a damn 401K! Ric has an IDK."

"IDK?"

"Yeah, an 'I Don't Know'. I don't know what the hell I'ma do when I retire because I don't have a 401K."

When she spoke those words, our roles reversed. I became the one who couldn't breathe because I was laughing uncontrollably.

"You're just gonna have to wait for Jesus to come back. He's the only man worthy of your standards and guaranteed to be faithful."

"I can't stand you," she said, trying to recover from her laughter. "There *is* a song about being happy with Jesus alone!"

Just then, Milky rounded the corner. We were going to Smyrna to look at the 1947 Cadillac we had restored for our dad as his birthday gift. For years, he's told us the stories of how his father bought a used one when he was five, and how he would help him fix it when it broke down. He credits that car as his motivation for going to work at General Motors—a career choice that afforded our family a comfortable living.

After attending a car show with Dante at the beginning of the year, I came up with the idea to find Daddy a 1947 Cadillac and make it like new. Willow and Todd agreed to contribute, and here we are ten months later. In two days, Raymond Thornton would be the happiest man alive.

"What's up, ladies?" Milky asked before setting her purse on the nearest chair.

"Same ol', same ol'. Trying to figure out the meaning of life," Dana replied. She rolled the ball and got a strike, which was enough to beat me.

Milky smiled. "Any luck?"

"Of course not." I turned to Dana. "Listen. Seriously, the moment you stop wondering and start realizing is the moment you'll be set free. I'm free as a bird."

I could tell Dana's mind was miles away. "You there?" I asked, sitting in the seat next to her.

"Ric's been cheating on me. There's no question. I say I wonder, but deep down, I already know. I just don't have the proof…and I don't know how far the cheating has gone." She spoke softly, and her zombie-like expression would've been scary if it wasn't so pitiful. Continuing her stare at nothing, she asked, "Why don't I feel free?"

Dana is too much of a good girl to handle my real answer, so I placed my hand on her knee and patted until my wrist became fatigued. For her, freedom would only come if she found a little something on the side or if she found the strength to leave Ric's sorry ass. I'm a lot of things, but a condoner of extramarital affairs isn't one of them. My situation is my situation—and many other women's—but I wouldn't hang a plaque in my office to congratulate myself on being an adulterer. It doesn't resolve anything within my marriage, but it keeps me sane and keeps me from becoming another disgraced wife of a celebrity. It's how I deal.

"You said the little girl denied anything happening between them, right?" I asked.

Dana nodded.

"You don't believe her, huh?"

"Naw. He probably has her trained. She's probably brainwashed into thinking I'm crazy and I'll go after her."

"Nah, he probably told her the truth—that your friend is crazy and will go after her," I said.

"Alright, I guess I'll go," Dana said as she stood and stretched. "Make sure you send a pic of the car to my phone."

"So what you gon' do, D? Are you gon' break the silence and finally say something to him?" I probed.

"I don't feel like being entertained by lies, so no. I'll just go to my room, shut the door, watch *Why Did I Get Married* a couple times, and drink vodka until I throw up." She tried eclipsing the sadness in her voice with laughter.

An aura of hopelessness swept through the room as Milky and I watched her leave.

"That sucks," Milky said, removing the hair band from her wrist and pulling her hair into a ponytail.

I changed out of my bowling shoes and into some sneakers. "She's not cut out for this. She's gonna say something. If she doesn't, it'll drive her crazy."

"Are we supposed to be cut out for this?" Milky asked.

My best friend's husband keeps shitting on sticks and telling her they're chocolate-covered pretzels, my sister is a walking ad for the magic of MAC makeup, and I'm now reaching the devil's drop on my marital rollercoaster. Are we supposed to be cut out for this? Probably not.

# DANA

If someone made a movie about my marriage, it would be called *Why Am I Here?* Sometimes I sit in the bathtub and ask myself that question, and each time, I don't have a real answer. It sounds generic to say, "Because I love him," but it's true. Then I ask myself, "Why do you love him?" and I can't find words to explain. I love him beyond a reason. That's poetic to hear on a soap opera, but painful to live out.

Each time I find something suspicious, I wonder if it's going to be "the big one". I almost hope it's the big one. I don't like going through his pockets, looking in his wallet, or searching his phone for texts and pictures. I've become addicted to it, though, because I always find something.

I accuse him of playing games, but I guess I'm playing one of my own. I don't win until I find solid proof that he's cheating on me. What kind of shit is that? I guess a part of me wants to believe he has only put out feelers to see if he still has it, as he's said in the past. I want to believe he hasn't gotten physical with any of the females in question. I'll stop while I'm ahead, because this is where I begin to sound stupid.

This is when I peg myself as "that person" in the movie theater who sits through the closing credits, afraid she's gonna miss something, determined to get her money's worth—the person everyone shoots questioning glances at on their way out, thinking, *It's the end, lady. Leave already!* Then the high-school-aged cleanup boy comes in wearing his unkempt uniform with his broom and standing dust pan in-hand, and politely says, "Ma'am, we're not showing a double feature today." I'll smile and say, "I know," and do the same thing the next weekend. There's no logic in the act, no rhyme or reason—just the definition of being a disgruntled wife, according to Crystal. *Why Am I Here?* coming to a theater near you.

The latest finding: two receipts. The receipts first drew my attention because he rarely keeps them. I expected to see the three-thousand-dollar camera he's been raving about on one of the receipts, but Frederick's of Hollywood doesn't sell those. Apparently, Ric purchased a two-piece set from there on December 13th. According to the other receipt, he also purchased body wash, body spray, and lip gloss from Bath & Body Works on the same day. I was certain that neither of those items was under the tree on Christmas day, and I was highly doubtful he'd buy that kind of stuff for his sister.

This time, I didn't go looking. I noticed the white paper when I dropped some change between my seat and the center console. I had cleaned my car out before the holidays, so the only other explanation for the receipts even being in my car was because Ric was driving it. He had the opportunity to use it while I was out of town with Crystal conducting business for Something to Do.

I was waiting for him to come out of Home Depot so I could gain some clarification. After a long five minutes, he returned.

"Damn, baby, sorry it took so long. They didn't have nobody workin' in the department. I had to go up front and

147

cuss the manager out just to get some help. They gave us this other can of paint for free," he said before settling into his seat.

"Is it a color we can use?"

"Yeah. We can put it on the walls in the laundry room or somethin'. I'll sell it if you don't like it." He laughed.

"Always tryin' to hustle somethin'." I held up the receipts. "These were tucked between the seat and the console. You must've dropped them."

He barely glanced at them. "I didn't drop nothin'. I don't even keep receipts."

"Hmm...I'm pretty sure you're the only person who has access to my car."

"You better talk to your girl, Crystal. Ain't that who has the third key?"

"Crystal has a Mercedes and a Hummer. Please tell me what the hell she needs my Camry for."

"That's not my business."

"You used my car while I was in Valdosta?" I asked.

"Dana, I'm not in the mood for this. We were havin' a perfectly good day until now."

"I just asked a question. You didn't even look at the receipts to see where they're from. This isn't meant to be an argument."

"Yes, it is. Everything you bring up is meant to be an argument. They must be from somewhere off-limits for you to say somethin'. And no matter what I say, you believe what you wanna believe. I'm tired of hearin' from you. Stop askin' me questions. I'm entitled to my privacy. I'm tired of you goin' through my shit."

"This is *my* shit! I thought I dropped something down there, and I know for a fact I didn't go to Frederick's and Bath & Body Works. You're tired of me going through your things at the house? Guess what? I'm tired of finding shit!"

"Everybody knows this is your car. It's funny how my stuff is ours, and your stuff is yours."

"If I had a responsible husband whose license wasn't suspended and who didn't sneak off like a teenager in the middle of the night, I wouldn't categorize the car as mine."

"I could say a lot of stuff is mine, too. You don't wanna get into all the things I bought for you while you were in school, though."

"You can get into it all you want, because I never asked you for a thing. That's why I don't ask people for nothin'. They always find a way to throw it in your face. Go 'head. Run down your list, because nothin' on it will hold any real significance. Have you bought me a car? House? You couldn't even put your name on the paperwork for any place we've lived because your credit is horrible. Tell me, Ric. What's yours? The clothes you bought me back in '96?"

"Man, look. The bottom line is you need to respect my privacy."

"No, the bottom line is we need to figure out who bought something from Frederick's since it wasn't me or you. There's no such thing as your privacy. When we got married, that was out the window. There's OUR privacy. What would you need to keep from your wife? What's so top secret?"

"It's about respect. Ain't nothin' a secret."

"I'll respect you when you give me something to respect."

"You need to watch your mouth. You don't talk to a grown man like that."

"You're a grown man?"

"Hell yeah."

"Right. A grown man with a dick that lives in Never Never Land."

149

"Man, whatever. If you feel like I'm cheating on you, Dana, do what you have to do. I'm not with this answering-to-you shit."

We arrived at the house, and our exchange never missed a beat. After he set the buckets of paint in the laundry room, he hightailed it for the computer desk.

"You don't have to answer to me. Ninety-nine percent of our arguments could be avoided if you simply clarify the subject at hand. I want you to answer me, not answer to me."

"You want an answer? Yes, the receipts are mine. I took the car and went shopping while you were gone, and I put the stuff up so you couldn't find it. I didn't want you to see it yet."

"Okay. Since you have it and it's hidden somewhere, pull it out. That's what it'll take to prove me wrong."

"Honestly, it's probably goin' right back to the store. You ruined the whole thing by comin' at me the way you did. Why would I give it to you now? It was for Valentine's Day."

"And you bought it in the middle of December while we were arguing? Any other year, you almost forget Valentine's Day."

"I was planning ahead for once. Now, it doesn't even matter because you're so fuckin' nosey."

I smirked. "So I'm being punished?"

He proceeded to browse the internet.

"There is no lingerie," I continued. "None here, at least. Has she worn it for you yet?"

"Who?"

"You tell me. You have the opportunity right now to end this argument, but instead, you tell me you're not gonna give me the satisfaction, as if I need to learn a lesson."

"You do need to learn a lesson. Trust your husband."

"Earn my trust back."

150

"I earn money at my job. That's all I have to earn. If you choose to be insecure, I feel sorry for you."

*And that's how much I mean to you*, I thought. *Why do I put myself through this torture?* I tucked the receipts into my pocket and stared at Ric's back. He was glued to the computer screen, further showing how irrelevant our conversation was to him. At that moment, I concluded I was done giving a damn, too.

*****

Every New Year, I resolve to have a better year than the last. That's it. This year, I've added something: get in shape. I'm far from being overweight, but as I move further into my thirties, I can definitely tell my body isn't like it used to be. Last year, I noticed my belly doesn't go down like it used to an hour after I eat. It stays put and doesn't look very flattering when I sit and a miniature roll folds over my pants. I've joked about it with Lorenzo, and he offered to help me tighten up.

I committed to working out with him three days a week in the weight room at the school, starting our first day back from Christmas break. As soon as the dismissal bell rang, I changed into my lycra workout capris and Lithonia Grove t-shirt, grabbed my water bottle, and proceeded to Lorenzo's coaching office.

When I walked in, he was seated at his desk with his back to me. "I'm ready!" I said.

"Alright. Give me one second." He sent the email he was composing and spun around to face me. "Daaaamn! Why do you need me again? I don't think Ric would be happy about you losin' none of that," he said, his eyes focusing on my thighs.

I giggled like a freshman getting complimented by the finest senior in the school. "Stop it. I told you I'm not big on

151

losing weight. I just want to tone up. And let's get this straight. I'm not doing this for Ric."

"Are you doin' it for me?" he asked with a smile.

"If your real name is Dana."

"Can a brotha dream? You could've just rolled with it and made my day."

"I think I've already made your day," I replied, turning around and pausing. "I'll meet you in the weight room."

I didn't have to turn around to see if he was looking at my booty. If the way he gawked when I was facing him was any indication, his eyes were surely on my lower frame while I wasn't looking. I won't pretend I didn't wear those pants on purpose. A girl likes to not only feel sexy, but to be told she is sexy from time to time. I got in trouble when I was seven years old for playing with fire. I guess I didn't learn my lesson.

We warmed up with dynamic stretches followed by five minutes of jumping rope. My new sports bra held my C's in place, but there was nothing I could do about my t-shirt sliding up to my waist when I was airborne. That gave Lorenzo an even better view of the backside I was known for in college.

The easy part was over. Lorenzo then directed my attention to the blackboard with an insane amount of exercises listed.

"Okay. You said you're serious about this, right?" he asked.

*What am I getting myself into?* I thought while nodding. "Just don't look at my booty when I'm doing my squats," I replied.

"I'm a professional, sweetheart."

"And you'll be professionally looking at my booty."

We both laughed, and that was the last of the fun stuff. From that second on, I was sweating, panting, groaning, and damn near crying. By the time we finished, I didn't want to hear a word about a bicep curl, pull up, squat, lunge, or crunch.

While I rested on a bench after completing my static stretches, Lorenzo came over and massaged my shoulders.

"Ah, thank you," I said, letting my muscles relax so I could enjoy his touch. "Oh, wait! I feel bad. You don't have to do that. I'm all sweaty and nasty."

"It's sexy," he replied.

I couldn't think of a good response, so I didn't say anything. When he was done, I thanked him again.

"No, thank *you*. It looks like Monday, Wednesday, and Friday are going to be my favorite days of the week now."

I smiled as I watched him walk away with effortless swag. *Mine, too.* I twisted my wedding rings around my finger and sighed. I once heard that lusting in your heart after someone other than your spouse is as much a sin as committing adultery. If Jesus were to come back right now, I'd go straight to hell.

# WILLOW (MILKY)

Vaughn asked me to stop by his parents' house to pick up some paperwork his father had forgotten. I hadn't planned on going into the office, but I opted to stop there briefly rather than have another night-long rematch with him. He was lucky I hadn't started bruising yet, because there was no guarantee the discoloring would stay within the confines of my sunglasses this time. Joseph had already suggested I stop taking the kickboxing classes (that I was never enrolled in) a few months ago, because it was apparent I wasn't good at the sport. Little did he know his son was the one practicing his kickboxing moves on me.

Since I didn't have a good lie ready for Joseph this time, I told Vaughn he would have to come out to the car to get the papers. He agreed because he's now in the remorseful phase of his tantrum. He's also into appearances and would not want his father to know the truth behind my sunglasses obsession.

I stopped by the house after dropping Venus off at preschool. When Mrs. Ella came to the door with a manila envelope, we greeted each other and then had a few moments of uncomfortable silence. I waited with my hand

154

outstretched, but she kept the envelope at her side, tapping it against her thigh.

"Do you have a minute?" she asked.

I hesitated, then muttered, "Sure."

Much like a child making his death march to the dreaded spanking area, I followed her into the dining room and joined her at the table.

*What is it now?* I thought while adjusting my posture and preparing to hear her latest gripe about me being a subpar wife and mother.

"You gonna rest your coat?" she asked gruffly.

I slid the cream-colored pea coat down my shoulders, but kept my scarf around my neck. Mrs. Ella stared at me with her arms crossed, never saying a word. I swore I heard a piece of lint hit the floor as we sat in silence.

Finally, she cleared her throat. Then she did it again. And again.

"Do you want me to get you something to drink?" I asked.

She pointed to my clothing. "When I ask you to rest your coat, I mean rest it. How rude can you be?"

I removed my coat completely and draped it over the chair beside me.

"Okay. I'll just come out and say it. Take off your scarf and those damn sunglasses. I know what's going on. What did he do? Choke you this time, too?"

Slowly, I unraveled the scarf and placed it with my coat. Shame froze my chin to my sternum and my eyes to my lap. Before I knew it, Mrs. Ella was lifting the shades from my face. I glanced with my good eye just in time to see her reaction to the golf ball that used to be my left eye.

She took in a deep breath before speaking. "Have you had enough yet?"

"What's enough? That part was never in our vows."

155

"If you dare to stick around long enough to find out, you'll skip right to the end of your vows, child."

*'Til death do us part*, I thought.

"You wanna know why I never liked you from the beginning?" Mrs. Ella asked. She paused to give me time to answer, but I wouldn't dare. "Because I don't respect you. I could tell from our first introduction that you have no backbone," she finished.

I clenched my jaw to keep from responding, which only made my eye throb more.

Mrs. Ella had enough to say for both of us. "Look at you," she snapped. "You just gon' let me talk to you any kind of way? Speak up for yourself. That's your problem."

Without much thought, I raised my head and snapped back. "You're full of it! Don't give me that BS about you not liking me because you don't respect me. You never wanted Vaughn with a white woman. I didn't have a chance from the second you laid eyes on me. If anything, you didn't respect me because of my skin color. That doesn't exactly make you a nominee for Person-of-the-Year, now does it?"

"It's about time! Thank you! I can finally give you more credit. Listen, Willow. I wasn't happy about my son marrying outside of his race. I'll admit that. But I had to get over it, and I did. If I didn't, I wouldn't be having this conversation with you.

"Vaughn has always been controlling. Mix that with him being spoiled, and there's a good chance for disaster. The determining factor on how he acts, though, is how you respond. Pastor said the other day, 'Don't complain about the things you permit.' You think about that. Open your mouth and be heard. Stop letting my son have his way with you. There's a limit to being submissive."

"With all due respect, I believe that will do nothing but make him angrier."

She threw her hands in the air. "I've said my piece. That's all I can do. Vaughn is my son and I love him, but he has a lot of growing up to do. I'll admit I'm somewhat responsible for creating the monster he is. Not that I've ever knowingly condoned his violent behavior, but when he threw fits as a child, he often got off with no repercussions. I have my reasons, but that's not to say I was right. The second time I saw you with a fat lip, I knew exactly what was going on. You had the first one when we had all that rain and the builders couldn't work, and the second one was around the time Vaughn's deal with Sherman fell through. It was obvious. He was taking his anger out on you when he got home."

My eyes watered as I recalled both incidents. She was right. The first time, I just had a fat lip from him slapping me. The second time, I had a fat lip and a bruise on my upper arm in the shape of Vaughn's hand and fingers that stuck around for two weeks.

Mrs. Ella peered over her glasses. "I'm gonna share something with you. You're Vaughn's wife, so you deserve to know this. I know the kind of woman you are, so I don't have to tell you that this isn't something you go telling all your girlfriends.

"I don't know if Vaughn has told you, but Joseph isn't his biological father. He adopted him when we got married. Vaughn was seven."

I had no clue, and the dumbfounded look on my face conveyed that. "Did he ever have a relationship with his father?"

She grunted. "His father had a relationship with him."

I looked into her eyes, hoping she would soon shame the thoughts that swirled in my brain. I'd been watching too many episodes of *Law & Order: Special Victims Unit*.

"My first husband was a low-down, detestable, downright nasty son-of-a-bitch. I didn't find that out until I caught him in Vaughn's room one night. He was supposed to be reading him a story, but when I cracked the door to see what was taking so long, he had my baby's five-year-old hand stroking him." Her voice became raspier with each word. The anger from her spirit attached itself to her every syllable, conveying the heartbreaking tone of a woman who wishes she had known better.

*Guess my instinct was right.* "Do you know how long that went on?" I asked.

"In court, he admitted to doing it for two years," she replied, wiping her tears as quickly as they fell. "I didn't tell you that to gain your sympathy. I just want you to understand the man you're dealing with. Instead of becoming more feminine, he became over-masculine. He always has to prove he's a man. Joseph did a hell of a job helping me raise him. He's a great man. He taught Vaughn how to be a great man, but Vaughn is still fighting an inner battle."

*And that inner battle turns into an outer battle*, I thought. Mrs. Ella had given me answers to questions I didn't know to ask. Vaughn's need to dominate doesn't just stem from him being younger than me. It's his way of validating himself as a man. The manhood and dominance correlation is fine with me, but Vaughn mistakes dominance for violence.

I felt like I had all the right tools to fix something, but the same person who gave me the toolbox locked it and kept the key. I couldn't approach Vaughn with my knowledge of his painful childhood. I couldn't even talk with him about his erectile dysfunction without his defenses going up.

That was the reason for my latest battle scars. I didn't get to the pharmacy to pick up his Cialis before they closed, and God forbid he'd actually go in and pick up his own prescription. He's so embarrassed about his usage of the drug that he has his prescription registered at a pharmacy thirty miles away from our house. So, when he couldn't get an erection after we bathed together, I got blamed. When he declined to use his pump because it made him sore last time, I got blamed. And when he accidentally dropped his last pill down the sink, I got choked.

"I know you love my son, but love doesn't hurt. Don't punish yourself because you want to prove a point. You confirmed your true feelings for him when you married him. I apologize for dumping all this on you unexpectedly, but when I saw you wearing sunglasses again, I had to say something. You never struck me as the kickboxing class type."

"Thank you," was all I could come up with as I stood to put on my coat and scarf. Mrs. Ella handed me the manila envelope, and for the first time ever, we shared a genuine hug.

"I can't tell you what to do or say, or whether to leave. You'll know when you've had enough, and you'll have all the right words. You're a woman of strong faith. Stay in prayer."

I've been in prayer. I've just been praying for what I want to happen instead of asking God for His will to be done. President Obama has us all on this quest for change. Maybe it's time for me to change my approach.

*****

Rebecca and her husband arrived at my mom's house on Sunday as scheduled. Asking her to come for dinner seemed much more informal than her coming on a weekday to sit in the living room and have an already uncomfortable meeting with heightened delicacy. Food naturally brings comfort and joy, so I was optimistic about the day. Vaughn and I dropped Venus off at his parents' house because we agreed she should not be exposed to what would most likely take place. Besides, I didn't want to lie and introduce Rebecca to her as "Mommy's friend". Like it or not, she was much, much more.

Mom and I greeted Rebecca and her husband, Dave, at the door. This time, her hair was pulled up, allowing me to see more clearly how much I resembled her. Even more noticeable were the bags under her eyes, which were later explained when she spoke of how they had barely gotten any sleep. The airport had lost their bags, and through the course of the ordeal, they'd only gotten two or three hours of sleep.

Dave looked annoyed as we all introduced ourselves. He had to be at least ten years older than her, and his attire screamed country club chump. Rebecca often answered questions for him because he was so antisocial. She asked us to excuse him because he was crabby when he's sleep-deprived. I wasn't sure I believed that. I know the difference between being crabby and being a jerk.

We made it through dinner without incident. Crystal was on her best behavior, making lighthearted conversation with Rebecca and talking with Dave about her foundation. She was the only one who got more than two sentences out of him because they had a common interest. He also heads a foundation, though his is geared toward children battling life-threatening or debilitating medical conditions. From what I could hear at one point, he gave her the name and email to someone who he felt would make a significant financial contribution to Something to Do.

Mom and Dad even kept their cool, although I know my mom was itching to dig into Rebecca. As soon as we cleared the table, though, it was on. The men, excluding my father, went into the den to give me, Rebecca, Crystal, and Mom some privacy. We moved into the living room to get out of the hardback dining chairs. Dad sat in his recliner in the corner, while the rest of us sat on the couches.

"Before I forget," Rebecca began, "here's a picture of Scott. You can have it." She pulled out a wallet-size senior picture of a handsome guy with black hair and gorgeous eyes. He sat on a stool, surrounded by baseball, basketball, and football paraphernalia.

I held the picture and smiled. I wondered where he was and what he was doing now. He looked genuine—like his soul was authentic. It showed in his eyes. I'm sure he has children, probably three—two boys and a girl—with a beautiful wife who knows he has another daughter that was "given up for adoption" when he was in high school. I imagined he tried looking for me a while ago, but didn't know where to begin. I could tell. I could feel it. My hunch will never be validated, though, because I wouldn't think of looking for him. I vowed I wouldn't look for either of my so-called parents from the moment I learned they didn't want me in the first place.

Mom thanked Rebecca for reaching out and acknowledged that she thought it was important for me to know where I came from.

"No. I owe all the thanks to you and your husband. She's beautiful. You've raised a fine woman."

Crystal spoke up. "So do you feel good about yourself now? You found your long lost daughter, showed her a picture of the other person who didn't want her, and now you expect to sleep better at night?"

Rebecca gasped, unsure of what to say.

"'Thank you' doesn't cut it, Miss Rebecca. Milky wasn't my parents' charity case. She was their child. They treated her no different than me and my brother. When we attended private school, so did she. When I got a three-hundred-dollar prom dress, so did she. When her heart got broken for the first time, that woman over there was the one who stayed up until three in the morning comforting her. Where were you? Where were you when she first realized she was

161

adopted and my mom couldn't answer her questions? Was that around the time you took the trip to Rome you were bragging about at the table? Or was that when you were auditioning for the *Real World*, getting pissy drunk on videotape?"

"I didn't share those stories to have them thrown in my face. I was trying to give you an idea of where my head was at during those days. You're throwing low blows. I didn't come here for this."

"So what did you come for, Rebecca? What did you expect?" Mom asked.

"I expected us to move forward."

"You moved forward after you left the post office. I had moved forward, too, until you contacted my mom and paused my progress. I thought you were coming to face the music, but apparently, some things never change," I said.

Rebecca pulled out her checkbook and twisted her pen. "How much?" she asked sternly. I frowned with confusion as I watched her date the "Footsteps" check. "Your married name is Townsend, correct?"

"Wait. What are you doing?" I asked.

"What does it look like? I'm writing you a check. How much do you feel I owe you for putting you up for adoption and ruining your life?"

As I digested her question, Rebecca impatiently completed the check and dropped it into my purse.

"This isn't about money. You still don't get it," Crystal said.

"So how do I replace time? You spoke of private schools and prom dresses. I can compensate for that. Tears, comfort, and questions…I can't do anything about those. I missed it. I get that. I owe her time, but she doesn't want it. So you tell me what you all want from me?"

Mom leaned forward. "Nothing."

162

"I want her to wipe that goofy smile off her face," Crystal said. She looked at Rebecca again. "Stop pretending this is a formal tea party and join us in reality. From the second you introduced yourself, you've had that fake smile on your face. You can't gloss over your actions. That's what's pissing me off."

"I think we've said enough," Dad said. "This woman didn't know what she was getting herself into. We've heard her out. Now let it be." He stood and extended his hand to her. "You have a safe trip back to New York."

"Thank you, Mr. Thornton," she said, rising from the couch.

Dave stepped into the room. "Are you ready?"

"One minute, honey. I was just gonna say goodbye to everyone."

"Cut the bullshit. You've already been dismissed. I heard everything they just said. Let's go," he grumbled.

"You were eavesdropping?" Mom asked.

"No. I was coming back from the bathroom, ma'am."

"Let's go, Janice. We're done in here," Dad said, leading her into the kitchen.

Rebecca slowly walked over to Dave and stood at his side. "I really enjoyed dinner," she called out before they left the room

Mom threw up her hand and nodded, expressing her thanks. I remained in my state of shock on the couch, with my eyes fixed on the dollar amount on the check she'd written.

"I told you this was a bad idea from the start. What the hell did you think would happen?" Dave raised his voice unnecessarily, getting my attention. I was sure he spit in Rebecca's face as he spoke, seeing that his lips were just an inch from her forehead.

"Folks," he continued, "we're sorry for wasting your time. Willow, I wish you the best, hun."

Rebecca didn't even turn around to say goodbye as he shoved her in the back. Vaughn and Dante came out of the den in time to witness the push.

"Whoa, my man! Is there a problem?" Dante asked.

"Everything is fine. We're heading out. You all take care," Dave answered. Rebecca was already halfway to their car.

The guys looked on suspiciously. "What is that about?" Vaughn asked.

Before any of us could answer, we heard yelling outside. Crystal was the first one at the window. "Oh my goodness! He's crazy!"

When I looked out the window next to her, I couldn't believe my eyes. Dave had Rebecca pinned against their rental SUV, holding her by her throat. I cracked the window so I could hear what they were saying. She was a "dumb bitch," a "stupid bitch," a "cunt," and "the dumbest smart bitch" he knew. According to him, she could never do anything right, including give him a child; but she thought it was a good idea to search for a child who is closer to her black parents than she will ever be to her, like that was going to fix everything.

"He's way outta line," Vaughn said.

"Why? 'Cause he's doin' it in front of people?" Crystal asked as she whisked by all of us and stormed into the driveway.

Dante followed protectively behind her. Vaughn and I followed suit, leaving Mom and Dad clueless in the kitchen.

"Can you please keep your voice down and watch your language around here?" Crystal said, startling Dave into letting Rebecca go.

"This really isn't your business," he said.

"It's my parents' property, so it is my business."

"We're sorry," Rebecca said.

"Why are *you* apologizing?" Crystal asked.

164

"We'll leave your property so it'll no longer be your business."

"Do that. And while you're at it, why don't you keep your hands off the lady," Dante said.

Dave smirked, and the two of them got into their car. As they backed out, I heard the voices of my high school classmates in my head. "The apple doesn't fall far from the tree!" Back then, they were just being facetious, but they spoke the truth. I looked at how Dave treated her and saw me and Vaughn. Sadly, Vaughn didn't see it.

When we were alone later that evening, he went on and on about how Crystal needs to mind her business, saying she was wrong for comparing him to Dave. I spoke up after he became too self-righteous, professing that he's a better husband than Dante will ever be.

Choosing my words carefully, I followed Mrs. Ella's advice and seized the opportunity to be heard. "Baby, Crystal didn't say that because she's jealous of what we have. That *is* how you sound when you lash out at me. And just like you told Dave, it's way out of line. Does Crystal see what you do to me? Not while it's happening, but you know she sees the aftermath.

"I think you let everything go as soon as you apologize, and it's that simple for you. You forget it ever happened. You see my bruises, but you block out the fact that you gave them to me. Just know that other people see what we think we're hiding so well, and you can't be mad about that. I don't deserve to be the woman who caters to your every need, yet gets called a slut or bitch when you've had a bad day. I don't deserve to be touched in an ill manner, either, and it's time I told you that. It wasn't okay the first time, but these instances have fallen out of the boundaries of what's understandable and forgivable."

He clenched his teeth, but unlike every other time I've seen him do it, he didn't have fire in his eyes. He shifted in his chair like he was uncomfortable, never saying a word. I looked on, worried that once it all sunk in, he would throw his worst fit ever.

On the contrary, he nodded his head and looked me in the eyes. "You're right."

That's more than I expected him to say and all he needed to say. I exhaled slowly, welcoming the feeling of relief into my potpourri of emotions. Time would tell if we'd turned over a new leaf.

If I never see Rebecca again, if I never hear from her again, it doesn't matter. She has done her part in impacting my life. She showed me yet another similarity between the two of us, though it isn't one to boast about. In a sense, she led by example during the altercation in the driveway. She showed me what I don't want to be. The apple doesn't fall far from the tree, but who says it can't roll a few more inches away?

# CRYSTAL

I reclined on the cushioned lounge chair and overlooked Condado Beach through the grey tint of my Gucci shades. They were the only thing I wore while basking in the privacy of the terrace attached to our suite. Eighty-four degrees of heat warmed my skin, giving me a uniform tan — no interruption from clothes.

Dante was still sleeping, part of his recovery process. He had about six drinks too many the night before, and he surely paid for it when he woke up at eight a.m. with a headache from hell and a gag reflex that only produced dry heaves.

We've been in Puerto Rico three days, celebrating Valentine's Day and his birthday in one whop. Though they are weeks apart, it was our best bet to combine the festivities before his schedule picks up again. He starts his heavy publicity touring the day after we get back since his new album's release date is Valentine's Day.

We're hopeful it will debut at number one. His two singles already have, and that's almost a sure indicator that the album will follow suit. Thankfully, that brought him out of the funk he lived in after not winning the Grammy back

167

in January. The last single went gold in a month and is on track to go platinum after the release of his latest single.

I'm debating whether I will join him on tour. I usually travel for half of the dates, but I've arranged for my girls at the foundation to take part in more potentially life-changing experiences, and I don't want to miss out on them. I'll make my final decision once I look at the schedule. I told him that I didn't want to see it until we finished vacationing. This is a pleasure-only trip, and the mere thought of business is prohibited. There's no doubt I'll make my presence known—especially for the big city dates—but I don't want to be there to scare away groupies or screw Nigel. I want to be there for my husband, and after the show, I want him to be there for me.

We've had a blast so far. He took me on a shopping spree on Ashford Avenue the first day and bought me everything I wanted. We've walked through the cave park, gone scuba diving and hang gliding, raced in the pool, and made love on the beach. Who knows what else we'll squeeze in during the next few days?

I'd be perfectly content staying in our room the rest of our trip. It's been so long since we've been wrapped up in each other with no distractions from our outside obligations that I had forgotten what it felt like. We've had time to look into each other's eyes and see the truths that link us and the fears that threaten to separate us. Sometimes, all you need is time to remind you of why you're together and why you always want to be together; time to remember your definition of love. Our relationship feels brand new again. We've smiled wider, laughed harder, and loved longer; and when I close my eyes, I swear I'm nineteen again and in love with the sexiest man in the country.

When Dante finally got out of bed, we started the day with a little sex in the shower and then headed out to have lunch. I'd designated the day as his birthday, so it was all about him. First, I treated us to massages. Then we went to a carnival where the natives put my little shimmy-shake to shame. If I could gyrate that fast, I'd lose five pounds in five minutes.

After the carnival, we returned to the room to put on our best threads and headed back out for dinner. At the restaurant, I presented him with the two watches I'd gotten him from Jacob & Co.—one for him to look at, and one specifically designed for others to look at. He raved over them, thanking me again and again.

"I'm so proud of you, baby," I said after he ordered our meals.

"Why you say that?"

"Look at you. You've been in this business almost fifteen years now, and you've only gotten better. This is one of those albums you can retire after."

"This is the album you had the most input on, too. Maybe I should've had you hang out in the studio with me more often."

"I told you all you needed was about three songs with autotune. You've already proven yourself as a vocalist. Now it's time to have fun with your voice. People can't get enough of that right now. I'll take my percentage later, thank you."

He laughed. "For what?"

"Creative direction. You just admitted that my input was a big part of your success on this album. Pay me like you pay everybody else."

"I'll pay you tonight," he replied with a smile.

"No, thanks. I don't accept currency from your sperm bank, sir."

After more laughter, he looked into my eyes much like he did when we went on our first date. "What if I really want to donate from there?"

169

I frowned, acknowledging the seriousness of his tone.

"Come again?" I asked.

"Do you still want kids?"

We hadn't talked about having children since he'd shot me down four years into our marriage. Back then, I was all about it. After years of independence, though, I'm not sure I can transition well into motherhood.

"Honestly, I haven't thought about it since you said you didn't want any," I replied.

"Well, I think it's time. That would be the perfect birthday gift for next year. What do you say?"

I picked up my wine glass, took a sip, and cleared my throat. "I say...I've read a lot and heard even more. Ms. Hunter seems to have been a part of your entourage, but it's funny she was never around when I was."

"Who is Ms. Hunter?"

"Oh, I guess you weren't interested in her last name. Katrina, your little hometown ho. I know people who know her, and I know everything y'all do when you're in Orlando. You wanna keep her in the mix? Take my ass out of it. I don't appreciate people knowing more about my husband than I do."

"I'll just say this. I'm sorry for disrespecting you, but it's not all like you think it is. To eliminate any doubts, though, I won't record in Orlando any more. That settles that."

"Does it?"

"Yeah! Do you really believe I'd choose anything or anyone over you?"

"I believe what you lead me to believe."

"Well, believe that you are the love of my life, and I want you to also be the mother of my children."

"I don't wanna hear shit else about these girls, Dante. I refuse to bring a child into some mess. I chose you, so I can handle your lifestyle. But a child? No. You need to be sure that you're done with all your Katrinas, because I don't endorse broken homes."

"You won't. There's nothing to hear. As a matter of fact, why don't you come with me on all the tour dates? Or at least the two Indianapolis ones for sure."

Little did he know, I was going to those anyway.

When we entered our hotel, all eyes were on us. I don't think anyone recognized Dante. They were just wondering why he was shirtless, strolling through the lobby. The alcohol increased my body temperature a couple degrees, too, but I didn't start stripping in the limo.

Dante leaned against the wall near the elevators while I spoke with the concierge. After I confirmed that everything was in place for our evening activities, we headed to our suite.

"Is there anything we're not supposed to eat or drink here?" he asked.

"I don't think. Mexico has the jacked up water, but we've only had bottled water here, too. Why?"

He ran his tongue across his bottom lip. "My lip is tingling. Maybe it was the champagne. You didn't change lip gloss or anything, did you?"

I laughed. "No. Maybe I'm just that damn hot. Got you all tingly inside."

"I'ma make you tingly inside," he said as I opened the door.

As I had requested, the hotel had installed a stripper pole in the middle of the bedroom, and there was a cake on the table near the couch. I pressed Play on the iPod dock, and our theme song for the night began.

"Happy Birthday, baby," I said, while stripping down to my sexy undies and mounting the pole.

Dante eased into the chair behind him and enjoyed the show. *Birthday sex. Birthday sex.* Jeremih's voice complemented my moves. Dante helped himself to the champagne next to him—the same kind he said tasted great with me the first time we tried it. I slid all the way to the floor, landing in a split. His index finger summoned me in his direction before my act was over, so I obeyed, crawling seductively to his chair and up his body.

I kissed on his chest to drive him crazy, and then whispered that I expected to see a tattoo of my lips there on my birthday.

"Whatever you want, baby," he replied, caressing my curves.

I moved up to his neck, and when he couldn't take it anymore, he stood up and carried me to the bed. He spread my legs so far apart, I felt like I was doing another split. Then, he devoured my young lady as if she were the last meal he'd ever have.

February 12, 2009 went in the books as our best night of lovemaking. We experienced ecstasy in paradise. He showed me that he knew my body—what it wanted, what it needed, what it could handle. I showed him that even if he had been sampling other women, they would never be me. My young lady isn't offered in generic substitute form.

The next morning, Dante entered our room carrying a tray with French toast, eggs, bacon, and orange juice. "Wake up, baby," he said sweetly as I sat up and rested my back against the headboard. I didn't even know he'd left.

"Whoa!" I said, as the headboard gave out and I fell back onto the wall. "What the hell?"

Dante laughed while I examined the damage. "Oops. Maybe we shouldn't have tried that last trick."

"You think, you damn animal?! I thought I heard it cracking last night. They're gonna charge us an arm and a leg!"

"You didn't hear nothin'. We were making too much noise."

172

"Whatever," I replied, accepting my breakfast with a smile. "Thank you, boo."

He leaned in for a kiss, but I stopped him with a stiff arm to his forehead. "What the hell is that on your lip?"

"Ha ha. Whatever, man. Give me a kiss. I brushed my teeth already."

"This ain't about your breath. You have a bump or something on the side of your mouth. You don't feel it?"

"What are you talking about?" he asked, looking at the mirror above my head for answers.

"It looks like a cold sore. Since when do you get those? Ugh."

"Huh?" Panicked, he rushed into the bathroom to get a closer look. "Shit! How did that happen?"

"I told you about sharing drinks and shit with people. That stuff catches up. Y'all steady poppin' bottles in the club, drinking from 'em, passing 'em around. I was trippin' when I told you that mess was nasty, though. Remember?"

Dante looked to be on the verge of tears as he carefully touched around the blister, making sure not to get too close. "Can you get 'em by drinking after people for real?"

"Yeah, if they have one, too, or are about to get one."

"Fuckin' Rocco. I think I saw something in the corner of his mouth, and I handed him my Henny."

"Or you can get it from kissing groupies," I said before stuffing my mouth with a forkful of French toast.

"Don't even go there with me, baby. You already know what it is. I know the rules, and we cleared all that up last night."

"Un huh," I said, recalling the tabloid pic that seemed to capture the prelude to a kiss with Naptown New Booty. "Well, you better call Dr. Reed and get that handled as soon as we get back. You may have to leave for your in-store early if it's still there by Saturday, because you'll have to run by Stacia's and spend some time in the makeup chair."

173

"*Grooming* chair."

"The cold sore chair," I said, unable to withhold my laughter.

"You got jokes?" he asked, running out of the bathroom toward me. He moved my tray to the floor and jumped on top of me. "What if you have to sit in the cold sore chair beside me?" he asked, while placing his lips less than an inch away from mine.

I laughed uncontrollably through my drawn-in lips, careful not to release them and make contact with his. He laughed, too, as he released my pinned down arms and got up.

I threw a pillow at him. "I think you just spit on me. Don't let me wake up and find a bump! I'll kill you *and* Rocco, or whoever you choose to blame it on."

"Not if I hide your gun."

"I have two. And even if I didn't, there's more than one way to skin a cat." I placed my plate back in my lap and thanked God we didn't kiss in the mouth the night before.

# DANA

"Happy Valentine's Day, Mrs. Hall," one of my students yelled as I walked to my car.

"Same to you!" I replied, as I placed my messenger bag in the backseat.

I then reached between the front seats and carefully placed my dozen red roses where the passenger would normally sit. I didn't want to risk the chance of them sliding between the boys' car seats and getting ruined in the back. I still couldn't believe Rashad bought them for me.

All day, I kept waiting to receive a page from the main office telling me that I had a special delivery. Ric isn't the flower-giving type, but with all the crap surrounding this day, I thought he'd surprise me by doing something out of the ordinary. Silly me.

During my seventh period study hall, though, Rashad, a former student of mine who is now a senior, walked in with a bouquet of long-stemmed roses. I stood behind my desk with my hands over my mouth, hoping he wasn't delivering them to one of the girls in the room.

"Happy Valentine's Day, Mrs. Hall. You thought I forgot, huh?" he said with a slick smile that only a handsome seventeen-year-old can display.

Rashad has flirted with me since his freshman year. He's a confident young man who has been in a little bit of trouble, but he has a heart of gold. I saw that the moment he introduced himself in my third period English 9 class. As did most of his male classmates, he took an immediate liking to me. I recognized that and was able to get him to also like English class. That year, my coworkers who had him in their classes nicknamed me "The Miracle Worker" because they couldn't pay him to keep his eyes open while they taught.

Even though he hasn't been in one of my classes for two years, he stops by my room every now and then to say hello and let me know how he's doing. He knows I care, and that means a lot to him. Early this school year, he came in my room to tell me he had broken up with his girlfriend of eight months. I joked with him, saying the next time I saw him, he'd be bragging about all the gifts he got her for Valentine's Day. That day, he told me I was going to be his valentine.

"I'm gonna hold you to that," I said playfully, never giving my words a second thought.

When he approached me with the flowers, I was speechless, embarrassed, and a little nervous. I thanked him and gave him a warm hug before he strolled out of the room feeling like a pimp.

The chorus-like sound from all the kids in my study hall saying, "Awwwwww," fed into my embarrassment, and the school's head gossiper confirmed why I was nervous when she said, "I didn't know y'all was like that, Mrs. Hall." The last thing I need is a rumor circulating that I have an inappropriate relationship with a student.

I didn't let those feelings overpower the warmth my heart felt. That was such a thoughtful thing for Rashad to do. Long stems aren't cheap, and though I have a pretty good idea where he gets his money from, he still didn't have to spend it on me.

Lorenzo teased me as soon as he spotted me in the hall with the flowers. "If I would've known you can take stuff from another man home, I would've gotten you that ring I saw."

"Shut up. If you really wanted to get me a ring, you would've bought it anyway, and I could've worn it from seven to three. It's only right since you say you're my school husband."

"Something tells me you probably would do that, you lil' sneaky thing. I think I like it." His smile barely revealed his gap.

"I have my moments," I replied.

"Well, damn. Can a brotha get a call the next time you have a moment?"

"Maybe if you would've gotten me some roses," I said with a wink as I walked away.

All of those thoughts entertained me on the drive home. I was sure to get a reaction from Ric when I walked in the house bearing a gift that wasn't for him, and I couldn't wait. If he knew what was best for his marriage, he would have the living room covered with rose petals, a hot bath waiting for me, and a babysitter lined up for the boys.

I entered through the garage and was surprised that Chase didn't greet me. Usually when he hears me set the alarm on the car, he waits patiently on the other side of the door to hug my legs. *This could be a good sign*, I thought while ascending the stairs. I placed the roses on the counter and yelled Ric's name. Then Chase's. Then Ric's again. I couldn't imagine where they could be, especially since Dalvin's bus would be arriving at the house in seven minutes.

I kicked off my shoes and ran up to the third floor. Nope. They weren't waiting with candy and flowers behind their backs, ready to say, "We love you! Happy Valentine's Day!" They were still nowhere to be found.

Before I knew it, Dalvin's bus had arrived; we'd finished his homework; I'd cooked him a quick meal; and we were in our respective rooms watching TV. The day was over. In the midst of all that, I had been calling Ric to see where he was with my baby, but he didn't answer his phone for two hours. When he finally answered, he had the nerve to have an attitude because one of the MARTA trains broke down, and he had been waiting for almost an hour for another to show up. After we hung up, I was certain romance wouldn't be in the air when he got home.

He walked in forty minutes later with a Fredrick's bag in-hand. "Here," he said, as if he were forced to write a thank-you note to the person who peed in his apple juice. Because he wasn't looking at me, the bag totally missed my hand and fell to the floor. He kept walking while Chase picked up the bag.

*Wow. A half-assed "Happy Valentine's Day" would've been nice.* I opened the bag and pulled out a one-piece nightie that had to be the most reserved item in the store. It was plain— no lace, no frills, no plunging neckline…nothing. The only thing that made it look semi-decorative was the pattern of hearts covering it. If it didn't have a Frederick's tag, I would've sworn he got it from Wal-Mart. I'm not an unappreciative bitch, so under another circumstance, I would've pretended I liked it. In this case, though, there was a problem. The receipt clearly marked his purchase as a two-piece set, and he sure as hell didn't hand me another bag from Bath & Body Works.

I walked over to the couch where he was lounging. "Thank you, but I can't accept this. This isn't mine." I placed the bag on the arm of the couch.

"What?"

"Where's the strawberry-mango lotion and body spray or whatever?"

"What do you mean?"

"You bought that stuff the same day you bought the lingerie—the real lingerie that's on the receipt."

He went into a rage as he explained how he dropped the bag of "smell good stuff" as he got off the bus, got pissed, and threw it in a nearby trashcan. He had an equally elaborate story for the lingerie, saying he changed his mind right after he bought the two-piece set, picked out the nonsense he'd given me, and asked the lady if he could just swap one for the other since they were the same price and he didn't have time to stand in line again. She agreed because she was too busy to be bothered, and that was that. Lies, lies, lies.

As with most of the stories he tells, could that have really happened? Absolutely. It's far-fetched, but possible. It's also coming out of Ric's mouth, so it's most likely a bunch of crap.

"Am I really supposed to believe that, or were you just testing me?" I asked.

"Why would I lie about something like that?"

"Hmm…let's see. Because you don't want your wife to know that not only are you screwing someone else, you're buying them fancy little outfits to wear; because you didn't have time to get to Bath & Body Works to get me the same stuff you got her; because if the truth comes out and I kick you out, you won't be able to live in LaShay's dorm room. Would you like me to go on?" I asked.

"I can't win with you. No matter what I say, you'll say I'm lying."

"And you know whose fault that is?"

"Mine. Everything's my fault, right?"

"Don't be mad at me because the shoe fits."

He nodded. "So you don't want your gift."

"Nope. It's not what was originally purchased, and the original purchase wasn't meant for me."

"You wanna talk about purchases? Who bought you roses?"

"It surely wasn't you, huh? How does a seventeen-year-old *boy* know how to put a smile on my face and you don't?"

"I don't put a smile on your face? I just bought you those shoes you were drooling over last week. You don't remember smiling?"

"I'm talking about today. This was the day you were supposed to prove me wrong. I was looking forward to feeling like a dummy after accusing you of buying something for another woman. What did you do, though? You brought me this sorry nightie and thought I'd believe that was what you picked up for me in December. I don't even think they put Valentine's Day stuff out in December!"

"That's a real sign of your true character. Because I didn't make you smile today, that erases all the other times. All I have to say is fuck you, Dana. You came up in here with flowers from another man, knowing damn well if I came in with a gift from a female customer, you'd tell me how disrespectful I am and I'd never hear the end of it. What kind of man do you think I am? Do you expect me to believe a kid gave you roses? One of those corny teachers gave those to you, and I guess it's fair for me to assume you're fuckin' him."

His tirade was comical until he started throwing illegal blows with his tongue. I kept a cool head until he said I've probably had a boyfriend at work for years and that Chase probably isn't his.

From the first time we saw Chase, we joked about how much lighter he is than Dalvin. Ric even joked in the delivery room, asking if there was something I needed to tell him. I really took it as a joke, considering how Chase is a spitting image of his daddy, just with my skin tone. Dalvin is

180

the opposite, a darker version of me. He has even continued to joke through the years, but again, I thought his words were all in good fun.

I asked Ric to repeat himself, and he did. According to him, I've always liked light-skinned men, and almost all the teachers I work with are light-skinned. That automatically means he was fathered by one of them. I don't know how he concluded that I've always liked light-skinned men, seeing that we've been together from the moment I was really into having a real boyfriend. Of course my elementary and middle school boyfriends were light, because that's what was in. If they didn't look like Al B. Sure, I didn't have any rap for them.

"You got me jumpin' through hoops and demandin' that I prove shit to you. I want you to prove that. Prove that he's mine."

The pressure I felt from my headache seemed to push the tears more forcefully down my face. *How can he say such hurtful things with a straight face?* Then I remembered that's what you do when you mean what you say. I walked away slowly, taunted by Ric's voice as if he had defeated me.

"Where are you going? You had so much to say. You don't wanna hear what else I have to say?"

I didn't know my heart could feel so much pain. I hurt for my baby boy. I hurt from the thought of him accidentally hearing the words coming from his father's mouth and understanding what was said. I hurt because, in my mind, I didn't want Ric to speak to or touch Chase again, and if I implemented that, it would hurt Chase more than anything. He adores his daddy, who all of a sudden questions whether he is his daddy.

I was in and out of our bedroom with a bag packed in seven minutes. I stopped at the hall closet to get another duffle bag large enough for the boys' things before proceeding to their room. I didn't make time to get my face

181

together before facing them like I usually do. They have rarely seen me cry, but I had to make an exception this time.

I stuffed their bag while being bombarded with, "Are we going somewhere, Mommy?" "Where?" "Can I take my DS?" "Are we gonna go swimming?" "Why are you crying?" "Are you sad?"

I didn't know where we were going. I'd figure that out once we were in the car. I knew I could stay at Crystal's if I needed, but she lives so far away from my job and the boys' school and daycare. The only other alternative off the top of my head was to call Lily and see if I could stay with her, but I didn't want her in my business. You don't have to be a rocket scientist to know there is trouble at home when a woman shows up on your doorstep with her two children.

As we walked by Ric, who was still lounging on the couch, he laughed. "So what's this supposed to mean? Why leave? That's stupid. I told you what you need to do for us to be straight on that issue. I know little man don't like needles, and they don't even use 'em no more. No hurt, no harm. Just a Q-tip."

I clenched my jaw, squeezed my babies' hands more tightly, and led them down the stairs. They both said goodbye to their ignorant father who only threw his hand up like they were his homeboys.

182

# WILLOW (MILKY)

Eighty-three thousand dollars. How do you write a thank-you note for that? When Rebecca wrote the check, I assumed it was an erratic move. She couldn't have really meant that. But when I called her, she told me that she had been saving the money for me since she started her career at age twenty-five. She started putting away two thousand a year, and when she found out she couldn't have children, she raised it to five thousand. Evidently, she did think of me over the years and had always planned to find me. I can't imagine how much money she spent on the private investigator who located my mom. Though money is certainly no indicator of love, learning that she'd planned on giving me the money regardless gave me a different perspective of her. She jokingly called it her "back child support" and said she was going to write the check at the end of what she thought would've been a more civilized evening.

"I have to say I feel weird accepting such a large sum," I said.

"Please keep it. I've had it stashed away all this time specifically for you. It's not meant to make up for what I did.

You can't put a price tag on a person. I know that. If you don't need it, put it away for Venus. For all I care, donate it to charity. It's yours. Please."

I respected that. Maybe I would donate the money to charity. Or I could start my own charity. I've been dissatisfied with many of the services or lack thereof for children with developmental disorders. What if I could bring more attention to the issue and help fund programs that would allow those children to have the same educational opportunities as their peers without feeling incompetent?

How about that? Rebecca had again unknowingly afforded me a monumental opportunity. First, I was able to speak with Vaughn about his violent spells. Now, I may be able to make a lasting difference in Venus' life. Some people aren't built to be parents, but they are still able to influence those around them. Rebecca is that person to me.

Before hanging up, neither of us promised to call again. Instead, we wished each other the best. This wasn't done out of hostility. I believe we reached an unspoken understanding. I'm pretty sure I'll call her when I decide what to do with the money. She needs to know that it will have a purpose, and that in turn, she has a purpose. I get the feeling that she only feels relevant when she's negotiating deals at her job.

Only my mother knows the amount of the check. Vaughn wasn't in the room when Rebecca gave it to me, and Crystal thinks I ripped it up. I followed my mom's advice to place the money in her savings account. She told me that every woman needs a stash of her own, and that was one heck of a stash. My mom has been saving for over thirty years, and she doesn't even have half of that sum put away.

I feel uncomfortable keeping the money a secret from Vaughn, but my mom has never steered me wrong. I trust her over everyone because she chose to make me a part of her family and teach me how to exist in this complex world. She was never a parent merely acting out of obligation, crossing off calendar days leading up to my eighteenth birthday. She has always acted out of love. She chose me.

Her nature is instilled in me. I guess that's why I stand by Vaughn. I chose him, and I choose to stay with him through these trying times because our marriage is more than an obligation to me. It's my life. I raise our daughter, cook our meals, and work for his company. Those three things are always a part of my day, always a part of my life. And now that Mrs. Ella has let me in on his haunting secret, I further understand my connection to him. In fact, the love I feel has grown stronger.

He must feel so empty and alone. Since he's a man's man, his pride won't let him share that experience. There's probably so much he'd like to express about that time in his life. I wonder what everyday happenings trigger memories of his father. He does a great job covering up the pain from his past with his exaggerated confidence and material possessions, but if he was stripped of those, he would see a scared, angry little boy when he looked in the mirror.

Though at the time I was too young to realize it, I was once a scared little girl. The person who was supposed to be there for me deserted me because she was scared, too. So, I know what abandonment feels like, and I don't want to do that to Vaughn. I equate it to kicking someone when they're down. No one should ever experience that. I will live out our marriage feeling confident that I didn't bail when things became complicated, and this is easier to do now that he has owned up to his violence and has since changed the dynamics of our relationship.

The upward swing in our momentum came just in time for Valentine's Day. Vaughn surprised me with a helicopter ride over the city and a candlelit dinner. At the restaurant, our waitress brought over a red and silver gift bag with our

185

dessert. She placed the bag near my glass and wished me a Happy Valentine's Day. After I thanked her, I looked at Vaughn suspiciously.

"What are you up to?" I asked.

He whistled and looked away as if he were innocent and uninvolved. I moved the bag to my lap and immediately saw a jewelry box that looked to be the signature Tiffany & Co. blue color. Once the box was in my hand, the words were clear as day and it was confirmed. I opened the box and saw the stunning gold crown key pendant and chain. The crown portion of the key was embedded with round diamonds that caused me to squint when the light reflected off of them.

"This is beautiful, baby," I said. "It's so unique."

"It symbolizes the key to my heart. You make sure you're careful with it," he replied with a smirk.

"Of course."

I almost forgot about the other gift in the bag. I pulled out the thin hardcover book and read its cover. *Reasons Why* was the title, and his name was listed in the bottom right corner. I frowned, thinking he couldn't have embarked on a writing career without me knowing.

When I opened the book, I saw thirty-five pages that listed reasons why Vaughn loves me. He found a company that allowed him to personalize his feelings in something much more memorable than a card. His reasons ranged from very silly to extremely sentimental as I flipped through the pages briefly.

My heart melted. A gesture of that magnitude is a great example of why I married him. He gave me something that would be around long after I leave this world. The book was something Venus could have as a symbol of the love between us. It could serve as a guide of sorts to what love should be. It sets a standard for the men who will come into her life years from now.

After dinner, we checked into the Westin in Buckhead for a night full of rekindled passion and much-needed pleasure. Everything went well. He didn't need a pump or a pill. He barely needed me to touch him.

My man was back. The eyes that used to glare relentlessly at me were looking at me with delight. The lips that spoke detestable words toward me were kissing me in the tenderest way. The hand that has struck my face was stroking my hair. I lost myself in the moment, hoping to never be found.

# CRYSTAL

Ever since I saw the picture of Milky's biological father, I've been disturbed. I didn't want to say anything then, but I'm pretty sure I know that guy. Life is full of coincidences, but I'm almost positive this is much more. I pulled my cosmetic dentist's business card from my wallet and tapped it on the table in front of me. *This is creepy*, I thought.

I stopped my nervous movement and stared at the script on the card: Dr. Scott R. Knight, DDS. Could there be another Scott Knight with blue eyes and a Ken doll smile? It's certainly a common name, but I can't help but wonder if the man who has been keeping my teeth looking flawless is my sister's dad.

Since the subject of adoption is often a sensitive one, I can't go in for my next appointment and say, "Hey! I know your daughter! The one you don't know." That probably wouldn't go over too well. And Milky has made it clear that she doesn't want to look for him. I think she's afraid he'll be like Rebecca; happy to see her doing well, but only interested in that moment—nothing long-term. I guess it's similar to seeing an ex unexpectedly, catching up over a quick lunch, and parting ways, never to speak again. You say, "Let's keep in touch," because it's politically correct, but you know you don't plan to. You want to, but you don't know what you'd talk about if you phoned. Years have gone by, and you find you have nothing in common. Something tells me Dr. Knight isn't like that, though.

I don't want to hurt Milky by digging into a wound that's trying to heal, but I can't continue to look at Dr. Knight without thinking he is the final missing piece to my sister's family puzzle. I glanced at my watch, aware that by two o'clock, I needed to have a plan.

For the first time in about a year, I made it to the office before my scheduled time. When I signed in, Malory, teasingly asked me if something was wrong because it's unlike me to be prompt.

"I like to mix it up every now and then. Keep you on your toes," I replied, laughing only half as hard as she.

The dental assistant called me back right away, and within minutes, Scott Knight was staring down at me with the "spotlight" in my face.

"You know what I'm gonna ask, right?" he said.

"How was my day?" I replied.

"Cut it out," he said, laughing and showing his naturally pearly whites.

I groaned. "No, I haven't stopped drinking the wine."

He warned me during my last visit to slow down on the spirits because they can cause permanent damage to my teeth. I figured red wine would, but my beloved Moscato can, also. He said I will see its effects over time...and my "over time" would probably come sooner than someone who generally just has one or two glasses at a social event twice a month.

"Are you gonna lecture me again?" I asked.

"Nope. I'm not your father. You heard me the first time. It's not my job to preach to you. I'm here to educate you on dental health, and most importantly—to you at least—make

189

your teeth look like you've never done an ill thing to them. Open up."

When he finished, he handed me a mirror. "Perfection," I said.

"You could've had that without paying for it."

"What's up with you and the speeches lately? Did you go to a conference and come back with a new outlook?"

He laughed. "No. I'm sorry. It's been a long day. You wouldn't believe some of the jobs I had to do today and how those people ended up in the shape they were in. You know I don't want you to stop coming to see me."

*There you go winking again*, I thought. "Yeah, I probably provide your children's breakfast and lunch for a month. That's why you wanna see me."

"I wish. You'd be surprised how much children eat—especially two teenage boys." He helped me out of the chair and handed my purse to me.

"I can only imagine. My brother, Todd, probably ate the same amount by himself. I don't know how my parents kept the cabinets stocked on their salaries."

"You'll see when you become a parent. Providing for your children is just what you do, no matter what the cost."

"Well, if I have any, I'm stopping at one. You have four, right?" I asked, leaning to get a better look at the family portrait at the end of the counter.

"Actually, five. My other daughter isn't in that picture."

*Ahhhh!* I screamed inside. Unsure of how to respond, I pulled out my phone and pretended to text someone. We started down the hallway. When he stopped to clarify some information with one of his assistants, I kept walking until I reached the checkout counter. I made small talk with Jessi as we waited for Dr. Knight to give her the billing form.

I had to ask the question of the day. I had to find out if he was as much of a candidate to be Milky's father as I thought. When he joined us at the counter, I used my most casual and forgetful tone to mask what I'd wanted to ask since he first told me to say "Ah" this afternoon.

"Oh! Do you know a woman named Rebecca? I don't know her last name, but she's from Indianapolis. Well, actually she's from a suburb of Indianapolis…Geist. I was talking about you working miracles on my smile the other day, and she said she went to school with a smart guy named Scott Knight. I told her you were a California boy, but I figured I'd ask."

He cleared his throat and kept his eyes on my chart as if he was looking for something. "It's possible. I'm originally from there. I only went to college in California. I knew a ton of Rebecca's, though."

"Oh, I'm sure." I nudged him on the arm. "I'm from Indianapolis, too. See? If you would've ever come to where the sistahs hung out, we may have crossed paths. We could've made magic together, Dr. Knight."

Jessi giggled and excused herself to go check an incoming fax.

Dr. Knight set his pen down and leaned onto the counter, overcome with laughter. "If I would've come to where the sistahs were and tried to talk to one of you, I would've either been beaten up by one of the brothas or arrested by one of the cops. Do you know how old I am?"

After Jessi returned, I paid her, and then Dr. Knight escorted me to the exit, which he never does. As we rounded the corner leading to the door, I was pretty convinced he was my guy. I was further convinced when he nonchalantly asked over his shoulder, "So how do you know this Rebecca?"

"Actually, my sister knows her. That was my first time meeting her."

"Oh, I see."

His understated disappointment didn't go unnoticed, along with the nervous tap of his hand against the side of his

191

thigh. "Well, if you think about it, ask your sister what her maiden name is. Maybe she does know me. I don't keep in touch with anyone from high school, though."

There were so many questions I wanted to ask, but I had already crossed the line between patient and doctor. If I went any further, I'd have to tell him everything, and that's not my place. So, I thanked him and left.

Having to share the amazing potential connection with somebody, I ran down the entire conversation with Dante. He half listened while smoothing his goatee and twisting his lips to the right repeatedly.

Unfulfilled and disappointed with his response, I joined him in the bathroom. "What are you doing in here? Looking for another cold sore?"

"That ain't funny."

"I didn't say it was. You tingling again?"

"I don't know, man. This shit is stupid. I'm not tryin' to go through this every few weeks or every month."

"Well, the only way you're gonna stop them is if you end your tour. Didn't you read the pamphlet? They're triggered by stress and fatigue. That's the definition of your career—a combination of those two."

"All it takes is one photographer to catch me out with a blister on the side of my lip, and that's it. People get cold sores all the time, but because I'm me, it's gonna be a big deal."

"You only need to worry if it becomes a big deal to me."

"It is! You won't even kiss me on the lips."

"Do you blame me? I don't wanna share cooties with you and whoever."

"Rocco. I told you he was drinking from my bottle. Ain't no 'whoever'."

"Right...Are you ready now? They have the car all packed. Grab your Abreva and let's go." I ran to escape his playful blow, almost running out of breath from laughing so hard.

We were on our way to Atlantic City, where Dante would perform the next night. Upon our arrival, we'd be celebrating our ninth wedding anniversary. We had already exchanged gifts, but I was hoping to see a silver 2010 Mercedes G550 in the driveway with a big pink bow on it when we returned from our trip. I've made it clear that I'm in love with the vehicle, and nothing says "I'm sorry for f'ing up our last year of marriage with my Naptown New Booty scandal" like a brand-new SUV.

I'm proud of us. We're still in the "different place" we discovered while in Puerto Rico. We're in love and meaning it. We've brought back the little things that made our relationship the envy of our friends, restoring my faith in him, even if I didn't have the same faith in our marriage.

I've been behaving while on the road with him, which is a first. Nigel and I have only hooked up twice—once in Cleveland and again in Seattle. Two out of twelve ain't bad. Dante has been coming back to the room like he promises and giving me all the attention I need. He's been what he promised to be nine years ago, and I've been what I've wanted to be for the past three years I've been allowing Nigel to get me off.

In fact, I believe I pissed Nigel off last week in DC when I turned down his offer to sex me while Dante was making an appearance at a club. I didn't want him—plain and simple. He joked with me about how I would be disappointed when Dante came back to the room with no energy left to work me the way I needed to be worked. But I then made it clear to him that I wasn't interested in being worked that night. I just wanted my baby to join me in the king-size bed so we could cuddle like we were in a twin-size one. I was looking forward to spending an intimate evening with Dante, not Dante, Jr. By the time I was done responding

193

to Nigel's hater-esque comment, he was very clear that he's my meat, not my man; my just in case, not just because...and he's only hanging on to that title by a thread after overstepping his boundaries.

I stared at Dante behind my oversized shades as Elgin drove us to the airport. I couldn't help but smile, thinking of the mini crush I had on him during his teenage days when he performed at Expo. Never in a million years would I have thought of us being married, but here we are. We've made it through nine years that exerted pressures most couples would've cracked under. That says something, but I'm not sure if it's anything worth hearing. Not yet.

I have no expectations for year ten. In a perfect world, Dante and I will still be frolicking in our bliss. In a perfect world, we would renew the honesty we shared when we first met fourteen years ago and compromise so our marriage won't just survive; it will flourish. However, we all know this isn't a perfect world. I would only be setting myself up for failure to expect anything other than the unexpected. All I can do is take responsibility for the things I can control and see what happens. If it helps, I look forward to seeing what happens.

# DANA

I was surprised to receive a phone call from my father on my way to work. We hadn't talked since November, and that was because I called him. We've gone through this since he and my mother split. He thinks I'm supposed to call him all the time as if he's been a model father, and I leave him waiting, because in my opinion, a real parent will have regular communication with their child despite the circumstances.

We have a love-hate relationship. I love him because he's my father, and we're similar in a lot of ways. I can talk to him uncensored, unlike my mother, and he usually gives me a great view of the male perspective without even realizing it. I hate him because he treated my mother like shit. From five to nine years of age, I witnessed him choke, slap, wrestle, and hold a gun to her. He's lucky I speak to him at all.

He asked how the family was, and I told him all about the boys' new milestones. I didn't mention Ric, so he asked specifically about him.

"He's alright. Same ol' Ric," I replied.

Dad pried until I opened up. Without going into too much detail, I told him I had put Ric out of the house. He had stayed out another night and came in the house hungover, so I told him to go back where he'd come from. Something—be it a bottle of alcohol, a blunt, a woman, or a combination of the three—had more priority over him returning to his household, and I could only play the fool once. First time, shame on you. Second time, shame on me. Or was that the third time? Regardless, that, in addition to his denial of Chase, was plenty grounds for his removal.

"I'm gonna tell you somethin', Noodle," he started. A sense of my five-year-old vulnerability came over me when I heard him use my nickname. "A man is gonna play. That's what we do unless someone stops us. You're not a stupid woman. Me and your mama didn't raise you like that. If he didn't bring his tail home one night, do you think he was laid up around a bunch of hard legs? There ain't nothin' I can do with the fellas overnight. I'll tell you that much. But I think you know that."

*I do,* I thought.

"Now, it's up to you to decide whether you want to keep him around. If you love him enough to make it work, then sit him down and tell him you ain't havin' that shit. He's either gonna straighten up or y'all can go your separate ways. Y'all are married, so you're supposed to work things out and make 'em better. Your mama never sat me down. She ran her mouth to her friends and walked around the house mopin'.

"Whatever you decide, I'll support you. I will tell you this, though. I always thought he was a little sneaky son-of-a-bitch. I believe he loves you, but that fool has as much business bein' married as I have bein' at a KKK meeting."

The conversation that was going so well had hit a brick wall. "So if you felt like that, why did you give him your blessing when he called and asked for my hand in marriage?" I asked.

Though Ric acts like he has no home training sometimes, he'll often do traditional things that show he was raised correctly. I remember telling him that he didn't have to call my father because it wasn't like he was an integral part of my life.

"Well, it seemed like you loved him, so I wasn't gonna throw a wrench in the plans."

"So you let me enter into a lifelong commitment with a man you felt was gonna play me?"

"Dana, if you already had your heart set on marrying him, there was nothing I could've said to change your mind. I wasn't even in touch with you when you first met him. You and I both know you wouldn't have paid one bit of attention to me."

"That's not true. Would I have leaned on your every word? Absolutely not. But you better believe your words would've been in the back of my mind, and I would've been paying closer attention to the things my *father* pointed out before I proceeded. Let's not act like I was in such a hurry to marry him that I would ignore the input of my parents."

True, my father wasn't around to intimidate the boys I dated during my teenage years. He wasn't there to point out the discrepancies that only another man can recognize. In other words, he wasn't there to share the game with me.

"Well, I don't believe that," he said.

"Looks like you'll never know what would've happened."

He had the opportunity to potentially save me from a world of hurt. Instead, he sat back with a bag of popcorn, waiting to watch the shit unfold. Now, he has so much to say and so many opinions to share after I've been married almost eight years. I swear too many people see the wedding ceremony as just a ritual. They hear the words that are spoken without listening. Everything is said for a reason. No, Ric and I didn't have a traditional wedding, but my mom and dad did. My dad heard their minister say, "Speak now or forever hold your peace." It is said for a reason. My take on it is this: If your lips were sealed before I got into it, why open them when I'm in it?

I don't blame my father for what Ric has done in our marriage, nor do I blame him for "letting" me get married. I do blame him for failing as a father...again. This is why my nose is buried in Steve Harvey's book every day during my lunch break. I'm hoping he can help me think like a man since my own father forgets to.

*****

I decided it was time for a vacation. After two months of training with Lorenzo and doing cardio work on my own, I was feeling like a new woman. With a few more weeks' work, I'll feel comfortable wearing a two-piece bathing suit again. Scratch that. I'll be ready to show off my new six-pack and firmer thighs. I mentioned it to the girls, and we agreed on the perfect time and place: June, the week of my birthday, in Vegas. Crystal was planning our soiree, so we met up to discuss logistics at my house.

She had already made arrangements to use Dante's plane and decided on the Bellagio for our hotel. I didn't know the difference between the Bellagio and Caesar's Palace, and I didn't care. I just wanted to get out of Atlanta and away from Ric. I heard Vegas gives you a sense that nothing matters except having fun, and that's exactly where I need to be. I'd return to the real world only when absolutely necessary.

Martha had compiled a list of all the shows and other happenings that would be taking place while we were there. Crystal gave me first dibs at choosing our itinerary since it is essentially my trip. I wanted to let loose, so I chose the male strip club, the pole dancing class, and the Keri Hilson concert. I also wanted to visit the wax museum and see the Hard Rock Hotel. She could fill in the blanks with whatever else she wanted to do.

"Sounds good to me," Crystal said. "We'll be able to do all that and then some. I'll get back to y'all with updates next week." She put her papers away and crossed her legs. "So...what's up? Anything new with y'all? We might as well make this a DWC meeting."

I laughed. "When isn't there something new with me?" I told them about my father calling and how upset I am with him revealing his gut feeling almost a decade into my marriage.

"Well, no one wants to feel responsible for breaking up an engagement or marriage," Willow said.

"I disagree. If anyone should feel responsible, it should be your parents. It's their job to look out for you. How would you feel if your mom said she thought Vaughn had a terrible temper but hoped she was wrong?"

"Mrs. Ella pretty much said that. I'm not upset with her for not telling me, though."

"She's not supposed to tell you. She's *his* mother, not yours."

"Forget all that. I wanna get back to the part where you said he's not around anyway. I thought he was just at work," Crystal interrupted.

"I put him out. He stayed out all night again, so I told him to stay out some more nights."

"Do you know where he was? Do you know where he is now?" Crystal asked.

"I still believe he was with LaShay. That could be where he's staying now, too. Who knows? He says he's at his other coworker's place. I just find it funny that when I called LaShay, she hung up on me," I replied.

"Wait. You called her?"

Yes, I played myself. I called LaShay looking for my husband. How silly is that? I had to check myself. If I don't know where he is and am convinced another woman does, that's grounds for reevaluation.

"I'll never do that again," I said. "All it did was piss me off even more."

"Do you know where she lives?" Crystal asked.

"I have access to that information," I said. "Why?"

"I can go get answers if you want me to. What kind of woman just hangs up the phone? If you're bold enough to fuck my husband, be bold enough to tell me. I know you wouldn't roll to her house, but I will. I've been itching to bust a bitch in the head."

"Stop it," Willow said. "That's not gonna solve a thing."

"She's right, but I'll keep your offer in mind," I replied. "Hell, I may be focusing on the wrong chick. He could be telling the truth when he says he's not doing anything with her. That doesn't mean he's not boning somebody else. He feels guilty about something. I told you he's giving me spending money for the trip, right?"

"Oh really?"

"Umm hmm. Says I deserve a break and that it's the least he can do."

"Well, he gets a little credit for that," Willow said.

"Ric has run out of credit with me, Milky. I'm talking bankrupt," I replied.

As the stories came pouring out, so did the alcohol. Crystal invaded my cabinet and came back with a bottle of sweet tea vodka. She spoke highly of Dante, but said he still has the secret phone. I wish she would just ask Nigel what's up with Dante and Naptown New Booty or any other person of interest. Contrary to what her mouth says, I know his alleged infidelity disturbs her. We never pry into each other's business, though, so I don't press the issue.

200

Out of embarrassment, I kept my other stories to myself. They don't know what Ric said about Chase because I didn't tell them. I didn't tell them because he's notorious for saying ignorant things to hurt me, and then apologizing once he's satisfied with the distress he caused. He's been apologizing for that since the day after Valentine's Day, but I'm not ready to accept.

I told him he has to start thinking before he opens his mouth. Maybe if he does that, he can only use "sorry" in his vocabulary when he is consoling someone about their loss of a loved one or after he bumps into someone in a congested area. But why tell the girls when I know I'll eventually accept his apology and let him move back in? Not because he'll say something profound to convince me, but because I know he didn't mean what he said. Try explaining that to someone after you've revealed just how far that same husband's ignorance stretches.

I'm a walking contradiction, a smart woman with dumb tendencies, but I'm not the only one. Whether I'm in the lunchroom at work, the salon, the parking lot after church, or standing in the grocery store check-out line, I hear stories of women who are unhappy in their marriage. We're a society of females who can share stories about the bullshit we've dealt with and then go home to wallow in it. Maybe we should just call ourselves flies.

"Do you miss him now that he's out of the house?" Willow asked.

I shrugged. "I don't know if I'd say that. I think I'm just used to him. He's my bad habit."

"Like biting your nails," she suggested.

"Nah...like grinding my teeth," I corrected before laughing. "Vaughn's been behaving?"

"Yes, he has. Seeing Rebecca and Dave really opened his eyes. He hasn't even harassed me about the Vegas trip."

201

"That's because he'll be spying on you the whole time," Crystal added. She turned to me. "He's not fooling me. That dude did not do a one-eighty overnight."

"Sounds like we're all in the 'to be continued' stage," I said.

"So what do you say, ladies? Two weeks? One week?" Crystal asked. "PRN?"

"I can't do too many more of these damn meetings. You're gonna turn me into a lush like you," I said, closing my eyes and melting into the couch.

"You *will* attend our meetings. This is a support group, dammit." She laughed as she raised her glass in the air. "We need a pledge."

"You are going too far," Willow said.

"Of allegiance?" I joked with a drunken smile. I placed my hand over my heart. "I pledge allegiance to the club of the Disgruntled Wives of America…"

With her glass still raised, Crystal continued, "…and to the husbands…"

"…who we love, but can't stand…" I helped.

Willow laughed.

"…one situation after another…"

I took a few seconds to think. "…until we're fed up…"

We exchanged blank stares. "Damn! It was just gettin' good," Crystal said.

"We only have a couple lines left. Think," I told her.

"Pursuing happiness and clarity for all." We looked over at Willow, who simply smiled and placed her hand over her heart, too.

"That's what I'm talkin' about, Milky!" Crystal exclaimed with her left fist in the air.

"Amen!" I added.

"Heffa, we ain't prayin'!" Crystal replied.

"Well, we need one of those, too."

After we finished laughing, Willow's tone changed to a more serious one. "We really shouldn't be laughing. Think about it. This is far from funny. We're supposed to be with these men forever."

"If I don't laugh, I'm gonna die from a nervous breakdown," I said. "I'll admit I don't laugh to keep from crying. I laugh so I don't cry as much. I laugh because when it's all said and done, I chose Ric, and despite all this shit that he's putting me through, I love him. I think he's screwing a teeny bopper, and I still love him. I kicked him out of the house, but next time you see me, he'll probably be back home. You can't tell me that's not funny."

"*Life* is funny, dammit! A lot of bad things are funny. Laughter is made for the strong," Crystal blurted.

I tried to make sense of it for a few seconds, but Willow interrupted my thought.

"What?" she asked with unmistakable confusion.

Again, there was an outburst of laughter between all of us.

"Shit. I don't know," Crystal replied. "I just wanted to say something."

Willow waved her sister off, then turned to me. "I get what you're saying, I guess. I just know that at some point, the comedy show has to end."

"It can only end when there's no audience," Crystal said. "Things are peachy with you and Vaughn now, but if he starts up again, are you gon' leave him?"

Willow stared at Crystal blankly. Her card was pulled, and there was no way to get it back.

"Well," I started, "looks like we all need to do some facial stretches, because we're gonna be laughing for a long time."

203

# DANA

"Hey, you, I'm having a moment," I said as soon as Lorenzo answered the phone.

"Huh?"

"You asked me to call the next time I had a moment, right? Remember on Valentine's Day?"

He chuckled. "Wait. You serious?"

"We have until nine o'clock. You comin' or what?"

"What's your address?"

I've been dreaming about Lorenzo since the Christmas party. As a married woman, I fought off the yearning to give him a taste, but if Ric can do what he wants, why can't I? I mean, I've been respectfully window shopping for years. Now, I'm window shopping with money in my wallet and considering trying on a few things. My inner good girl has her breaking point, and Ric took her there when he gave me that phony lingerie. As much as I've tried to forget about it, I can't. And his most recent slumber party "at his boy's house" only made my suspicions worse.

I didn't expect Lorenzo to bring refreshments, which means I surely didn't expect to be tipsy in an hour. I can't front, though. From the moment he stepped in the door, his intentions were clear. He was freshly showered and rubbed with Dolce & Gabbana. His hug was much warmer and lasted four times longer than the five-second good-to-see-you ones we exchange at work. And because he didn't give me the six-inch courtesy, I felt his semi-hardness upon contact. In my mind, I was well aware of what would go down later, but I wasn't willing to admit it until the Cîroc kicked in.

Nothing about our private party was planned. As most cheaters say, it just kind of happened. Lorenzo walked with me to my car after school and said he'd see me later. I opened my mouth and said, "Six o'clock?"

He raised his eyebrows. I responded with a smile and drove away. He thought I was kidding. I did, too...until I picked up the phone at five and called him.

He made our drinks, and we sat on the loveseat in the living room. I rested my feet in his lap while we watched *Love Jones* and chatted about the layoff rumors circulating around the school.

I mentioned I enrolled in the doctorate program at Georgia State, and he was excited to hear that. He has been thinking of doing that, as well, but still isn't sure if he wants to go into administration. That's what I like about him. Yes, he's fine and sexy, blah, blah, blah; but he can also hold an educated conversation without misplacing "big" words and talking in circles.

As the movie went on, Lorenzo kept asking me to recite some of my poems for him. I made the mistake of revealing that I write poetry during one of the scenes, and he seemed very intrigued by that. I refused each time he asked, thinking of how embarrassed I would be doing such a thing in my living room.

I forgot how sexy *Love Jones* is. I squirmed a few times, pretending not to be turned on by Darius and Nina's connection and pretending not to be turned on by the man sitting inches away from me. After another Cîroc and white grape juice mixture, though, I stopped pretending.

I was ready to fulfill his request for the poem. When given a choice of topics, he opted for "something sexy" and I gave it to him. I went all out, reciting my sexiest poem, "Lady in the Streets." As I spoke, his hand moved up and down my calf, later reaching as high as my thigh. If he didn't want me before, he certainly wanted me after hearing that.

"Come here," he said.

I took his hand and he pulled me toward him. We kissed. For a while. And it was succulent...and sensuous...and tempting.

"Wait right here," I said as Lorenzo sank more comfortably into the couch.

Now, I was suddenly ready to go through with what was barely a plan to begin with. Sure, inviting Lorenzo to the house was wrong. I accept that. It was my bad-girl scheme. Ha, ha, ha, look what I did. Another man was on your couch. But after I staggered my way to the bedroom and searched through my closet, I committed to take my scheme to another level.

I retrieved the bullshit nightie Ric gave me on Valentine's Day from under a pile of sweaters. As I shook the wrinkles out, I smiled. "I *do* have a use for you," I said, slipping out of my jeans and tank top and into the simple number. The bottom hem reached my thigh just an inch below my cheeks, allowing a peek at my lacy magenta boy shorts if I walked too fast or barely bent over. If that wasn't enough, my cleavage offered an open invitation for his tongue to travel between the girls and stop to play for a while if he felt like it. A couple squirts of Burberry completed my outfit as I stood in the mirror to admire myself.

*Thirty-two with two kids and I still look good*, I thought, before blowing into my palm to check my breath. Then it dawned on me. We were both drinking, so our breath smelled exactly the same. Ready to go, I pulled my *Slow & Easy* CD from my panty drawer and took one last look in the mirror. *He thinks he's the only one who wants me? Ha!*

When I reentered the living room, Lorenzo's bottom jaw dropped. The candles provided just enough light for him to enjoy the view. He could pat himself on the back for helping me give my thighs more definition and my booty a little lift. I proceeded first to the CD player, then turned to face him. With the remote in my hand, I stood in front of him and stared seductively—the way I've been wanting to for a while now.

"Damn," he said. His facial expression looked like Dalvin's when he first saw Mr. Incredible at Disney World. He reached for my thigh, and I grabbed his hand lightly.

"One rule. Keep your hands to yourself." *For now...*

"You're not playing fair."

I raised my index finger to my lips, not saying another word. As soon as I pressed Play, it was showtime. He sat on the couch and enjoyed my presentation. Unsure of what to do with his hands, he periodically reached for me, but remembering the rule, he would return his hands to the cushions. Before we reached the middle of the song, though, he'd found a new place for one of his hands: in his pants. The more I swiveled my hips, the more aroused he became.

Before I knew it, I was straddling him and his hands were stroking my back down to my thighs. R. Kelly continued to whisper "You know I can't see nothin' wrong wit' a little bump and grind, baby" into our ears, egging me on to take my tease to the next level.

"You're driving me crazy," Lorenzo whispered. "You gotta get up."

"Or what?" I asked.

He pressed my hips into his lap. "Or I'm gonna have to do somethin' with this." He slid his hand between us and pulled out inches of hardened meat.

I stared at it as it rested on his stomach, thinking of how great it would feel inside my love when the curved portion turned the corner and tapped on my spot—the spot that would send both of us to ecstasy.

He lifted me off of his lap and pulled my panties down. Before I could protest, his face was lodged between my thighs. When he came up for air, he licked his lips and looked into my eyes. His fingers still played with my love as he told me how beautiful I am and asked if I was sure I wanted to make love.

"I know *she's* ready," he said, referring to mini me, "but are you?"

I guess I was, because I found myself on the floor feeling the heat from his touch and the candle wax he let drip onto my thighs. I closed my eyes and scratched at the carpet, but much like my hormones, I couldn't get a grip on that either.

Since he was using props, I joined in. Refusing to be outdone, I went to the kitchen and came back with a container of honey. Only this time, I wasn't pouring it into my tea. Add the ice leftover in my cup, and we were indulging in a buffet of aphrodisiacs. Add the Trojan Ecstasy condom, and we were indulging in each other.

*What am I doing?* I thought. Sex with Lorenzo solved nothing. It wasn't like I timed it so Ric would walk in on us. Even if I had, I wouldn't have gotten any satisfaction out of hurting his feelings because he would've killed me and Lorenzo before I could've said, "Na na na, boo boo!"

I pretended to be into it, though it was obvious Lorenzo was having much more fun than me. He grunted, moaned, and squealed as he hovered over me, humping and sweating. I sobered up when a drop fell from his face onto

208

mine, repulsed because only my husband was supposed to sweat on me.

Damn my conscious! If I didn't have one, I think I would've actually enjoyed myself. Our night together was morally wrong, but vengefully excusable in the *Woman Scorned Handbook*. When he entered me, it felt like he swelled even more, filling me to capacity. I shuddered with satisfaction and moaned in his ear, hoping he didn't hear my teeth chatter. He had my body twisted into positions it had never been in, taking in his manhood at every angle possible. He was aggressive, but tame; anxious, but cautious; dominant, but considerate. And there was no denying the sexiness of his strength. He's in such great shape that he could've done pushups to enter and exit me. At one point, we were in the missionary position, and he scooped me up effortlessly, placing me in his lap for a ride that was so sensual that it will forever be ingrained in my memory. The only thing Lorenzo did wrong was not be Ric...and that was enough to ruin the experience.

All in all, my mission was accomplished. I gave away my love to a man who appreciated it. On three occasions, I've dressed up for Ric, planning to show him a great time, and he has ignored me or criticized the outfit. The last time I wore my black get-up, I approached him from behind as he sat at the computer desk and asked him to help me with something. When he turned to see what I wanted, he saw the flyaway apron babydoll. He laughed, but I wasn't offended. It's what he usually does when I surprise him. It was when he doubled over with laughter after looking at my marabou slippers that I got pissed.

Actually, I was more hurt than anything. I was trying to switch things up. Usually, I'm just barefoot, but the heels took the sexiness of the babydoll to another level. Or so they were supposed to. The mockery didn't stop there, though. He asked me to hold on "a few minutes" because he had to finish looking something up on the internet. When I confirmed that he was serious, I turned my half-naked tail around and went back to our room to change.

He came to see about me after talking on the phone, watching the news, and making a sandwich, two hours later. I made sure I was awake with eyes that didn't look like they were crying. He sat beside me and touched my sweatpants, jokingly saying they were just as sexy as the babydoll and that my plan didn't work to turn him off. Well, he had turned *me* off. So, count that as the first time I denied him sex in eight years of marriage.

Lorenzo helped me clean up the scene of our crime. It took us twenty minutes to pick the dried candle wax from the carpet, so I'm glad we had forty minutes to spare. Instead of flushing the condom down one of my toilets, he wrapped it in a paper towel and stuffed it in his pocket. Before he left, he gave me the sweetest hug.

"I wish you were mine," he said as we let go.

I smiled and adjusted the bottom of his shirt. "I'll see you on Monday, sweetie."

He kissed my forehead and left.

I leaned against the door, drained of my energy and integrity. The satisfaction I craved only lasted for two minutes of the twenty-five-minute act, and I was now left feeling unfulfilled...and drunk. Revenge is supposed to be sweet, but all I tasted was vodka.

I removed the nightie and balled it in my hand as I trudged upstairs to take a shower and brush my teeth. Ric would be home in fifteen to twenty minutes, and I planned on being asleep.

When I climbed into bed, my cell phone buzzed on the nightstand. I read the text message from Lorenzo. *FYI, that was much more than just a moment to me. Goodnite, luv.*

How do you tell someone you used them to get back at your husband without hurting their feelings? I brainstormed for a few seconds, and after I still came up with nothing, I simply powered my phone off and closed my eyes.

# WILLOW (MILKY)

Robyn spun my chair around, and I looked in the mirror apprehensively. I was pleasantly surprised to see an edgier, sexier me. I had already planned on coloring my hair, but I didn't think of cutting it until Robyn showed me a photo of Victoria Beckham looking fierce in the cut that was short enough to call a bob, yet long enough to extend about two inches past my jawbone. Without trying, she had me convinced that I would look cute in it, and after a ten-minute deliberation with my less adventurous alter ego, I decided to go for it. Summer is here, and I wouldn't mind a new look. Besides, I think brunettes look better with short hair than blondes anyway.

She cut the medium-length bob in an angle, giving me short layers in the back and long layers in the front. She'd warned me that once she started cutting the layers, there wouldn't be much for me to do if I didn't like the style, but I encouraged her to snip away. If it turned out horribly, I'd just have to obtain an affinity for hats and big earrings until my hair grew back.

"Well?" Robyn asked.

I turned to see my left profile. "I love it! I can't believe how different I look," I said while admiring my hair's new, sleek texture.

"Your husband is going to be all over you when he gets home from work."

Yes, he was. He had a late meeting, so I made sure Venus was tucked in her bed by eight, and I was clothed in my sheer white bra and panties by a quarter after. I met him at the door with a kiss that said more than hello.

He reciprocated the kiss, but quickly pulled back to examine my hair. "What did you do? I thought you said you were just coloring it?"

I explained the impulsive moment with a smile that was smacked off my face before the period reached the end of my last sentence. That was the most unexpected blow he's given me since the very first time.

I thought we were past that. My last black eye was at the end of January, and here it was June. We've had two weekend getaways since then, dined out more often than usual, made love without a hitch ninety percent of the time, and resumed our movie nights on Saturdays from the comfort of our cozy bed. Never ever did I expect to see the back of his hand coming at my face.

"Don't you ever take my money and do some shit like that!" he yelled.

*Great. I guess the meeting didn't go well*, I thought.

"I didn't use *your* money, as you call it."

"All the money you have is my money. That's my company you work for. If my dad doesn't sign your checks, you don't get paid."

*Right. And that's why it's your dad's company and not yours.*

"Why did you cut all your hair off? You look fuckin' baldheaded."

213

"All my hair isn't gone. You're being dramatic. I wanted a change...and I like it."

"Who else likes it? Did you do this for another man?"

"WHAT?" I exclaimed. "Don't even go there, Vaughn. Pick up a recent magazine, and you'll see Victoria Beckham rocking this same style."

"Did I ever tell you that I like Victoria Beckham? Do I give a damn about Victoria Beckham? Hell no. You never cared about her either, so who does? Since when do you model yourself after celebrities?"

He breathed hot air from his nose onto mine, waiting for answers to absurd questions I refused to entertain.

"I swear to God, Willow, if I find out you've been messin' around on me, you better go to the nearest plastic surgeon, change your face, and disappear."

"Why does everything I do have to be about you? I didn't cut my hair to please you or to spite you. *I* liked it, so I took a chance." I looked down at my bra and noticed the left cup was stained with blood that dripped from my lip. "This is uncalled for. This is what I mean. You're no better than that idiot Dave."

"And you're no better than your mother. I bet you have another baby out there somewhere. Put some fuckin' clothes on. You're not turnin' me on. You're makin' me sick. You think I don't notice shit, but I do. You don't even feel the same no more. I didn't say nothin' because I thought it was my imagination, but the truth always comes out."

*Probably because when you can't get it up, I have to use my vibrator that's much thicker than you.* "You're bipolar," I said, bracing for another hit.

He pushed past me, knocking me down. I landed awkwardly on the bottom two stairs and was briefly paralyzed by the sharp pain that shot up my spine. When I was able to move, I walked to the laundry room and pulled some jean shorts and a t-shirt from the dryer. All of my shoes were upstairs, so I also grabbed a pair of socks and left the house just like that to avoid Part Two of his mania.

*****

Crystal came to the door in her swimsuit as Martha stood nearby with wide eyes. She looked me up and down. "What the hell?"

I stepped inside and grabbed a handful of my hair. "Don't you like this cut, especially with this color?"

"Yeah, it's cute, but the color doesn't draw as much attention as the bloody red hue on your busted lip. Get in the damn house."

She pulled me by the arm, and we traveled to the pool room. She unfolded a towel and used it to replace the wet one around her waist. She then opened the freezer in the kitchenette and filled a smaller towel with ice. "Here."

I held the wrap against my lip and sat on the bench.

"How many more times, Milky? Do you have a quota to meet? Are you trying to set a world record for taking the most shit?"

"This came out of nowhere. I don't even know what to tell you right now."

"Look at what the hell you have on. Where are your shoes? This is stupid. I'm tellin' Mama," she said, standing, I assumed, to go get a phone.

"No!" I begged, grabbing her arm and yanking her back onto the bench. "That's not your place. I'll tell her when it concerns her. Every couple reaches bumps in the road. Have you told her the truth about Dante and Naptown New Booty? You didn't tell her you think he really cheated."

"Don't compare us to y'all. This isn't a bump in the road. It's a bump on your face. How many bumps will it take before you decide you've had enough or at least give his ass a matching bump?"

215

"I took my vows seriously, Crystal. God doesn't honor divorce just because times get hard."

"Last time I checked, God didn't honor domestic violence, either. Even if I go along with your bump in the road metaphor, your bumps are more like big-ass potholes that catapult your ass out the car, and your silly ass keeps walking back to the car to see what'll happen the next time you reach a pothole. This shit is beyond out of hand. I'm beginning to think you're suffering from an ongoing third-degree concussion, because your brain is clearly traumatized. Has he ever DDT'd you? Maybe you need a CT-scan."

We used to watch wrestling faithfully as children, so I immediately recognized her quip. It seemed she was full of them today.

"I don't come to you to be criticized, Crystal. There was a time when you would listen because you knew that's why I came to you. Nothing has changed on my end. I just need you to listen. Maybe you should do that instead of cracking jokes."

"Well, that's some selfish shit. And if I was joking, I'd be laughing right now. *Maybe* I can't handle just listening to your stories of being pounded on. Maybe that shit gets old to me, even though it seems brand new to you every time you relay it. And maybe, just maybe, I have more self-worth than you, and I'm hoping you'll ask me if you can borrow some."

"Wow," I said, removing my keys from my purse before flinging it onto my shoulder. Though I tried to leave before my face turned red and my tears fell, the tickles I felt on my cheek were a clear sign that I was moving too slowly. Crystal's words had never stung this much in the past.

"Are you crying?" she asked with more disgust than sympathy.

"I don't have anything to say to you right now," I replied on my way to the door.

216

"But you'll go home and lay up with Vaughn, right? He'll be gyrating on top of you tonight after he apologizes, right? My words make you want to leave me alone, but his fists don't give you that same reaction? Get out of my house. You'll never know what hurt is until you feel what I'm feeling right now. I can't believe you."

I didn't bother taking the long way to the front door. Instead, I exited from the pool room. As the door slammed behind me, I released the sobs that were caught in my throat. I can't explain why I feel the way I do. I don't know why I still love Vaughn through all the pain he's caused me. Crystal's probably right. Mrs. Ella's right, too. I'm a glutton for punishment. I have justification to leave my marriage, but I haven't done it and don't have any plans to…and I can't explain why outside of saying I love Vaughn with all my heart. Humph. Perhaps that's my issue. I gave him all of my love and forgot to save some for myself.

I drove home in silence, thinking of the word God had just given, thinking of how I was still going to ignore it or at least downplay it because it's not what I wanted to hear.

217

# DANA

We purposely flew at night so we'd land in Vegas when The Strip was lit. I tried not to gawk at the illuminated signs and fancy architectural designs as I looked out the plane window, but my eyes had never seen such a sight. Crystal and Willow were right. I was in love with the city already.

A limo met us at the airport and drove us to our private villa at the Bellagio. Even though Crystal has been married to Dante for quite some time and has the best of everything, the magnitude of her status was clearly beyond my perception until we took the private road that led to our personal paradise.

"Well, what do you think, birthday girl?" she asked as we stepped inside the house.

"I can't believe you did this for me," I said behind the hand cupped over my mouth. "I thought we were getting a suite inside the hotel. This is a house!"

She winked. "I told you we were doing it big."

"This is humongous, not big," I said, admiring the welcome presentation of fresh fruit, nuts, and chocolates.

"You did go all out, sis," Willow said, pivoting on her left foot to get a panoramic view.

218

The place was over-accommodating. The three bedrooms were sufficient, but the seven bathrooms made me feel like we should have a rotation to make use of them all or at least walk in and flush the toilet a couple times a day in the extra ones. The dining room looked like it could have been modeled after the Queen of England's, with its exquisite place settings, bronze candle stands, and European-style décor.

My eyes subtly seeped orgasmic tears as I toured the space. I felt like I was sleepwalking, exploring a dreamland while awake. I admired the place with all of my senses, inhaling the scent from the fresh flowers situated in the foyer, satisfying my tactile cravings with a stroke of the velvety couch, relishing the barely audible hum of the lights in our private pool, tasting the sweetness of the good life.

Crystal gave us a verbal itinerary for the following twenty-four hours. We would freshen up and hit The Strip for some warm-up gambling, come back for a few hours of sleep, wake up to breakfast prepared by our personal butler, and enjoy two hours of free time to make use of the pool, whirlpool, workout facility, or home theater. After that, we'd get our massages and then return to The Strip.

Crystal's rules: limited cell phone use, no watches, no husbands, no limits. We were there to have a good time, and distractions from that goal were prohibited. I had one rule of my own for Crystal and Willow: no arguing. They had agreed to squash their differences for the sake of my birthday, but I made a secret bet with myself that Crystal would breach that agreement by day two.

After choosing my room, I decided to make use of the dresser that was provided. Why live out of a suitcase when you don't have to? I unpacked the main compartment and then checked the smaller ones to make sure I didn't forget to remove anything. As I smoothed my hand over the upper pocket on the outside of the luggage, I felt something. Its measurements seemed to be similar to a deck of cards, but it felt much too hard to be such an item. I unzipped the pocket expecting to find one of Chase or Dalvin's toys, but found a mini-DV videotape instead.

I didn't remember ever putting it there, and it wasn't labeled. I shrugged and placed it back in the pocket, figuring I could play it when I returned home. For all I knew, it was a blank tape that the boys placed there while they were playing one of their secret mission games.

Crystal came into the room and grabbed me by my wrist as I considered other ways the mystery tape could've gotten into my suitcase. "Come here." She led me into the bathroom and pointed to a little door that looked similar to a mini refrigerator. "Open it."

Thinking I would find bottles of wine, I grasped the surprisingly warm handle and pulled. Instead, there were four perfectly folded towels inside. It was a towel warmer— the one thing Crystal has wanted Dante to get in their bathroom for what seems like an eternity. I laughed.

"Tell me that is not the shit," she said matter-of-factly. "They're in every bedroom."

"Your whole house is the shit, Crys. No...*both* of your houses are the shit."

She laughed. "You know what I mean."

When she first told me about having a towel warmer in her house, I thought it was totally ridiculous. After seeing that one, though, I couldn't wait to feel that warm Egyptian cotton wrapped around me when I stepped out of the shower.

"They do feel nice," I said, resting my hand on the top towel.

"See? If you didn't clown me so much about wanting one, maybe you would've gotten one for your birthday."

"Shut up," I replied. "How are you gonna get me one when you haven't gotten yourself one?"

220

We laughed again. I felt like we were back at IU in our dorm; silly, carefree, and ready for adventure.

"Where's Milky?" I asked.

"She's probably hiding in the courtyard behind a bush, talking to Vaughn. Let me go find her. Can you be ready in twenty minutes?"

"Yes!"

I could've been ready in ten. I was so ready to be free, so overdue for unadulterated fun. This trip was right on time. Quickly, I freshened up and met the girls at the front door. Ric called just as the Hummer limo arrived.

"You just caught me. I'm about to turn my phone off. What's up?" I asked.

"Damn. It's like that?"

"This is my vacation."

"Alright then. I didn't want nothin'. I got your message sayin' you touched down, and I was just checkin' on you. We just got in from the Fun Center."

"Okay. I'll call the boys tomorrow. Kiss them for me."

"No kisses for me?"

I hung up as if I didn't hear him and pressed the End button until the phone powered off. Less than ten minutes later, we were getting dropped off at Mandalay Bay to let the games begin.

We returned to the villa at 4:30 a.m., and I crashed before I could change clothes. I woke up six hours later to the smell of home fries and biscuits. Still dressed from the previous night, I washed my face and ventured into the common area to see who was throwing down in the kitchen. *I forgot Crystal said we have our own butler*, I thought, while waving to the stranger at the stove. He asked if I cared for an omelet, and after I glanced at the one on Willow's plate, my answer was, "Yes," without a doubt.

We were out the door by one and had hit three casinos by five. I'm not a gambler, but I love the atmosphere. There's

221

a certain rush that comes with being in the casino, and it makes you want to participate in the action. Lucky for me, the action was putting more money in my pockets.

As we sat at the Blackjack table with an older gentleman from Australia, I delighted in people-watching, sipping free drinks, and stacking chips. I was on a roll, even though I really didn't know what I was doing.

I was startled by a strong vibration in my lap, followed by my text message tone. I pulled the phone from my purse and read a text from Lorenzo. *You've got the best trainer in the world. Flew all the way out here to make sure you're keepin' that booty poked out.*

It was our inside joke I usually laughed at, referring to the correct posture for performing squats. This time, I couldn't laugh.

"What in the world?" I mumbled.

"No cell phones at the table, ma'am," the dealer snapped.

I apologized and placed the phone back in my purse.

"What was that all about?" Willow asked.

I sighed. "I guess Lorenzo's here."

"Here in the Mirage, or here in Vegas?" Crystal inquired.

"Vegas. I can't believe this," I said, massaging my brow.

Willow's eyes narrowed. "Have you been holding out on us? What's up with you two?"

I doubled down on my hand at the suggestion of the dealer and won big. "Y'all know I've had a crush on him since we met. That's old news. But things are a little different between us now."

"How different?" Crystal asked.

"We've spent a lot of time together over the past few months, so naturally, we've become closer."

222

"Vertical-hug close or horizontal-hug close?" Crystal asked. "Wait. You can do that vertically, too. Okay…church-hug close or hotel-hug close?"

"So it's no coincidence that he's here," Willow gathered.

"I'll be damned. You gave it up to ol' Lorenzo. Quietly, that was a long time coming. Was it good?" Crystal asked before I could answer either question.

"Huh?"

"This is me, sweet pea. You had that same look on your face when you didn't want to tell me you screwed Eddie our sophomore year. You can't fool me. Ric ain't here. Answer my question. Was it good?"

I glanced at the dealer, who tried her best to act like she wasn't listening. "Not really. I don't know. Maybe it was, but I didn't do it to get off. The whole thing was about revenge."

"Oh, no, Dana," Willow groaned with disappointment.

"So when was this? We need to wrap this game up so we can go talk," Crystal said. "I feel like I've read the last chapter of a book I didn't know the title of."

"You haven't missed much. It was one time. Like I said, I was trying to get back at Ric."

"Vengeance is mine, sayeth the Lord," Willow said.

Crystal leaned closer to Willow. "And I love the Lord, but I will punch you in the face if you quote another scripture while we're in Sin City."

"Trust me. God and I had a long talk after the deed was done. I felt like hell," I directed at Willow.

"I can't relate to that, honey. I feel great after I get done with Nigel," Crystal said, fanning herself as Willow sucked her teeth. "Don't judge me. I'm a descendent of Eve. It's her fault I like forbidden fruit."

"You are going straight to hell for that one," Willow replied.

"No, I have to stop and pick up Vaughn first."

I tuned them out as my phone vibrated again. I wanted to leave the table so I could text Lorenzo back, but I was on fire. As I hit hand after hand, my mind entertained a number of scenarios about how his presence would affect my Vegas experience.

"I can't imagine why he would seriously travel here. I was just playing when I told him he should come, too," I thought out loud.

"That good-good got him sprung!" Crystal said as she accepted another drink from the waitress dressed in a red and black leotard, fishnet pantyhose, and stilettos.

I laughed and shook my head. "Whatever. It can't be that good if my husband is out chasing new booty." I paused to place my next bet, and after I set it down, I had a revelation. "That's it! I'm Lorenzo's new booty. I forgot what that feels like. Ugh," I groaned before collecting my winnings. "I don't know if I'm in the mood for this. I don't need a stalker."

"*New* booty doesn't make a man fly across the country, boo. *Good* new booty...will. You must've pulled out your bag of tricks!"

*Maybe a couple*, I thought as I recalled my strip tease and the trail of honey I traced with my tongue.

"Listen here, rookie," Crystal said, wrapping her arm around my shoulders. "You have to prepare for stuff like this. There's always a chance that you'll give the goodies to a dude who's just plain crazy or who isn't used to gettin' the good-good. Now you have to pray that he falls under Category B. That's what you get for withholding information. You're trying to dabble in an area you know nothing about. You *know* you should've talked to me first."

"Sign up for her class, Adultery 101: Techniques of the Master, for only $99.95," Willow said, rolling her eyes.

Crystal stopped just before she took another sip of her drink. "Or she can take your class for free; Punching Bag

301: Mastering the Art of Escaping a Choke Hold. I'm sure you'll even throw in 101 and 201 as an added bonus if she wants to learn how to make the perfect ice bag or cover up a black eye with one hand tied behind her back."

"What a bitch," Willow said.

"Don't start none, won't be none," Crystal replied.

"Ladies, ladies, come on now. We discussed this. This is my birthday trip. No drama allowed. Low blows are banned."

I silently thanked God that I'm an only child as we cashed out at the table and went to redeem our winnings.

*****

My fear that Lorenzo was a clingy and borderline psycho man was settled once I finally spoke with him. His frat brothers had access to an extra buddy pass if he wanted to join them for a bachelor party, and he accepted. I was pleased to hear he didn't follow me to Vegas, though he admitted he ultimately based his decision on my presence.

I invited him to the villa that night. After introducing him to the girls and giving him a tour of the inside, we made drinks at the bar and ventured outside. As we circled the terrace, I showed off the topiary shrubs and private pool as if it were mine.

"Did you bring a bathing suit?" he asked.

"Yeah, but I'm not much of a swimmer. I just brought it so I can show off my new figure," I replied.

He laughed. "Are you gonna use that fitness room while you're here?"

"I already did this morning, thank you very much."

"That'a girl."

"Wait! You were gonna make me workout?" I smacked him on his chest. "I thought you just wanted to take a casual swim."

225

"Nothing's casual about me except my clothes, sweetheart."

He looked into my eyes, and I got the feeling he was talking about the night he viewed as magic and I viewed as a mistake.

"Go hard or go home, huh?" I said with a nervous laugh.

We sat at one of the patio tables, and he pulled out a deck of cards. When we had talked earlier, I told him how I won a little money playing Blackjack, but that I was afraid to play again because I only had luck on my side. I have no clue about the actual strategy of the game. I just know my cards need to equal twenty-one or get pretty damn close. After a half-hour crash course, I knew all about bust cards, doubling down, and when to split. I felt confident enough to hit the tables again in the morning when we headed to MGM. I wanted to call for the limo right then, but figured I shouldn't be in such a hurry to lose my money.

"Are they expecting you back any particular time?" I asked.

"Nah. The party isn't until tomorrow night," he replied.

I offered him another drink, but he declined, saying he had been drinking all day at the casinos. I could relate, so I grabbed us a couple bottled waters from the mini refrigerator on the deck.

We shared a chaise and watched the water flow down the waterfall and into the pool. Its sound promoted tranquility, a feeling that had become so unfamiliar to me. I lounged between Lorenzo's legs with my head resting on his chest. He wrapped his arms around my shoulders, clasping his hands between my breasts.

"I know they do quickie weddings here. You think they do quickie divorces?" he asked, while running his fingers up my forearms. I chuckled. "I'm for real. You're perfect. I can't find a woman like you to save my life."

226

I closed my eyes and listened to his heartbeat accompany the rest of his words. The vibration from the bass in his voice nearly lulled me to sleep as we talked about our futures and shared our wildest dreams. Lorenzo's appeal lies in his authenticity and his quest to be more than a great man. He strives to be phenomenal, and a phenomenal man is a keeper. Too bad you can't keep what you don't have.

We fell asleep in the cabana, but woke up at about three. Lorenzo spent the rest of the night in my room, in the bed…with me. Our night was one of innocence. He held me securely between his bulky biceps, and I held on to the feeling he leased to me. Intimacy happened in Vegas, and I didn't want to leave it there. If what happens in Vegas stays in Vegas, maybe Lorenzo and I should've been applying for Nevada driver's licenses and looking at houses.

# CRYSTAL

Dana came outside as I was getting out of the pool. I had been out there since eight o'clock because I wanted to get in a good swim before breakfast. As I expected, I exited the water feeling revived and ready for another fifteen-hour day on The Strip and at the outlet mall.

"I don't know why you didn't seriously pursue swimming after college," Dana said as I dried off. "It's nine in the morning, and you're out here like a little fish."

"I don't know any swimmers who are millionaires," I replied. "I like it this way. Sometimes when you make a career of doing something you love, you end up hating it. Too much pressure. Takes the fun out of it."

"I guess."

"So how was your night with Lorenzo?"

"It was nice." Her smile portrayed something much more than nice.

"I knew it! You ain't gon' learn. Keep on, and he'll show up at your house unannounced," I warned.

"We didn't do anything, Crys. Well, we connected on a level I wasn't expecting to reach, but we didn't get sexual. He barely kissed me."

Hearing the limo pull away, I squinted at Dana.

"I swear! We didn't. It was so pure, Crys. I can't believe I was thinking he came out here on some stalker stuff."

"But he stayed the night, right? Did he sleep with you?"

"Yes, but he was a gentleman. If I'm guilty of anything, it's intimacy. Lying beside him felt natural. We talked until we fell asleep. He knew just how to hold me, and he didn't let go of me until a half hour ago."

"You dig him. It's more than a physical attraction. It's all in your voice."

A sigh escaped her lips. "The crazy thing is I could place him on reserve if I wanted to. If I say the right things, Lorenzo would wait for me to get a divorce so we can be together."

"Whoa! Divorce? That's what you're on now?"

She shrugged. "Let's be honest. It's only a matter of time. I hope it doesn't come to that, but slapping Ric on the wrist every time he fucks up has gotten old. You know what this feels like? I feel like I'm unhappy with my cell phone carrier, but since I've been with them for so long, I feel a sense of loyalty and am unsure if I wanna leave."

"For fear the other carrier will give you the same problems?"

"Right. Or better yet, I feel like I'm locked in a contract with my carrier, and I have this other carrier wooing me with features I can't access right now. If I terminate my contract early, I lose. If I wait it out, knowing I'm leaving that company anyway, I win. No penalties."

"Damn, D. I didn't know you were really thinking of letting Slick Ric go. I'm not about to lie and say I'm sorry to hear it. I just want you to do what makes you happy."

"Nothing's in stone. I'm just evaluating the situation and weighing my options."

229

"There's nothing wrong with that. And you'll have plenty of options swinging their ding-dings in your face tonight at the strip club."

We giggled like school girls at the cafeteria table, unable to contain ourselves. I stretched my arms to the sky and squinted to avoid being blinded by the morning sun.

"I'ma go see if Milky is still alive. We might as well get our showers, and I'll page Gustavo so he can come make us breakfast."

"That's what I need to talk to you about real quick. Y'all can't be—"

"I'm done. I promise. I'm not gonna spoil your birthday trip," I replied.

"Yeah, that, and I want to talk to you about what's going on with her. I was gonna bring it up when y'all got into it before the trip, but I didn't want to overstep. After y'all gave the dealer a show at the table, though, I figured I better say something.

"I know she pisses you off, but you need to be more sensitive toward her," Dana said. "You're killing her with your shots about domestic violence."

"I try, D, but it's hard. Have you ever had to sit back and watch someone you love endure constant abuse? I was sensitive the first few times. Now, I'm just pissed."

"To answer your question, yes, I have. My father whooped on my mother ever since I can remember. I've seen the other side. It's not easy. She's not living in blissful ignorance, Crys. She's confused. She's scared. Most of all, she's still in love. My mom left when she was ready. When she knew she was strong enough to stay away, she left and never looked back. *Please* be more sensitive to Milky's situation."

I didn't know Dana's mom had been through that. Just looking at Ms. Bell, you wouldn't guess it.

"How do you know when to step in?" I asked. "I'm afraid he's gonna go too far one day."

Dana shrugged slowly. "I can't tell you that. It was different for me because I lived in the same household. I was able to run interference when things escalated. That's your sister. I can't tell you to stop being protective. Just watch how you speak to her, because if she stops confiding in you, you'll really be in the dark and have no way of determining whether you should intervene."

She was right. I'd been hitting my sister with gut punches and expecting her not to block them. I'd gone from tough love to ruthless love and was pushing her away.

*****

"Oh, hell no. Wait, ladies. I have to change," I told them, removing my heels. We were congregating in my room because I was the last one to get dressed, as usual.

"Why? That catsuit is hot," Milky said.

"Thank you, but the camel toe is not! Look at this!" I practiced a few dance moves for them. "The men will be grabbin' at my young lady instead of my booty, girl."

Dana doubled over with laughter, almost falling to the floor. I changed into Plan B, an even hotter silver mini dress that didn't shy away from showing my long legs.

Lonnie met us at the villa just before the limo showed up. He's a makeup artist I met at a video shoot when Dante first started out. We clicked like two old girlfriends and have stayed in touch ever since. I always link up with him when I'm in Vegas so he can show me a good time. I warned the ladies that they had better have their walks down, because on any given day, if Lonnie was feeling fierce, he'd work the hell out of some heels and put a woman to shame. They understood what I meant when he arrived wearing a black sequined top that was unbuttoned, baring his smooth chest, and skinny jeans with black rhinestones on the pockets.

"Y'all ready to shut this city down?" he asked after the introductions.

"Hell yeah. Let's do it. Where to first?" I asked.

"We'll hit Palms since there are so many options. I like to start off with Rain. There's so much damn energy in there, you can't help but shake your ass, honey."

While we were in the limo, my phone rang. Milky rolled her eyes, while Dana sang along to the "Boyfriend #2" ringtone.

"Let me guess. It's Nigel," Milky said

"Girl, yeah. I forgot my phone was even on," I replied before turning it off. "I don't have no kids, and I definitely ain't answerin' it in the club."

"You still turnin' that cutie out?" Lonnie asked.

I responded with a wink as Milky groaned.

"What's wrong? Posh Spice don't like your little yum yum on the side?" he asked. Dana and I fell out laughing, and Milky couldn't help but laugh a little, too. "Don't hate, honey. You better find you a little sexy somethin' out here who'll bend it like Beckham. Ow!" he said, then struck a pose with his hands in the air, lips pursed, and hip shifted to the right.

"I'm married," Milky replied.

"Umph. Is he?" He giggled. "What's his name? I may know him."

"Okay, too far," I intervened, still laughing.

Minutes later, we were at Rain, strolling confidently to the front of the line. We stayed for about an hour and then moved on to Ghostbar. We went straight to the V.I.P. area to avoid the crowd. I danced in place with my drink near the top of the steps and briefly glanced around to see if I recognized anyone.

When I turned to ask Lonnie if the tall guy in the corner played for the Celtics, he was covering his mouth as if he were shocked. I followed his eyes and saw a girl's head buried in some guy's lap.

"These broads are nasty out here," I yelled in his ear. "I know that stuff goes on in V.I.P., but back home, they at least try to be more discreet. Damn!"

I tapped Dana on the arm and pointed in the couple's direction, and she directed Milky's attention to them. Over the spectacle, I walked toward the rail and looked down at the sea of people, thinking of how hot they must have been. It was so packed there was barely room to dance. I turned to comment on the drag queen in a hideous hot pink outfit, but saw that everyone was still looking at the live porno.

"Will y'all stop staring at them?" I shouted from three feet away.

Just then, the guys that were blocking my view walked away and I could see that the man being pleasured was my husband. The girl slid up his body and planted kisses all over his face. For the first time in my life, I wished someone had put a hallucinogen in my drink. She whispered something in his ear and kissed him in the mouth. He signaled for her to wait, then handed her money from his pocket. She kissed him again on his cheek before grabbing the tray on the nearby table and loading it with empty glasses. I took note of her outfit and compared it to those of the women working the area near one of the bars on the lower level. She worked there!

Dante checked his pants for spillage as I obstructed the slut's path.

"You need something to wash that down with?" I asked as Dana, Milky, and Lonnie nervously looked on.

"Excuse me?" she said, scrunching her face.

"That sperm you just swallowed. His tends to be a little extra salty," I replied. As soon as she opened her mouth to speak, I doused her face with the remainder of my Apple

233

Martini. "Thirsty ho." Since there was no room on her tray for my empty glass, I threw it at her nose, hoping I broke it.

Before she could get her bearings together to react, I was in Dante's face. "Hey! Fancy meeting you here. I thought you were supposed to be in L.A."

"Hey...baby...I meant to let you know we stopped here first. I just got caught up with—"

"Getting your dick sucked?"

The wrinkles in his forehead did a poor job of conveying his phony confusion. "What?"

"You know the rules, huh? Since when is getting your dick sucked publicly *and* without a condom on the list of allowable behavior? Are you still wondering why I don't do it anymore?"

"Crystal, let's not do this here," he replied nervously.

"And she did that shit so well you had to tip her! I don't think you've ever handed me anything but a towel."

The deejay got on the mic. "Hey, laaaadies! I just got word that ya boy Dante is in the building! Show him some love! You know how we do in Vegas," he said before playing Dante's newest single.

The spotlight reached us as I took off my ring. "I'll tell you what. When she comes back with your next bottle, give her this. If she's that damn bad, she deserves to be tipped for life."

I threw the ring straight up in the air and started to walk away. Dante grabbed my wrist and yanked me toward him. As I fought to break free, I accidentally backhanded him. With no regrets, I shot him a venomous glare.

"Get back to your hoes."

Members of Dante's entourage looked on with wide eyes. The dancers shook their heads as if they knew he'd get caught one day. The girlfriends of the bass player and keyboardist called out to me. Nigel came into view as I tore past the girls who were waiting to get a closer look at Dante.

234

I pushed away his outstretched hand, but didn't ignore the concern in his eyes. Later, I would be more rational, but at the time, they were all a part of Dante's circus, all for him and against me.

Knowing and seeing are two totally different monsters. I've known about Dante's whorish lifestyle since college. Many of the stories, he told me himself. But when I looked over and *saw* him, my knowledge became a reality. It was much like knowing that since you've been eating French fries every day you've gained weight, and then looking in the mirror after a few years and seeing that you're obese. Knowing comes from learning, but believing comes from seeing.

Lonnie, Milky, and Dana followed me outside, unsure of what to say. I leaned against the building and touched up my lipstick as we waited for our limo.

"Say something," Milky prompted. "That girl was on your man in the club. Please say something. You're too quiet. You're scaring me."

I blotted my lips. "He's not my man. He's just my husband."

"What?" she and Lonnie asked simultaneously.

"Wow. I think I actually know what you mean. That's the perfect way to put it," Dana said.

"I just have legal bragging rights to him. He's my glorified boyfriend." I turned to Lonnie. "So where are we going next?"

"To the damn police station if this limo doesn't hurry the hell up." He pointed discreetly to the squad car that pulled up with flashing lights. "That hussy probably called the boys on you."

Our getaway car arrived seconds later as the two cops entered the club. Dante came outside with Manny, his head security guard. "Crystal!" he yelled just as I placed one foot inside the car.

"Unless Ashton Kutcher is about to run down this sidewalk and say I've been Punk'd, you can turn back around," I replied. "You don't have a thing to say to me."

He approached me, stopping just outside of my arm's span. "We have to talk. I'm staying at the Hard Rock in the Altered States Penthouse." He dug in his back pocket. "Here's the key."

I stared at it, tempted to accept it, but afraid of what I might do with it. "If you value your life at all, you'll put that back in your pocket. Manny, to ensure his complete protection, you may wanna sleep with him tonight. I'm talkin' in the same bed. We've stayed at the Hard Rock plenty of times, and I know a few of the managers. I don't need a key if I wanna get to him. Feel me?"

"Yes, ma'am. I think we should go back in, Mr. Moss. Try to enjoy the rest of your evening, Mrs. Moss."

I thanked him and looked at Dante one last time. "Zip up your damn pants," I said before joining everyone else inside of the vehicle.

Dana rested her hand on my thigh. "Crys, let's just go back to the house."

"Why? Because of this? Un uh. If y'all are tired, that's different, but that monkey and his bitch ain't stoppin' our show. I don't do that sulking mess. Been there, done that; bought the t-shirt and wore it 'til it was faded. It solves nothing."

"I hear that, honey," Lonnie cheered.

"Is Tao poppin' tonight?" I asked.

"There's only one way to find out," he said. "Driver, we're going to the Venetian."

I pretended to be brave and unaffected because Milky and Dana look to me for strength, but I was sick inside. I needed to keep the party going, though, because once it ended, I would feel the pain.

I see now why some of the industry wives are addicted to pain killers. They must think OxyContin, Vicodin, and Percocet can ease the pain in their hearts, but the pills only alter their state of mind. Contrary to what seems reasonable, heartbreak isn't on any doctor's list of chronic illnesses. If the ladies took a moment to think about it, they're addicted because they're chasing relief that isn't there.

Quite frankly, I would need anesthesia to ease this pain. Knock me out and give me a drug to erase my memory, too. I'm not sure if I would wish this feeling on my worst enemy, because it's almost unbearable to pretend it is bearable. The only thing that was keeping me together was the constant flow of alcohol—the Novocain equivalent for my heart.

Tao was live. I substituted sweat for tears as I partied with the twenty-something'ers like I was one of them again. Dana and Milky even let loose and joined me on the dance floor for a while. Lonnie spent most of the night in the corner with some aspiring model gentleman from California.

We wrapped things up shortly after three. Lonnie stayed behind with his new friend, while the girls and I went back to our villa. I kept the smile on my face until I reached my room. As soon as I closed the door, I lay on the bed, buried my face in the pillow, and screamed.

Meanwhile, Dante was still texting me. I made the mistake of turning my phone on during the ride home, and it beeped continuously with missed messages from him in a two-hour span. There were even a couple messages from Nigel, asking if I was okay.

At this point, Dante was only repeating himself. I'd read all the other ones. He was sorry. He made a stupid mistake. He got caught up in the moment. He'd had too much to drink. He was only at the Palms in the first place because he was recording in the studio on the premises. He was gonna call me, but got sidetracked by a group of fans. He wants me to come to his hotel room, even if it's to kick his ass. Where

237

am I staying? He'll come to me. Why won't I at least talk to him?

How many times can you ask the same questions? Apparently a lot. I wasn't going to reply, but I wanted to get one thing out before I turned my phone off: *I'm on vacation. Why don't you text the girl who was sucking your dick?*

In the shower, I combined my tears with the water like I wanted to hide them from myself. I stood in place with the showerhead aimed at my neck and chest. The lukewarm water attempted to cool down my temperament and warm my cold spirit. It didn't help much. I could've moved the handle to either temperature extreme and felt nothing. Nevertheless, in the morning, I'd have to let it go. Crying about things you can't control only makes you lose focus of the things you can control.

Farah never touched on this when we talked about industry wife etiquette. I planned to call her in the morning to see if she had any advice to lend. Unfortunately, marriages in the world of entertainment are similar to games of strategy. My next move would set the standard for my future dealings with Dante, and it needed to be a power move. The one move I was sure of was the one I was going to make to the bed. The sooner I could get to sleep, the sooner I could dream about something less painful, like a leg amputation or hysterectomy.

*Goodnight, pain. I'll feel you in the morning.*

# WILLOW (MILKY)

*Dirty Dish* printed a picture of Crystal's wedding ring lying on the floor of the V.I.P. area next to a broken glass. BET News reported that Crystal assaulted the girl we saw performing oral sex on Dante and fled the club shortly after. TMZ had reports of the girl filing charges against Crystal and posted an exclusive twenty-second clip of the act that someone captured on their cell phone. Though it was poorly lit and unsteady, one thing was clear: some girl's head was bobbing up and down in a man's lap. And since I was there, I knew it was who they claimed it was. The most disturbing exposé, for Dante at least, was TMZ's exclusive side-by-side pictures of him and the girl from Indianapolis that showed they have something in common: cold sores. I didn't believe that one. I've never seen Dante with a cold sore, and if he ever did have one, so what? Cold sores are common. Just because they're associated with the herpes virus doesn't mean they're related to sex.

I swear ignorant people should be banned from communicating sometimes. Because of the pictures that were most likely altered and a fabricated story of Dante's relationship with that girl, my sister's life had become a

239

mockery for the media. We usually talk every day. Yet, since we've returned from Vegas, I've talked to her only once. And that was because I drove to her house and pounded on the door until Martha let me in. I found her upstairs in one of the guest rooms, sitting at the computer desk, working on a spreadsheet. She acted as if nothing was wrong and said she just had a ton of work to catch up on after coming back from vacation. She asked if I could come back or call later because she didn't have time to waste. Now, a week later, she won't answer either of her phones, and LaToya said she hasn't been working with the girls at Something to Do.

So much for 'what happens in Vegas stays in Vegas.' I even found out my privacy was invaded when Vaughn made comments about outfits and shoes I wore there while we lay in bed on the night of our return. He calls my stilettos "ho shoes" because the heels are so high, and since I wore them while I was in Vegas, that must've made me a ho. I can only wear those shoes when I'm not with him because he has a complex about his height. I'm 5'9" and he's 5"11", so I'm limited to a two-inch heel when we go out. I remember trying a three-inch pump one evening and being tripped because I was "trying to make him look like a little man."

He seemed to be amused by all the information he knew about the shows we attended and the casinos we frequented, but I didn't find a thing funny. He had someone spying on me the whole time as if I'm not trustworthy. What a slap in the face. I have been too honest according to most standards, totally embracing the oneness of marriage…except for the secret money on the side I've put away. I'm glad I did. I don't feel guilty now that I've learned my husband doesn't trust me.

I was by far the best-behaved on the trip. At the strip club, I purposely sat behind Dana and Crystal so any action that came our way would be directed at them. At the nightclubs, I stayed in V.I.P. and danced by myself. At the casinos, I gambled conservatively and drank responsibly. I bet the spy was bored out of his mind watching me do a bunch of nothing.

When I asked him if he had someone spying on me here, he winked at me and said, "You never know who's watching, doll. Just make sure you stay on your best behavior."

I was flabbergasted. I didn't need to ask, "Or what?" because I already knew. The thought alone of someone misinterpreting an innocent exchange between me and another man elicited a chill through my body that almost sent me into hypothermia.

*****

Dana and I rode the elevator to the twenty-third floor as Crystal had instructed. Her phone call was cryptic and way too vague, but I was happy she had finally reached out to us. Neither of us knew what we were in for, but the answer was only a few steps away. We approached room 2309, and before we knocked, Crystal opened the door.

"Hey, ladies! I hope you're hungry. I made pasta salad."

"Is this a suite?" Dana asked as we trekked through the foyer and reached the lavishly furnished living area.

"Apartment," Crystal answered.

"Okay, you said that like we attended your apartment-warming party. What is this all about?" I asked.

"It's my escape. I've had it since March. Dante doesn't even know about it."

"My laundry room is my escape," Dana joked.

"Well, this is your escape now," Crystal replied. She pointed to two keys on the dining room table. "Those are for y'all."

Dana picked up her key immediately as I continued to question my sister. "What does this mean? Is this your first step toward leaving Dante?"

She finished loading the dishwasher. "Nope. It's an escape, just like I said."

"You saw him with another woman," I reminded her.

"Doing what I already knew he was doing. His only infraction was not wearing a condom while she did her thing."

"So if it's not a big deal, why are you here?" I asked.

"Because I'm overwhelmed with tabloid information right now, and if I'm around him, I may mess around and hurt him. You know I keep my baby loaded," she replied, referring to the gun she keeps in the bottom drawer of her nightstand.

I ran my hand across the marble countertop, trying not to look as uncomfortable as I felt.

"Well, I like your escape," Dana said.

"Y'all can use it any time. Bring the kids. The sofa lets out into a bed."

We were careful to let Crystal lead the conversation about the turmoil in her marriage. It seemed the only good news she shared was that the girl from Vegas had dropped all the charges against her.

"If the paparazzi spot Chris and Rihanna together again, the attention will shift back in their direction and I can go back home. They aren't letting up about Naptown New Booty, and Cheyenne said she dropped out of school because of all the media exposure. When a bitch goes into hiding, there's more to the story. I'd much rather remain in the dark about the whole thing at this point, because I'll be forced to make a decision."

"What's so wrong with that? That decision wouldn't even be hard. Stay or go? I don't see you staying," I said.

"No. Kill him in his sleep or while he's awake. That's the choice I'd have to make."

"I'd go with awake," Dana said.

"How is it that all three of us are unhappy? I feel like I should have researched the odds before I dove in," I said.

Dana nodded. "But the heart doesn't work like that."

"Doesn't it feel like you invested in a shitload of stock when it was worth thousands, and two weeks later, the market crashed?" Crystal asked.

"The only thing left to do then is fire your broker," I added.

Crystal turned to Dana and said, "You hear that? Did you catch that neck roll? Is my Milky getting her mind back? Is ol' Vaughn about to be fired?"

Laughing, Dana agreed with a nod.

"I'll admit I used to think pain is temporary but marriage is forever. Those days are gone. I guess I've had enough," I replied.

"If you're still guessing, you haven't had enough," Crystal said.

"No, I'm just stuck between if and when. I've done everything I can to help keep our marriage afloat, but I can't do it alone."

"Ain't that the story of my marriage," Dana agreed. "I'm not saying I'm the best wife, but I'm a damn good one. I cook, clean, take care of the boys, work a full-time job, *and* screw him on the regular. What the hell else does he need?"

"It's what he wants," Crystal stated.

"If he wants anything else, he's screwing a man. I give it to him however he wants, whenever he wants it. I have him convinced that I actually enjoy fellatio; we've experimented with almost every toy in the book; I stay wet; and I stay groomed. Hell, I walked around feeling like a nine-year-old for months because he asked me to wax everything. If that's not enough, I've even survived the anal sex he wants to perform at random. Tell me *that's* not taking one for the team."

"I mean, all men want more. Too much is never enough. Men aren't monogamous creatures," Crystal further explained.

"I don't believe that. How is that true when we're all supposed to be made in God's image?" Dana asked.

"You might wanna save that question for the angel directing traffic at the pearly gates. Do I look like one of the disciples?"

Dana burst into laughter. "I'm just saying I'm tired of understanding Ric's shortcomings. I know he's King Fuckup, and I know shit happens, but when shit lingers, it's time for a change. I'm not old school. I know couples who've been married fifty years, but it's just a number rather than an accomplishment. Back in the day, women shot their men for cheating on them and went on like nothing ever happened — like their husbands didn't have a few illegitimate children running around the same city. Then, the church honors their anniversary as if their marriage is really something to admire. I'm sorry, living in the same house for fifty years but sleeping in separate rooms for thirty doesn't count. I'm not gonna stay around for the sake of saving face. I want the real thing."

I nodded. "Mrs. Ella gave me some words from her pastor a long time ago. He said, 'Don't complain about the things you permit.' Vaughn is an asshole because I've never told him to stop being an asshole. Until a few months ago, I hadn't demanded any different from him. He's a great man, but I make up excuses for his behavior sometimes when there is no excuse."

"But after you did demand that he change, he still played knick-knack on your face after you cut your hair, and you're still there."

"Crystal!" Dana chastised.

"I wasn't tryin' to crack a joke. Y'all need to face it. There's no nice way to say, 'You got punched in the face.'

244

My question is, are you going to stop complaining or stop permitting?"

I didn't look up from my plate. "Both."

I've done an assessment. As the years have gone by, my battles with Vaughn have become greater in number and increasingly threatening, outweighing the good times as well as my tolerance. The last time he hit me, he didn't even show remorse.

For the first time in our four-year marriage, I've thought of leaving, if only to give him time to evaluate whether he wants a wife or a sparring partner. After he told me I was being followed in Vegas, I realized he's really crazy—not just insecure. I can handle insecure, but crazy folks should be under the care of trained professionals.

Crystal turned to Dana. "By the way, you owe me a hundred bucks."

"Why?" she asked.

"Remember our bet in college? You said you would never let a man put anything in your booty—not even his finger—and I said you would eventually. Don't think I wasn't paying attention while you were venting."

"Shut up. I am not paying you for that," Dana said.

"I accept checks, but prefer cash. You're lucky I'm not adding interest."

We laughed, but I became distracted by the televisions when I noticed a breaking news banner on the screen. "Wait. Turn that up real quick."

Crystal picked up the remote and increased the volume. The three of us sat in shock as the reporter announced that Michael Jackson was just pronounced dead after being rushed to the hospital in cardiac arrest. She was looking for someone else to take the spotlight off of Dante, but never did she imagine it would be the King of Pop and it would be because he died. No one said a word as we listened to the horrifying news. It was a tragedy to the world of music and

245

the millions of fans who grew up singing his songs and emulating his dance moves...including us.

"Well, Crys," Dana started, "I think the media is done with you and Dante."

"Yeah, but for once, I don't feel like toasting to that."

*****

"I think you're rushing her. She'll only get frustrated in kindergarten. She's not ready," Vaughn said after I told him how my meeting went with the child advocate and members of the elementary school's administration. We were discussing educational alternatives for Venus that would give her the learning support she needs while keeping her in the least restrictive learning environment.

When we first discussed kindergarten in the IEP meeting and she later underwent the screening, the school suggested she wait another year to allow her more time to mature. I would've agreed to that if Venus didn't have special needs, but that's what an IEP is in place for. It's an individualized education plan. It is the school district's responsibility to come up with a revised curriculum for her. My sentiment is, figure it out. I refused to let them undermine her intelligence by recommending she stay in preschool. No. They're going to do their jobs and give my baby a fair chance.

Vaughn would rather baby her as much as possible and handicap her abilities than let her strive to excel. He's been against speech therapy from day one, saying she'll talk when she's ready. It's as if he ignores her diagnosis. I wish it was that simple. I wish Venus was *choosing* not to speak correctly.

He has never stopped me from taking her to therapy, but he hasn't attended a session; and when I come home and report major milestones she has reached with her oral motor skills, he chalks up the success to her "growing up."

I listened to him go on and on about my "horrible" decision until I couldn't take any more. "If you feel this strongly, why haven't you been around for any of her evaluations or therapies? The only doctor appointments you attend are the ones where you get to be her hero after she gets a shot. What about the ones where I have to hear how far behind her speech is on the developmental chart? You're never around to hear the doctor explain her condition."

"Because I know my daughter, and I don't need no evaluation to tell me nothin'. Every child matures at a different rate. I don't believe in this miracle therapy you think you've found. I believe in God."

"And I don't?" I asked. *I guess since you've come back to church a few times, you feel qualified to challenge my faith,* I thought.

"I can't tell. Stop tryin' to fix her like she's broken. You always talk about what God can do, but you're steady tryin' to help Him. That's why I don't support all that crap you take her to. Now you're tellin' the people who do this for a living that she's ready to advance after they clearly told you she isn't."

"I'm not trying to help God, but God helps those who help themselves."

"What scripture is that? Is that in the Book of Willow?"

I shook my head with disgust. "You're in denial."

Before I knew it, we were engaging in our ugliest argument yet.

"Denial? You're the one in denial. You walk around here letting people call you something you're not every day. My stomach turns every time Crystal or Dana says that 'Milky' bullshit. You're a white girl from a rich neighborhood. Accept it. Your slutty-ass mama just didn't want you to cramp her style, so she left you outside. If she hadn't, you'd be somewhere with your rich white friends, looking for a rich white man to spoil you. You probably wouldn't have spoken to the Thornton's if you were standing next to them. I'm not gon' let you transfer your identity issues to our daughter. She is who she is."

He didn't stop there. He said it's not in my genes to be a good mother, and if Venus only had me to rely on, she'd be in trouble; said I'm lucky he saw past my flaws and was willing to work with me; said my graphic design skills are mediocre, but he lets it slide because I'm his wife; said I'm the only white girl he knows that is no good at performing oral sex and that's why he has trouble getting erections; said he probably should've listened to his mother and married a 'sistah'.

I felt like he'd been compiling a list of ways to demean me and pulled it out at that moment to see if he could break my spirit. It worked. As I absorbed the blows of his verbal abuse, I grew helpless and became speechless. I tried looking away, but he would adjust so we were face to face again. He wanted me to say something so he could strike me. He wanted to hurt me. He didn't understand he already had. His words evoked emotion in me that his hands never had.

When he finished taunting me, he went upstairs to take a shower and go to bed. Like usual, he won't go to sleep until I'm in the bed next to him. So, I put on my nightgown and joined him a half hour later. When I was sure he was fast asleep, I eased out of bed and tiptoed to my closet.

With my shaking hands, I reached under my pile of handbags and pulled out Crystal's gun. I had taken it the last time I was at her house, right after Vaughn told me I was under surveillance. My intentions were to have it for a week or two in case I needed to protect myself, but as I wrapped my hands around the cold metal, I was well aware that my intentions had changed.

I walked to his side of the bed and stared at him. He even looked like a haughty jerk in his sleep. He was so comfortable and carefree, sure that his passive, Christian

248

wife wouldn't want to harm him after his vicious statements. Well, everyone has their breaking point, and I had reached mine.

I pointed the gun at Vaughn's forehead, fighting to hold it steady. *Let's see if the devil does a better job of sucking your limp dick when you go to hell*, I thought, as I stroked the trigger with my index finger.

I could almost see the devil and angel sitting on each of my shoulders as they debated on whether I should go through with it. Vaughn's voice overpowered theirs, though, as I recalled the barrage of insults he shot at me. Was I just supposed to be the white girl who gave him great head? Was I just his trophy all these years?

*You'll never touch me again*, I thought as I closed my eyes and prepared to pull the trigger.

"Mommy, my belly hurts," Venus said as she entered our room.

The sound of the door opening woke Vaughn and startled me. I held the gun behind my back, hoping the questioning look in his eyes had nothing to do with him seeing the weapon.

"Baby, Mommy already gave you medicine for your belly before bed. Remember? Hold on. Let's try something else."

"What are you doing over here?" Vaughn asked.

"She's saying her stomach hurts, but I think she just wants to sleep in here," I whispered as I knelt onto the floor. "I'm looking for Poofy so she can go back to her own bed. I think she had him in here earlier."

Poofy is Venus' favorite bear, and I knew he was in her playroom next to her kitchen set. As I pretended to look under the bed for the bear, I slid the gun toward my side, praying it didn't hit my nightstand. In the meantime, Vaughn invited Venus into our bed and told me not to worry about it.

249

I breathed a quiet sigh of relief as I returned to my side of the bed, and again, when he was snoring, I left the bed and hid the gun. Of all the voices I heard during my moment of rage, God's turned out to be the strongest. He spoke through my daughter, stopping me from probably making the biggest mistake of my life.

# CRYSTAL

I purposely turned the television off when Dante walked onstage. It was his turn to sing in tribute to Michael Jackson, and I wasn't interested in watching. We still aren't speaking, and every time I look at his face, I think of the expression he had when the girl was pleasuring him in Vegas.

I needed to relax in the tub anyway. I had a hell of a workout earlier, and a little soak in the Jacuzzi tub with some Epsom salt sounded like an orgasm waiting to happen. Fully embracing the freedom of my apartment, I walked into the kitchen and poured a glass of wine, backtracked to the living room to get the latest issue of *Essence*, and headed toward my room to run the water...in the nude.

Twenty minutes later, I eased into the water, letting my body gradually get used to the extra hot temperature. I paused a few seconds longer than normal when I lowered my young lady into the steaming liquid. She was more sensitive than usual, but just on one side. I wondered if the cheap-ass toilet paper at the airport was the culprit. Earlier, I had used the bathroom there when I went to pick up a guest speaker for the girls at Something to Do.

251

Once I was submerged up to my neck, I'd forgotten all about the uncomfortable tingle. The massaging effect from the jets served as a pleasurable distraction. When the weird sensation returned, I was convinced that the Epsom salt was only irritating the abrasion. I placed my finger in the fold and applied pressure to block the water. The quick fix would've been to exit the tub, but there was no way I was getting out before my feet and hands were wrinkly.

I explored the area by gently rubbing my finger back and forth, and it felt swollen. I jumped from the sudden pain when I reached what felt like raw skin. "What the hell?"

I reached for my handheld mirror. Something wasn't right. I don't wipe that damn hard, no matter how hard or soft the toilet paper is.

After I hoisted myself out and brushed away the bubbles, I sat on the edge of the tub and spread my legs. I positioned the mirror at an angle where I could get the best view, and instantly, I was displeased with what I saw.

I wrapped my towel around me and stomped into the living room. Sat at the computer desk. Breathed fire. My Yahoo image search brought up countless pages of results for genital herpes. Many of the photos were gruesome, like the person saw the blisters and figured it'd be cool to see how many they could stand before having to go to the doctor. But on page two, I saw a photo that made me wonder if I'd accidentally activated my webcam and taken a picture. Sure enough, the barely visible ulcer just inside my labium was looking more and more like herpes. Fucking herpes!

"I'll kill him," I grumbled as I went to WebMd.com. I had a pretty good idea of what the symptoms were from hearing some of the other industry wives talk, but I needed to be sure. All of my symptoms matched—the tingling, the damn sore, and the fact that Dante has been getting cold sores like pimples lately. I never let him kiss me anywhere when he had them, so I couldn't understand how he could've transmitted the virus to me unless he has the virus above and below his waist.

I could've thrown up all over my keyboard. Did I miss something? Out of habit, I always look at Junior before he enters me. My aunt told me to do that as part of her I-know-you're-gonna-have-sex speech when I went off to college. She told me not to be afraid to ask questions about skin texture, and to investigate any blemish that didn't look quite right. They were wise words, and I lived by them.

As I read more on the website, I confirmed what I already knew to be true: the virus can be transmitted through oral sex. That knowledge was the basis for me requiring Dante to wear a condom when getting head from groupies. If a girl had a cold sore and sucked on him, he could easily get some sores on Junior. What I never thought about, though, was the possibility of the virus being transmitted with no visible symptoms present. At that moment, I convinced myself that Dante had given me herpes while we were in Puerto Rico—when he thought the champagne was making his bottom lip tingle; when he ate me out like I was the last meal he'd ever have. It was five months ago, longer than the "usual" window for symptoms to appear, but I'm sure that can vary. One of the triggers for an outbreak is stress, and up until three weeks ago in Vegas, I had been stress-free. If my theory was true, my body was responding to the tabloid reports, even though I had been pretending I wasn't affected.

I opened my towel and looked down again. You're not supposed to get a venereal disease from your spouse. You get a venereal disease from the random person you stupidly had unprotected sex with without knowing their last name. Wrong.

When I shuddered, the towel fell to the floor. I was exposed, and so was Dante. I could now believe without a doubt that he'd been kissing Katrina Hunter, aka Naptown New Booty, and that every released photo told the story of a married celebrity who had lost all respect for himself and his wife. And though he acted selfishly, we're sharing the media attention and blisters that can come and go as they please for the rest of our lives.

I allotted myself five minutes to cry away my anger and humiliation, but took ten instead. After the ten minutes went by and my temperament didn't improve, I had to reach out to someone. For the first time since I've been married, I had to call someone and admit that I'm not invincible, that I don't have everything in perspective, that my insightful ass needed to be enlightened.

"I don't know what to say, Crys," Dana said on the other end of the line. I called her because she's also dealing with infidelity or at least the suspicion of it. "Oh my God. I'm speechless."

"This would be so different if he had been getting cold sores since I met him, you know? Or even if he'd gotten 'em from drinking after his band member for real. But, no, this shit was brought on because he was kissing a bitch he sang to onstage."

"You know what I'm gonna say, right?" she said softly.

"If it has anything to do with my part in this, save it until after I light candles and meditate. I've got to come down from this shit, and I'm not even close to doing that. You're my girl, but anything you say in his defense right now can and will get you cussed out."

"I'd never defend someone who's wrong. Have you talked to him yet?"

"No. I'm still at the apartment. I don't wanna call him. I'm going to the house to chat with him when he gets back from L.A."

"Are you sure you're ready to confront him? Why don't you wait until you have a clear head?"

254

"Are you serious right now?" I asked.

"You're right. I forgot who I was talking to. Just try to keep your hands to yourself. Okay?"

*****

After I came back from the doctor, I pulled into the driveway and parked as close to the house as possible. I then walked to the garage and opened three of the doors. One by one, I drove each vehicle toward the front of the house and parked them around the semi-circle. I exited Dante's Hummer and retrieved one of the aluminum bats that were still in the trunk of my Mercedes from the Something to Do softball game a month ago. The slogan for the blue pills I had to get is "Take charge," and you better believe that's what I planned to do…the Crystal way.

Starting with the Bentley, I busted every window and light on every car except my Mercedes. I gave my Hummer a few extra hits since he had it customized for my birthday—the same birthday that marked the beginning of him swapping spit with Naptown New Booty.

I entered the house and told all the employees to go home—even our cook, who was in the middle of grilling salmon. I found most of them in the rooms with a view of the front of the house, where they acted like they weren't just watching me destroy the cars. A few were reluctant to leave until I threatened to fire them for insubordination. I warned them all that if they spoke to the tabloids, their heads would end up like the headlights. That wasn't a threat; it was a lifetime guarantee.

Tote bag in-hand, I walked upstairs thinking I would find an enraged Dante at the top. On the contrary, he was still in bed with his head under the covers. Jetlag from the trip had him sleeping soundly. That was just fine.

I pulled the candles from my bag and set them around the edges of the bed. Saturating the sheets just enough to not

255

wake him, I traced Dante's lower body with lighter fluid and then made a trail leading to the candles.

He stirred slightly as I lit each wick, but didn't awaken until he moved his leg and felt dampness. He propped himself on his elbows and squinted in my direction. "What the hell is goin' on?"

I'm sure he wanted to believe the candles were set up because I was being romantic, but he knows me too well. I had barely looked at him, much less talked to him since his little stint on the V.I.P. couch.

I maintained my position, standing at the foot of the bed. "Guess what? I just came back from my gynecologist," I began, smiling. "And instead of her telling me I have a baby growing inside my belly, she told me I have herpes growing inside my coochie! Would you believe that? I asked you for all kinds of shit for Valentine's Day, but you decided to give me something that would last forever. Herpes, the gift that keeps on giving. Are you gonna go all out five years from now and give me the killer?" The smile never left my face and the phony excitement never left my voice.

"How could that happen?"

I turned on the fans centered above our bed on each side of the ceiling mirror so the flames would dance a little. "Well, when you kiss hoes in the mouth and then come home and eat your wife out, those types of things happen. Good thing you didn't let *that* one suck your dick without a condom on, huh? Then you'd have issues down there like me, not just on your face."

"Crystal, you know none of this was intentional. I never put my mouth on you when I had that shit."

I dug into my tote bag and tossed three pamphlets at him. "Read up on your disease. You might learn something."

"What's the deal with the candles? And what's that smell?"

256

"Lighter fluid. We're one, right? Since I'm feeling the burn, why shouldn't you?"

The phone rang, and Dante ignored it until I told him to pick it up. "Yeah...Huh?...Whose cars? How did anybody get past the gate without you knowing?" A few more seconds went by, then Dante glared at me. "No, I'll handle it." He hung up and yelled, "You're goin' too fuckin' far! You busted the windows in all the cars?"

"Almost all of 'em."

"What do the cars have to do with anything?"

"I'll bust up everything on this property. Try me. I've been supportive of your career, understanding of your career. I've compromised the values I grew up with for you—because I loved *you*, not this shit." I picked up the bat and swung behind me, breaking a decorative vase into a thousand pieces. "And this is what you do to me. Because you refused to follow a couple simple rules, I can now relate to the bitches whitewater rafting and climbing mountains in those stupid-ass commercials."

"How was I supposed to know all this would happen? You're purposely wreckin' shit to get back at me, but I didn't purposely give you nothin'."

"Say it out loud. Herpes. You gave me herpes. Well, I guess I should say y'all gave me herpes." I pulled out his secret phone and scrolled through his contacts. His eyes were far from squinted once he realized it was his phone. "Let's see..."

"What are you doing?" he asked.

"It's only right that I call and thank Miss Katrina. A note would be too informal."

Before he could lunge forward, I had the pistol from inside my Hummer in my hand. "What? You 'bout to snatch your ho hotline phone from me to protect that bitch?"

"I'm tryin' to protect you."

257

"Too late," I said after I pulled out the pill bottle and shook it. "You didn't think I knew about the phone, did you? So damn slick, you done messed around and got caught slippin' on your own oil."

I put the gun down. Picked up the bat. "It's all good. I'll give you your phone back. I transferred the numbers to my BlackBerry months ago."

Like it was a softball, I tossed the phone in the air and hit it. Dante blocked its flying pieces with his hands and accidentally knocked down two of the candles. He picked them up and blew them out before the flames reached the lighter fluid.

"You're crazy! Don't touch nothin' else of mine!"

"See how emotional you are about the shit I destroyed? You're throwing a fit because it's gonna cost you money to repair or replace it. But you gave me a fuckin' disease that's hangin' in there for the long haul, and all you can say is, 'How was I supposed to know?' You've destroyed my life as I knew it, and you're more concerned with how much you have to put out to replace all this overpriced shit. Fuck me, right? Your money can't fix what you've done to me, but fuck me. I'm just crazy. I'm not hurt. I'm crazy."

"You're being irrational."

I nodded slowly. "Tell you what. I'll show you irrational. Since I'm in this situation as a result of you being impulsive, I'm gonna be impulsive, too."

I turned the fans on high, causing the flames of the candles to extend above the glass rims that housed them. I put the tote bag on my shoulder and held the gun in my hand.

"You did what you did at the time because you wanted to. This is what I wanna do."

I tipped over the candles closest to me, creating a line of fire that ended between his legs. Then, I pointed the gun at his reflection in the mirror on the ceiling and fired one single shot. Huge shards of glass fell onto the bed as he attempted to roll away. Within seconds, the bed was on fire and he was on the floor screaming from the pain of the glass that was embedded in his skin. I ran into the bathroom and got the rubbing alcohol from under the sink. Walked back to where he lay. Doused it onto his open wounds. He screamed every profanity at me, though most of his words were drowned out by the smoke detector's beeping. Before I left, I grabbed what was left of his secret phone's keypad and tossed it at him.

"Maybe you should call Katrina."

*****

Sheila, Dante's publicist, called my cell phone early the next morning. Like everyone else, she'd heard about my demolition and was in damage-control mode. While she's in her office, her job is to rally for Dante and protect his image. However, since we've become close over the years, I knew our conversation would be much different when she called again after-hours as Sheila, my girl.

Her reason for calling? They were setting up a press conference for Dante to confirm his indiscretions and make a tearful apology to his faithful fans, his family, and most of all, his loving wife—the shit all the stars do to protect their images. Cue the chili pepper to throw in his eyes and a well-practiced speech written by a stranger, and in a few months, he would regain his number one position on the charts and in the hearts of the silly hoes that would still do him in a heartbeat. Sheila wanted me to attend.

"Uh unh, Sheila, you know better than that."

"I know this is hard, Crystal—"

"Do you? Did your husband give you herpes, too?"

Her professional tone never changed. "These calls are the most difficult to make. Ultimately, it's your decision, and

259

I totally understand why you would be reluctant to go to the press conference."

"I'm not reluctant. I'm not going. This ain't no Vanessa-Kobe shit. If I show up at the press conference, I'm grabbin' the mic and tellin' it all. It's public knowledge that I'm still with him, and that's embarrassing enough. I'm not about to be on national TV looking like the stupid, passive wife. I'm a lot of things, but a dumb bitch isn't one of them. You don't want me there unless you want a show."

"Well, you know we're denying the STD rumors."

"That's great for the image of Dante, the singer. More power to y'all. I hope the people believe your lies. If it was just a rumor, I wouldn't have a bottle of blue pills prescribed to my alias in my medicine cabinet, Sheila. You two handle the Hollywood version of the story without me. In the real world of Alpharetta, Georgia, that sloppy bastard gave me herpes. That's my story, and I'm sticking to it. If you need a statement from me, release this: 'The reports are true from *Dirty Dish* to TMZ. Dante acquired herpes from Katrina Hunter of Indianapolis, Indiana, and gave it to me with a smile. I would've shot *him* instead of his reflection, but I wasn't sure if I'd have time to clean up the scene before our security guards arrived.'"

# DANA

"Okay, baby. I'm so, so, so sorry," I said, blowing past Ric and entering our bathroom. "She's a total wreck. Her mom and dad just heard the news, her girls from the program have been blowing up her email inbox, paparazzi is posted up outside her house...I'm afraid she's gonna lose it. Well, I guess she already lost it when she destroyed all that stuff, but you know what I mean. Anyway, all I have to do is change real quick, and I'm ready. My clothes are laid out, so it'll take me all of ten minutes. I know we were supposed to go to the four o'clock movie, but I checked the listings on my phone, and there's a seven o'clock show. The runtime is only an hour and forty-two minutes, so we'll still make it in time for our dinner reservations."

Crystal had called at a quarter 'til two, asking if I could come to her apartment. The news about her latest fight with Dante had spread like a wildfire, and she needed to vent. Ric and I were just sitting around, waiting to go to the movies, so I drove over there to listen. I didn't expect to stay almost four hours, but when your best friend is in distress, you can't just leave in the middle of her tirade. I was afraid if I didn't stay to hear her out, she might've returned to the mansion to finish it and Dante off.

I knew Ric was pissed, but I figured when I returned, I'd stay as upbeat as possible, not give him a word edgewise, and pray that my positive attitude rubbed off on him. On the contrary, it rubbed him the wrong way.

I exited the bathroom and proceeded to the dresser to squirt on the perfume he bought me as an anniversary gift. "I'm ready, baby."

"So you think you can just leave in the middle of what was supposed to be our day to go be with that bitch, and I'm supposed to just roll with the punches?" he asked. "It's our fuckin' anniversary!"

"Ric—"

"Don't 'Ric' me. I don't give a damn if her house was on fire. I'm your husband, and this is where you were supposed to be. You didn't even ask me if I minded you leaving. You *told* me you had to go and you'd be right back. You showed me where your loyalties lie. You shoulda married her. Take her ass to the movies."

I threw my head back. "That's not fair. Ric, I apologize if I hurt your feelings by leaving. You're right. I didn't ask you. I guess I was just trying to hurry so I could get back in time for us to go out. I was in a tough spot. My *best friend* just learned she has a lifelong STD, and the whole world knows, too. She was freakin' out. She never freaks out. When she called me, I instinctively went to see what I could do to help. If that's wrong, again, I apologize."

"She whistles; you run—tongue out, tail wagging. You left me sittin' here like a dummy, flipping through channels, watching the time go by."

"Ric, we didn't even have anything planned until four. You act like we were doing something and I was like 'Peace' right in the middle of it."

"We were spending time. And you tell me I don't get it. Looks like you don't know what a relationship is."

I chuckled. "Oh, our time together is important to you on our anniversary, but you don't care about it any other day of the year. Are we going or what, Ric?"

"Hell no. Ain't nothin' to celebrate. Fuck this marriage," he said before recommencing his channel surfing.

*My sentiments exactly.* "At least you finally said it out loud," I said, then left the room.

I really didn't mean any harm when I left the house earlier, but at this point in our marriage, I don't harbor much sympathy for Ric. Sure, if we name a victim in this incident, he would be the one. But he had some nerve to act as if my mishandling of that situation trumps his mishandling of me for the better part of our union.

Nowadays, I'm not interested in making Ric happy or making things "right". I'm confident that I've done that for years. I used to cater to him in spite of. Now I only cater to him because of. If he would rather pout in the room while watching Discovery Channel, so be it.

I've found myself dealing with everything I said I wouldn't in my marriage. This isn't life. It can't be. And if it is, I don't want it. Crystal's woes could easily be mine. I've found condoms in Ric's jeans—the ones he was "holding for Moe", who also happens to be married. I know he barely wears his wedding band. I've kept up with his emails and seen his flirty exchanges with LaShay and other random chicks. I've wondered what sparks him try new positions with me, unable to chalk up his actions to simple spontaneity. Though he thought he was hurting me by canceling our plans, I begged to differ. Perhaps he was doing me a favor.

When Crystal was crying to me earlier, I thought about my visit to the gynecologist for my annual exam two months ago. I'd talked to the doctor about my recurrent bacterial

263

infections, secretly worried that maybe Ric was cheating on me. She was adamant in assuring me that the infections are prevalent in African-American women and are usually not sexually transmitted. After she performed the pelvic exam, she mentioned they no longer automatically test women over age twenty-five for STDs, but they would do it by request. I waved my hand as if I didn't believe Ric has been unfaithful, and with a laugh, she replied, "I didn't think you needed that. We just have to tell everyone. I've shared the same disclaimer with sixty-year-old women."

I don't know why I didn't speak up and ask to be tested. Embarrassment, I guess. She knows I'm married. She delivered Chase and Dalvin. Saying I need to be tested is the same as saying, "I think Ric is mixing my juices with his co-worker's." I guess I was afraid to speak up, too. If any of the tests were to come back positive, what would I do? How badly would that hurt? How would I refrain from doing what Crystal did to Dante?

I put a reminder in my phone to call Dr. Leslie as soon as her office opened on Monday. I wanted to schedule an appointment and have those tests done. Denial was getting me nowhere, and I couldn't let fear or discomfiture keep me from learning valuable information. Best case scenario, I'd be mad at myself for spending an extra ten dollars for a co-pay toward a visit that returned all negative cultures.

I knew this was coming. After I came back from Vegas, Ric was way too gentlemanly, way too accommodating, way too husbandly. How dare I think happiness was our final destination? I didn't. I just enjoyed our stay there while it lasted.

His actions almost came across as phony—like I was being paid counterfeit attention. And so I braced myself for the fallout. That's why his outburst didn't hurt so much. But believe me, when someone says 'Fuck this marriage' and you're married to them, it still hurts like hell. I, too, say fuck this marriage, but I say it with pain in my heart.

*****

August came quickly, and my grueling schedule distracted me from my failing marriage. I started evening classes for my PhD two weeks after we resumed at Lithonia Grove, and I was still squeezing in time to work out with Lorenzo. Consumed with studying, grading papers, being Mommy and a best friend, I don't have the time to care about Ric and have retired from being his wife. Well, technically, I've given my two-week notice, but he hasn't noticed it. I don't check any of his accounts or look through his pockets. I don't ask who he's talking to for hours. Doing so would only deter me from bettering myself, which, as bad as it sounds, is what our marriage had temporarily done already. I'll find out what I need to know. I've prayed about it and let it go. The Lord knows what I need to hand Ric his pink slip, and my fingers are ready to dial the lawyer's number as soon as I get that information.

Lorenzo and I have been spending a little more time together. Sometimes he'll meet me at the restaurant near the school and we'll grab a quick bite, or we'll go to the park on a Saturday morning to run. We've continued to keep our exchanges innocent, but I'm certain we're guilty of having not-so-innocent thoughts.

Ever since we spent time together in Vegas, I can't stop wondering what life would be like with him. Then again, I used to daydream about life with Ric when he was an ambitious military man with his head on straight. Whoever coined the phrase "Things change" ain't never lied. I could be smitten by Lorenzo's representative.

I'm sleeping with the enemy, but this isn't a movie. I've been singing the same song for years, so I'm long overdue for a new tune—not a remix. I'd rather feel lonely alone. I can be torn down by strangers. I don't need a husband to help with those things. Ric shouldn't be the one calling my decision to return to school "stupid" because it requires him to come home on time and take care of his sons. Lorenzo shouldn't be the one asking me how I did on my paper, and he shouldn't know all the hilarious stories about my sixty-year-old teacher who wears the same wool skirt every day, never minding that it's summer. Or should he?

It's hard to say. I don't think I even want Lorenzo—not to the extent that I would leave my marriage and bank on greener grass. He represents happiness, and I want to be happy. He symbolizes my possibilities that I deserve more. I can decide where he stands in my life when I'm a single woman. I've known my worth all along. Now it's time I act like it.

# WILLOW (MILKY)

Vaughn walked in as Venus and I reviewed the alphabet. He looked on with a proud smile while we rejoiced over her latest accomplishment. She said the letter "G" clearly for the first time—one of the many goals we'd been working toward since she started speech therapy at age three.

Thank God for her, because once again, she's been the only reason we smile around each other. He clapped after she and I finished the "We Did It" dance, getting her attention. Within seconds, she ran and jumped into his arms.

Seeing their interaction brings me joy. Vaughn is extra careful with her, undeniably showing she is the love of his life. He used to look at me that way, but I'm starting to believe he only needed me to birth her. Now that I know more about his childhood, I can see him wanting to be the best father he can be. No. *Needing* to be the best father he can be.

So where does that leave us? Right where we are. Stagnant. I'm prepared to change that status, though. I was gonna change that status the night I pulled the gun on him, but my God is a savior, and He sent my angel in to stop me.

267

I knew then it wasn't the right solution, but it was the easiest solution.

Once I started thinking with my brain cells instead of my emotions, I made a decision. It was time to go. Separation could only do one of two things: make him appreciate me or make him appreciate life without me. It's a risk I was once afraid of but am now willing to take.

In the week that had passed, I'd taken my money out of our joint account and had been gradually moving some of my and Venus' clothes. We were going to stay in the apartment Crystal has at the W. I thought she would've been staying there, but the last time I'd talked to her, she said she was going to spend some time in Indianapolis.

I'd written Vaughn a three-page letter expressing my past and present feelings, as well as my hopes for our future. I requested that he see a psychologist to help him sort out his issues resulting from his father's perversion if he chooses to work things out with me. I'd already cleared the mention of it with Mrs. Ella, and in her words, "He can't continue to hide from the truth." To assure him I would never keep Venus from him, I also included a schedule that allowed us to alternate weeks of physical custody, detailed with suggested exchange locations in well-lit, heavily-populated areas. In the morning after he leaves for work, I'll put the letter on the island in the kitchen, remove the rest of my necessities, and head to my new residence.

"Do you have any plans tonight?" he asked, still holding Venus.

"No. Why?"

"I think we're overdue for some alone time. I've had enough of walking around the house not speaking. You?"

I smiled. *How does he do that?* I thought. His spontaneity is such a lovable trait that I didn't dare consider turning him down.

"I've been thinking about you all day. I already called Mama, and she said she'll watch Venus. I'm about to run her over there now. Cool?" He bit his lower lip the same way he did when I met him at the job fair.

*I'm such a sucker.* "Cool."

I was reclining on the chaise reading the passage for Tuesday's bible study when Vaughn returned. I wanted to make sure I completed it before our make-up evening started. I was interested in seeing how things would go, thinking that surely God was intervening before I made my move.

It surprised me that he didn't enter with flowers, but my tinge of disappointment left when he knelt at my feet and pulled off my slippers.

"Just what we need...a little privacy," he said before placing my big toe in his mouth and swirling his tongue around it.

"I like privacy," I replied, closing my eyes to savor the satisfaction.

"Me, too. I told you I've planned this all day. I almost left work early."

He had to know I was secretly craving him, too. We hadn't made love in almost a month because he was either out of town, arguing with me, or unable to get erect. He massaged my feet for a few minutes.

"You're tense, babe," he said, running his thumbs up and down my instep. "What's on your mind?"

"Nothing now. You're making it all better."

His hands traveled to my calves and my shins. Slow strokes sent my body into total relaxation as I eagerly waited for him to give one particular muscle its attention.

"Are you sure?" he asked, trickling his fingers back down to my feet. In one motion, he gripped my ankles, stood up, and snatched me out of the lounge chair. The foot of the chaise stopped my head from hitting the floor. "I make it better now, but you were gonna shoot me a couple weeks ago."

Shell-shocked, I didn't have a great answer, so I just said, "No."

He stood over me, straddling my legs. His smirk looked overwhelmingly intimidating as he looked down at me. "You thought I didn't see it, huh? *I* thought I didn't see it for a while. Then it hit me today as I was sitting at my desk. I thought, 'Vaughn, she had a gun pointed at you while you were sleep. That's not safe.'"

My throat became so dry that I couldn't swallow for about twenty seconds. I was totally thrown off. When he didn't say anything at the time I had the gun or the next day, I was certain he didn't see it.

"I didn't point it at you," I lied.

"Right...because my baby came into the room. What is that called? Divine intervention? Isn't that something? You're the one who always goes to church, and I'm the one who gets the miracle."

At that moment, I looked at my husband and saw pure evil. I saw the face of Satan. "Vaughn—"

"Don't call my name! Where's the gun?"

It was in the bathroom buried under the tampons and maxi pads I store in a plastic bin—the perfect hiding place because the concept of women having a period freaks him out.

"I don't have it anymore," I replied.

"Don't lie to me, bitch. You were bold enough to pull it out then; go get it now."

"I don't want it. I don't want to use it. That's why I got rid of it."

"Why did you have it in the first place?" he yelled.

"Look at you! Look at how you treat me! That's why I had it. I was scared for my life."

270

He jerked me from the floor with one hand and glared at me with empty eyes. "I don't believe you. Tell me where the gun is." The sting from his backhand set my cheek on fire, and its force sent me back to the floor. "You scared now? Get up!" he shouted.

*Not anymore. Lord, I promise if you deliver me from this devil, no deception will ever bring me back*, I prayed as I used the couch to hoist myself up. A passage from Acts, Chapter 18 popped into my head. All I could remember of it was, "Be not afraid, but speak, and hold not thy peace."

"I don't want to do this, Vaughn. I can't fight you. We both know who's gonna win. I'll leave...whatever you want."

"It's not that simple. You tried playing with big boy toys. Now you get to go toe to toe with a big boy. Nobody has ever pulled a gun on me until the other night, and I'll be damned if it wasn't my own wife! Nah, Willow...*Milky*...you want me dead. You wanted to kill me. I can't walk around God's green earth knowing that someone wants to kill me."

"If you're treating people right, they won't want to kill you."

"You ungrateful, nobody bitch! I treat you like a queen. I gave you your job. I keep you in those designer labels. I put you on my father's private jet to go where the hell you want, and you just said I don't treat you right?" He charged at me until I backed into the wall.

"None of that entitles you to put your hands on me. You've also given me black eyes and migraines. You keep me in designer makeup because I'm covering up your dirty work. Is that how you treat a queen? I'm a queen who has a lifetime supply of Royal ice packs," I yelled. "If you would talk to me about your insecurities instead of taking your frustrations out on me, we wouldn't be doing this."

271

"Ah, you wanna talk back?" he said, placing his hand on his hip. "Go ahead. What else do you have to say?"

I watched his hands carefully so I'd know when to duck. "I know about your real dad. I know what he did to you, and I know that's why you act out. I'm not the one you should be mad at, though."

Emotion reappeared on his face as he let my words seep into the crevices of his brain. I took advantage of his solemn moment to ease my way out of his reach and hopefully, out the door.

"I don't want your stuff, Vaughn. Keep this house, your daddy's plane, and every single article of clothing you bought me. I just want to go," I said, raising my hands to signal surrender.

His eyes remained focused on the floor as I reached for the doorknob. I turned one more time to see what he was doing and met his fist. I wanted to scream, but I couldn't open my mouth widely enough. An excruciating pain shot through the perimeter of my gums, causing immediate salivation. I couldn't really swallow, so I just spit, only see the oozing liquid was blood and not saliva. I cupped my hand under my chin with one hand and held my throbbing jaw with the other.

I could only see Vaughn clearly through my right eye, and he was beyond enraged. Like a demon, he growled and then slammed my head against the door. The last thing I remember is the pressure of his thumbs against my carotid arteries and his fingers squeezing the back of my neck.

When I came to, it took a while to get my bearings. I was lying on my stomach in the most agonizing pain I've ever experienced. My whole face felt like it was on fire, and my left arm was numb. My mouth felt the worst. Imagine someone slicing your gums with a razor, then pouring acid into every laceration. I could see that my shirt was covered with blood on my chest and left sleeve, and so was my hair. I listened for a few seconds to determine whether Vaughn was still there, but the only sound I heard was the faint hum of the refrigerator.

*What did he do to me?* I thought, while trying to get up. No luck with that. I quickly learned that my left arm was not just numb; it was immobile. Something had to give. If I didn't get help soon, I was afraid it would be too late. I wasn't sure if "too late" meant death or permanent damage to something because I didn't know what all Vaughn had done to me, but I knew pain like that came with serious consequences.

Through my haze, I was able to spot the large C's on my Coach bag near the front door just three feet away. Though I moved in slow motion, I propped myself up using my right forearm and scooted across the hardwood floor until I reached the purse. Without looking inside, I rummaged through it until I felt my cell phone.

Unable to hold myself up any longer, I rested my forehead on the floor, pressed Crystal's speed dial button, and placed the phone on the floor under my mouth.

Once she answered, all I could do was grunt because my jaw was too frozen to mumble.

"What are you saying?" she asked. "What's wrong with you?"

I tried again.

"Hell? Is that what you said? Is somebody playing on my sister's phone? What the hell?"

One more time, I attempted to scream, "Help!" but the newly falling tears combined with the pain and swelling only made me sound worse. I hung up on her and then took a deep breath.

*You can do this,* I said as I mustered a little more energy to text her. *Help…at home…call ambulance.*

273

# CRYSTAL

I changed into my Nike tracksuit and threw on some sneakers in record time. My mind and heart raced each other as I replayed Milky's voice and text message in my head. I frantically searched my nightstand drawer for my gun, knowing damn well I didn't move it. With no time to waste, I didn't spend another second searching for the weapon. I still had the other one in my purse, and it's just as powerful. I was anticipating the opportunity to make Vaughn a human shooting target, because I was sure his ass had something to do with my sister's cry for help. On my way out the door, I told Martha to be on standby with bail money, because if my instincts were correct, Vaughn was going to pay for whatever damage he had done...and not with money.

I wiped the sweat from my forehead when I pulled into the driveway. The strong, rapid beat of my heart had turned into an irregular, nervous flutter, and I prayed I wouldn't walk in and witness some grotesque murder-suicide scene— a bitch move I wouldn't put past Vaughn. *Shit! I forgot!* Before I exited the car, I called 911 as Milky had requested in her text.

274

With my finger on the trigger, I used my key to enter the house. Immediately, I gasped. Milky was lying face down near my foot. There was blood everywhere—in her hair, on her clothes, and all over the floor. She must have dragged herself to get to her phone judging by the red trail smeared across the hardwood.

"Milky!" I screamed as I knelt to see if she was breathing.

She grunted, but didn't move.

"I'm here, sweet pea. The ambulance is on its way. You hang in there, okay?"

I didn't want to touch her, afraid I would cause more harm than good. So, I surveyed the scene a little more, looking for answers she was unable to provide at the time.

"Did Vaughn do this? Where is that motherfucker?" I yelled.

Milky pointed her quivering index finger toward the door.

"Son-of-a-bitch. If he didn't drive off a bridge somewhere, he better be on his way to do so. I swear to God I have a bullet that wants to live right between his eyebrows."

As I paced, I noticed something white near the wall. When I leaned over to get a closer look, I threw up. It was one of Milky's teeth. Once the paramedics arrived, the extent of her injuries was painfully clear. The left side of her face was severely bruised and three times its normal size. Five of her teeth were missing, which explained the blood, and her left shoulder was dislocated—we assumed from the impact of her body hitting the floor. If I hadn't found her myself, I wouldn't have believed the battered woman was my sister. She was totally unrecognizable.

Five hours had passed before Milky was resting semi-comfortably in a hospital room. They had us wait longer than usual because I requested a private one. I also requested that they didn't release information on her. That is, when anyone called, they were to say they had no one there by that name.

The police had come to get a report, but due to her injuries, she was unable to tell them what happened. I gave them my account, which didn't amount to much, and they said they'd return the next day to see if she could provide a written statement. That was great. I wanted them to get to Vaughn quickly so his uppity ass could sit in a dirty cell where his new friends would give him the beating he'd given to Milky. I have friends in high places who know people in low places—every jail and prison in Georgia. His fate could definitely be arranged.

Dr. Simon, the oral and maxillofacial surgeon that works in the same building as Dr. Knight, performed the surgery on Milky's jaw. He said it was severely damaged, but he was confident she would have a speedy recovery. "Speedy" is a subjective term, because to me, having your teeth wired together four to six weeks is a long time.

Since I had all the information I was going to get for the night, I made the call I could no longer avoid.

"Crystal?" Mom answered. Her whisper-like tone indicated she was already asleep.

I looked at my watch. "I'm sorry, Mama. I forgot how late it is. Umm…I don't want to get into this over the phone. Can you come to Northside? I'm out here with Milky."

"Northside, what?"

"Hospital, Mama. You and Daddy get your clothes on and come out here. Vaughn did it."

"Vaughn did what?"

"Nevermind, Ma. I'll call you in the morning."

She's always been loopy when she's awakened unexpectedly. She'd hang up, go right back to sleep, and then call me in the morning to ask if our conversation was part of her dream. It was for the better. I would've had to cuss the staff out if she and Dad were denied seeing their daughter because it was after visiting hours.

Milky stirred as I texted Dante the latest news about her. He had called the house, and Martha told him how I'd left in a hurry. When he reached me, I was following the ambulance to the hospital. I gave him a quick explanation of what I'd walked in on, but had to go after about five minutes. He was in Indiana at our other house, but had just texted to let me know he was making arrangements to return to Georgia within a few hours.

When I looked at Milky, she was reaching for her face. Her less swollen eye widened to its capacity and displayed the horror she felt—most likely due to the fact that she could hold her hand four or five inches from her face and feel her cheek. I stood up just as she attempted to speak, just as she began to panic.

I reached her bedside, and she clenched my hand.

"You're fine, sweetie. Look at me," I said. She stopped grunting and blinked away a tear. "They wired your mouth closed so your jaw could heal. He broke your jaw, Milky."

"Hurts," she managed to say.

"Maybe they can give you more pain medicine," I said before pressing the call button for the nurse. Something told me she was referring to her face *and* her heart, though.

Once they upped her dosage in the IV, she calmed down. I knew I only had a few minutes before she'd fall back asleep. So, I told her that the police were awaiting her statement and asked her to think of any places he could've run off to so they could bury his ass under the prison for attempted murder.

"Oh, and you know I'm telling Todd, right? I'm not covering this shit up no more. Mom was sleep when I called, but her and Daddy will know in a few hours."

She pointed to her cell phone, which was in my hand. I kept it there all night in hopes that Vaughn would try to reach out to her.

"What?" I asked. She kept pointing to it. "You want me to call Todd now?"

I opened the phone and realized the damn thing was on silent the entire time. There were six missed calls from Todd and one text. My little sis had revenge on her mind. That was clear when I looked at Todd's text that read, *Been calling. If I don't hear from you by morning, I'm flying out there.* That was in response to her *Think Vaughn just tried to kill me* text.

My smile reeked of vindication. Todd went from barely knowing who Vaughn is and having no clue he'd been abusing our sister to reading that he tried to kill her. Milky knew that would send him from zero to one hundred in a millisecond. Milky knew there was no going back after that. She knew it was time for Vaughn to get fucked up. Just hurting him wouldn't be enough justice. I was amazed to see that she'd also managed to take a picture of her face with the phone, but it never went through. Perhaps she lost consciousness before she was able to send it. If it had reached him, Todd may have beaten us to the hospital all the way from Arizona.

"I wonder why he didn't call me," I said, while checking my call log. I knew I hadn't missed a call, though. Then, it hit me. Dante and I had changed our numbers after the herpes disaster unfolded, and I had only given the new numbers to Mama, Milky, Dana, and LaToya so far.

I called Todd right away, and he answered after the first ring. After I gave him the rundown, he scolded me for not giving him my new numbers.

"I'm glad you didn't call Mama."

"I wasn't tryna upset her if she didn't know what was up. Plus, it was late. Why did you change all your numbers anyway? Groupie shit?"

278

"Yeah. He had a persistent bitch," I replied, thankful he'd given me an out.

It would only be a matter of time until Todd found out the whole truth, but until then, I was safe…or should I say Dante was safe. With his football workouts, camp, and team meetings, Todd has no time to watch BET, and he wouldn't have caught the gossip on the radio because he only listens to his iPod in the car.

He wanted to come to Atlanta the next day, but I told him to wait until Vaughn surfaced. I had a plan and was pretty sure if we all followed it, he would come to us…no effort needed. I gave Todd strict instructions not to call or text Vaughn, no matter how tempting it was. I needed him to think this incident would blow over like all the others. If my guess was right, he'd put out some feelers after two weeks, no more than three. From there, Operation FHU (Fuck Him Up) would be in motion.

# WILLOW (MILKY)

Four days in the hospital, two weeks of bruising, three weeks of unrelenting pain and swelling, and five weeks on a liquid diet. I sat in Dr. Simon's waiting room, hoping he'd remove the wires today. During my visit last week, he said the x-rays looked good, but he wanted to give my jaw another few days to heal.

Next, I'll be moving on to a cosmetic dentist who will replace the spacers that are preventing my teeth from shifting with fake teeth. Yippee! More surgery. Oh well. I'll do whatever it takes to not have my baby look at me like I'm Godzilla. She's doing better since the bruising faded and the swelling decreased, but she still won't look at me longer than five seconds.

I think I've forgotten how to chew food or talk with my mouth open, but I've mastered the art of functioning with my jaw wired closed. I've become so good at conversing through clenched teeth that I sound normal, and I've convinced myself that the chocolate Ensure tastes like a Steak N' Shake milkshake.

I most look forward to gaining a few pounds. I've lost twelve that Mom says I didn't need to lose in the first place, so I'm sure she has some dishes in mind to help bulk me up a little. Though solid food will be much more fulfilling, I think I'll continue to make the variety of smoothies I concocted when I need something a little different. I've had both successful and unsuccessful mixtures of fruit during this time, but it was the least I could do to keep things interesting.

It's difficult to make lemonade when life hands you lemons. I've even tried making lemon pie, but neither have turned out right yet. I don't understand God's purpose for this—not yet. Though the physical pain has passed, my heart is still in distress. I feel like I was attacked by a stranger.

Never in a million years could you have told me this would happen and I would've believed it. There goes my judge of character. Makes me question my psychology degree. Makes me thankful I didn't go into counseling and advise people on what to do in their lives.

I'm not heartbroken or sad. I'm two emotions beyond infuriated, and I can't shake the feeling. I hope Vaughn stays away, because I only have retaliation on my mind. I won't be satisfied until I see him in searing pain. Usually I would pray such negativity away, but I don't want to yet. It's on my list of things to do, but I haven't set a target date.

Vaughn has reached out to me, but I don't answer. It's my form of self-control. He's apologized forward and backward...in English, Spanish, Latin, and French...with bass, tenor, alto, and soprano tones. It all means nothing to me. The only communication he's received in return was a text message asking how he expected me to talk to him with a broken jaw.

I don't know where he is. Mrs. Ella says he's definitely not in Georgia, and he's smart enough to stay away from Nevada, too, since it's like his second home. Knowing his scary self, he's either in another country or in some random state like South Dakota, where he's hoping no one will get wind of who he is and what he has done. Little does he know he isn't on *America's Most Wanted* or anything even close. Again, that's how vain people react. He thinks he's important enough for the police to have organized an extensive search.

Speaking of Mrs. Ella, she and Joseph came to visit me every day I was in the hospital, and she called each day thereafter for two weeks. She would've come to see me at home, but I couldn't risk her knowing where Crystal's apartment is. She claims she has only talked to Vaughn once, and says he only called to tell her he'd "messed up big-time" and because she'd told me his secret, it was all her fault. I don't know whether I believe her. I want to, but blood is thicker than water. She owes me nothing.

Mom sat beside me and watched *As the World Turns* on the screen mounted on the wall in front of us. She hasn't let a day go by without coming to see me, even if she makes up a generic excuse to explain her presence. Somehow, she's found a way to blame herself for this. She thinks she should've seen Vaughn's other side and warned me before it got to this. As a mother, I can understand. It's my job to make sure nothing or no one harms Venus until she's eighteen, but it's my instinct to protect her from all danger as long as I live. I wish Mom would take it easy on herself, though. She's done more than enough for me from the moment she held me in her arms. It's my turn to do something for myself.

The nurse called my name, and after sitting in the room for another twenty minutes, Dr. Simon came in.

After a quick examination, he jotted a few notes in my chart and opened a drawer to access his instruments. "It's your lucky day," he said with a smile. "Let's set this baby free."

"I know you can't really tell, but I'm smiling," I replied.

282

He laughed. "I know. As weird as it sounds, you'll have to strengthen your jaw muscles. They've been doing minimal work for over a month. Claire will give you a list of exercises that will help."

I was so glad Crystal wasn't there. She wouldn't have been able to resist suggesting a perverted exercise or two.

After removing the wires, Dr. Simon asked if I wanted to look in the mirror. I declined. I haven't looked in a mirror since the day I was released from the hospital.

"You look great. I promise I didn't disfigure you. I think I did a hell of a job if you ask me," he joked.

"I'm sure you did. I'll look when I can smile and not resemble a jack-o-lantern. How long will it take to get that ball rolling?" I massaged my sore cheeks, amazed at how weak they felt.

"That depends on which dentist you consult. I have a colleague who shares a building with me in Buckhead, and he's the best. He's the one who placed the anchors in your jaw for your implants. Of course, I recommend that you follow-up with him, but you're free to choose whoever you want."

I vaguely remember him speaking with me and Crystal about the doctor when I was in the hospital room recovering from surgery, and I guess I gave him consent to dig into my jawbone. But things were just now becoming clearer as Dr. Simon praised the other doctor for his wonderful contributions to the world of cosmetic dentistry. He told the same success stories that existed only as residue in my brain before today. Bits and pieces were familiar. All of it was useless information. Then he handed me the business card.

Dr. Scott R. Knight was the dentist extraordinaire's name. The card served as my time machine, rewinding back to those four fuzzy days in the hospital. That man came into my room. I remember. I didn't see his face clearly. I didn't see anyone's face clearly because my one eye was still swollen and the other was on hiatus thanks to the drugs they were pumping through my IV. He came my second day there. Rebecca was there, too. She had flown in from New York because Crystal made an unauthorized call from my cell phone to tell her what happened. I didn't want her there. It wasn't her place to show up. She had given up her rights to be my heroine.

From what I can recall, Dr. Knight didn't stay long. All he did was stop in briefly and part my lips to check out the damage, so I thought. That fifteen-second "procedure" probably cost five grand. I remember Crystal calling his name like it was their class reunion and he was walking by as if he didn't know her. He must've asked why she was there. Silence followed her proclamation that I'm her sister. That was the only time I felt someone was more confused than I was. After she joked about our resemblance, she asked if he'd gotten her message.

The only other thing I remember is Rebecca reentering the room after stepping out to make a phone call. Crystal introduced Dr. Knight. Dr. Knight repeated Rebecca's name. Rebecca gasped. More silence. Or maybe I just fell asleep again. Until Dr. Simon handed me the card, I thought the whole thing was a dream.

"If you say he's the best, that's who I want," I said.

*****

I didn't call Rebecca and question her, or ask Crystal why she didn't tell me her dentist's name. No one knew I had an appointment with him. I wanted to go in blindly and alone, with no preconceived notions or expectations. I've looked at his picture probably fifty times, so if it was him, I would know. He already knew of me. I just didn't know what he knew me as.

When he approached the chair I reclined in, he introduced himself and gave me a firm handshake. His eye contact was brief, but his temperament was nothing short of friendly. He got right down to business, checking my x-rays and then my mouth. While he looked inside with the little mirror, he made small talk.

"Willow. That's a unique name. I think you're the first patient I've had with that name, and I've been doing this for fifteen years."

I grunted to simulate a laugh.

He removed the mirror. "How did your parents come up with that?"

I looked into his eyes. "From what I hear, my parents used to make out by a willow tree near their high school. I guess I'm a reminder of what happened once making out turned into something else."

He smiled. "They told you that?"

"I heard. You know my sister, right?"

"Yes. Crystal."

"So you've probably deduced that one of us is adopted."

He tapped his instrument on the table and nodded quickly.

"Like I said, I've heard. I'm like an actress. I can come up with my own backstory and be whoever I want."

"I'm sorry. I didn't mean to bring up a sore subject."

"Don't be. It's not sore anymore. I'll be thirty-two in a few days. I'm numb."

He was a spitting image of the high school jock in the picture Rebecca gave me, thirty years removed. Without asking him one question, I was 99.9% sure he is my biological father. I wasn't sure if he was playing games, but in case he was, I played along. A lot of people seeking general conversation with me start with an inquiry about my name and follow with apologies once I say I'm adopted. I didn't know his angle, but by the time I would finish interrogating Crystal and Rebecca, I'd know the mystery of Dr. Scott Knight.

He helped me to a sitting position and directed me to an area obviously designed solely for consultation. Placing a model of a mouth between us, he explained that the process to get my implants was going to be a long one—about ten months. I almost cried when I learned I'll have to walk around toothless at least two more months before I can get temporary crowns. And that's just for the three lower teeth. The two implants at the top can't be touched until the end of February. It's September. They might as well have kept my jaw wired shut, because I'll barely be opening my mouth anyway.

I could feel more hate rising in my spirit. Vaughn got me good. The attack has been over. Everything has healed for the most part. He has vanished. Still, he's able to disturb my life for practically another year. The girls at the MAC counter can't fix this, and neither can an ice pack. I hope God gets him first, because if given the chance, I will accept the opportunity to disturb his life, as well.

# DANA

"Are you all packed?" my mother asked on the other end of the phone.

I internalized a sigh. "Yes, Mother."

Hell no, I wasn't packed. And what did it matter to her? I don't prepare for trips two weeks in advance like she does. I'm a last-minute person when it comes to things like that, and she knew that before she posed the question. Shoot...I still have another load of laundry to do that contains some of the clothes I need to pack.

The boys and I are traveling to Indianapolis to see her for the weekend. About a month ago, her landlord called and told her he was selling the house she's in, and now she has to find a new place. Since I didn't go home in July as I had originally planned, I figured I could go now and be of some help.

My mother doesn't handle change well. So, instead of searching the phone book for senior living housing or some kind of gated apartment community, she has sat around the house fussing about her situation to her friends and crying helplessly in her spare time as if that's going to fix her predicament. I took the liberty to research a few places a

287

while ago and printed out the info, but her phone call reminded me to retrieve the papers from my desk drawer and put them in my suitcase.

"Un huh…Oh yeah?...Umm hmm…Really?...Oh…" I half-listened as she went on about some drama that took place at the church meeting. I went to place the papers in my laptop bag but changed my mind. I would have enough clutter with our boarding passes and the essays I would have to grade. Instead, I unzipped the top front pocket of my suitcase and placed the papers inside. "Shiii…sheesh!" I said after jamming my finger against something inside.

*The videotape*, I thought, as my mother asked what my problem was. I'd forgotten all about it. That goes to show how thorough I am with unpacking. It's right up there with folding clothes on my list of things I hate to do. I was lucky I didn't find a couple outfits from the Vegas trip in the main compartment.

With the phone tucked between my ear and my shoulder, I ventured into my bedroom to get the video camera. I pulled the cords from the bag and connected it to the television. Mom was still running her mouth.

When I pressed the playback button, I only saw a black screen, and it sounded like someone was fiddling with the camera. *I knew it*, I thought, while shaking my head and walking to the dresser. I figured I could at least pack some underwear while I was on the phone and feel somewhat accomplished. Just as I thought, it was one of the tapes Ric let the boys use when they called themselves making movies like Daddy. They usually ended up capturing the floor or the lens cap.

About a minute into it, I heard what sounded like a handclap, then a moan.

"What's that?" my mom asked. She heard it loud and clear because the volume was cranked up from Ric's last viewing of *106 and Park*.

288

I didn't answer her as I faced the screen and saw a female's ass, my video camera strap, and someone's penis ramming into what I like to call "the wrong hole". I couldn't answer her. I managed to press the off button with my trembling finger before the phone dropped to the floor. I was right about the origin of the clap I heard. It's just that his hand was slapping her behind. I lost all feeling in my body except the overwhelming thump of my heartbeat—my only indication that I was still alive.

Then he spoke. Asked her if she liked it. Asked her if she could handle it. Asked her if it was "in that ass" as if he didn't already know. I stared at the images, regaining my sensation—feeling the heartbeat that felt like it had traveled to my throat, becoming short of breath. The more I attempted to breathe through my mouth to encourage calmness, the worse my tremors became. I was infuriated beyond explanation; physiologically affected and psychologically challenged. I wanted to turn it off, but I couldn't stop watching.

I wasn't trapped in a nightmare, fighting to wake up. I was conscious and alert, watching the ultimate horror movie starring my husband. Ric was thoroughly enjoying himself, cheering himself on. The mystery ho cheered him on, as well, praising his endowment and calling him "Daddy".

Reading the time and date stamp made my stomach turn, but seeing the strap from my camera get trapped between their sweaty bodies and realizing he wasn't even wearing a condom was enough to induce vomiting. I barely made it to the toilet before chucking up the Boston Market meal I had for lunch. I've never felt so drained...of everything. I had no energy, no tears, no words, no strength. So, I sat at the base of the toilet and laid my head on its seat. Let the numbness set in. It felt great to not feel.

I wanted to pray. I tried to pray. But all I kept hearing in my head was, *That motherfucker.* He was having sex with that

289

girl when he was supposedly at the latest training session for BlackBerry phones back in January. He set that up so sweetly, too, because when he came in the house that night, he handed me the latest model of the phone. *That motherfucker.*

I returned to the bedroom in time to see position number two, which consisted of her performing oral sex on him. His moans of enjoyment only added fuel to my fire as he called out her name, petted her on the head like a good dog, and whispered, "That's a good bitch. That's the bitch I know." Seems like Marisa was a bitch I needed to know, too.

By the time they reached position three, I was talking to God. Ric had placed the camera on the bed to capture both of their faces, and I was through. I regained every emotion with a renewed intensity. As if Jesus was sitting in front of me, I spoke aloud.

"Lord, help me. I'm gonna kill him." For a while, everything went black, but my eyes weren't closed. "I...am...going...to...kill him." I meant it. I scared myself, because the logical part of me had been flushed down the toilet with my lunch, and there was nothing left but rage.

I paced in front of the television, oblivious to the multiple times my mother called, deaf to the sound of the boys' voices as they came upstairs to play in their room.

I fast-forwarded the scene, looking for the end, only to find two other videos of two more females engaging in similar activities with my single husband. Seconds into Part Three, I flung the remote control toward the TV like it was a boomerang, knowing it wouldn't return to my hand. It did exactly what I wanted it to do: destroy the high-definition screen. It signified the point of no return—the destination Ric had driven me to; my wardrobe consisting of only a blindfold and my heart that I wore on my sleeve.

The boys pounded on my door. Dalvin sang my name over and over, while Chase cried. The noise from the broken

TV probably scared them half to death. I didn't respond as quickly as I normally would have. In fact, I didn't budge until Chase sounded like he was going to throw up from crying so hard. As soon as I opened the door, they grabbed my legs and asked if someone was breaking into our house. I reassured them that we were safe and then told them to get their shoes on. We had somewhere to go.

Once they were in their car seats, I proceeded to the corner of the garage where Ric keeps his Rubbermaid bins. A year ago, I saw him digging in a particular one that contained his belongings from his time in the Air Force. He looked like he'd hit the jackpot when he pulled out a videotape then, and when I casually strolled out there to see what he was looking at, he buried it in the bin and wrestled with me. "Leave me alone," he said playfully. "Ain't nobody thinkin' 'bout that tape. I was just lookin' for an old picture of me and Wilson standing next to the first jet we worked on. He called me earlier today. I told him I'ma get a duplicate made." He held the picture up so I could see.

For some reason, I kept wondering about the videotape, though. I never pressed the issue then, but I had every reason to now. And I didn't need him to grant me access to it. I guess it was my lucky day, because I also found a few pictures of naked girls sprawled out on a bed. I guess I was supposed to give him credit for not having them on our bed. I held the pictures like a deck of cards as I scanned for a familiar face. Lo and behold, LaShay was in the bunch.

*That's it*, I thought as I closed the bin and kicked it to the side. At first, I was getting in the car to go for a drive and think of my next move. When I saw LaShay, I had a specific destination in mind. The boys complained of being hungry, so I took them to the KFC nearby. On the way there, I called Ms. Gladys and asked if she could watch them for a couple hours.

"Sure, sweetie. Is everything okay?"

I thought I had steadied my voice enough to sound normal, but apparently, I hadn't. "Yes, ma'am. I just have to make an important run. Something just came up, and it's best that the boys don't come with me."

"Is there anything else you need? Any other way I can help?"

I took in a deep breath and exhaled. "Just pray for me...please."

I tried to avoid her when I let the boys out of the car, but she came outside. After she told the boys to go inside, she looked me in my eyes. "I don't know what's goin' on with you, and it's not my business, but don't go do nothin' foolish. Only one thing will make your eyes turn that hue of red and flush all the emotion from your face. He's not worth you going to jail and losing these babies. You understand?"

I nodded and gently patted the hand she placed on my shoulder. "I'll be back by eight o'clock. If I'm not, call the police and tell them I was last at City Mobile in Gwinnett."

Before I left, I ran into my house and copied the footage onto my laptop and my external hard drive. I'm sure my divorce lawyer will want me to have hard evidence that our marriage has been a mimicry of all things real.

*****

Ric was surprised to see me fling the glass door open. There were six customers in the store, and he and LaShay were busy helping them. I walked straight to his office and dropped my purse on his desk.

He excused himself and rushed into the room. "What's wrong? Where are the boys? Somethin' happen?"

"Un uh. Go take care of your customers. I'll wait."

He frowned, but hurried back out to close the deal with the wealthy-looking gentleman in the sweater vest. I searched the control panel for the TVs, looking for A/V ports. Once I found them, I pulled the video camera from my purse and connected it. After experimenting with a few switches, the screens in the sales area went from showing City Mobile commercials to showing Ric smiling into the camera while humping the last girl on the first tape.

Once I heard the first moan, my job was done. I picked up my purse and stormed out of the office. The customers' faces all displayed the same expression: a lot of shock mixed with a little disgust. Ric was horrified. When he looked up to see what the customers were gasping at, he saw his face and heard his voice demanding the ho to keep saying his name. He sprinted into the office and turned off the screens. By that time, two of the customers were heading out the door.

"Just so there's no confusion, folks, that footage was not taken on a phone," I said.

The young guy looking at the iPhone looked disappointed.

"However, I'm sure Cedric here can help you pick the phone that can give you the best video quality if you're interested. And his sidekick here can tell you which one takes the best still photos." Ric tore out of the office as LaShay stood near the counter looking like a deer in headlights. He clamped his hand around my bicep and flung me into the corner in the back of the store.

"You don't come into my store startin' shit."

"And you don't come into my life startin' shit. You wanna show your ass *literally*? Well, this is how I show mine. If you don't like it, call security, you nasty son-of-a-bitch."

As I walked past LaShay, I grabbed her by the throat and dragged her a few steps. "If I wasn't a respectable woman, I'd fuck you up. How many times did I talk to you about dealing with my husband? It's alright. You better pray your naked picture doesn't end up being posted on every bulletin board on Georgia State's property. If you haven't

293

done it already, go 'head and fuck him. He's a free man now."

I took one last look at Ric, who stood with his lips tight, breathing through his nose as if I was supposed to be intimidated. I waved them both off and left the store. His delayed reaction was to run after me, but I was already backing out of my parking space. He learned quickly this wasn't one of those occurrences he could fix when he attempted to stand in my way and I hit his left thigh.

When he screamed, I didn't even check my rearview mirror. When he called, I acted like I didn't hear his ringtone. I went straight to Ms. Gladys' house and got the boys. Willow said she would keep them overnight at Crystal's apartment, and that was perfect. I needed to be able to yell at their daddy without worrying about my volume.

I stayed around and talked to Willow for about an hour. She looked surprisingly well. The swelling in her face was gone, but the bruising was still lingering around her jawbone. She said it was because the doctor keeps aggravating it when he works on her teeth. Then, she told me she thinks he is her father. I tried my best to stay tuned in to her story, but I couldn't stop thinking about the videotapes. She noticed.

"I know everything isn't okay, so I won't ask that," she started. "Are you gonna be alright?"

My lip trembled before my tears fell. I couldn't answer her, so I just shook my head.

"What can I do?" she asked.

I continued to shake my head and then pointed at the boys, who were coloring with Venus. "Thank you," was all I could get out before I signaled that I would call her and rushed out of the apartment.

*****

294

"All this time you've been trying to break into the movie production business, and I'll be damned if this doesn't make complete sense. Guess you left out the part about producing porn. Wait! You're a jack of all trades. You're the producer, director, camera 1 & 2 operator, *and* the star." I clapped with insane enthusiasm. "Now that's talent."

"Man, that was a long time ago. You trippin'. That's old," is all Ric had to say when I got home.

His facial expression disgusted me. He wore a genuine smirk, and his eyes danced in all directions, making sure not to stop to look at me.

"Well, excuse me. I haven't found the new release yet."

"There ain't no new release."

"So that's it? The tapes are old. That's your final answer?"

"Yes! I don't need to phone a friend or do fifty-fifty. What else do you want me to say? We were goin' through problems anyway. You kept threatenin' to leave me and shit. So, when the opportunity arose, I took it."

"*Did* I leave you, though?"

"You might as well have. You were walkin' around the house wit' an attitude for like a month."

I laughed. "Unreal."

"What do you want from me, Dana? If I say sorry, you ain't gon' accept it."

"I don't want shit. You have to be the nastiest, most disrespectful, uncouth, inconsiderate son-of-a-bitch I know. And I married your ass. I knew you did your dirt in the past, but I couldn't have predicted this with a crystal ball. You slid up in each of those bitches with no condom, no fuckin' consideration for your wife who was putting her lips on that same dick."

"Don't play me like that. I didn't do that and come home to you. We never had sex after I did that."

"Maybe not that same night, but that doesn't make it okay. Diseases don't wash off in the shower. You know what makes this even more hurtful and demeaning? *Everything* you did with those girls, you've done with me. So, that means you're just greedy. Greedy and disgusting. That 'big gift' you were working on for me for Christmas...What was it? AIDS?"

"I know you're mad, but you're going too far."

"You went too far, you nasty fuck. You were busting through assholes in almost every flick—one of the most common forms of sex associated with AIDS. 'Merry Christmas, baby. I wrapped my dick in a red bow for AIDS awareness. I wanted to get you something you could have forever,'" I said, mocking his voice.

Again, he smirked as if he was amused.

"And that shit's funny to you?"

"Man, you're wild. No, it's not funny, but none of those girls had a disease."

"And how do you know this?"

"None of them had a disease...period."

"So I guess your dick is an STD test dipstick."

"That's real cute."

"Not nearly as cute as you worshipping Girl Number Three's ass in the video."

"So I guess this is it, huh? I'm sure you hate me."

"That word doesn't even scratch the surface of what I'm feeling."

"I don't want you to feel that way, though. Hatred isn't good for your health."

"Neither is unprotected sex. You leave my health concerns for me and my doctor to worry about. Excuse me," I said, before walking by him and retreating to the office.

For a while, I just sat on the floor with my knees to my chin and back against the wall, looking into the darkness. *What is happening to me?* I thought as more tears welled up. I let them fall. I wanted every bit of pain to leave my body, and if the tears were its only method of transportation, so be it. It was time to face the facts I had been seeking. I was right. He was cheating, and I'd finally caught him. I won the game. Time for my victory song.

Meshell Ndegeocello's husky voice crooned lyrics that made my heart feel a hundred pounds heavier. *I remember when you filled my heart with joy. Was I blind to the truth, just there to fill the space?...I've allowed you to make me feel so dumb. What kind of fool am I?*

"Fool of Me." I needed to hear it. I set it to repeat and listened to its honesty for over an hour. I wanted to torture myself with the words that told my story. I wanted to get tired of hearing it so I'd never want to play it again.

When my "woe is me" party ended, my head still wasn't very clear. I still wanted to get a knife from the kitchen and stab Ric relentlessly in the heart so he could feel my pain. If I didn't leave, I was afraid I would really do it.

I sped down I-285 at 2:17 a.m. with the windows down, blasting Keri Hilson's "Energy". Her volume was at thirty, and mine was at forty as I belted out every lyric. Most were unintelligible because I was forcing the words through the gigantic lump in my throat.

My logical self made a guest appearance halfway into my second trip around the huge circle. I remembered my babies needed school clothes for the next day, so I stopped at Wal-Mart to get them emergency outfits and the toiletries they would need when they woke up. When I left the store, I started my journey back downtown to the "escape". My presence there would be a win-win. I would be with my boys, and I could be trusted with the knives.

# WILLOW (MILKY)

Just as Crystal predicted, Vaughn contacted me again. It had been a few weeks since he'd left a voice message, and I thought I'd blown my chance to find out where he was. To his surprise, I answered his phone call.

He stammered for a while and then finally got to the point. He had come to town to turn himself in, but wanted to see me and Venus first. I shut down the visit with Venus immediately. He seemed to understand that I didn't want to confuse or upset her, but insisted on seeing me. Supposedly, he wanted to face his demons like a man, see just how good he got me. His story still contains the part where he blacked out and can't imagine how he could've harmed me in such a way.

I told him that his attack was a blessing in disguise because it led me to my biological father. After my first visit with Dr. Knight, Rebecca and Crystal had affirmed my suspicions that he is *the* Scott Knight that would've been on my birth certificate if I had been born in a hospital like most babies.

"I wish I could've been there with you when you discovered that," he replied.

"And I wish I wouldn't have found out the way I did."

"I never put two and two together."

"Huh?"

"Nothing. So will you meet me somewhere? All I want is ten minutes of your time. You name the place."

"Where are you staying?"

"At one of my properties."

"I'll meet you there. I don't like being in public. I'm still missing teeth, you know."

"Should I prepare for Todd? Is he gonna come with you to knock my teeth out?"

"Todd is in-season. Besides, why would I give you a heads-up? You didn't give me one."

"Touché." His tone had become more relaxed, as if he had charmed me into seeing him. Little did he know, I'd been waiting for his invitation.

*****

"I don't have time for all of these questions. Are you coming or what?" I asked.

"Hell yeah, I'm comin'," Crystal replied.

"I'm outside. Let's go."

She looked confused when she walked out and saw the Infiniti with tinted windows. I cracked the window and rushed her inside. Once she closed the door, I explained the situation. I'm convinced Vaughn has had someone following me for weeks, and I wanted to throw them off so he wouldn't have any suspicions about our meeting.

There have been too many occasions where I've seen the same woman in too many different parts of town during too many times of the day. She thinks she's keeping a low profile, but since I know Vaughn is a psychopath who had surveillance on me in Vegas, my senses are much more keen. I hear footsteps from further distances, see shadows I never noticed before, and take note of faces I would've barely

299

PORTIA A. COSBY

glanced at under other circumstances. When Vaughn said he didn't put two and two together during our conversation about Scott Knight being Dr. Knight, I took that as confirmation that he was having me followed. That set me off.

I rented the car under Rebecca's name, and wearing a wig and sunglasses, I rode in a cab to pick it up. Once I had the car, I didn't return to Crystal's apartment. Instead, I went to Wal-Mart and picked up a few things—random things—that would keep our visit interesting.

"So what's the plan?" Crystal asked.

I shrugged.

"You don't know? What the hell, Milky?"

"I'm playing it by ear. You said you wanted to roll, right?"

"Uh, yeah, but I thought you at least had a general idea of what you were gon' do."

"You hate him, right?" I asked.

"Hell yeah."

"Me, too. Now's your chance to show it. Just follow my lead. Whatever you do, don't shoot him. He doesn't get off that easy."

"I think you're scaring me, but I kinda like it," Crystal said.

As we had discussed early in the day, she called her friend from the Cobb County Police Department and told him we were five minutes away. He was going to park discreetly in the area and be ready to arrest Vaughn after we were done "defending ourselves".

I called Vaughn just before we pulled into the housing plan. He answered after three rings, out of breath. "Hey. Are you on your way?" he asked.

"Actually, I'm pulling in now. I got done with everything earlier than I expected. Don't tell me you're out and about."

300

"No, no. Well, I'm not at the house. I'm in the fitness center. You can come here, though. It's after hours, so we'll have privacy."

Vaughn is a creature of habit. I knew he'd be working out. It's what he always did at nine o'clock. "Perfect," I said after we hung up.

Crystal and I blended into the night with our black attire. I closed my lips tightly, careful not to let the cool air blow through my teeth. My gums were already aching as if I hadn't taken Vicodin an hour earlier. The pain fueled my fire as we entered the fitness center and found Vaughn bench pressing.

He laughed when he saw Crystal. "How did I know you wouldn't be alone? You still can't do things by yourself, huh?"

He completed a few more reps and placed the bar on the rack. I got Crystal's attention and prayed she would understand our next move based solely off of my eye movement.

"Did you come to shoot me, Crystal? I'm not Dante. I'll press charges." He laughed as he lifted the bar again and began another set.

She laughed with him. "I know you're not Dante. His dick works."

"Willow, I asked to speak with you—not your peanut gallery. You can leave now." He grunted as he pushed the weight off of his chest.

On my cue, Crystal joined me behind the bench as Vaughn lowered the bar to his chest again. As if we'd planned it in the car, we pushed down on the metal rod, making it impossible for him to move it and difficult for him to breathe.

"I'll leave when I get ready," I said. "After what you did to me, do you really think I would show up alone?"

He used his limited oxygen supply to laugh again.

301

"And how could I leave without you seeing your body of work?" I leaned over and smiled three inches from his face. He couldn't hide his horror. "What's wrong? I thought we were laughing?" I spat between his eyes before standing upright again.

"Looks like I'm not the one you should worry about," Crystal said.

"Okay. You've made your point. Get this thing off me."

"Was it that simple for you? Don't you think you'd made your point when you yanked me from the chaise lounge? No, you had to play dirty. You wanted to fight me like a man."

"You know what triggered that. You brought that up on purpose."

I retrieved the Wal-Mart bag that rested near my foot. "I brought it up on purpose, but not to undermine your manhood." I pulled out the package of hot dogs and tore it open. "Back then, I wanted to help you. Now, I want to demean you." I dangled a hot dog near his lips. "Remember when you said I'm the only white girl you know that can't suck dick? Why don't you show me?"

He folded his lips inside of his mouth, and a tear ran from his right eye into his ear.

"Don't be shy," I said.

Crystal gave me a questioning look before I asked her to punch him in the stomach. I had never told her the story Mrs. Ella told me. That would make for great conversation during the ride home. As soon as she punched him, his mouth opened involuntary. I interrupted his loud groan with the placement of the hot dog on his tongue.

"Show me what I did wrong. You should know, right?" I moved the meat in different ways, simulating oral sex as best I could. I added three more hot dogs because I wanted to see how many his mouth could hold. Sick, I know.

We let go of the bar just before Vaughn's air supply was depleted. His arms shook like twigs holding a cement platform as he racked the weights. He turned his head to the side and let the hot dogs fall onto the floor.

"You're fuckin' crazy."

"No, you're crazy to think you can beat me unconscious, leave me, and then call with a few tearful apologies like all should be forgiven. Maybe *you* should've gone to the nearest plastic surgeon, changed *your* face, and disappeared," I said, referencing the advice he had once given me in the event that he ever caught me cheating.

"You'll get yours," he threatened as I walked away from the bench.

I picked up a ten-pound free weight and dropped it directly onto the useless meat between his legs. He squealed like some unidentified animal, locked his ankles around the bench, and took it with him to the floor.

"I just did," I replied as Crystal's friend and his partner walked in.

"Bet it'll swell now," Crystal said.

"Vaughn Townsend, you're under arrest for attempted murder, fleeing the scene of a crime, violating a P.F.A...." The list went on.

We gave our report to the officers of how Vaughn tried to attack us and we had no choice but to retaliate. They were glad to take him away since they had been looking for him for two months. I could only hope they had a cold cell and a horny cellmate waiting for him at the jail.

Crystal drove me back to her apartment and ended up staying. I slipped deeper and deeper into a state of inertness as the night progressed, overcome by emotions I've never felt. I rarely ever drink alcohol, but I raided Crystal's bar and downed a half bottle of Strawberry Smirnoff in less than an hour. I couldn't believe what I had done. It was cruel and

303

merciless. It was sadistic. It was satisfying. That was the scary part.

I now know what temporary insanity feels like. Even as I sat on the floor and leaned against the bar, a certain amount of justification remained. My mockery of his childhood trauma was a low and mighty blow, but after all I've endured, it was long overdue. He tried to take everything from me—my will, my self-respect, my love, my worth. Physically and emotionally, he tried to destroy me, but he says he loves me. I hope he takes the express route to hell.

# CRYSTAL

Well, Dante pulled it off. It's been four months since the press conference, and ninety percent of his fans still love him. The other ten percent don't necessarily hate him. They're just indifferent. Hell, he isn't their husband. Why should they care about what he did to me? He can still sing, and he's still fine as hell...now that his first-degree burns and lacerations from the glass have healed.

His P.R. team had him play that pitiful, sorrowful, remorseful husband role to a tee at the press conference. As fate would have it, I ended up helping him, even though I refused to attend. The injuries I caused made him look like a man down on his luck, a man who looked like a victim. He spoke softly, cleared his throat to fight tears, and played with his hands as he addressed reporters and television cameras. When they asked why he didn't press charges, he stressed that the stories were all embellished because no one was there but me and him. When they asked where I was, Sheila quickly reminded them that he was not answering any questions about me out of respect. Said I've been through enough.

I love how I'm so deserving of his respect now. I'm such a beautiful, irreplaceable black queen, owner of the best coochie ever made, goddess of his world. What the hell ever. I mean, I am all those things. That's why he married me. But evidently those attributes don't hold much weight because here we are. Or rather, there he is and here I am.

It's all good, though. You can't make a deal with the devil and then be surprised when he takes you through hell. I didn't create the monster Dante is, but I'll take the rap for being one of his enablers. I have every right to still be angry about the herpes thing, but in my eyes, I have no right to leave.

I take that back. We all have choices, and I technically have the right to leave. Still, I choose to stay. He wants me to stay, even after all the damage I've done. I guess he figures no groupie will want him now that he has the big H. Let him tell it, he wants me to stay because I have his heart and he can't function without me. He wrote those lyrics for our wedding day song, and he sang them like he meant them. But somewhere between the ending applause and now, he forgot how to live up to his words, and I forgot how to care that he didn't.

I'm no hypocrite. I, too, have been an adulterer. Nigel was my late-night snack for years. I'm not hung up on Dante cheating. I'm pissed because he lied repeatedly about his relationship with that girl, and for whatever reason, for whatever amount of time, she meant something to him. His sudden affinity for the Florida studio last year was proof of that. Kissing her was proof of that. Protecting her from my phone call was the tip of the iceberg. I need more time to figure out how I feel about that. Maybe if he goes into rehab, I'll believe he has changed. All the celebs go to rehab for something, right? There has to be a center for liars.

Nigel wasn't important enough for me to lie about our relationship. If Dante would've ever asked if we were screwing, I would have come clean. Nigel knew this, and he knew the repercussions. He had more to lose than me. That made me significant to him. He was simply convenient for me. We still talk—at least once a week—but it's all talk. He tells me how miserable Dante is without me, and I can hear the hateration in his tone; his hope that I stay away permanently to teach Dante a lesson. He's always said my husband doesn't realize what he has, but he's sure not attempting to ride the Crystal train anymore. Seems his shining armor is being repaired and his horse is suddenly unavailable. Hmm…I wonder why. It's all fun and games until somebody gets a disease. Note to self: Go in on his ass the next time he calls talking that bullshit.

I used to think you had to be a nasty girl to get nasty-girl acne, but I'm definitely not that and I definitely have it. When I first went to the gynecologist in total panic mode, he shared a shocking and oddly consoling statistic with me. He said one in four adults have herpes. That means that out of my closest friends—Dana, Milky, and LaToya—I'm the one of us four taking it for the team.

After hearing of some of the reckless sexual behavior my girls at Something to Do have engaged in, I fear it's even more common in teenagers. I'd rather not shout it from the mountaintop, but I plan on speaking with them about this once I find a little more nerve. They look up to me, and I guess educating them could be the one positive thing that comes from this ordeal. Like Dana said, they need to hear the truth from me. They need to know I'm still the woman they respect as a mentor, big sister, and mother figure.

I'm not crippled by this. I don't have a blanket of bumps all around my pelvis. I don't pop pills every day. Though it's a serious disease that is technically in my system forever, life goes on. I don't have to put the shit on my résumé or anything. The doctor even said I may stop getting outbreaks altogether. I didn't know that was possible. I'll be damned if I'm not becoming one of those people in the commercials.

Dante's been going all out. Back in September, he bought me the G550 Benz SUV for my birthday. I had been drooling over it since it came out, but he never entertained my interest. I would've destroyed the cars and the house a long time ago if I had known that would get me the vehicle. He even had the towel warmer installed in our bathroom. I'll tell you. People don't pay attention to you until you go crazy.

I've been living in our house in Indiana for a couple of weeks. I felt more comfortable leaving after I knew Vaughn was locked up and my sister was safe. I'm going back to Atlanta. I just don't know when. It'll be soon, though, because this snow and bitter cold is for the birds. I forgot how different November is here.

This is Indianapolis, where the major stars play for the Colts and the Pacers. Dante's hometown fans love and support him, but not enough to focus on whether I've moved back to the area. I appreciate going to the store without people really noticing who I am. I can walk around my property without fear of the paparazzi hiding in my bushes, waiting to snap a picture of me so they can Photoshop it and say I'm pregnant with a baby that will have herpes, too. Dumb stuff. And my friends here see me as Crystal Thornton, the chick they skipped class with—not Crystal Moss, the chick married to a star. They're unaware that one call to any gossip mag revealing my whereabouts could pay their bills for a couple months. Thank you, God.

Before I left town, Dante sent me a picture message via phone with a caption that read, *I told you I'm serious.* When I opened it, I saw my lips tattooed on his chest, over his heart, and his hand holding the piece of paper I'd kissed a long time ago. In college, every time I wrote him, I put on a fresh coat of lipstick and planted a kiss just under my name. I had asked him to get the tattoo as my anniversary gift two years ago, but he came up with some lame excuse. Then, he said he would get it, but only from some parlor in New York. Of course, whenever he was in New York, his schedule didn't allow for a tattoo. I mentioned it again when we were in Puerto Rico, but still nothing happened. I think the ink was supposed to persuade me to stay in town, but the gesture came after I had already made up my mind.

I had moved back into our house prior to that because Milky and Venus were using the apartment. Dante tried his best to accommodate our living situation so I could have my space and still enjoy the comfort of our home. In order to keep me around, he had moved out of our room and into one of the other bedrooms in the west wing of the house.

For a while, life there was tolerable. I enjoyed driving my fancy truck and wrapping myself in warm towels. It wasn't until he was home five days in a row that I became uncomfortable. I realized I had returned while the wound was still open and bleeding. Thought I was tough enough to handle it. Was clear that I wasn't by day two. So, I avoided him. I would call Martha to see where he was so I wouldn't run into him. I would text him when I absolutely needed to communicate with him, even if he was within earshot. I would eat my meals in my room. It was stupid, and I felt childish. Now I'm here and I feel incomplete, but I can't decide whether it's because of our time or our love.

He thinks I'm never coming back, and I like it that way. Everything has come easy to him in his life, so it'll do him some good to sweat a little. He's not sure what to make of my state of mind, and I'm not either. I'm confused about how we will overcome this, but I'm sure I still love his disobedient ass. Whether I like it or not, he has my heart. If he would stop trying to solve things the celebrity man-whore way and get back to the basics, he can have all of me again. I can consider not just moving back to Atlanta, but moving back into our house. These are desperate times and he's certainly taking desperate measures; but I need him to acknowledge that desperate measures should also include a certain amount of sentiment. He's on track with the tattoo.

# DANA

My phone lit up, showing another text message from Ric. He was on his way to bring the boys home. Like a model father, he has been picking them up, taking them to the library for homework and reading time, feeding them, playing with them, and returning them to me. My only responsibilities have been bathing them and tucking them in. I think I'm supposed to be impressed, supposed to see this as his atonement and forgive him. Too bad I'm not.

I resent that he's still so comfortable. Sure, he's affected by my decision because I took away home base, but that's about it. He calls and tries to hold conversations like everything is cool. He tells me he loves me, even though he knows he'll only get silence in return. He's not hurting. He's just waiting for me to get over it so he can come back.

When he arrived with the boys, he told me they were ready for bed because they'd been to the YMCA and showered once they got out of the pool. The boys begged him to tuck them in, and with my go-ahead, Ric was heading upstairs with Chase on his back and Dalvin holding his hand.

311

He came back down twenty minutes later. "You look nice," he said with a look that used to break me down.

"Thanks," I replied with no real appreciation.

Shot down once again, he shrugged and said goodbye. It was then that I decided to implement a plan I'd been devising for a day or so. I knew it would affect him, if not hurt him, and though it was juvenile in nature and not fully planned out, I was sure to get a satisfactory amount of pleasure from my act.

Before he reached the door, I asked, "Do you miss us?"

"Yes, baby. You know I do," he said, his eyes looking like a child waiting for a surprise. He anxiously walked toward me, stopping at a safe distance.

I made it obvious that I was looking at what I used to call mine as I stared at his crotch. "How much do you miss me?"

He grew instantly, and I rested my index finger at the corner of my mouth like the porn stars do.

"Show me," I said, pulling a condom from my back pocket. I'd had the same one in my pockets the previous two days, but this time, I also had the guts to go through with it. He looked shocked when I presented it to him, but he knew better than to question why he needed to wear it.

Our clothes were barely off before he penetrated me. My mini-me gave him the genuine hugs my arms could only fake as he moaned instantly with pleasure. I closed my eyes and pretended it wasn't him for a little while. With his every stroke, I made it my business to massage his hardness with my vaginal muscles and the natural lubricant within.

"Damn, baby, you *did* miss it," he whispered. "It's so warm."

"You ever heard of a warm welcome?" I whispered back, then hiked my legs over his shoulders so he could go deeper.

312

"I knew you'd give it to Daddy again. This is all mine." He hit it hard a few times because he couldn't resist, then stopped. "Wait. You gon' make me cum too fast, baby."

*Stupid fucker*, I thought, as he exited me and prompted me to get on top. He pulled me to his face first, treating my clitoris like it was an ice cream cone on the hottest day of the year. Once I got mine, it was time for him to get his.

I took a deep breath, then placed him inside of me. Staring at his closed eyes and open mouth, I rode him like a wave and ran through a near-psychotic range of emotions. I was aroused, angry, pleased, and repulsed, fighting the flashes of Ric and his amateur counterparts performing the same act.

He fought to keep quiet as I maneuvered my legs into a position he and I had never tried—one I didn't know existed until earlier in the year. His breathing became heavier, and his nails dug into my hips as he neared his climax. He sputtered sweet nothings between breaths, begging for my forgiveness, proclaiming me to be the best at everything, promising me a world he can't even afford to put on layaway.

I stared at him, waiting for just the right moment. When it arrived, I asked, "Does that feel good, baby?"

His body jolted but stayed in rhythm with mine. "Yes. Yes, baby."

I picked up the pace, determined to drive him insane. I leaned over and placed my lips beside his ear. "Good. Lorenzo taught it to me. Damn teachers," I whispered.

Before my words could register, Ric was ejaculating, and I was dismounting him. He was too weak to swing on me, too shocked to speak, and too cool to show his embarrassment.

"Let yourself out," I said, while rounding the couch and starting down the hall.

The only thing I heard was a grunt of amusement as I made my way upstairs to lock myself in the master bathroom. Though Ric has never been violent toward me, there's a first time for everything, and I wasn't gonna welcome the opportunity with open arms or an open door. I even waited to hear the door close and went through the house with my baseball bat to survey the scene before washing up and preparing for bed.

Ric never has to admit he was hurt by what I did. I know him well enough to have noticed the subtle emptiness of his eyes when he came down from his peak. He may even think I lied just to get back at him. Regardless, he'll always wonder, and those nine minutes will forever be etched in his memory.

*****

I met Crystal for drinks the next night at a lounge downtown so we could discuss why I had been M.I.A. She was in shock when I told her about Ric's feature films.

"I can't believe you didn't call me!"

"Girl, you have your own stuff goin' on."

"Whatever! I would've been happy to transfer my psychosis in Ric's direction. You're too nice to *really* act up."

We paused our conversation to accept our meals from the server. When he walked away, Crystal pointed her chopsticks at me. "Don't ever act like I'm too wrapped up in my own madness to talk to you. You've known me too long."

"It's not just that. I needed to sort through things by myself. I had to mourn the death of my marriage. You'd think it would be easy to accept its demise since I watched it deteriorate for eight years."

"If it starts off being easy, your marriage never meant anything in the first place. It gets easier, I'm sure, but it's not supposed to be a joyous occasion." She tasted her sushi and

314

dabbed the corner of her mouth with the teal napkin. "We save the celebrating for the one-year anniversary of your freedom. Vegas, baby!"

We shared a laugh that drew the attention of those in our vicinity.

"Really, how do you feel? Are you alright with your choice?" Crystal asked.

"I feel like I didn't have a choice. I'm too intelligent to watch my husband's infidelity on tape and stick around because he says he made a horrible mistake. I have more respect for myself than that."

"You have to stay true to yourself."

"Exactly. And that boy had me acting twelve shades of foolish. You know it's time to go when you find yourself acting completely out of character," I replied. "I've gotta get back to me."

I then told her how I assaulted LaShay in Ric's store, and how I rode around at 3 a.m. looking for him with the boys in the car a few days after that. She most appreciated the story of my revenge sex.

"I cannot believe you did that! What a way to ruin an orgasm." She placed her hand over her heart. "I have to say I'm proud. I hate the circumstances that brought this side out of you, but I love the woman you're becoming. They say there's a blessing in the storm, and I think you've become much stronger from dealing with his shit."

I laughed. "You can't talk about a blessing and cuss in the same sentence."

"Oops!"

We were two hours in but just getting started. We moved to the bar and let the spirits flow freely. In turn, my emotions flowed just the same.

"Remember how you told me to believe half of what I see and none of what I hear? You need an addendum for that. Believe half of what you see unless that shit is on video.

Do you know some of those dummies didn't even demand that he use a real video camera? He had files from his phone hidden on our computer. How are you agreeable to letting a virtual stranger use his cell phone to film your face—your mouth—getting stuffed with his...Ahhh, it's unreal!" I screamed.

Crystal slid her glass in front of me, and I finished the last of her drink in one gulp. She signaled for the bartender to bring us another round. "Make hers a double." She turned back to me. "So where is he these days?"

"Somewhere kickin' rocks. Shit, I don't know and I don't care. I swear if he was on fire right now, I'd spit a half shot of vodka on his ass and drink the rest."

"Ooookay?!" Crystal exclaimed, clanging her glass against mine.

"Do you know how hard it is to look in the mirror and realize you're just as responsible for the pain you thought someone else caused you? Why wouldn't Ric think he could get away with this? He's gotten away with everything else. I've *let* him get away with everything else. I've swept so much shit under the rug, and now there's no more room."

"I'm glad you're accepting your part in this, but let's not get too carried away. He's manipulated your relationship since I've known you. How many times did I have to make you hang up on him in school 'cause he was stressing you out with his grandiose lies? That fool got comfortable and somehow believed you were weak enough to stay for the long haul, no matter what he did. 'For better or for worse' doesn't translate to 'Let him fuck around all he wants, and then document the shit on videotape as proof that he can get away with anything.' He thought he had you brainwashed, but somebody's apparently brainwashed him into thinking he's irreplaceable."

"Cedric Hall and irreplaceable? Aren't those synonyms?" I hung my head and chuckled. "I guess I should

316

raise my hand as the responsible party. I put his ass on a pedestal for years because I thought that's what a woman did for her husband. I thought if I did my part, he'd reciprocate. But the truth is he's a sorry-ass excuse of a man. I can say that out loud now because he's no longer *my* sorry-ass excuse of a man."

Crystal cracked up while I took a sip of my new drink. "Uh oh. I can feel it. You're about to go *in* on Slick Ric."

"I'm just stating facts. He surrounds himself with naïve little youngsters because they're the only ones who look up to him and feed into the bullshit that comes out of his mouth. I can name one friend his age, and if they talk five times a year, that's a surprise.

"He's a joke to anybody who has good sense. Sittin' up tellin' Dante what kind of car he'll be driving next year because he'll be a millionaire, when he doesn't even have a valid license! How 'bout you stop talkin' about it and be about it? Surprise the man and show up at an event that only millionaires go to. That'll let him know you're in his league.

"And it's not like he doesn't have the talent. He's just so caught up in his dreams that he never wakes up and does what's necessary to bring them into fruition. You can't tell he's an intelligent, aspiring filmmaker if you watch him bop around town in oversized t-shirts and baseball caps like he's nineteen. I told you I nicknamed him Peter Pan 'cause he refuses to grow up."

"He's probably been bopping right by potential investors, too," Crystal added.

"Right. But according to him, he was a project kid and he'll always 'keep it real,'" I mocked, using air quotes. I downed the rest of the drink. "I loved him, though. I sure did. I saw what he used to be and what he could be, but I ignored what he is. I get it now. Roger that. You have to love the person, not their potential."

"Over and out!" Crystal said.

As if cued as a needle drop in a movie, the intro to "What's Love Got to Do with It" blared through the speakers around us. We looked at each other and cracked up.

When my laughter faded, I asked, "How can you love someone and hate them at the same time? Why doesn't Tina touch on that?"

I glanced up at Crystal, who was still wearing her sunglasses at eleven o'clock at night in a dim restaurant because she didn't want to be recognized as Dante's wife. Behind the shades, I knew her eyes mirrored mine. Glassy.

"I should know, right?"

"Okay, your turn. What's up with you and Dante? I've kept up with y'all through TMZ while I was in seclusion." We laughed. "I called Milky to see how she was, and she told me to make sure you tell me the latest Vaughn story. Her mouth was still sore from the implants."

After another two hours, we were all caught up...and emotionally depleted. Again, we both downed our drinks and made them our last. I had drowned in my sorrows enough. The time had come for me to face the bitch named reality instead of turning my back every time she appeared. It was time for me to let go of the memories that used to be and see the tomfoolery that took place over the years for what it was—a virus that infected our marriage, a recurring problem that would temporarily subside, only to return again in a mutated form.

For years, I was hung up on not wanting to start over. I still feel that way, but the feeling is no longer factoring into why I should stay married. It is now number one on my "Why I Should Stay Single" list. I don't want to go through the whole girl meets boy thing again, learning a new man's flaws and mannerisms, dealing with an ignorant baby mama, crazy ex-girlfriend, or needy ex-wife. And the idea of getting used to another man's morning breath or sweaty stench is revolting. It's too much work to learn when he is lying versus when he's telling the truth, how he likes his food cooked, what makes him happy, what pisses him off, and what saddens him. I put in years of effort doing those things with Ric, and I'm tired. I'm tired of loving, done with caring, through with the rigmarole that relationships yield. I don't want to let anyone else into my heart or into my boys' lives because we may get hurt again. I consider love to be an action word, and I gave all I had. If I can get a refill on eBay, perhaps I'll reconsider.

If…okay, who am I kidding? *When* I do decide to reenter the dating pool, I'm not following my heart again. I did that the first time and ended up five miles outside of hell. I'm letting my mind lead the way—do what it does best: make decisions. My heart can stick to pumping blood.

# DANA

He's a thirty-seven-year-old fuckup and I hate him. I'm far from disgruntled; I'm disappointed...with myself. Ric has been true to himself, and I was the one totally out of my element, adapting to his disrespect and selfishness. I'm disgusted—sickened by his carelessness, burning with so much hostility that I could stand by a tree and start a wildfire. I'm disenchanted. The harshness of reality makes no provisions for the idealistic. I would rather not have learned that the hard way.

Some would say I should be happy I'm not burning with gonorrhea or breaking out with blisters like Crystal, but my heart is now plagued with distrust, and I have to learn how to get past that if I ever want to let another man in. There's no pill or shot to help those symptoms, now is there?

This hurts...more than I'll admit to anyone. Some people get married to take advantage of the tax breaks, so they can have medical insurance, so they can have legitimate kids, or so they can simply have a wedding. I married for love. I married my first love, and look what happened. I'm now a single mother of two, forced to wear a smile and be strong in front of my boys so they don't fall apart. I have to answer the same questions everyday: Where's Daddy? When's he coming home? Why doesn't he live here anymore? What did you do? Is he mad at us? What if we promise not to be bad anymore?

I feel stupid for having dealt with Ric beyond his first occurrence. Crystal and Willow argue that I'm not, so I guess I have the symptoms of being an idiot without the diagnosis. Ric had been lying to me since the day we met, and a house built on a janky foundation is destined to fall at some point. I should've known that. I did know that, but I didn't know of the lies until I was in too deep.

Sometimes I still close my eyes and see what my marriage was supposed to be like. I see Ric as a Master Sergeant in the Air Force. I see us living in a four-bedroom house with a two-car garage and fenced-in backyard for our Black Labrador. I see him proudly introducing me to his friends and coworkers—even the females. I see him putting his family first instead of himself. I see joy instead of pain. I see success instead of failure...and then I open my eyes.

*****

It was Christmas Eve, and the boys were fast asleep. I had just placed their presents under the tree and assembled Chase's train set when the phone rang. I stared at the caller ID, eagerly waiting for the voicemail to pick up Ric's call. By this time, his mother had surely opened her anonymous gift in keeping with family tradition. She and Mr. Hall open their gifts on Christmas Eve and let everyone else open theirs on Christmas day.

Ric and I normally travel to Pittsburgh with the boys every other year, but because of the circumstances, I refused to go. Ric was too much of a coward to face his family with just the boys, knowing they would infer my absence was due to something far different from the flu. I sent gifts from me and the boys on one day, and the anonymous gift a week later. Mrs. Hall had probably just finished cussing Ric out, and he was all set to do the same to me.

Instead of leaving a message, he called again...and again, I didn't answer. That process continued at least three more times, and then he knocked on my door. I hooked the chain before opening it.

"Yes?" I said pleasantly.

He held up a piece of paper with the image of the DVD cover I asked Milky to design. I put a little something together to commemorate the beginning of his film career, using the footage I found and his editing software. I purposely had her keep the cover classy so his parents would proudly put the disc in their player to watch in front of everyone. After much contemplation, I settled on the title, *Definition of a Man*. Someone must have faxed him the image so he could see for himself.

"This is funny? You hate me so much that you'd do this to my parents?"

"I don't know what you're talking about. Do what?"

"Let me in," he demanded.

"It's two in the morning. No. The boys are asleep."

"Dana, if you don't open this door, I'm kicking it in."

I let him in once he began jerking the door, but kept the cordless phone in my hand in case I needed to dial 9-1-1.

"Are you that hateful? My nieces and nephews were in the room when they put that DVD in! You've gone too far. You ruined my Christmas and my family's!"

"You ruined my *life*! Wanna trade?"

"Have you lost your mind?"

"No. I've lost my husband."

"You don't have to lose me."

"Oh yes, I do."

"Everything's out in the open now. I did my dirt, and you did yours. You pulled your little prank with the DVD.

322

We're even. Now it's time to sit down and fix this thing. This is out of hand."

"This 'thing' you speak of is—*was*—a marriage. And, baby, I'd have to put in about eighty hours of filming and let you see a private screening of other men giving it to me raw to be *almost* even with you. Don't ever compare an indiscretion to a total mockery. I had sex with Lorenzo to foolishly get back at you. I didn't even enjoy myself. I wasn't praising him on film."

"That's what I mean. You always try to downplay the shit you do. Wrong is wrong."

"You're right about that, and I can admit I was wrong. I can also admit that it wouldn't have happened if I wasn't convinced you were out sharing what was supposed to be for me. Yes, it was childish of me to do what I did, but at the time, I felt justified. You didn't even have a reason other than wanting to see if you 'still had it'. How many coochies does it take to figure that out? That question should've been answered before July 21, 2001."

"I just believe we need a little time. I know you won't be ready to come back to me right away. It may take a year, but I'm willing to put in the time. I wanna stay married."

"Of course, you do. You got your way throughout the whole marriage. Why the hell would I stay? Stay for what? More humiliation?"

"For love. And I wouldn't humiliate you. I've changed."

"That's what you inadvertently said before the Justice of the Peace, but you probably didn't realize what you were saying because you were daydreaming about your next flick. I don't love you. I never did love you. I loved the man you introduced me to when I was seventeen. He was the shit. You're a piece of shit. You're all of a sudden a changed man after the truth has surfaced, but your ass was just in preproduction for your Porn Star Audition Series Part 36.

Changed man? You changed alright—changed your hiding spot for your evidence.

"Had me walking around town like a damn fool. You're laughing out loud, laughing your ass off all over the internet and in your little texts to your girlfriend, and I can't get a fuckin' smile in person. You're sharing fantasies on cheating sites that I didn't even know about. Naw, boo. Idiot Season is over. If you didn't have enough fun with me over the eight years it lasted, I don't know what to tell you. Your longstanding permission slip to treat me like shit has been revoked."

We went back and forth, and then he finally changed the subject. "On the real, though, you need to call my parents and apologize. They didn't have nothin' to do with this. That was very disrespectful of you."

"*You* need to apologize. I didn't manipulate that footage and make it look like you. It *was* you, and according to your speech when I found the shit, it wasn't a big deal. Remember that? The girls didn't mean nothin', so that made it excusable. I thought you'd want to show off your movie-making talent. After your stint in film school, you finally have something to show. When my gag reflex stopped functioning, I stepped outside of myself and recognized how impressive your body of work is. I even sent a copy to Kandi and Rhonda at Dante's PR firm in case they're interested. You can thank me later."

His facial expression transformed to a somber one. "Dana, I don't wanna do this. It's killing me to see you like this because I know it's all an act. You're not comfortable with what you've done. This ain't even how you operate."

I dropped my hands from my hips and leaned against the couch.

"I wanna make this right. I can't live without my family."

"You were living without us all over the tapes, weren't you? Ric, save this shit for the next dummy you get with."

"Baby, Dana, I'm goin' crazy without you. I've never begged for anything in my life until now. Please."

"You've *been* crazy. You had me, and you treated me like a no-name ho you use on an as-needed basis. You want a PRN wife. When I wanted you to care, when I wanted you to beg, all your cocky ass could do was smirk and shrug your shoulders."

"Just tell me what to do and I'll do it. I swear. I can't lose you."

"Rewind time back to 1993. Otherwise, there's nothing you can do for me except pick up your favorite pen and sign the papers when they arrive."

He raised his voice. "I'm NOT living without y'all. All I have is my family. I'd rather be dead."

"Well, I'd be happy to kill you, but our boys need their mommy to parent them face to face, not from behind bars."

"So it's that easy for you? I'm serious. I'm no good without y'all. I haven't eaten in days, and I'm barely sleeping."

"Sleep deprivation and starvation? That's a slow march to death. I suggest you get with one of your immature buddies and borrow his gun. I hear putting it in your mouth is pretty much a surefire way to go. Or just grab a good knife and slit your wrists. Be sure to cut vertically and not horizontally. Good luck."

As quickly as his tears welled up, his eyes filled with anger. "Alright. That's how you want it?"

"That's how it is. That's how you made it."

"Cool. I'll see you in court. I'm getting custody of my boys. Young men need to be raised by a man."

"So why are you going after them? You're not a man. What can you teach them? How to cheat on their wives? The

325

fastest way to catch an STD? How to live beneath your potential?"

After going back and forth for a while, he finally left. He knows there's nothing he can say to change my mind. The only way I'll consider taking him back is if God himself comes down to Earth, walks him over to me, and says he's ready to be a real husband. Until then, I'm good.

Okay, maybe I'm not good, but I can fake it 'til I make it. He'll never know, but yes, I still love Ric. Although I've tried, apparently, I can't flip a switch in my heart and turn off my feelings for him. He's the only man who knows me. He didn't have to ask about the scar on my knee because he was there for my ACL surgery in high school. He already knows my favorite drink because he introduced me to it. He knows that if my right ankle is shaking, I'm pissed. No one else ever had the opportunity to be what he has been to me because he had me on lock at age seventeen. Even the guys I went on dates with in college only got a piece of me.

I will probably always have love for him, but love isn't a good enough reason for me to stay. I won't say Ric never loved me. I believe he loved me the best he knew how. Unfortunately, his penis didn't get the memo his heart was trying to send. His betrayal was undeniable, so leaving was easy. Now comes the hard part: coping.

There are certain things you can't tell your friends. Things like how you occasionally watch one of the videos of your husband fucking someone else to rekindle your hate for him when you feel yourself weakening; or how you accidentally get turned on because the penis you are watching was once yours and brought you so much pleasure; or that you're now in therapy because you're sure you must be mentally disturbed to torture yourself with such a practice, alternating between feelings of pleasure and pain inflicted at your own will. Those are things you can't even share with your parents—things no one will

326

understand unless they have lived through it; things that only prolong the healing process.

My mind is in such an abstract place these days. I wasn't supposed to feel confusion once I left him, or so I thought. This is the part where I'm supposed to feel free. I remain semi-sane, though, because I know that eventually I *will* heal. At some point, I'll delete all the videos. At some point, the wounds won't keep opening up. They'll merely be scars that will hopefully fade away with the memory of the pain they caused.

Months ago, Willow shared words that always stuck with me, and I'm proud to say I have accepted my part in my unhappiness. It's time to turn in my membership card for the "club" and move on. No more complaining about things I permit. I'm finally done; still battling love's changes, but free of regret. My sixteen-year journey with Ric played a huge part in me becoming the woman I am today. The only thing left to do now is learn how to walk correctly now that the monkey is off my back.

I used to pray for God to save my marriage, but I should've been praying for Him to save me. He wasn't going to save something He wasn't a part of in the first place. He's now giving me what I need instead of what I asked for. I just have to remember…it's a process.

# WILLOW (MILKY)

Praise God! I am no longer disgruntled. I'm free. My heart and mind are clear, no longer bound by the restraints of a false perception of love. The Bible says God doesn't honor divorce, but He's a forgiving God. I have faith that He'll let this one slide, so to speak. If it's not in His will for the disunion to occur, it won't...for reasons I probably wouldn't understand. In the meantime, I have met with a family law attorney and filed the necessary papers to get the ball rolling.

Vaughn is still in jail awaiting trial. His lawyer was able to get the attempted murder charge dropped to second-degree assault, which could get him anywhere from two and a half to five years in prison. My attorney looks for him to serve at least three and a half years once the other charges are considered.

He's written me twice. Once, to tell me how much he hates me; and again, to tell me how sorry he is and that he's been talking to a counselor in jail about his experience with child molestation. I responded to the second one. Commended him for taking that step. Wished him the best.

Chastised myself for wanting to ask if he'd met a nice gentleman in there.

I'd be lying if I say I don't have love remaining for Vaughn. I married him, so I will always feel something. It's just that disdain weighs in much heavier on my heart's scale. I still pray for him. I still talk to Venus about him. I can love him from afar.

Joseph and Mrs. Ella have approached me a few times, offering to pay for my dental implants on behalf of Vaughn. I asked them to keep their money and only worry about Venus. I want to be responsible for the bill. I want to remember not to let myself be a victim again. I've spent the majority of my life fighting so much to show how strong I was that I didn't recognize my weaknesses.

Throughout this ordeal, starting with when I learned the extent of my injuries and ending with Vaughn's arrest, I've grown to respect the importance of peace-of-mind. I've realized that it's priceless, a figure no one can write on a check or withdraw from an ATM. It's the one thing I need that Vaughn can't provide, and the fact that I *can* is priceless.

I can't remember the last time I visited the MAC counter at the mall or wore sunglasses on a foggy day. I've pitched all of the icepacks that were in my freezer because they were taking up valuable space. I wear heels almost every day now—the high ones—just because I can without bruising Vaughn's ego. Venus thinks playing dress-up is my favorite game, too, because I'll often wear them in the house with pajama pants and a tank top on. The simple things in life are the ones we take for granted. They're the ones that play a significant part in our lives. I thank God for the chance to appreciate them.

*****

On the way to the dentist office, I seriously mulled over telling Dr. Knight that I know he's the man in the senior

329

picture I keep in my jewelry box, the man who gave me the striking blue eyes that neither of his other children have. He seems like such a great man—just like I had already imagined—intelligent, family-oriented, and successful. I have every confidence that if I would've come along when he was twenty-five and more established, I would be walking into the office asking if my father was ready to see me.

I didn't want to rock the boat, though. As I did for my first visit, I signed in like every other miscellaneous patient and called him Dr. Knight. Impersonal? Yes. But he must want it that way. Crystal told me that he knows who I am. And that's okay. For what it's worth, he's taking care of me in some capacity, and that's more than either of us ever expected.

He was able to put in the two temporary crowns at the bottom, and said my gums at the top were healing well. In three weeks, he wanted to see me again so he could decide when he would put those crowns on. The process of regaining my smile reaped far more benefits than cosmetic fulfillment. The old teeth that couldn't be saved were a part of the former me. Now I'm a new person who will soon have new teeth to go along with my new attitude and new outlook on life. It's a great beginning to a new year. I tested out my smile when he handed me the mirror. Slowly but surely, it's getting there. I'm getting there.

When I approached Jess to make my next payment, she wouldn't accept my check. "The doctor has instructed me not to collect payments from you anymore," she said.

"What? Why? Does he need more money upfront? He's still gonna see me, right?"

She shrugged. "I assume so. He told you to schedule your next appointment with me, right?" I nodded. "I can go ask him if you'd like, just to make sure."

"Please."

She spun around in her chair and stood quickly, nearly colliding with Dr. Knight. "Mrs. Townsend is confused about the new payment arrangement," she said. "Would you like to speak with her about it?" Before he answered, she walked away.

He looked nervous as he approached the counter. "Willow, what's your schedule like this afternoon? Are you available around four o'clock?"

"Yes, but I don't understand. Do I have to come back?"

"Actually, I'm making the appointment with you. You name the place. This is so awkward, and it's all my fault, but...I'll just say this for now. I don't charge my children for dental work."

"Four o'clock it is," I replied.

# CRYSTAL

I pressed the intercom button as I stretched my free arm toward the ceiling. "They finished servicing the pool yesterday, right?" I asked Dante.

"Yeah. You comin' over?"

"Yeah."

"Oh! I meant to tell you Tre called and said I got the Grammy nominations for Album of the Year and Best Male R&B Vocal Performance." I hadn't heard that childlike giddiness since he'd had his first sold-out show nine years ago. With all the industry buzz surrounding his *Crown Me* album, this year, he was almost guaranteed to win both.

"Oh, I'm sorry. You've reached the wrong extension. You're evidently looking for the Caring Wife department. This is the I-Don't-Give-A-Damn department," I responded.

He continued to page me as I strutted to the bathroom in the nude. Really, I do care and I would like to have my man back, but I learned early in life that you can't always get what you want.

There's nothing like a good old-fashioned STD to change your way of thinking. My attitude has been revised since I witnessed Dante cheating and subsequently became a member of the blue pill club. Lenience is appropriate in some situations, but marriage isn't one of them. Of course, I learned this nine years into mine...the hard way. I suppose the lesson wouldn't have been as effective if it was delivered the easy way. I'm not the most religious person, but I know God, and I know He has a way of reminding us that He's in control. Since I still haven't had another outbreak, I wonder if getting the disease was a wakeup call, a nudge.

We made our own rules for our marriage, and that type of behavior can't be rewarded. We now have a choice to make: stay in the same mess, leave the mess, or clean up the mess. I'm willing to clean up the mess, but I won't do it alone. Dante has some serious changes to make in his career before we reach the road to reconciliation.

Since he's lost my trust, I feel there are certain situations he shouldn't place himself in. He still uses the argument that the partying and late-night studio sessions are a part of his professional obligations, though. I've accepted that, and he has to accept that I'm his wife in name only now. As far as I'm concerned, he's married to his music, and I will no longer be his patient mistress.

That doesn't mean I'm leaving him, though. Why would I leave? To prove a point? To who? He was wrong, and so was I for giving him the rope to hang himself with. Now, we have to live with our consequences. Because of the time and energy I've invested in him and the public humiliation I've endured, I refuse to get a divorce, refuse to leave the mess. I've spent years walking on red carpets, flashing rehearsed smiles, probably passing some of the hoes he screwed. He doesn't get off that easy. He damn well deserves to walk on eggshells at home with steel-toe boots on. I dare him to crack one.

Disgruntled? I'm beyond that. I'm disconnected, disengaged, disinterested in anything involving him. Well,

I'm conditioning myself to take on that attitude. I live in the guest house now because I don't want to feel like I did a month ago when we shared the main one. Really, I don't want to feel anything—not from him. I have my friends to keep me happy, random strangers to piss me off, my foundation to keep me busy, the evening news to make me sad, and a box full of toys to make me cum.

I've remodeled everything in the house, making my new lifestyle complete. Nothing has anything to do with music. Allowing its presence would be too much like inviting "the other woman" to dinner. I don't even have an iPod dock or radio here. There are still many luxuries I enjoy at the main house, and it's fortunate that our property is so large, I don't have to run into Dante if I don't want to. When I do, I don't get upset. The wound is healed now.

I returned to the intercom after I put on my swimsuit. "Whatever you do, make sure you don't let them put you in skinny jeans when you perform that night. You looked a hot mess on *106 and Park* last week. It was embarrassing," I said.

"Aw, how sweet. Are you worried about my image?"

"No. I just don't want to be around while you wear pants that look like they came from your second grade back-to-school collection."

He laughed. "I don't know. I may have to wear some again if they get you to talk to me. I miss hearing your voice, baby, even when you're using it to insult me."

*Here we go*, I thought. I ended our exchange there before the vulnerability in his voice got to me.

As I drove the golf cart to the pool, my stylist called, requesting my presence at her studio. From Cavalli to Versace, she'd already selected my potential gowns for the show. She wouldn't reveal colors or styles. Instead, she gassed me up, saying I would outshine most of the female artists as I prepare for my husband to walk away with two of the night's major honors. She is a fashion genius. For the past five years, she has laced me from head to toe, giving me the hottest diamonds and stilettos to accessorize my gorgeous gowns, and I knew she wouldn't let me down this year. My marital controversy would have all eyes on me, so I had to look fierce. The glamorous lifestyle is about the only thing I still enjoy about my marriage, so I told her I'd see her at two o'clock.

I thought about not showing up for the Grammys, but in the industry, appearances are everything. I won't walk the red carpet, but when the cameras cut to Dante during the announcement of the nominees in his categories, everyone will see me and know that we're still together. We'll send a message without saying a word, even if it's a total lie.

*****

I was totally comfortable at the ceremony. It's an environment where I knew I wouldn't be judged. The great thing about the entertainment industry is that everyone has secrets—some revealed to the public and some still hidden. It's like a secret society. Everyone has something they're not proud of. Only a few people brought up the disease. Even then, it was inadvertently through a Keep-Your-Head-Up speech.

Dante put on a killer performance and walked away with both Grammys. When the cameras cut to a close-up of my face, my smiles were genuine and my pride was deeply rooted. I've seen him work for this since we were barely legal, and he deserved every accolade given to him.

I hung out backstage, waiting for Dante to finish speaking with the press. While there, I turned away a few lurkers who asked for my reaction to his wins. They only wanted drama, and I wasn't going to give it to them. I barely listened to the question-and-answer session as I texted back and forth with Dana. When I tuned back in, they were wrapping it up.

"Alright, guys. One more question, and I have to go," he said.

"What's next for you, Dante? When can we expect another hot album?"

"Actually, *Crown Me* was my last album. I'll never leave the music business, but I'll be working behind the scenes. I appreciate all the love from my fans, but it's time to move on."

There was a choral gasp, followed by camera flashes that created a strobe effect. Dante looked at me briefly and then turned his attention back to the stunned audience.

"I don't get it. Is this you wanting to bow out while you're on top?" the reporter from BET asked.

"No. This isn't about me…for once."

We locked eyes like we did when I stood backstage at his concert at IU on the day we met. His decision is worth more than the Benz truck. It's more meaningful than his tattoo. It means I'm worth the sacrifice. It means he does love me more than his music. It means he knows that deep down I still love him.

In time, it'll mean we will share the same house, the same bed, the same feelings…again. Correction: The feelings will never be the same. Sometimes similar is all you're gonna get. Sometimes almost *does* count.

Farah, who was nearby watching her husband's backstage interview, rushed over to me. "Girl, what did you do to him? That's a major move. Do you know how much your life is about to change?"

"I loved him. And I think he's finally realized how much."

336

# DISCUSSION QUESTIONS

1.  Do you think each woman made the right decision?
2.  What are your feelings about Vaughn and how his childhood experiences affected his temper?
3.  What are your feelings about Crystal's rules for Dante concerning what constituted as cheating at the beginning of the book?
4.  In marriage, do you believe there is no excuse for divorce?
5.  Dana crossed the line with Lorenzo. Do you feel she was justified?
6.  Do you think any of the women brought their problems on themselves?
7.  In your opinion, was Ric truly remorseful?
8.  Why do men cheat?
9.  Why do women cheat?
10. Should adultery be a deal-breaker?
11. Dana was upset with her father for not speaking up about his feelings toward Ric before their marriage. Was she justified? Do you believe in the statement *Speak now or forever hold your peace*?
12. Is there such thing as a happy marriage? Define happiness.
13. What do you see in Dante and Crystal's future?
14. There are a lot of couples who are unhappily married. Ideas on why they stay together?
15. If you could add anything to the traditional wedding vows, what would it be?

## I FORGOT MY GLOVES

Nobody told me that I was here to fight
'Cause maybe if I'd known, I would've been alright
Last night I suffered from a severe case of fright
From the forty-seven seconds my left eye lost its sight

But I've been blind for nine years
Ignoring the warnings of my peers
My tears formed a black curtain that hid all of my fears

I was forced in a ring with no trainer or coach
I had no adequate time to even plan my approach
Like a roach, I love the darkness, but when the light comes
I choke
Frozen in place with my back against the ropes

I became a human punching bag
A role so sickening, the memory makes me gag
My eyelids sag, I could grace the cover of a boxing mag
With blows to my head that make my thought processes lag

Who would've guess that I'd learn to spar
Or that I'd leave in the middle of the night with
What I could fit in my car
Now I'm up to par—the only memory of you, a scar
Washed my sorrow down, then threw it up at the bar

So come at me again
This time I'm prepared
I thank God every day for my life that was spared
My temper is flared, and I'm no longer scared
Can't imagine how the two of us ever were paired

A heavyweight and a lightweight
Supposedly fighting in the name of love
But if you really cared anything about me
You would've told me I forgot my gloves

## APOLOGY NOT ACCEPTED

Sorry gets old, and my heart's grown cold
Watching the web of your lies and deception unfold
See I bought what you sold,
but rotten shit is destined to mold
Like that yellow-coated necklace you could've sworn
was real gold
Disappointed…
but impressed
I didn't read you like the rest
Blinded by love, knew no negatives
Only wanted to believe the best
But shit's heavy on my chest
I used to wear it like a vest
Bulletproof, but not fool-proof, 'cause it never passed the test
Until now
It's real now, 'cause I recognize the game
Thinking back on shady nights and familiarizing names
You've pulled too many fast ones
So you can go as quick as you came
I'm not forgiving or forgetting, so it'll never be the same
There's no longer a "we"
There's a "you" and an "I"
If that's ignorant, let me sit in my bliss
as I count the tears you cry
Some say it's never too late, and you chose to believe
Well you better jump off that bandwagon,
get your money back and leave
Now you're going through withdrawal
Why? 'Cause you've no longer injected
Shots of poisonous words that'll leave my heart unprotected?
Well how does it feel to be the one who's neglected?
You can beg, plead, and cry all night long
Apology NOT accepted

339

## WELCOME TO THE CLUB

Welcome to the club of disappointment and lies
Where wedding rings and smiles are a part of the disguise
Where yes means no and no does, too
And communication no longer involves "us two"
Where boo-boo's get kissed but never seem to heal
Where nerves become sensitive, but somehow never feel
Where your husband's not your man
And your wife's not your boo
And your best conversation takes place when you screw
Where the fire's gone out and there's nothing left but smoke
Where the busted antique lies that you refuse to admit is broke
Where time never flies and hearts don't grow fonder
Where Facebook friends and Google maps lead to where you wander
Where closed mouths still eat and open ones do, too
Where you realize you're an animal and you're living in a zoo
Where vultures prey and dogs collect bones
Cats retract claws and black snakes moan
Where i's don't get dotted and t's don't get crossed
Where souls are given and common sense is lost
Where love is given and pain is returned
Where you escape from the heat or stay and let it burn

## ACKNOWLEDGMENTS

God has a funny way of changing our plans. I didn't originally set out to write this book. I was actually doing extensive research for the third book in my series when I abruptly halted the project and decided to tell these three women's stories. I'd had too many conversations with my girlfriends about relationships and marriages gone wrong. We spent hours sharing stories, awaiting epiphanies, plotting revenge, and threatening to leave. Months later, we'd get on the phone and do it again. It became almost comical, but none of us are comedians. After encountering virtual strangers over the years and exchanging small talk, I realized that being disgruntled is unfortunately more common than rare. I realized it was a story I wanted to tell. Thank you, God, for realizations.

For seeing my vision and helping make this possible, I want to thank my editor, Carla Dean, and my graphic designer, Keith Saunders. There are others I would like to thank for everything they have been to me and done for me. Mom, for having a good feeling about this one, and for her patience once again; my daughter, Amari, for her hugs and smiles, and for the obvious pride she shows when she wears her "Cosby" shirt. I love her for being who matters most in my life. I must also thank my Advisory Board for being just as supportive for this book as they were for the first, if not more. Special thanks go to Ericka Elder and Roswitha Odiko for spending their valuable time reading and critiquing my first draft. DISTINCT Incorporated, for selflessly giving their time and support at ALL times and for their genuine understanding. I look forward to taking this to another level. To my other friends and family members who have been a part of my journey, thank you. I certainly can't list everyone without running the risk of forgetting a name, so insert yours (here). Last but not least, I want to acknowledge YOU. You know who you are and what you have done.

9 780982 301326